∽THE [...] OF WAR∽

COMMANDER RAFAEL SIMS: An Alabama-born navy man destined for the cause, he plays two sides in a dangerous game . . . and with two remarkable women.

SARAH HAMMOND: The daughter of a prosperous shipping magnate, devoted to the pursuit of peace, her heart guides her into a top-secret mission . . . and toward a perilous act of betrayal.

LOUISA LEE PHOENIX: A Lee of Kentucky, cousin to Robert E., she lives her life with reckless abandon—using her beauty, wits and passionate fire as a weapon in defense of her beloved homeland.

MAJOR ROBERT ANDERSON: Though sympathetic to the South, he is a man of unwavering principle—and determined to fulfill his sworn obligation to the Union . . . even if it pushes his nation into war.

AND

PRESIDENT JAMES BUCHANAN: Considered an inept, inadequate leader, he must hold together a disintegrating country. And with only weeks left in office he decides to make a stand—at a vulnerable garrison in Charleston harbor called Fort Sumter.

IRONCLADS

MAN-OF-WAR

LARRY NAMES

AVON BOOKS ◆ NEW YORK

IRONCLADS: MAN-OF-WAR is an original publication of Avon Books. This work has never before appeared in book form. This work is a novel. Although this work refers to some actual events and historical figures, the circumstances surrounding them are fictional.

AVON BOOKS
A division of
The Hearst Corporation
1350 Avenue of the Americas
New York, New York 10019

Copyright © 1995 by Larry D. Names
Published by arrangement with the author
Library of Congress Catalog Card Number: 94-96270
ISBN: 0-380-77619-7

First Avon Books Printing: March 1995

AVON TRADEMARK REG. U.S. PAT. OFF. AND IN OTHER COUNTRIES, MARCA REGISTRADA, HECHO EN U.S.A.

Printed in the U.S.A.

RA 10 9 8 7 6 5 4 3 2 1

To the memory of a great lady,
Sarah Chase Hammond,
my great-great-great-grandmother

The only way to win a war is to prevent it.
—GEORGE C. MARSHALL

1 ～

Thursday, December 20, 1860

Broad Street buzzed with anticipation. Thousands of people—a majority of them Charlestonians, mostly all Southrons if not South Carolinians, with a sprinkling of Northerners present on business or just out of curiosity—awaited word from within St. Andrews Hall. Inside, delegates from every district in the state were meeting in convention, transferred to Charleston because of a smallpox epidemic at the state capital of Columbia. They had but one purpose: to make history.

David F. Jamison, the president of the Convention of the People of South Carolina, banged a gavel and called the session to order. The gentlemen so gathered fell silent. Jamison ordered the reading of the Ordinance of Secession that had been drafted by the state's leaders. With stoic posture, all listened. Shallow, orderly debate followed, then Jamison called for the question. In alphabetical order, beginning with John H. Adams of Richland District and ending with Henry C. Young of Laurens District, the one hundred sixty-nine representatives present cast a unanimous ballot in favor of splitting the Union of 1787.

The word was announced to the citizens outside, and a mighty shout notified those farther away that the deed had been done. Like the breath of a firestorm, the news spread rapidly through the city, penetrating luxurious drawing rooms, echoing through offices on Lawyer's Row, even causing German merchants to close their shops and join in the spontaneous celebration. Cannon roared. Flags of every description save one—the Stars and Stripes—hung from balconies, flew from poles, or were draped from windows. Grog shops and taverns overflowed. The printers and editors of the Charleston *Mercury* leaned through the building's windows and tossed out hastily printed sheets that read, THE UNION IS DISSOLVED. Bedlam reigned in nearly every corner of Charleston. But not everywhere.

Built in the Greek Revival style, the four-story Charleston Hotel, with its imposing colonnade of fourteen Corinthian columns across its front, offered the only sanctuary of sanity within the city. On the second-floor piazza enclosed by iron railings stood a small conclave of Northerners—among them, a single woman and an arms merchant, both observing the chaos below on Meeting Street.

Sarah Rebecca Hammond, twenty-six and blessed with brunette hair in silky curls, an apple-blossom complexion, and a fair figure, gripped the iron railing so hard that her knuckles paled from the pressure; the only outward sign of the agitation beneath her factitiously calm facade. Her beauty suffered but one flaw, a nose slightly too large for her face; however, a genuinely infectious smile of straight ivory and pavonine eyes possessing a watery mirth easily distracted the viewer from the imperfect proboscis. God save the suitor who mistook her loveliness and casual gaiety as signs of a mediocre mind. Much to the contrary, she disguised a great intelligence and an ingenuous pragmatism with typical feminine wiles as a ploy to trapping men into making fools of themselves over her, and once they did, she dismissed them as inferiors, feeling a sympathetic pity for their wives or the women whom they would one day lure into marriage or some other sort of stylized debauchery.

Standing beside her, Captain Adam Colt of the Patent Fire Arms Manufacturing Company of Hartford, Connecticut, marveled at the revelers below and counted them as so many buyers for his firm's revolvers. First cousin to Sam Colt, the inventor of the first practical revolver, he had come to Charleston to sell guns to the Carolinians, counting on the Southrons to bolt the Union and to arm their own military as quickly as possible with the best arms available, meaning Colt revolvers and rifles.

"This is only the beginning," said Colt without turning to face Sarah. "Before the winter is through, many of the other slave states will pass similar resolutions and withdraw from the Union. You can bank on that, Miss Hammond." He turned to her, grinned sardonically, and added, "And no doubt your family will."

"As will yours, Captain Colt," said Sarah icily. "I don't doubt that most of our northern businessmen are planning to profit from the secession of South Carolina and the other Southern states. Isn't that what all this business is about, Captain? Money."

"I thought it was about slavery and states' rights," said Colt, partly fearing Sarah for being so astute with her statement and partly mocking her for invading the realm of men: politics.

"For decades, Captain Colt, Southern wealth has maintained and supported our nation," argued Sarah a bit testily, as if she were a schoolmarm making a point to an illiterate parent, "and now because of the spread of railroads and all the industries that they have spawned, the majority of American wealth has shifted to the North. The Southerners don't believe this, however. They still believe that the Federal government can't survive without the Southern economy. Tragically, too many of these fools hold the same beliefs as my distant cousin. They believe that cotton is king and that the North dare not make war on cotton.''

Colt's face showed his surprise as he said, ''Distant cousin? Don't tell me you're related to that nefarious scoundrel.''

''Distantly,'' said Sarah, sorry that she had mentioned the family connection to the former United States senator and one-time governor from South Carolina and the author of the infamous ''Mud-sill'' speech in Congress.

Two years earlier on March 4, 1858, Senator James Henry Hammond had stood before the United States Senate and declared:

> In all social systems there must be a class to do the menial duties, to perform the drudgery of life. That is, a class requiring but a low order of intellect and but little skill. Its requisites are vigor, docility, fidelity. Such a class you must have, or you would not have that other class which leads progress, civilization, and refinement. It constitutes the very mud-sill of society and of political government; and you might as well attempt to build a house in the air, as to build either the one or the other, except on this mud-sill. Fortunately for the South, she found a race adapted to that purpose to her hand. A race inferior to her own, but eminently qualified in temper, in vigor, in docility, in capacity to stand the climate, to answer all her purposes. We use them for our purpose, and call them slaves. We found them slaves by the common ''consent of mankind,'' which, according to Cicero, ''lex naturae est.'' The highest proof of what is Nature's law. We are old-fashioned at the South yet; slave is a word discarded now by ''ears polite''; I will not characterize that class at the North by that term; but you have it; it is there; it is everywhere; it is eternal.
>
> The Senator from New York said yesterday that the whole world had abolished slavery. Aye, the name, but

not the thing; all the powers of the earth cannot abolish that. God only can do it when he repeals the fiat, "the poor ye always have with you"; for the man who lives by daily labor, and scarcely lives at that, and who has to put out his labor in the market, and take the best he can get for it; in short, your whole hireling class of manual laborers and "operatives," as you call them, are essentially slaves. The difference between us is, that our slaves are hired for life and well compensated; there is no starvation, no begging, no want of employment among our people, and not too much employment either. Yours are hired by the day, not cared for, and scantily compensated, which may be proved in the most painful manner, at any hour in any street in any of your large towns. Why, you meet more beggars in one day, in any single street of the city of New York, than you would meet in a lifetime in the whole South.

Yes, Hammond had spoken some truth; the lowest class of the North did exist at the mercy of the capitalists and on an economic level lower than that of Southern slaves. However, he had omitted the two intangibles that placed the lowest class of the North above the South's slaves; Hammond had failed to mention that the poor of the North and West possessed inalienable freedom and the opportunity to advance their lives, to raise themselves to higher social and economic levels, whereas the slave of the South had no such liberty or option to rise above the present station that was his purely by accident of birth.

Abolitionists had turned Hammond's argument against him and his fellow slaveholders by enjoining the Republicans to employ his reference to Northern whites as being a lesser class than Southern Negroes. Throughout the campaign of 1860, they had portrayed the Democrats as the party of the wealthy, who not only held the Negroes in perpetual servitude in the South but also treated the workers of the North with base con-

tempt. Their tactic worked, and Abraham Lincoln won
the election. It worked too well. Lincoln's election had
forced South Carolina to carry out its threat to withdraw
from the Union, an act that James Hammond had proposed for three decades since South Carolina led the
Nullification Movement against the Federal government
under Andrew Jackson, the irony being that Hammond
was the scholarly son of a schoolteacher from Massachusetts and a descendant of William Hammond of
London, whose sons came to America as part of the
emigration of the Puritans, a race who despised slavery
and the nobility of England—the antecedents of the Old
South's aristocracy, the very social stratum in which
Hammond aspired to become a leading integral slaveholding member.

Sarah Hammond sprouted from the same family tree
as her notorious Southern cousin, far removed though
he might be, but her connection to James H. Hammond
was much greater than the familial bond of bearing the
same name. Her family did business with him.
Grudgingly.

The advent of railroads had changed America forever, and at the vanguard of this industrial metamorpho-
sis rode two branches of the Hammonds of New York
and Massachusetts, both headed by offspring of Gideon
Hammond, one from each of his two marriages. Asahel
Hammond, the first son of the first marriage, built a
financial empire in Boston, and Gideon Hammond Jr.,
eldest son of Gideon by his second wife, Sarah Chase
Hammond, did likewise in New York by funding the
construction of railroads, then taking possession of
them for pennies on the dollar when their builders failed
to make good on their debts. Oftentimes, these half-
brothers clashed and competed for the basest of reasons: lust.

Widower Gideon Hammond and Sarah Chase published their intention to marry in the fall of 1792 in a

quasi-Quaker ceremony at Foster, Rhode Island. She was eighteen, and he was thirty-four. Their marriage wasn't official until January 29, 1793. Their first child, a daughter, was born in August of that year. They named her Freelove for good reason.

Asahel, Gideon's fourteen-year-old son by his first marriage, knew that reason, and he wanted to cash in on it. Sarah repulsed his adolescent desire for her, but Asahel wasn't one to give up easily. With all the tenacity of his Puritan ancestors, he tried over and over to bed Sarah and never succeeded. Like many obsessed people who can't get what they want, he took the opposite approach and tried to destroy Sarah for denying him. His lies about Sarah to his father accomplished only one thing: his banishment from Gideon's household. Asahel went to Boston, where he entered the banking business.

Asahel's lust for his stepmother never abated. Neither did his hatred of her for turning his father against him, or so he imagined.

When the first iron ribbons began stretching across South Carolina, Gideon Jr. provided the financing by giving the Southern entrepreneurs a lower interest rate than Asahel had offered them. Angry over losing the loan to his half-brother, Asahel went to South Carolina to see about building a competing line. Instead of competition, he discovered opposition to the first road, and leading the attack was none other than distant cousin James Henry Hammond, a young planter with great political ambitions. Asahel plotted with James to stop the railroad, but they failed because Cousin James, in spite of all his high-minded rhetoric to the contrary, had his price. In this case, it was interest-free money for the expansion of his plantation and a factor who would deliver his cotton to Europe for the lowest possible rates. The shipping agent was Gideon Jr.'s younger brother, Levi.

Sarah Chase Hammond, the matriarch of the family—for she bore Gideon Sr. eleven children who reached their majority and gave her dozens of grand-children—masterminded this defeat of Asahel. This was not her first besting of him, and it wouldn't be the last. Over the ensuing years, they continued to do battle in the financial markets, and more often than not, Sarah's sons came away with the greater profits.

Witnessing many of these events firsthand was Levi's youngest daughter, Sarah. Because business kept Levi away from home for months at a time, little Sally, as she was called in the family, spent most of her formative years in the country home of her grandmother, who tutored her namesake on the pitfalls of dealing with men in business. The granddaughter learned her lessons so well that by her fourteenth birthday, the elder Sarah pressed Levi to take Sally with him on his next voyage to Europe and involve her in the daily dealings of inter-national trade. Reluctant at first, Levi agreed and soon came to realize that his daughter possessed the same great penchant for commerce that his mother had shown so often over the decades. His confidence in her abilities grew with each season until she reached her majority, when he felt comfortable enough with her to send her to Europe in his stead to negotiate with the English and French merchants.

With the passing of her grandmother in 1856, Sally Hammond announced that henceforth she wished to be called Sarah by all family members with the exception of her father, to whom, woman or not, she would always be his little Sally. She also made it known that she had accepted a position as clerk in her Uncle Gideon's bank, where she intended to experience the world of finance from the ground up. She learned that business rapidly, and within three years, she moved from clerk to cashier to accounting supervisor to loan proces-sor to loan officer. Satisfied that she knew as much about banking as she wanted to know, she resigned and shifted her interest to railroads and travel.

During her excursions across the United States, Sarah discovered the rift between North and South to be deeper and more treacherous than many people, particularly the politicians, had previously thought. First, Senator James Henry Hammond's infamous "Mud-sill speech" inflamed the Northern press and inspired the South, then John Brown's attempt to start a slave rebellion created a panic in the South and encouraged the abolitionists to become bolder than ever with their vitriol against the slaveholders. Next came Lincoln's nomination and the failure of the Democratic party to remain united against the fanatics who would achieve freedom for the slaves at any expense, even if that cost should include the total destruction of a great portion of the nation and its people. In reaction, South Carolina and other slave states threatened to dissolve the Union and take up arms to defend themselves in the event that the free states refused to let them withdraw peacefully.

Following her grandmother's first rule of business, Sarah tried to anticipate the future and profit from it. She saw a national cataclysm that could destroy her family's fortune or enhance it, depending on which steps were taken. In conference with her father, Uncle Gideon, and other family members in their businesses the week after Lincoln's election was made certain, she reviewed recent history and offered her predictions on the year ahead. After a general concurrence with her evaluation of events past, present, and yet to unfold, she outlined a three-step proposal to profit from the coming war between North and South. Her father and uncle proudly put their stamps of approval on the plan, then Sarah startled them by saying, "Although I wish you all well, I cannot in good conscience participate in this profiteering from the suffering of others. As you all know, I subscribe to the doctrines of Mr. William

Lloyd Garrison. Being so inclined to pacification, I have
determined that I will do all that I can to prevent this
war, and if hostilities should erupt, then I will do all
that I can to bring them to a quick end.''

Then it was Sarah's turn to be surprised as Uncle
Gideon rose and said evenly, ''If our mother taught us
nothing else, she did teach us to be a people of peace.
Sarah, I believe I speak for all gathered here when I
say we will support you in your efforts to stem this
tide of war. We offer you our hearts, our prayers, and
our fortunes. Whatever is necessary to prevent the shedding of blood. Just tell us what you need from us, and
it will be yours.''

With that, Sarah revealed how she hoped to prevent
a war. ''First,'' she said, ''we must keep in mind that
our primary purpose is the prevention of bloodshed, no
matter which side we have to betray to achieve that
goal.'' Silence for a moment, then general concurrence.
She continued. ''Being quite realistic, I don't hold out
much hope of total success, but we must try.'' Other
family members offered to channel their thoughts,
words, and deeds toward the same end. Sarah concluded
by telling them of her personal plans for the month
ahead, saying, ''I will go to South Carolina because that
seems to be the center of the secessionist movement.''

And so she went to South Carolina, ostensibly as the
agent of the Levi Hammond Shipping Line, but in reality with a hidden agenda that she hadn't even trusted
to any member of her own family. She was not surprised to find Colt and other representatives of munitions manufacturers ahead of her, circling the capital in
Columbia like so many vultures waiting for the carcass
to gasp its last breath. She met with Governor Francis
W. Pickens and let him know that her father's shipping
company would continue to do business with South
Carolina's planters, carrying their cotton to Europe, and
in the same breath, she offered to make her father's

ships available for importing whatever the government of his state considered necessary to maintain its sovereignty.

"Even if your country should be opposed to such trade?" inquired Pickens.

"Not all of my father's ships fly the flag of the United States, Governor Pickens," replied Sarah.

Pickens smiled, nodded, and understood. As far as he was concerned, they had an understanding.

As far as Sarah was concerned, she had opened a very important door.

Before smallpox drove the secession convention out of Columbia, Sarah removed to Charleston, where she set up her headquarters at the Charleston Hotel. She placed advertisements in the Charleston *Mercury* and the Charleston *Courier* on behalf of her father's shipping line and her uncle's banking interest, but instead of using their New York offices, she listed the address for Gideon Hammond & Company as No. 5, rue de la Paix, Paris, France, and the ports for Levi Hammond Shipping Line as Liverpool, Northampton, and Le Havre. Plainly, she was announcing the Hammonds' intention to continue doing business with the South, secession or not.

Secession it was. Now Sarah had more decisions and moves to make. Unwilling to waste a single opportunity, she excused herself from Captain Colt's presence and returned to her room on the third floor.

During her first incursion to the South the previous year, Sarah chose as a traveling companion her first cousin John Burch, oldest son of her favorite aunt, her father's youngest sister, Ruth Ann. Cousin Jack, Sarah's near equal in age but much less experienced in the ways of the world, having been born and raised on a farm in Pennsylvania, now resided in Ohio, working as a common laborer. He was the oldest son of Joseph Burch, a ne'er-do-well fortune-hunter who frequently left his family to fend for themselves while he sought adventure; first in Texas, arriving there shortly after Houston defeated the Mexicans at San Jacinto; then, in the Mexican War as a scout for General Taylor; and later joining Fremont and other explorers surveying routes for a transcontinental railroad to the Pacific. Sarah hoped to expand her cousin's horizons and possibly inspire him to reach for a higher latitude in life.

While in New Orleans, she coaxed Burch into attending a slave auction. She argued that she couldn't oppose slavery unless she knew more about the peculiar institution. The experience shook her deeply and changed her life forever. Seeing human beings paraded and inspected like cattle and horses penetrated her armor-plated sensibilities. She wanted to halt the entire proceeding and set those poor people free, but being perfectly practical, she knew that she could do little short of purchasing every man, woman, and child, putting them aboard a ship bound for a Northern port, and setting them at liberty once they were on free soil. Even an act such as that would constitute a cruelty against those folk. Instant freedom without a job and a place to live would be worse than slavery. With this reality facing her, Sarah turned to leave the auction, only to have her weepy gaze met by the defiant stare of a woman of similar age standing in line waiting to be sold to the highest bidder. Sarah stopped, unable to look away from this coffee-complexioned slave. What is it about her? wondered Sarah. Something noble. Something honest and forthright. Something regal even.

"You, girl!" barked a man holding a coiled whip in his right hand. "Lower them eyes! You ain't up to Virginny no more. Down here, niggers got to respect their betters." He shook the black leather snake at her.

The young woman lowered her head but not her eyes, her aspect becoming all the more fierce with pride in

who she was and hatred for what she was: a slave, a
captive, a stranger in a strange land.

Sarah sensed a link to this woman, a bonding of
sorts. She felt outraged when the slave driver spoke so
harshly to the woman. "Wait," she said to Burch. "I'm
not ready to leave after all, Jack."

"I said to lower them eyes, you black bitch!"
growled the slave driver. He allowed the whip to uncoil
at his side.

Sarah gave the woman a slight nod as if to tell her
that it would be all right to look down, that if she did,
Sarah would not think the less of her.

The woman obeyed, although not because she feared
the lash; she knew perfectly well that her price would
plunge if he struck her in full view of the auction. She
obeyed because she, too, could feel a connection with
Sarah, and the empathy of their joining, as ethereal as
it might be, guided her action much more than the slave
driver's gruff voice and hateful command. She waited
a moment, then peeked at Sarah again. Yes, she
thought, the white lady is still here. She ain't leaving
me. Not my friend. A tingle of emotion rippled through
her as the oddity of that thought struck her. It com-
forted her.

"Go on, girl," said the slave driver. "Get up on
them steps. You're next on the block."

Sarah watched the slave climb the steps to the platform, the chains around the woman's ankles rattling
only slightly as she mounted the stairs. She has so much
grace, thought Sarah. Such beauty in her movements.
She must be the daughter or granddaughter of some
African king. She has such dignity.

"Next," said the auctioneer, "we have a female
house servant. Leastways, she was back in Virginia till
she got uppity with her mistress." He turned to her and
said, "Go on now and get up on that block so as the
gentlemen can see you better." As the slave complied,

he addressed the bidders again. "Her name is Rowena. She's only eighteen years old, and she's in perfect health." He lied on the first count; Rowena was actually twenty-two years old, but slave women that old fetched lower prices because their best breeding years would be fewer. "Matched with the right buck, and she oughta produce good field hands for more than twenty years. Just look at them hips. Just right for child-bearin'." He surveyed the audience, then asked, "What am I bid, sirs, for this fine nigger wench?"

The bidding started at one hundred dollars, rapidly rising to three hundred before anyone dropped out. At four hundred, only two men continued to bid. As soon as it appeared that one would go no higher, Sarah entered the competition.

"Four hundred twenty-five!" she said loudly.

A silence shrouded the audience.

Rowena gasped, held her breath, and hoped.

"Pardon me, ma'am," said the auctioneer, his face painted with a patronizing grin, "but ladies are not permitted to bid at this auction."

"I see," said Sarah, feigning the drawl of Southrons. "Forgive me, sir. I am a stranger here and unaware of the customs."

Rowena exhaled and slumped.

"It's quite all right, ma'am." He bowed at Sarah, then resumed his business. "I have four hundred. Do I hear four ten?"

Sarah turned to Burch and said softly, "Make the bid, Jack. Bid four ten for me."

"What?" muttered Burch.

"Bid four ten," she repeated with a touch of urgency in her voice.

"I don't have that kind of money," protested Burch, "and you know it, Sarah Hammond."

"But I do, Jack. Now bid for me."

"Goin' once," said the auctioneer.

Sarah glared at Burch.

Burch frowned.

"Goin' twice."

"Bid, Jack."

Burch raised his hand and said, "Four hundred ten."

"Goin' three—"

"Four hundred ten!" shouted Sarah.

Rowena's heart leaped.

The auctioneer grinned his patient, patronizing smile at Sarah and said, "Ma'am, I already told you that ladies ain't permitted to bid at this here auction."

"Yes, sir, I know, but I'm not bidding. He is." She nudged Burch to step forward.

"Is that right, sir?" asked the auctioneer, shifting his view to Sarah's cousin.

Burch looked askance at Sarah, then focused on the auctioneer. He nodded and said, "Yes, sir, it is. I bid four hundred ten dollars for that Negress."

Rowena rippled with excitement.

The auctioneer scanned the other bidders but avoided making eye contact with the man who had bid four hundred. He cleared his throat and said, "Very good, sir. I have four ten. Will anyone make it four twenty?" He surveyed the bidders for a taker.

The gentleman who had bid four hundred twisted up his face sourly, threw up both hands with disgust, and mumbled a few well-chosen epithets that only the men around him could hear clearly. They chorused their agreement and urged him to protest the new bid. He chose not to make any more fuss than he had already.

With raised eyebrows, the auctioneer said, "Goin' once." He looked to the other bidders for aid but received none. "Goin' twice." Another empty search for help. "Goin' thrice." He took a deep breath and finalized the transaction. "Sold to the young gentleman with the lady."

Sarah smiled at Rowena.

Not knowing why, the slave woman felt a surge of joy at being sold to Burch. Something, a premonition, intuition, or merely a prayer of expectation, something told her that this man—no, the white lady, yes, the white lady—that this white lady would be her angel of deliverance, her savior, the instrument of her rescue from bondage.

"Now what are you gonna do with a slave, Sarah?" groused Burch.

"Buy her some new clothes," said Sarah evenly.

Obtaining Rowena at the slave auction proved to be the easiest part of Sarah's relationship with her. Gaining her trust and friendship tried Sarah's heart, soul, and conscience. Taking the first step toward reaching an accord, Sarah ordered the leg irons removed from Rowena's ankles, then made the introductions. "I am Sarah Rebecca Hammond of New York, and this is my cousin, Mr. John Burch of Ohio." When Rowena did not raise her face in response, Sarah said, "Please look at me when we are conversing, Rowena. It would make it so much easier for both of us to see inside each other."

In all her life, nobody had ever said anything like this to Rowena. Not only were Sarah's words foreign to her, Sarah's tone and inflection were also a new sound to her ears. Possibly her mother and father had spoken to her with such gentle sincerity, but that had been so long ago that she only vaguely remembered their faces, never mind recalling their voices. Slowly, she lifted her face to meet Sarah's gaze. Yes, the eyes said, the voice was true. The anger brewing within Rowena fizzled to a flat calm.

"As soon as the legalities can be conducted," said Sarah, "you will become a free person. Until then, we must get you some new clothes and prepare you to be free. Are you agreeable to this, Rowena?"

Knowing no other way to reply, the slave said, "Yes'm, missy."

Sarah shook her head and said, "No, do not address me as missy or ma'am. My name is Sarah, and you will call me by my name from this moment forward."

"I don't think that's such a good idea, Sarah," said Burch. "Leastways, not in these parts."

"Jack, I will not be a hypocrite," she protested.

"Mr. Burch be right, Miss Sarah," interjected Rowena. "White folks down this way ain't gonna tolerate no nigger callin' a white woman by her Christian name. Leastways, not without puttin' a *miss* or somethin' of the kind in front of it."

"You have a point, I'm sure," said Sarah, "but you must begin now to think and act like a free person. Do you understand?"

"Yes'm, Miss Sarah."

Sarah sighed and said, "I suppose Rome wasn't built in a day. All right then. We'll work on it."

And so they did. Sarah continued to insist that Rowena address her by her first name only, and Rowena continued to use the title of *miss* whenever they were in the presence of other people—free or slave.

As soon as they arrived in New York, Sarah informed Rowena that she was a free woman. "My father's lawyer will take care of the legalities to ensure your liberty," she said. "There will be no worry over some slave hunter coming North and claiming you under the Fugitive Slave Law. You can rest assured of that. Therefore, you are free to strike out on your own or you may remain with me as my employee."

"Employee, Miss Sarah?" queried Rowena, reverting to her former status of kowtowing slave.

"Yes, Rowena, employee."

"I ain't sure what that means, Miss Sarah."

"It means you are a free woman. Free to stop calling me Miss Sarah and start calling me Sarah. Free to be

paid to work for me, if you want to work for me. Free
to work for somebody else, if you want to work for
somebody else. You can make your own choices now,
Rowena. I am offering you the position of handmaid.
I will pay you five dollars each week and provide all
your living and travel expenses. The choice is yours,
Rowena.''

"Five dollars? Is that a lot?"

Sarah smiled and said, "We will teach you to read
and write and to cipher numbers. Then you can determine whether five dollars is a lot of money or not."

Rowena nodded sternly, then added, "These livin'
and travel expenses, Miss Sarah? What be them?"

"You will live in my apartment with me at no cost
to you. Also, I will expect you to go with me wherever
I go, and I will pay all the expenses of traveling with
me."

Rowena accepted the position, and she went along
with Sarah on all her travels, including her latest trip
to the South.

Being all too familiar with the present political mood
of the South, Sarah advised Rowena to remain in their
hotel room instead of joining her on the piazza to observe the impromptu celebration on the street below.
"You can watch from the window," said Sarah, which
was exactly where Rowena was standing when Sarah
returned.

"Those people down there have all gone crazy," said
Rowena, much of her slave accent now absent from
her speech, thanks largely to Sarah's tutoring and her
exposure to Northern voices. "Do you think we're
safe here?"

"You needn't worry about such things, Rowena,"
said Sarah as she sat down at the writing desk. "Not
yet anyway. For the moment, these fire-eaters still need
us." She took up the pen and opened the inkwell. Care-

fully, she wrote the note. No salutation. No signature. Only a terse message.

Remain here. Send word by our ships only. Make contact with D. Be cautious. God preserve us.

Sarah proofread the note before blotting it. She folded it in half and inserted it into an envelope. "Take this letter upstairs," she said, offering it to Rowena, her gaze serious and calculating. "You know which room."

"Yes, of course," said Rowena, accepting the envelope.

Letter in hand but hidden in the folds of her skirt as she walked, Rowena left the room and ascended the stairs to the fourth floor. Nobody in sight. No matter. Few white people would pay her any mind, even if they should encounter her in the hall. She approached the door to room number 412, stopped in front of it, and looked up and down the corridor. Still nobody. She stooped and slid the note under the door. Coming erect again, she moved away toward the stairway, strolling casually as if she had not a care in the world or a secret to hide.

2

Friday, December 21, 1860

"Disunion!" cried the newsie. To punctuate the lead story of the day, twelve-year-old, freckle-faced Jimmy Eagan held aloft a copy of Walt Whitman's Brooklyn *Daily Eagle,* a dozen more sheets tucked under his left arm. "South Carolina convention votes to leave Union!" he shouted, his breath clouding in the winter air as he waved the newspaper for further emphasis.

A mustachioed gentleman wearing a charcoal-gray plug hat approached young Eagan. "I'll take one, boy," said the businessman. He dug a three-cent silver out of his right vest pocket and held it out to the newspaper vendor.

The youth lowered the latest edition of the *Eagle* and handed it to the buyer. "Here you go, gov'nor," he said, his tone cheerful and colored with the brogue of the Emerald Isle. He accepted the gentleman's coin. "Thank you," said Eagan with a broad grin and a touch of the bill of his tattered brown motorman's cap, "and merry Christmas, sir." He dropped the money into his right coat pocket, jiggled the cash just to hear the comforting sound it made, then pulled another *Eagle* from his dwindling supply and renewed his heralding of the headline that had all of America and much of the rest of the world talking.

Secede. Secession. Secesh. Words that had only recently come into the common usage. They sounded as foreign to the newsboy as the growing myriad of languages and dialects spoken by the hundreds of immigrants who landed daily at one dock or another in New York's bustling harbor.

Secession. The very idea inflicted alienation, fear, and hate in the hearts of most thinking men and women throughout the no longer United States, but not to all. Some felt otherwise.

"Union dissolved!" cried the newsie. "South Carolina leaves Union!"

Eagan's voice carried upward to the second-story windows of the brownstone behind him, permeating the glass and echoing into the dreams of two exhausted lovers dozing after their morning tryst. The woman stirred only enough to curl into a fetal position while pulling the deep blue comforter over her auburn tresses in an effort to shut out the outside world. She emitted a whimper of displeasure and buried her head in the pillow. The man lifted his eyelids languidly, exposing a pair of cobalt irises to the dim light of the bedroom. The white tongue-and-groove slat ceiling above him filled his view, but he failed to focus on it, choosing instead to concentrate on the voice of the boy hawking newspapers on the street corner below. His eyelids fluttered as he strained to hear better. When he couldn't discern the exact words floating up from the street, he decided to rise. Sinewy, tall, handsome, naked, he threw back the satin quilt and slipped quietly from the full-size featherbed, taking care not to disturb his mistress. He grabbed a maroon silk dressing gown from the back of the bedroom chair and donned it. He tied the belt as he walked to the window. Parting the drapes with both hands, he scanned the street below and spotted the

newsie immediately. He couldn't read the headline on
the newspaper that young Eagan held over his head,
but he could hear the boy's pronouncement that the
Union was dissolved.

So they've finally done it, he thought. He heaved a
sigh. So now it begins. South Carolina today. Which
state tomorrow? Georgia? Alabama? Mississippi? How
soon before all the slave states leave the Union and
unite as a new nation where the people shall retain the
right to nullify the acts of government? And once that
nation is established, will it be allowed to live in peace?
Or will there be war between North and South? A shudder of foreboding uncertainty rippled the nape of his
neck, causing an involuntary hunching of his shoulders.
He twisted his head to shake off the ill feeling, but it
persisted, shrouding his features with a pall of gloom.

The newsie glanced up at the window where the man
stood staring out at him. Eagan recognized the watcher
as Rafael Sims, the naval officer whom he had first
seen entering the apartment house two weeks earlier.
Although Sims remained inside less than an hour that
day, his mere presence in the neighborhood had roused
the vendor's curiosity about his identity and purpose
for being there. A few quick questions put hastily to
the gentleman upon his leaving the building, and Eagan
learned that the stranger held the rank of commander
in the United States Navy and that he had come from
Washington City to inform Mrs. Phoenix, the lady who
lived on the second floor, that her husband's ship, the
corvette *Levant,* had failed to arrive at Panama City on
its routine patrol from the Sandwich Islands and was
feared lost at sea. When the commander returned the
next day, the newsboy figured Sims had some new information about Master Phoenix for Mrs. Phoenix, but
Sims dashed that idea when he informed Eagan that the
lady needed comforting, thus his reason for staying the
entire afternoon. On the third day, the lad concluded

that she must be very distraught because Sims failed to exit the apartment house until early evening. After that, Eagan couldn't say when Sims left the building on his nearly daily visits because he went home before the commander made an appearance on the street again, if he made one at all.

Eagan made eye contact with the watcher, waved a copy of the *Eagle* at him, and shouted, "South Carolina secedes!" Sims released the drapes, vanishing from the newsboy's sight. The youth shrugged off the mild rebuff and went about his business. He couldn't swear to what was happening behind the woman's closed doors, but he had a fairly good idea, knowing as much about the Phoenixes as he did.

Dawson Phoenix, an officer with the rank of master in the United States Navy, and his wife, Louisa, had rented a flat on the second floor of a three-story brick apartment house two and a half years earlier, only a week after Jimmy Eagan took up selling the *Eagle* on the corner of Bedford and Rodney in the Williamsburgh neighborhood of Brooklyn. They moved into their new residence with little fanfare, but not without the notice of the block's other residents. The Phoenixes, their drawls giving them away as Southerners, became the primary subject of local gossip for several days afterward due to their sudden absence from public view. Dawson departed immediately for sea duty aboard the corvette *Levant,* and Louisa, exhausted and distressed by the long trip from Charleston, took to bed, effectively denying her new neighbors the opportunity to learn anything about her and her husband. Speculation about the newcomers spawned dozens of rumors, nearly all untrue, of course. After a week of being turned away from the Phoenix household by Louisa's black serving girl and thus being forced to sustain the suspense of knowing nothing concrete about this couple other than the fact that he was a naval officer, a trio of well-intentioned ladies finally gained admittance to Louisa's parlor to welcome her to the neighborhood. Delighted to have the company and now recovered from her bout with depression, Louisa made up the lost time by releasing her innate tendency to be talkative and her uncontrollable desire to be the center of attention. In the course of an afternoon, she revealed as much of her personal history as she wanted the ladies to know at that time.

Louisa Lee Phoenix was born in Wayne County, Kentucky, the youngest child of John Lee, a veteran of the battle of New Orleans and second cousin to the Revolutionary War hero Henry "Light-horse Harry" Lee of Virginia, and Tabitha Francis, whose father, grandfather, and uncle fought in a Virginia militia unit during the Revolutionary War and who, through her mother, Nancy Ann Mounts, was descended from Christopher Mounce, the Delaware Swede and legendary colonial frontiersman who prevented hundreds of colonists from being massacred by a war party of Nanticoke Indians; Mounce led a handful of fellow woodsmen on a foot race through the Maryland forest warning the imperiled settlers of the approaching danger and gathering them into an army to defend their settlements. When James Fenimore Cooper's *Leatherstocking Tales* reached print, descendants of Mounce, including and especially the Francis clan, made claims that the author had based his character, Natty Bumppo, on their illustrious ancestor. True or no, the possibility enlivened many a conversation on cold Kentucky nights when the Lee and Francis families gathered around the home fires to tell stories of their famous forebears.

As most fathers are wont to do with their youngest offspring, John Lee had indulged Louisa as a child, and like so many other parents, he lived to regret the many favors that he lavished on her. The sweet, lovely daughter who hugged him without coaxing, who giggled at his every tease, who idolized him without expectation, who sided with him at every turn, that same strawberry-blond angel metamorphosed into a headstrong, auburn-haired young woman whose raging passions belied the morality that her mother had been so certain was bred deep in the souls of all her children, as testified by Louisa's older brother, the Right Reverend Robert M. Lee, an assistant Methodist minister to a flock of God-fearing folks in Edmonson County.

As he watched his favorite blossom from little Weezy to Miss Louisa to Miss Lee, John Lee began to dread the day when one of her many suitors would win her heart and take her away from his household for good. He approved, however, when David Gray, a young man of sturdy stock and economic potential, asked for her hand in marriage. Louisa marked her seventeenth birthday in the last week of May 1851, then wed Gray on the first Saturday of June. Before the nation could celebrate its diamond jubilee a month later, she sued for divorce on the grounds that Gray had "failed to fulfill his marital obligation as a husband." In other words, as Louisa confided to her childhood friend Edie Crane, "No kissin', no huggin', no touchin' or feelin' like the other boys was always tryin' to do to me when they'd take me down to the holler for some sparkin'. No, ma'am, not Davy Gray. He'd just climb on, jump a couple of bumps, let out a grunt, roll off, and fall asleep afore I could even start breathin' hard. He weren't no fun at all."

John Lee railed at Louisa for leaving her husband after only a few weeks. Tabitha intervened. "You've got to give it a longer try, darlin'," said the mother. "Marriages ain't made in heaven like it says in the fairy tales. They take lots of hard work and sweat and tears to make them come out right." Louisa countered with, "I know all about that work, sweat, and tears business, Maw. I was willin' to work hard and get up a good sweat with Davy atop me, but he just couldn't keep it up long enough, and that's what drove me to tears.'' Aghast at her daughter's attitude, Tabitha washed her hands of the matter. Louisa got her divorce, and John Lee banished her from his hearth.

William and Sarah Skaggs, Louisa's brother-in-law and sister, accepted Louisa into their household in Brownsville, Kentucky, but the restraint of living in a minister's home proved too trying for her. Within a few weeks, she sought reconciliation with her parents through her brother Robert. "No," said the father, "not as long as her behavior is no better than that of a common tavern strumpet on the Natchez Trace." To which, Louisa responded, "Pa must be an expert on the behavior of a common tavern strumpet on the Natchez Trace to say something like that. I wonder how he learned so much about their behavior. Must've been on some of those timber raft trips to New Orleans he took without Maw." The implication brought gasps from every member of her family except her father. "That girl is too smart for her own good," said John Lee, "and too rough. She needs honin', refinin', the kind of refinement she can't get here in Kentucky. She's goin' to my cousin Henry's in Virginia to learn to be a lady."

And so she did.

Henry Harrison Lee and his wife, Loretta, a Randolph by birth and a third cousin to her husband, opened their Caroline County plantation home to Louisa that autumn. Childless themselves through thirty-two years of marriage, they had become over the years the unofficial foster parents to many of the children of friends and family, taking them into their home and hearts and giving them the love and guidance that the petulant girls and recalcitrant boys felt their natural parents had been denying them since birth in favor of older siblings. Upon first welcoming their young cousin to Ferncliff, Henry made an aside to his wife: "You certainly have your work cut out for you with this one, my dear. I've seen corn cobs with smoother edges than she's got." Loretta replied sweetly: "I don't see her that way at all, Mr. Lee. I see her as a caterpillar that wants to be a beautiful butterfly." And with that attitude, Loretta commenced the remaking of Cousin Louisa.

As could many of the finer families in the Old Dominion, the Lees and Randolphs traced their ancestry to the cavaliers of King Charles I who sought refuge in the Piedmont of the southern colonies from the tyrannical rule of the Roundheads of Cromwell. They brought with them from England their breeding, their customs, and a nobility of character in a society of affluence and gentility. These traits of culture and the peculiar institution of slavery gave rise to an aristocracy of tobacco and cotton planters who created a civilization unique in itself in that it provided its members with wealth, education, and leisure from birth for those who chose to remain within its social and geographic confines.

It was this heritage that Loretta Randolph Lee wished to impart to Louisa, and much to her credit, Louisa accepted the tutelage of Loretta and the traditions of her lineage without pause and with all the enthusiasm and vigor of a religious zealot given the key to heaven's gate. From the very first day, Louisa concentrated on speaking correctly, walking with grace, and practicing the manners of the genteel order which she so ardently desired to join. Additionally, she learned to sing with the sweet clarity of a scarlet tanager, to play the piano with the touch of a lyrist, and to dance with the harmony of motion of a swan gliding over a still pond. Moreover, she read; she read everything in the Lee library that time would allow, from Voltaire to Jefferson, from Shakespeare to Cooper and Dickens. As Cousin Loretta stated it so succinctly, being pretty wasn't enough to be a real lady. "A pie with no fillin' is only so much crust."

A year passed, and Loretta decided that the time had come for Louisa to be introduced to polite adult society. She accomplished this task when she and Henry made their annual Christmas visits to the homes of their relatives in the surrounding counties; they would take Louisa with them, and Louisa would be afforded the opportunity to practice everything that Loretta had so painstakingly taught her during the months since her arrival in Virginia. They would culminate the holiday trip at Arlington, the home of cousin Mary Lee Fitzhugh Custis, the wife of George Washington Parke Custis, the grandson of Martha Dandridge Custis Washington and adopted son of the first President of the United States.

Seeing so many mansions awed Louisa, but the first sight of the Custis home left her breathless. Arlington had been built by George Custis after his grandmother's death when Mount Vernon, the only home he had known until then, reverted to the Washington family. The house, named after an old Custis residence on the Eastern Shore of Virginia, was distinguished more for its site on the hills overlooking Alexandria and for the impressive columnated portico than for any interior beauty or convenience.

Mary Lee Custis had given birth to four children during her life, but only one had reached her majority. This daughter was Mary Anne Randolph Custis, who had married another Lee cousin, Robert Edward Lee, a son of the Revolutionary War hero Henry "Light-horse Harry" Lee and a third cousin to Louisa. Robert E. Lee was a brevet colonel in the army, presently assigned to the Military Academy at West Point as its superintendent. Nearly every year since their marriage in 1831,

Robert and Mary Lee had returned to Arlington with
their children to spend the winter months with Mrs.
Lee's parents. This particular season, Loretta and Henry
learned at the last home they visited before departing
for Arlington, the colonel and his wife would not be
present, as the colonel's duties demanded that he remain in New York.

Henry and Loretta had hoped to introduce Louisa to
her cousin Robert and his family for several reasons,
not the least of which was the fact that Robert, like his
father before him, was a war hero, having fought with
great distinction at Cerro Gordo, Contreras-Churubusco,
and Chapultepec during the recent Mexican War. More
so, they wanted her to meet Robert because he epito-
mized everything good about the Southern aristocracy.
He stood five feet ten and one half inches tall, with
brown eyes that sometimes seemed black, and with
abundant ebony hair with a wave that some women
envied. He possessed dignity in his open bearing, and
his manners were considerate and ingratiating. He had
candor, tact, and a good humor that easily won and
held the friendship of others. In short, he was a Lee.
Their hope had been that Louisa would see the virtue
of Robert's conduct as well as his family's behavior,
and that Louisa would wish to emulate it and them.
Disappointment that the Robert E. Lees would be absent from Arlington clouded the last day of travel for
Henry and Loretta until they arrived at the mansion
overlooking Alexandria and learned that not all of Robert's family had gone with their parents to New York.

The oldest daughter of Robert and Mary Lee was
Mary, born between brothers George Washington
Custis Lee, known as Custis, and William Henry Fitzhugh Lee, known as Rooney. Although only thirteen
and eleven respectively, Annie Carter Lee and Eleanor
Agnes Lee had already begun to bloom as young ladies
of position. They were the fourth and fifth children of

Colonel Robert and Mary Anne Lee, while preceding
Robert Edward Lee Jr. and Mildred Childe Lee, named
for the colonel's sister. Of the older offspring, only the
oldest was absent. "Custis," explained Henry Lee, "is
followin' in his father's footsteps. He's a cadet at the
Military Academy at West Point, New York, where his
father is the commandant."

"Mrs. Lee and the two younger children are with the
colonel in New York," said Loretta.

Louisa was happy to find that Mary was the same
age as she was. Upon introduction, they became fast
friends as Mary took charge of Louisa, determining that
they should be together nearly every minute of the Kentucky cousin's visit.

Of course, the Caroline County Lees proved not to
be the only guests at Arlington that Christmas season.
On the second morning of their intended three-day stay,
Robert's older brother, Commander Sydney Smith Lee,
and his aide, Ensign Francis Dawson Phoenix, called on
George and Mary Custis, ostensibly as a purely social
function as they passed through Alexandria on their
way to Ravensworth, Smith Lee's home in Fairfax
County. The truth be known, the commander hoped to
play matchmaker by introducing Phoenix to his niece
Mary. He hadn't counted on the presence of any other
young ladies in the Custis household upon their arrival.
Especially, he hadn't expected to find anyone as lovely
and as provocative as Louisa Lee from Kentucky.

Neither had Phoenix. He wasn't exactly smitten with
Louisa at first sight, nor she with him. Neither was he
attracted instantly to Mary Lee, in spite of her obvious
infatuation for him.

Francis Dawson Phoenix, handsome with amber-
flecked green eyes; thick, curly, strawberry-blond hair;
nearly six feet in ramrod-straight height, hailed from
Maryland, the youngest son of an artillery officer who
fought at Fort McHenry, when the British bombarded

the historic bastion and Francis Scott Key wrote the immortal words to the the *Star Spangled Banner.* Because his older brothers had chosen the law or the army for their careers, Phoenix ran away at the age of fourteen to join the navy, starting out as a cabin boy aboard the U.S.S. *Massachusetts,* where he progressed to seaman within a year. Recognizing Phoenix as an intelligent, natural-born leader, the youth's captain recommended him for appointment as a midshipman, and President Tyler signed the order making Phoenix an officer and a gentleman at the tender age of sixteen. After four years at the lowest rank, he was promoted to ensign. Now twenty-six, he had recently been assigned to serve as aide to Commander Lee in Washington.

Mary Lee fawned over Phoenix in the few hours that he spent that day at Arlington. Much to Smith Lee's chagrin but to Loretta's delight, Louisa also showered him with attention, although her initial motive for doing so sprang more from a natural spirit of competition with Mary than from any physical attraction for the ensign. Adding her own touch of spice to the contest, Mary Custis seated Phoenix between the girls at the dinner table, then watched with glee as they dueled for his attention, neither one able to gain the upper hand. The three of them melded into a unit as they strolled about the grounds after the meal, Louisa clinging tenaciously to his left arm and Mary squeezing his right. Regretfully, Phoenix had to leave later that afternoon to accompany Commander Lee to Ravensworth, but he promised to return as soon as he could. That was the next day, when he took leave of his superior's hospitality for the company of the young ladies at Arlington.

Mary and Louisa had stayed up late the night before talking about Phoenix and wondering when and if they would ever see him again and conjecturing which one of them he would choose to court, if, of course, such was his intent at all. Both girls came to the same conclusion, although neither of them spoke it openly, that he would opt for Mary over Louisa because of the simple fact that she was still a maiden and her Kentucky cousin had been despoiled and had the pall of divorce shadowing her past. Both were wrong.

Phoenix rode up to the house, knocked at the door, was ushered into the foyer by a liveried servant, and was greeted by George Custis. The ensign came straight to the point. "Sir, I have come to call on Miss Lee," he said. Custis ordered a servant to fetch Mary. "No, sir," said Phoenix. "I meant the other Miss Lee." Custis frowned, but he changed the order to the slave and sent for Louisa.

Although he admired the Lees as one of Virginia's and thus the nation's great families, Dawson Phoenix harbored no secret desire to become one of them. He felt much like his mother's aunt, Margaret Leatherbury, the youngest child of another prominent Virginia family. In 1808, in spite of her kin's opposition to the union, she married John Hallet, an able-bodied seaman with much promise and dreams aplenty. When her relatives pointed out how much she would be giving up in order to settle down with Hallet on some distant frontier, she replied, "I would rather be the head of a new generation in a new country than the tail end of an old generation in an old state." They settled in Texas, and the last Phoenix had heard of Great-Aunt Margaret, she had founded a town in that state.

Ensign Phoenix called on Louisa at Henry Lee's home in Caroline County nearly every Sunday throughout that winter and into early spring of '53. She had no other suitors for the very reasons that she feared Phoenix would prefer Mary over her; therefore, she encouraged him to return every week. When he proposed marriage on the first Sabbath in May, she accepted without hesitation, knowing that her most likely alternative would be to return to Kentucky and eventually marry some uncouth widower whose first wife had died either in childbirth or as a direct result of having endured too many pregnancies. She wrote to her parents and informed them that she intended to marry Phoenix before the year was out; they would be welcome to attend the wedding if they so wished. John Lee wrote back that she would have to marry her naval officer without them being present as the journey over the mountains to Virginia would be too arduous for him and her mother, who were both over sixty years old now.

The following Christmas season Ensign Dawson Phoenix and Miss Louisa Lee exchanged bands of gold and spoke their matrimonial vows in the sight of God and as many Virginia Lees and Maryland Phoenixes as could be squeezed into Ferncliff mansion for the occasion. The wedding party carried into the New Year, lasting until the third day of January, when the newly-weds were finally allowed to leave for their honeymoon, a week in Charleston. They rode in a stagecoach to Richmond, where they took the cars to the South Carolina city, arriving there late on the fourth instant and checking into the American Hotel on the southwest corner of King and George Streets. Unlike her first night of marriage with David Gray, Louisa expected little if anything from Dawson Phoenix. Admittedly, he was older than Gray had been, and his realm of experience was certainly greater than Gray's, his having been a sailor and naval officer who had taken liberty in nearly every port on the eastern seaboard and Gulf Coast as well as several Caribbean stops. Even so, this was no reason for her to expect any more from husband number two than she had received from number one. Within an hour of locking the door of their room behind them, Louisa realized that she had greatly underestimated Phoenix. As she wrote to Edie Crane in Kentucky, "Dawson touched me in ways and places that I had only dreamed about before our first night in bed together. I got me a real man, Edie, and I am in love with him."

Louisa's wedded bliss lasted less than six months. Her husband had a mistress. The sea.

Dawson Phoenix, born on the shores of Chesapeake Bay, grew up watching the tall sailing ships entering and leaving Baltimore harbor, and the very sight of them awakened in him a primitive wanderlust inherent to all men descended from the food gatherers and hunters who followed the great herds of long-vanished prehistoric beasts and, in so doing, discovered distant mountains and valleys and oceans that tantalized their curiosity and led them to invent boats if for no other reason than to make more discoveries beyond the blue horizon. He dreamed of seeing new lands and new peoples, and like Alexander the Great, who wept when he feared that his father would leave him no countries to conquer, he worried that every corner of the world would be civilized before he could navigate the globe. Running away to sea as a teenager was expected of Dawse. Upon finding the note that said his son had left home to see the world, his father had expressed surprise that he hadn't done it sooner. Feeling the salt-air breeze on his face with the land at his back for the first time convinced young Dawse that he had made the right decision. The life of a sailor would be the future for him.

After twelve years at sea, Ensign Phoenix accepted assignment to be Commander Sydney Smith Lee's aide in the Navy Department in Washington. Only a few weeks afterward, he learned that Commodore Matthew C. Perry's Pacific squadron would be sailing the next year for the Orient with the express purpose of opening diplomatic and trade relations with the emperor of

Japan. Phoenix placed a request with his superiors to be transferred to Commodore Perry's command, but it was denied on the grounds that the squadron had no open officer billets. Greatly disappointed, he considered resigning his commission and applying for his master's papers on a merchantman. Commander Lee talked him into postponing such a rash decision until after the holidays when he would be thinking with more clarity.

The ensign chafed at his desk until he found diversion in Louisa Lee.

The intent behind Commander Lee's introduction to Mary Lee had been so transparent that Phoenix dismissed her immediately as a potential companion for life. Mary was less attractive than her cousin, too giddy, too religious, and she was the daughter of a ranking officer in the army, a situation that would only bring him grief in the future in that he would cease to be his own man but would become a social-climbing toady, or at least he feared that he would be perceived as such by many of his fellow officers.

On the other hand, Louisa Lee intrigued him. Upon staring into her chestnut eyes for the first time, he recalled hot Caribbean nights with olive-skinned Cuban beauties, their white cotton *blusas* open to expose full, rounded, hard teak-nippled breasts and their deep purple *faidas* pulled up around their midriffs revealing silky smooth thighs with deceiving strength. When she spoke, her words and voice fell softly and huskily on his ear, pronouncing her to be a woman secure in her femininity and not a girl still trying to choose between adolescence and womanhood. She moved with much the same grace and charm as most Southern belles, but a slight hitch in her step suggested her possession of a natural copulatory rhythm to her hips, and this also stirred memories of starlit Havana, swaying palm trees, and rum and coconut juice drinks that fueled lusty fires. A physical attraction, however, was insufficient cause for him to return to the Custis household on the second day. He needed more, and he received it when Commander Lee informed him that Louisa was a young woman already despoiled in a foolish marriage. Lee's revelation added spice to his inclination to see Louisa again to learn more about her—from her rather than from others.

Dawse Phoenix courted Louisa Lee, and as he came to know her better, he fell in love with her. He concluded that she had slept with at least one man, possibly more as indicated by the way she kissed him so passionately; she hadn't learned about tongues from that backwoods lout who had enticed her to run off with him, then used her like some grog shop trollop too drunk to do anything except lie on her back and take it for two bits a throw. Her experience, he decided, was a good thing; she would have something with which to compare him; and he intended to give her a night of passion that would forever burn in her memory if not in her loins. He succeeded.

Like all good things, the honeymoon for Dawse and Louisa Phoenix came to an end when they returned to Washington and set up housekeeping. Dispatches from the Orient reminded Phoenix of the adventure that had escaped him, and again he requested a transfer to a ship in the Pacific fleet, only to be denied once more. As consolation, he received promotion to the rank of master, adding a narrow stripe to the broad ribbon on his coat sleeve. With the new rank came new responsibility and a new duty assignment: the navy yard at Gosport, Virginia. The move put him closer to the life that he loved so much, as it allowed him to sail aboard repaired ships on shakedown cruises as inspection officer.

As for his wife, Louisa settled into married life with ease and even became pregnant by the time of their first wedding anniversary. All seemed to be progressing well until the spring of '55 when an epidemic of yellow fever broke out in the vicinity, taking the lives of hundreds of people, especially children. Master Phoenix was at sea when the deadly scourge struck, but Louisa wasn't so fortunate. She contracted the disease, and in the delirium of the fever, her baby, a boy, came early, three months early, too soon to be expected to live for more than a day or two; he lived three days, long enough for Louisa to survive the crisis of her illness but not long enough for Dawse to return to port and set eyes on his son just one time. To make their tragedy worse, the doctor informed Louisa that she would never have another child.

Distraught over losing their son and the distressing news that they could never have another, Dawse focused on advancing himself in the navy. He rose early and worked late, avoiding Louisa at every turn and ignoring her when they were together, although not realizing the hurt he was causing her. If a temporary assignment to another duty station came open, he volunteered for it, the last one taking him to Charleston for three months before Louisa joined him there for the remainder of the year's duty. When a billet for a master at the New York Navy Yard in Brooklyn became available in the spring of '58, he applied for the post and received it. Dawse went to New York ahead of Louisa, and as soon as he located an apartment in the Williamsburgh neighborhood of the city, he sent for his wife. Within hours of Louisa's arrival in Brooklyn, Dawse's longstanding request for sea duty was granted, and he was ordered to report to Panama City, where he would go aboard the corvette *Levant* before it sailed for the Sandwich Islands in October. He packed his seabag and took a steamer for Chagres, Columbia, where he would make the crossing of the Isthmus of Panama to the Pacific port.

Dawse's quick departure and being left alone in a strange city brought about the illness that put Louisa in

bed for the first week of her life in the North. Of course,
she blamed her incapacity on exhaustion caused by the
trip from Charleston, or such was her excuse to the
ladies who called to welcome her to the neighborbood.
After their visit, Louisa determined that she would
make the best of her situation—with or without Dawse.
She made every effort to be the good wife left behind,
at least in the eyes of the other navy wives living in
the area, by attending all the social functions associated
with the shipyard and the military posts scattered
around the harbor, and she wrote to Dawse weekly,
whether she received a letter from him or not. When
Dawse was due to return home for a month of leave in
the summer of '59, Louisa waited anxiously on the pier
with the wives and families of the other officers and
men, and when he came down the gangplank, she
greeted him with open arms and passionate kisses. To
her joy, he reciprocated. They relived their honeymoon
for the first week of his furlough, and everything
seemed to be right with Louisa's world again. Then
Dawse went down to the docks. He went every day.
Early. And he stayed late. And again Louisa saw little
of him. Then he boarded a steamer for Chagres to return to his ship. The following summer he came home
on another leave, and history repeated itself. Louisa had
her man for a week, then he started visiting the docks.
At the end of a month, he was gone again, leaving
Louisa bitter and angry with him. She determined that
the first man to strike her fancy would be welcomed to
her bed. That man turned out to be Rafael Sims.

Sims turned away from the window, his conscience
bothering him. His view fell on Louisa in the bed. What
am I doin'? he asked himself. She's the wife of a fellow
officer, and I'm a married man. I must be insane. I
must be . . .

Louisa stirred, the newsie's high-pitched cries finally

interfering with her dreams, urging her into coming awake. As the reflex of a sated woman, she stretched out a bare arm and felt the vacant space beside her, hoping to touch the man who had brought her so much pleasure these last two weeks. No Rafe. Her head turned aside, eyes opening, looking to confirm his absence. Sure enough, no Rafe. She propped herself onto her right elbow and scanned the room until she saw him standing near the window. "There you are, you sly devil you," she said, her lips spreading into a lascivious grin.

"Yes, my dear, I am still here," he responded softly. Although I don't know why, he chastised himself.

Eagan's voice forced its way through the glass and into the bedroom. "South Carolina secedes! Union dissolved!"

Louisa's eyes widened with hope, fear, and exultation as they were drawn to the window for an instant before refocusing on Sims. "Is it true?" she gasped. "Have they done it?"

"Apparently so, my dear," said Sims.

Louisa threw off the quilt, exposing her nude body without shame to this man who had explored every inch of it with gentle caresses and savage kisses. She jumped from the bed and bounded across the room into his reluctant arms. "Oh, Rafe, they've done it!" she chortled. "They've declared their independence from these Yankee tyrants. Soon we'll all be free again, won't we?"

"It's too soon to tell," said Sims gravely.

Surprised by his statement and his tone, Louisa pulled away to arm's length and said, "Whatever do you mean, Rafe darlin'?"

"I mean that South Carolina has seceded and only South Carolina. This doesn't necessarily mean that the other slave states will follow."

"But of course it does. They're sure to follow."

Sims released her. "Yes, some of them are sure to follow. I know that Alabama will leave the Union at the slightest provocation from the North, and so will Mississippi. Senator Davis has said so. The others? I can only speculate about them. I've had no contact with their men of power." He noticed Louisa's naked form for the first time. Embarrassment crimsoned his cheeks. He looked away, moved past her, picked up her bathrobe, and handed it to her. He began pacing as she donned the garment. "I can only speculate about their intentions. Secretary Floyd has let it be known to many Southern officers in both the army and the navy that he expects them to follow their native states when they leave the Union, but I know that not all of my fellow Southerners will go the way of their home states. Many will remain loyal to the army or the navy of the only country they have ever known."

"But most will remain loyal to their states, won't they, and secede with the rest of us?"

"I would suspect so, although I couldn't tell you which ones at this time. I can't even tell you which side I'll choose when the time comes to make the final decision."

"What?" gasped Louisa. "But I thought you would surely go with Alabama when she leaves the Union. Have you changed your mind, Rafe darlin'?"

Sims ceased to pace, looked evenly, straight into Louisa's eyes, and said, "I've not yet made up my mind."

Louisa glared back at him, giving no quarter until a single thought barged into her consciousness. "I see now," she said. "It's your wife, isn't it, Rafe? Didn't you tell me that she was from Ohio?"

"That's right, she is. Cincinnati to be exact."

"And I suppose she's against the Southern states leavin' the Union."

"No, that's not quite it. She's opposed to *my* leavin'

the Union, and she has a very good point. The navy is the only life I've known since I was seventeen years old, and to give it up at this point as a matter of principle does seem a bit foolish. At least, so it would seem from Annetha's point of view."

"But not from yours?" queried Louisa.

"No, not from mine." He resumed pacing. "I am an officer and a gentleman sworn to uphold the Constitution of the United States of America and sworn to support the Federal government created by that very Constitution. But how can I do that when this very same government that I am sworn to support no longer abides by the Constitution that I am also sworn to uphold? My conscience tells me that the new government with this man Lincoln as president will only further the abuses already heaped upon the Southern states by the Northern-controlled Congress. Even if Alabama should remain in the Union, I certainly can't take up arms against my brothers from South Carolina and any of her sister states that should choose to join her in the formation of a new nation on this continent, and that is exactly what I will have to do if I should remain in the navy. As a Marylander by birth and an Alabaman by choice, I can't stand by idly and let Lincoln and his Black Republicans continue to tread over my fellow Southerners. No, the only course for me is to resign my commission if Alabama should leave the Union."

"And your wife?" taunted Louisa. "What of her feelin's on this matter?"

Sims went to the window, parted the curtains, and stared out at the street below. He focused on Jimmy Eagan as the newsie sold his next-to-last copy of the *Eagle* to a passing businessman.

As soon as the transaction was completed, the youth glanced up at Sims, waved the remaining newspaper at him, and shouted with a certain grating arrogance and defiance, "South Carolina secedes from Union! Civil war threatened!"

Softly but firmly, Sims said, "There comes a time when a man must place his country before his family."

3～

As his custom had been since his earliest days in the
United States Navy, Commander Rafael Sims awakened
before dawn to exercise his body and his mind in preparation for the coming day. This morning he took his
daily constitutional from the bachelor officers quarters
at the New York Navy Yard down to the landing at
the foot of Fulton Street, where he could meet the ferry
from Manhattan and purchase a morning edition of the
New York *Times*. Although the *Eagle* would soon be
available on the streets of Brooklyn, he felt the *Times*
would give him more information, especially details
from the South, which the *Eagle* often abridged or
omitted completely. True, the *Eagle* and Brooklyn were
pro-slavery, pro-South, anti-Negro, and anti-Lincoln,
which usually suited Sims and others of the same ilk,
but the *Times* presented a balanced account of the news,
especially in reporting the momentous events then shaking the United States.

Sims arrived at the landing just as the boat from New
York tied up at the dock, its steam whistle blowing
a shrill announcement of its arrival. Dozens of varied
commercial conveyances lined the right side of the
street, their drivers clustered in knots on the sidewalk.

The horses sneezed and whinnied and occasionally pounded a shoed hoof on the cobbled street in an expression of eagerness to be moving again if for no other reason than to stay warm against the morning chill. The teamsters all held cups of steaming coffee in one hand and burning tobacco of one form or another in the other, as evidenced by the glowing red dots in front of their shadowy faces, the slow fires so very visible in the predawn light each time one of those rugged men inhaled the weed. They waited patiently in the cold, damp air to board the ferry for its return trip to the South Street docks, where they would scatter to the various markets of Manhattan, although a majority of them would repair to the Washington Market on the Lower West Side. They passed the time conversing about the current status of the nation, or as Sims gathered from their localized palaver, the condition of the remaining Union now that South Carolina had declared itself separate from the other thirty-two states.

In a group to themselves on the left side of the street where the *Times* wagon would soon emerge from the ferry stood the newsies, more than two dozen of them, a few drinking coffee, more smoking cigarettes in an effort to exert their claims to manhood and to maintain their stations in the neighborhood pecking order. They waited patiently for their newspapers, the oldest of their number boasting of taking the ferry over to South Street in lower Manhattan and sampling a two-bit waterfront whore the previous night, while the younger boys listened in awe. Among the latter was Jimmy Eagan. He failed to notice Sims, as he was too intent on hearing the ribald details of the older boy's escapade.

Sims didn't distinguish Eagan from the other lads as he took up a position near the newsboys where he could watch the longshoremen secure the hawsers around the piles and the docking lines to the deck cleats. His eye caught sight of the boat's nameplate on the side of the superstructure, and he noted that the moniker, *Union,* possessed a ring of irony. A wry smile curled the corners of his mouth. How soon, he wondered, before this *Union* would see its last days?

A deckhand cranked the winch that lowered the loading ramp, and as soon as it touched the dock, a second man unhooked the rope gate and walked it to the other side of the boat, where he coiled it quickly and deftly against the bulkhead. The winch operator signaled the teamster of the lead wagon waiting to debark the ferry to move ahead. With a snap of his whip, the driver put his team into motion, and a snort-groan-cloppity-clop later, the mercantile ambulance rattled down the ramp to the dock, then up Fulton to any one of the markets located in Brooklyn's more than two dozen neighborhoods. Other wagons followed the first until finally the *Times* van clattered down the ramp to the dock, drove up the short distance to where the newsies waited for it, and stopped close to the sidewalk.

Sims watched and listened as the boys surrounded the rear of the wagon, each holding up at least two dimes, the minimum amount of a purchase, to buy a supply of newspapers to resell throughout the day until the afternoon editions were due to hit the streets. Two men, one lanky, the other stout, both unshaven and dirty-faced with smudges of printer's ink on their cheeks and foreheads, transacted the business of wholeselling newspapers to the street vendors from the rear of the van, the taller fellow taking the money and the shorter handing out the "exact" number of papers purchased at the rate of a penny apiece. These were good times for the newsboys, as the reading public craved every tidbit of news of the South's move toward total separation from the North and West; thus, each lad bought ten or twenty copies more than he normally would. In this microcosm, bad news was good for business.

Jimmy Eagan stepped up to the wagon to take his turn. He held out a silver dollar and said, "I'll take a hundred, Mr. Blodgett."

Sims recognized the newsboy and decided to buy a copy of the *Times* from him.

"A hundred, Jimmy?" queried Blodgett, showing his long, tobacco-stained teeth as he spoke. He wore a tattered wool watchcap to cover his balding pate. "Are you sure about that, boy? You usually only take twenty."

"Yes, sir, I know, but everybody wants to read about the Southerners leaving the Union, now don't they, Mr. Blodgett?"

"Yes, I guess that's right, Jimmy, but this is Saturday, you know, and the paper's got a four-page supplement to it today. That makes twelves pages in all. That's a mighty heavy load for a bucko your size, Jimmy. Are you sure you can handle it?"

"Positive, sir," replied Jimmy, showing the man respect only because to do otherwise would result in decidedly less favorable treatment. "I'll take a hundred."

"Well, all right, if you're sure about this."

"I'm sure, Mr. Blodgett."

Blodgett turned to his helper. "Give him a hundred copies, Charlie."

The assistant counted out ninety newspapers and handed them to Eagan. "Here's your hundred, Jimmy," he said.

Eagan accepted them with a grunt at their weight, knowing the count to be ten less than he'd requested. That was another facet to this business. The newsies paid for ten copies and received nine. That was nine cents for the *Times* and one penny for Blodgett and Charlie, payment that ensured each boy of a corner all his own and enough copies to make a few pennies for himself every day, should he sell out, that is. "See you

Monday morning, Mr. Blodgett," he said just before turning away toward the sidewalk.

"Good luck to you, Jimmy," said Blodgett. "All right, who's next?"

As the remaining boys crowded closer to the wagon, each eager to replace the previous customer, Sims emerged from the shadows to greet Eagan as he stepped onto the sidewalk. "Need some help with those, Jimmy?" he asked.

Surprised by the officer, Eagan stumbled at the curb and lost control of his load for a brief second before righting it again. "Commander Sims, sir!" he gasped. "You gave me a start."

"Now I didn't mean to do that, Jimmy," said Sims, "but I have to say that you have also surprised me. I thought you only sold the Brooklyn *Daily Eagle* in Williamsburgh."

"Oh, no, sir, Commander Sims. I've been selling the *Times* for the past four months as well. I've got me fifteen regular customers that I deliver to each day between here and Fort Greene, and I sell the rest along with the *Eagle* on me corner up in Williamsburgh. Not everybody in Brooklyn is for slavery and the South leaving the Union, you know."

"No, I wouldn't expect so, Jimmy," said Sims sternly, feeling that the youth had given him a gentle verbal jab, which, intentional or not, he didn't like but absorbed. After all, Eagan was only a boy, a Northern boy, an Irish boy. What could he know of the great dispute between the two sections of the country? And of his knowledge, how much of it could be within his understanding? Sims decided against retaliating.

Eagan shifted the weight of newspapers to make them easier to carry.

"Let me help you with those, Jimmy," said Sims.

"Thank you, Commander Sims, but I can manage these."

"Nonsense, young man. Let me help. I'm goin' the same way as you are. I'd be delighted to help until you can manage on your own."

"All right then." Eagan held out the newspapers to Sims. "You can carry some, if you like."

Without counting, Sims took half the stack and tucked them under his left arm. "Lead on, Jimmy."

They began walking up Fulton Street.

"What are you doing down here this early in the morning, Commander Sims?" asked Eagan. "Mrs. Phoenix throw you out on your ear last night?"

Sims glared at the newsie and said, "My relations with Mrs. Phoenix are none of your business, Jimmy."

"I didn't mean nothing by it, Commander."

They walked on without speaking until they came to the Brooklyn Hotel and Eagan halted at the front door. "I've got seven customers in here, Commander. You can come in and wait in the lobby while I deliver me papers upstairs, if you want to."

"Thank you, Jimmy. I'll do just that."

They entered the hotel. No clerk occupied the registration desk at this hour, and the lobby was otherwise unoccupied.

"Have a seat, Commander," said Eagan, taking an easier, more familiar tone with the officer, "and I'll be back in a few minutes. Read a paper, if you like. It's on me."

"Thank you," said Sims. "I think I'll do just that." He surveyed his surroundings: carpet of deep cardinal with a gold fleur-de-lis pattern, oak registration counter, stairway to the upper stories, hallway to the dining room, a potted palm in the only corner suited for it, two maroon damask armchairs flanking an oak coffee table opposite the front desk, white molded ceiling, four-lamp gas chandelier, and gas lamps in the center of each old gold-papered wall, all the lights at half-flame. He put the newspapers on the table and eased himself into the right chair. He picked up a *Times* and scanned the front page.

The lead headline read:

THE NATIONAL CRISIS

Followed by:

PROCEEDINGS OF THE SOUTH CAROLINA CONVENTION

The third header interested him the most:

THE APPOINTMENT OF COMMISSIONERS TO PROCEED TO WASHINGTON

He skipped down the column of type to the first mention of the commissioners. "The Convention is now on its second balloting for three Commissioners to Washington. R. W. Barnwell was elected on the first ballot. A. G. McGrath and J. L. Orr stand the best chance." A "declaration of causes" that precipitated South Carolina's move to separation was printed in smaller, bolder type two paragraphs below, the list running the remainder of the first column and partially into the second. At its conclusion came an additional note on the commissioners. "The second ballot for the other Commissioners to Washington was unsuccessful. On the third ballot, Ex-Gov. J. H. Adams, and Ex-Congressman J. L. Orr were elected to act with Mr. Barnwell as Commissioners to treat with the United States."

Sims mulled over this fact, concluding, These gentlemen will need all the assistance they can get if there is to be peace between the states. He resumed reading, the following articles reporting the reaction to South Carolina's withdrawal from the Union in other Southern states and cities. In order came Charleston, Baltimore,

New Orleans, Mobile, Montgomery, and Pensacola, the last three of particular interest to Sims. All stated much the same thing: The secession of South Carolina was hailed with wild enthusiasm, bold speeches, and hundred-gun salutes. He passed over the remaining reports from other states and cities and read the article headlined:

OUR WASHINGTON DISPATCHES

Two items in its text proved of interest to Sims. One confirmed his own suspicion that the congressional delegations from Alabama and Mississippi would remain in Washington until their state governments acted on secession, while the other announced the resignations of Lieutenants Dozier and Hamilton and several acting midshipmen, all from South Carolina, from the United States Navy.

I should confer with Senator Houston and Senator Clay as soon as possible about my own future with the navy, thought Sims, looking up from the newspaper. Maybe I should speak to Senator Davis as well.

Jimmy Eagan came bouncing down the staircase. "All done here," he said as he approached Sims.

The naval officer stirred from his reverie, stared at the newsie, and thought, I can't talk to any of them from here in New York. Time to be going home.

"Find anything interesting in the paper, Commander?" asked the newsboy.

"Most of the front page concerns itself with the secession of South Carolina," said Sims, replacing the copy atop the stack on the table.

"How about you, Commander Sims? Are you gonna secede with the other Southerners?"

"My state hasn't seceded, Jimmy," replied Sims, not wishing to commit himself one way or the other to anybody, not even a newsboy, just yet, contradicting his words to Louisa Phoenix the day before. He rose from the chair.

"Which state would that be, sir?"

"Alabama," said Sims as he picked up the pile of newspapers and tucked them under his arm again.

Boy and man started for the front door, exited, and continued walking up Fulton Street.

"Do you think Alabama will secede, Commander?" asked Eagan before they had gone another block.

"I think all the slave states will leave the Union if an accommodation can't be reached in Congress in the next few weeks."

"An accommodation, sir?"

"Yes, an agreement whereby the Northern states will agree to abide by the present statutes concernin' slavery and whereby they will promise in the future not to interfere with slavery in the slave states and in the territories of the West. Also, there is the matter of the tariffs."

"I don't understand what that is, Commander."

"Tariffs, you mean?"

"Yes, sir."

"Tariffs are taxes on imports and exports," said Sims. "The Congress passed laws requirin' tariffs on many of the items imported and exported by the Southern planters. These taxes were then spent in Northern states to build public, military, and naval works, and many Northern businessmen prospered at the expense of the Southern planters. This system has been in place for more than forty years, and every new tariff is more oppressive to the South than its predecessor. Compound the tariffs with the question of slavery, and the South has plenty of reason to secede from the Union."

"I see," said Eagan. "I think. I'm from Ireland, you know, Commander, and I don't quite understand all this business between Northerners and Southerners. I'm guessing that it's something like back home where the

English lords own everything and we Irish got nothing. Me dad calls the English oppressors and tyrants.''

"And what do your people back home do about their oppressors and tyrants?'' asked Sims.

"Some bow down to them. Some fight. And some pack up and leave the country.''

"Well, that's what the Southern states are tryin' to do here, Jimmy. They're tryin' to leave the country.''

"Sometimes the English won't let people leave Ireland.''

"Then what happens?''

"They fight.''

"That's what will happen here, Jimmy, if the North doesn't let the South leave peacefully.''

"No foolin', Commander?''

"No foolin', Jimmy.''

Eagan let out a low whistle as they turned a corner and headed toward the navy yard. "That ought to sell a lot of newspapers,'' he said quite seriously.

Sims made no reply, concurring in his mind with the lad's conclusion.

As the eastern sky brightened with the new day, the newsie delivered copies of the *Times* to the remainder of his regular customers, finishing before they reached the entrance to the navy yard, where Sims halted to bid him farewell.

"It's been a pleasure to walk with you this mornin', Jimmy. I've enjoyed our conversation very much.''

"The pleasure was mine, Commander. Thanks for carrying me papers all this way.''

Sims dug into the coin pocket inside the waistband of his trousers to retrieve a five-cent piece. "I'd like to buy one,'' he said, holding out the nickel for Eagan.

"No, sir. You keep your money, and take a paper on me. Call it pay for carrying all those copies this far.''

"That's very generous of you, Jimmy, but I insist

that you take the money. This might be the last copy
of the *Times* that I'll be buyin' for a while.''

"Really? Are you going back to Washington soon?''

"Today, if I can take care of a certain delicate matter
this mornin'.''

Eagan grinned and asked, "Do you mean Mrs.
Phoenix?''

Indignation raked the hackles of his neck as Sims
said, "A gentleman does not discuss private relations
with the fairer gender, Jimmy. Always remember that.
A lady is a lady is a lady. Remember that, too.'' He
thrust the nickel into Eagan's coat pocket, took a *Times,*
and said, "Good-bye, Jimmy.''

Feeling a bit chastised, Eagan said meekly, "Good-
bye, Commander Sims.'' He watched as Sims strutted
to the front gate to the naval reservation where the
marine guard saluted him by shifting from "parade
rest'' to "present arms.'' "Now ain't that something?''
whispered the youth to himself, awed by the respect
shown to Sims by the handsomely uniformed sentry.
He heaved a wistful sigh, thought, Someday I'll be
getting that kind of respect, then went about his
business.

Sims returned to the bachelor officers quarters, where
he ordered a steward to pack his bag for the train trip
back to Washington. After a breakfast of fried eggs,
buttered bread, hot oatmeal, and coffee, he presented
himself to Commodore Andrew Hull Foote, the commandant of the New York Navy Yard, in the latter's
office to announce that he had completed his tasks in
New York, ostensibly the inspection of navy piers and
warehouses, besides being the bearer of sad news for
Louisa Phoenix and the wives of two other officers
aboard *Levant;* therefore, he wished to take his leave
of Foote's command. He stood at attention in the com-

modore's presence and did not speak unless asked a question.

"I suspect this will be the last time that we should ever meet, Sims," said Foote. The commodore's heavy jowls and baggy basset eyes painted him melancholy much of the time, but today he appeared more forlorn than ever. "I would assume that you will go with your state should it secede." He shook his head slowly. "These damn politicians will get us all killed before they find a solution to the mess that they've created. Hundreds, thousands, possibly tens of thousands of good men will have to die because those bastards in Washington can't sit down at the same table together without arguing about slavery and taxes." He raised up one cheek and blew wind. "Sorry about that, Sims, but if I mind my manners, the gas builds up inside me until my heart starts pounding the hell out of my ribs. A most uncomfortable feeling. I would choose to die in battle rather than to die from gas crowding my heart. I most likely will not be given that opportunity, however. I'll just sit here in this office and fart myself to death, while younger men like you become heroes and villains on both sides of this damnable, inevitable war facing all of us." He picked up a pen in his right hand and the document that would permit Sims to return to Washington in his left. "I wish you well, Commander." He signed the orders, blotted his signature, and handed the paper to Sims. "Have a good trip back to the capital."

Sims took his orders, thanked Foote, and returned to the bachelor officers quarters to pick up his travel bag. As he emerged from the barrack, he pulled his overcoat tighter around his neck against the rain that had begun to fall heavily. With everything in order as far as the navy was concerned, the time had come to tend to that final delicate item on his agenda. Valise in hand, he left the navy yard and caught a crowded streetcar for the house on the corner of Bedford Avenue and Rodney Street in Williamsburgh.

During the ride, Sims gave thought to the meeting ahead of him. He had come to New York as the messenger of tragic news for the wives of three officers serving aboard the missing *Levant,* and as an added duty given to him by Secretary of War Floyd, he was to inspect the navy's piers and warehouses in New York harbor. The latter assignment pleased him because he knew that Floyd was hoping to locate misplaced military and naval stores that could be removed to Southern posts and ports, and it gave Sims the opportunity to serve the Cause. The former task held no such pleasure for him until he met Louisa Phoenix. He had spoken briefly to the first two wives, then left them to bear their grief and worry on their own. Not so with Louisa. She had displayed much less emotion when he gave her the news about the *Levant* being late to port and feared lost at sea. Her restraint induced him to stay longer with her than the others, and it piqued his curiosity to return the next day. She was younger and prettier than the others, and she had no children. More than that, Louisa possessed a provocative air about her, an aura of sensuality, confirmed by her captivating behavior on his second visit. As he called on her a third time, Sims questioned his own motives. Was he succumbing to her charms? Or was he merely lonely? Away from his wife for too long? Was he trying to prove to himself that he was still a man who could conquer women at will? Was it his age or his ego? Had he seduced her? Or she him? The answer, he felt, rested somewhere between the two questions.

The streetcar driver clanged the bell and announced the intersection where Sims wanted to get off. As the public transport slowed to what was considered a safe speed for debarking, he stepped down to the street, stumbled a pace, then made it to the sidewalk. He crossed Rodney Street, his thoughts still whirling around the vivacious woman who lived on the second floor of the corner house.

In Louisa Phoenix, Sims had found a kindred spirit. For several months, he and his wife had debated the dispute between North and South, she playing the devil's advocate while he expounded all the reasons for the Southern states to withdraw from the Union. As convincing as he thought his arguments to be, none convinced her that he should follow Alabama if that state should secede. She remained adamant in her belief that he would be throwing away his career and their future if he should make such a risky move. Such arguments never entered into his conversations with Louisa. After they learned that they were both Southerners, their talks turned to the state of affairs between North and South, and to their equal joy, they discovered that both favored secession to remaining subjugated by the North. This mutual feeling sparked an excitement in them that brought them closer as people and as man and woman. The fire within their souls for the Southern Cause spread to their loins, and they united in a lusty struggle that both felt would culminate in glorious victory.

As he took the stairs up to her apartment, Sims reached the conclusion that the flames within him for Louisa had subsided. He knocked on her door, wondering whether her fire had cooled as well.

The door opened, and standing there was Hattie Jones, Louisa's middle-aged servant, in reality a slave but masquerading as a free person of color because Louisa had coerced her into the charade by threatening to have Hattie's children sold south if Hattie should make any attempt to gain her freedom or if she should reveal her true level of servitude. Averting her eyes from the commander's face as soon as she recognized him, Hattie welcomed Sims and invited him inside.

"Has your mistress arisen for the day?" asked Sims.

"Yessuh, she has," replied Hattie. "I'll go tell Miz Phoenix yo' is here, Commander Sims. Won't yo' make yo'self comfortable in the parlor, suh?" She backed away a few steps before turning aside to let him pass.

"Thank you, Hattie," said Sims. "I'll just leave my bag here." He put the valise on the floor beside the door and went to the parlor to wait for Louisa.

The living room was very spacious, with two brocade sofas, matching wing chairs, mahogany coffee table as a centerpiece, Persian carpet covering the majority of the hardwood floor, fireplace dominating the most interior wall, and two long windows looking out onto Bedford Avenue. A door to the left side of the fireplace led to the kitchen, and a second on the right led to the dining room. A third door in the wall opposite the foyer opened into a short hall to the bedrooms.

Louisa emerged from the kitchen, wearing a blue dress adorned with the blue and white palmetto cockade of South Carolina. "Why, Rafe darlin'," she cooed, "you've come so early today." She put her hands on his chest, expecting him to embrace and kiss her.

Sims did neither as he said, "And I'll be leavin' early as well, my dear."

A cloud darkened Louisa's face. "You will?"

Sims took her elbows in his hands, less as an act of affection than as a defensive measure against her possible negative reaction to his next pronouncement. "In fact, my dear, I'm returnin' to Washington today."

"But why? I thought you would be stayin' at the navy yard until after the New Year."

"Events are movin' more rapidly these days, Louisa, and I feel my place is in Washington where I can do the most good for the South."

"Where you can do the most good for the South or where you can be with your wife and children?" she asked bitterly, leaning away from him.

"There is that consideration as well," said Sims firmly, "but it isn't the only one. South Carolina is sendin' commissioners to Washington to negotiate the peaceful transfer of Federal property to the new republic. I might prove of some service to these gentlemen while they are in the capital. At the very least, I would like to make my report to Secretary Floyd as soon as possible. I only came by to bid you farewell."

"Oh, I see." She withdrew gently from his hold. "Will you be returnin' to New York in the near future?"

"I think not, Louisa."

She turned away from him. "Then we are at an end?"

"These are troubled times, my dear. Who is to say whether this is the end or just a beginnin'? Not I."

"Nor I." She twisted to look at him over her shoulder. "I wish I could be goin' with you to Washington."

"That is not to be, Louisa."

"Yes, of course it isn't. It's only that I wish to be near you, Rafe darlin'."

"And I with you, my dear," he lied to soothe the pain that he imagined she must be feeling, "but we must consider the Cause of Freedom before our personal desires."

"Yes, of course we must." She turned to face him fully again, heaved a sigh, forced a smile, and said, "I sometimes wish I were a man so that I might do more for the South."

"There are many ways that a woman can be of service to the South," said Sims, glad that their conversation had taken this tack. "If war should come between the states, you could be the South's eyes and ears here in New York. Who can tell at this juncture how important that would be to the Cause?"

Louisa's face brightened. "Yes, of course," she said.

"I could keep you informed about developments at the navy yard."

"Yes, of course you could," said Sims, seizing the idea with enthusiasm. "And there's the movement of ships from this harbor."

"Yes, especially warships. I could keep you informed about their movements as well."

"Yes, an excellent idea, my dear."

"But how would we accomplish this, Rafe?"

Sims twisted his brow in thought. "I'm not sure," he said. "I've never had to deal with this sort of thing before. I suppose we could use the mails, but that would take too long. We could use the telegraph, but that would prove too expensive in the long run."

"Not if we kept the messages short," interjected Louisa.

"But if we were to keep the messages short, we might not be able to relay as much information as we'd like." He shook his head. "No, this matter is too important for us to decide on how to deal with it at this time. We must give it some thought."

"Yes, of course, but at the very least we will remain in contact and occasionally see each other."

"Yes, I suspect so, my dear."

"Oh, Rafe darlin'." She threw herself at him, putting her arms around his neck and kissing him furiously.

Sims responded in kind, the fire for her and for the South burning brightly within his loins and soul, respectively.

4〜

Sunday, December 23, 1860

President James Buchanan had won election to the presidency of the United States because he was a Northerner who believed that the South had rights, even if one of them was the right to enslave a people who failed the test for Caucasian purity. He supported the South, although he was personally opposed to the very peculiar and demeaning institution of slavery.

When selecting a cabinet to aid him in the governing process, Buchanan chose men from both sides of the legendary Mason-Dixon Line. He picked Lewis B. Cass of Michigan for secretary of state; Howell Cobb of Georgia for secretary of the treasury; Isaac Toucey of Connecticut for secretary of the navy; Jeremiah S. Black of Pennsylvania for attorney general; Jacob Thompson of Mississippi for secretary of the interior; and John B. Floyd of Virginia for secretary of war. Three Northerners and three Southerners. Balance. Equal representation for the two sections of the nation, which Buchanan maintained when Cass resigned and he chose Black to succeed the Michigander, then appointed Edwin M. Stanton of Pennsylvania to replace Black as attorney general; and when Cobb quit to join the secessionist movement in his state, Buchanan tabbed

Philip F. Thomas of Maryland to take charge of the treasury.

Buchanan had possessed no misgivings about the state of the nation when he was inaugurated in March of 1857. He knew from the start that his presidency would be sitting atop a political powderkeg that could explode with the smallest spark of temper from either side, and he wanted nothing more than to keep the United States united for the length of his term. He achieved this goal for three years, nine months, and sixteen days; then South Carolina seceded. From that moment, keeping the states from going to war with each other became his new challenge. Little did he realize that half of his cabinet officers had been undermining his efforts all along.

Chief among these destructive forces was John Floyd, the planner and schemer who manipulated the military for his personal gain as well as for the benefit of the South. For the past year, Floyd had been removing arms, ammunition, and stores from Northern armories and warehouses to posts in the South and Southwest. Specifically, he had ordered the transfer of 135,430 muskets from the Springfield, Massachusetts, arsenal to various points in Dixie. For this, the Mobile *Advertiser* thanked Floyd on its editorial page: "We are much obliged to Secretary Floyd for the foresight he has thus displayed in disarming the North and equipping the South for this emergency." Floyd had done little of this maneuvering in absolute secrecy. Ostensibly, when questioned about his motives, he replied that the weapons were being strategically placed in preparation for a possible war with Spain over Cuba, a conflict much desired by expansionist Southerners wishing to spread the so-called benevolent brand of American slavery to maltreated Spanish slaves. However, he continued covertly to transfer munitions and weapons to southern

and southwestern forts after the threat of collision with
Spain had passed.

Many prominent Southrons inside and outside the
Federal government had been fully cognizant of Floyd's
movements prior to the remarks in the Alabama newspaper, but none of them objected or revealed knowledge
of his strategy to anybody who couldn't be trusted ex-
plicitly to keep it secret from the Northerners in Buchanan's administration. Included in this close-knit
circle were several Southern senators who could be
counted among the "fire-eaters" demanding the separation of the slave states from their oppressors in the
North. Not given the privilege of joining Floyd's cabal
were officers of the army and navy, because including
them might subject them to charges of treason and con-
spiracy to overthrow the Federal government, and this
would never do, because the South would need these
men when the time came to form an army and a navy
for the new nation that Floyd and his confidants were
certain would be forthcoming in the land of cotton.

Not content to restrict his activities to the military,
Floyd thought to bolster the South's naval potential as
well. Normally, the secretary of war had no control or
say over the navy, his concern lying solely with the
disposition of the army, its men and facilities, with the
secretary of the navy handling everything pertaining to
ships and ports as well as the men and officers who
manned them. Realizing that the South had a longer
coastline than the North and thus would need a strong
navy to protect it, Floyd hoped to move naval stores,
weapons, munitions, and ships to Southern ports. To
achieve this goal, he circumvented Secretary of the
Navy Isaac Toucey by informally requesting Captain
Duncan Ingraham, a fellow Southerner, to send a South-
ern-born-and-bred officer to New York to inspect conditions in that port. Ingraham chose Commander Rafael
Sims for the task.

Sims empathized fully with Floyd in particular and the South in general, and he was completely aware of the secretary's strategy to arm the South against her Northern aggressors. Although he remained an officer and a gentleman in the United States Navy, he accepted the assignment without trepidation, although cognizant that the information he would garner in New York was intended to aid a future Southern nation, and with that thought still guiding him, he hastened to Floyd's house on I Street to give an oral preliminary account of his findings on the condition of the navy's piers and warehouses in the vicinity of New York harbor.

A white-haired male slave in the typical colonial costume of house servants answered the door. "Yessuh, may I help you?" he asked, eyes averted as supremist whites demanded of blacks in order that they might be shown proper respect by a folk that they considered their inferiors.

"Commander Rafael Sims to see Secretary Floyd on a matter of naval business," said Sims.

"Please come in, sir," said the butler, his accent Southern but refined compared to that of field hands because masters and mistresses desired their house servants to be clean, civilized, and conversant in the English language as proof of their masters' cultured superiority. He stepped aside to permit Sims to enter the foyer, a small room with a long hallway running the length of the house from one side of it and a staircase leading to the second floor on the other, and as soon as the commander had come inside, he closed the door behind this latest guest. "I will announce you to Secretary Floyd, sir. If you will please wait here, sir?"

"Of course," said Sims. He removed his hat and waited.

The servant moved down the hall to the third door on the left, knocked twice, waited to be summoned inside, then opened the door and entered. In a moment, he reappeared behind Floyd, a man with determined features: strong jaw, aquiline nose, firm mouth, black walnut hair that covered the top half of each thick-lobed ear, brown eyes that offered the viewer no intro-spection to the soul, large head set on narrow shoulders that had never known manual labor, stature of medium build and height.

Sims came to attention as if encountering a military or naval superior, which, technically, Floyd happened to be, although he was a civilian and his primary gov-ernmental concern lay with the army. The officer re-mained rigid until Floyd released him from the courtesy.

"Good to see you again, Commander," said Floyd, smiling and offering his hand in greeting. "How was New York? No doubt very cold."

Sims shook hands with Floyd and replied, "Not as cold as I expected for this time of year, sir."

Floyd broke the grip and said, "When did you return to Washington?"

"I arrived late last night by train and went directly home, sir."

"And how is your family? Hale and hardy, I trust."

"My wife and children are just fine, sir."

"Well, what brings you here on a Sunday afternoon?"

"I thought you would like to hear of my findin's in New York harbor as soon as possible, sir."

Floyd's face brightened even more. "Ah, yes. The piers and warehouses inspection. Of course, of course. Come into the library with me, Sims. I have other guests who might wish to hear your report as well."

Sims hesitated. "Other guests, sir?" he queried, his voice barely able to disguise his sudden agitation.

"Senators, Commander," said Floyd as if that made everything all right.

"I wouldn't wish to intrude, Mr. Secretary," said

Sims, glancing at the butler standing behind Floyd. Servant or slave, the man still had ears and a mouth and the capability to speak out of turn.

"Nonsense, Sims," said Floyd. "You won't be intrudin' at all." Noting the direction of the commander's look, he turned to his servant and said, "That will be all, Silas. Be sure that we are not disturbed for any reason."

"Yes, sir," said Silas, bowing and backing away from Floyd and Sims. He retired down the hall, taking the second door on the right to the kitchen.

"Now come with me, Sims," said Floyd. "I'd like you to meet these senators, if you haven't met them already."

Sims followed Floyd down the hall to the library. The officer entered first as his host stepped aside courteously. Much to his surprise, the commander recognized all three gentlemen seated before him: Senator Clement C. Clay from his own state of Alabama, Senator Lewis T. Wigfall from Texas, and Senator Jefferson Davis from Mississippi.

Floyd closed the door behind them and said, "Gentlemen, I would like you to meet Commander Rafael Sims, who has just returned from completin' an assignment in New York."

"I am very much acquainted with Commander Sims," said Clay, a stout fellow with thick red hair, bulbous nose, weak chin, and flabby features everywhere else about his person. He made no move to rise from his wing chair. "We hail from the same state. How nice to see you again, Sims!"

Sims offered a stiff half-bow to Clay and responded, "The honor is mine, Senator."

"I also know Commander Sims," said Davis. He left the upholstered armchair, rose to his full height, and offered a bony hand in greeting to the naval officer. "How are you, Commander?"

"I'm fine, sir," said Sims, shaking hands with Davis.

"I ain't had the pleasure of makin' the commander's acquaintance," said Wigfall, rising from the other wing chair and extending his hand in friendship. A fire-eater of the first class, he looked more like a frontier brawler than a United States senator. Broad shoulders, barrel-chested, large head, heavy black beard and mustache, sharp blue eyes, a Scot descended from a survivor of the Spanish Armada. He presented a meaty hand that told a tale of years of labor carving a plantation from the wild country of Texas. "You look very familiar to me, sir. Where might we have met afore?"

"I am posted here in Washington, Senator Wigfall," said Sims. "Perhaps you've seen me at the Navy Department or in the halls of the Capitol when my duties have taken me there. I know that I've seen you on more than one occasion."

"And that's how you know who I be?"

"Yes, sir."

"Now ain't that somethin', sir," said Wigfall with a friendly smile. "How do you do, Commander Sims? It's a pleasure to make your acquaintance."

"How do you do, Senator?" said Sims, accepting the grip. "The pleasure is mine, I assure you, sir."

Davis and Wigfall returned to their chairs, while Sims remained standing in the presence of men he considered his ranking superiors.

"Now that we've completed the introductions," said Floyd, stepping around the large oak desk and sitting down in its straight-back chair, "let's get down to the purpose of the commander's visit this afternoon. As I stated before, Commander Sims has recently returned from an assignment to New York. I sent him up there to inspect the navy piers and warehouses around the harbor, includin' the New York Navy Yard at Brooklyn. Commander Sims has come by to give me an account

of his inspection tour. I thought you gentlemen might
be interested in hearin' what he has to say."

"Yes, certainly," said Clay.

"Agreed," said Wigfall.

"Yes, Mr. Secretary," said Davis, "I too would like
to hear the commander's report. Tell us, Commander
Sims, how are conditions in New York harbor? As far
as the navy is concerned, I mean."

"All things considered, sir," said Sims, "I'd have
to describe them as adequate. Every pier that I saw was
in good condition, and the warehouses were also in
good condition. Only one that I saw needed any immediate repair."

"What about their contents, Commander?" asked
Floyd. "Were they full of naval stores and the like?"

"Not really, sir. I'd have to say that many of them
are near to bein' empty."

"Would you say they held enough materiel to outfit
and supply a large naval expedition, if there should be
a need for one on short notice, that is?" asked Floyd.

"No, sir. The quartermaster would have to buy most
of the needed materiel for any emergency expedition."

Floyd exchanged glances with the senators, then
asked, "What about the navy yard at Brooklyn? What
condition was it in, Commander?"

"Commodore Foote has matters well in hand there,
sir," said Sims. "The drydock was in perfect order,
and the yard workers were busy refittin' only one ship,
the steamer *Wyandotte,* which I understand is due to be
sent to Pensacola, Florida, in the near future."

"You have notes and figures for everything you saw,
ain't you, Commander?" asked Wigfall.

"Yes, sir."

"How soon before you'll have your written report
ready?" asked Floyd.

"I can have it on your desk the day after Christmas,
sir," said Sims.

"Very good, Commander," said Floyd. "I'll be lookin' forward to readin' it."

"How long was your inspection tour of New York harbor, Commander Sims?" asked Davis.

"A little more than two weeks, sir."

"Did you have a chance to meet any of the people there?" asked Davis. "Other than navy personnel, I mean."

"A few."

"And how was the talk of South Carolina's leavin' the Union?" asked Davis. "Was there much opposition to it?"

"The newspapers expressed varyin' opinions on it, Senator. For the most part, I would say the Northerners are indifferent to South Carolina leavin' the Union. Some are opposed to the dissolution of the Union, and some have even said that the North will be better off without the Southern States."

"And what is your opinion, Commander Sims?" asked Wigfall. "How do you feel about South Carolina leavin' the Union?"

Sims fixed his gaze on Wigfall's right eye and said, "I am an officer in the United States Navy, sir, and therefore, I am not entitled to express my political views."

"Very well put, Commander," said Davis. "A very wise position to take, as well. Havin' served in the army myself, I concur that an officer's first duty is to the country whose uniform he wears for as long as he wears it. Wouldn't you agree, gentlemen?"

Floyd cleared his throat nervously and said, "Yes, of course, Senator Davis."

"Yes, of course," said Clay.

"I didn't mean for you to dishonor yourself, Commander Sims," said Wigfall sheepishly. He looked askance at Davis and added, "I was merely curious about your opinion. I meant no offense."

From this exchange, Sims concluded that Davis held the reins of power within this room, possibly within the entire infrastructure of Southern politics. Davis had impressed him in the past with fiery speeches in the Senate and with his dignified bearing, but the commander had never before realized how forceful a man the senator happened to be. His respect for Davis increased considerably.

"No offense taken, Senator," said Sims.

"Well, thank you for comin' by, Commander," said Floyd. "I look forward to readin' your report on your inspection of New York harbor." He stood up, came around the desk, reached for the door handle, and said, "I'll show you out myself, Commander."

"That won't be necessary, sir," said Sims. "I know the way." He turned to the trio of legislators. "Gentlemen, it was an honor." He bowed to them, straightened up, faced Floyd, and added, "Mr. Secretary, I will deliver my report personally to your office the day after Christmas." Without further ado, he left.

As soon as he heard the front door close behind Sims, Floyd returned to his chair behind the desk and said, "I have to say that I'm quite disappointed with the commander's report. I'd hoped for more. Or at least, I'd hoped that there would be an abundance of naval stores in New York that could be transferred to one of our Southern ports."

"I believe it's too late for maneuvers such as that, Mr. Secretary," said Davis. "Our immediate concern is with the forts at Charleston."

"Yes, of course, Senator," said Floyd. "As you know, last month I replaced that Yankee Colonel Gardner with Major Robert Anderson as the commandin' officer at Fort Moultrie. Anderson is a Kentuckian, and his wife is the daughter of General Clinch of Georgia."

"Yes, I know Anderson," said Davis. "Our paths crossed a time or two when I was in the army. We served together in the Black Hawk War. He contracted cholera but survived. A good Southerner and a good officer, but he's not a man to commit treason against the uniform he wears."

"Do you think he'll do the right thing when the time comes?" asked Wigfall.

"Do you mean, will he surrender the forts when the South Carolina authorities demand them?" asked Davis.

"Yes, precisely," said Wigfall.

Davis looked at Floyd and said, "What do you think about that, Mr. Secretary?"

"I believe he will," said Floyd.

"But you ain't sure if he will?" queried Wigfall.

"Let me say that I feel more comfortable with Anderson in command than I felt with Gardner down there."

"But you still ain't sure about his politics, are you, John?" asked Wigfall.

"He'll do his duty, I assure you, Lewis," said Floyd.

"Yes," said Davis, "but will his duty be to the army or to the South?" His eyes skipped from blank face to blank face about him without finding an answer to his question. He smiled sagaciously at Floyd and added, "Perhaps Major Anderson should be given a direction for his duty to take as a measure of assurance."

"Do you mean that I should order him to surrender the forts to South Carolina?" asked Floyd. A cold sweat beaded on his brow, and his hands became clammy. He wrung them to alleviate the condition.

"Not exactly," said Davis. "Perhaps a communication tellin' him not to endanger his command or something of the sort."

A sigh of relief hissed through Floyd's lips. "Yes, of course," he said. "I think I know what you mean, Senator." He pinched his lower lip between the thumb and forefinger of his right hand as he gave the senator's suggestion some consideration. A thought came. He pulled a sheet of notepaper from a short stack on the upper left corner of the blotter, drew the pen from the inkwell, and wrote rapidly. When he finished, he replaced the pen meticulously in the inkwell, held up the paper, and said, "How does this sound? Of course, it's only a first draft, but you . . ." His voice trailed off as he noted the expectation in the eyes of the senators. He cleared his throat and read. " 'In light of the recent events in South Carolina and considering the mood of that state's government, you are hereby advised it would be senseless for you to make a vain and useless sacrifice of your life and the lives of the men under your command, upon a mere point of honor.' "

"That sounds pretty good to me," said Wigfall, grinning like a black bear who'd just found a log full of honey.

"I concur," said Clay sternly.

Davis said nothing, merely nodding slowly, a twinkle in his eye and a small smile curling the corners of his mouth, satisfied that Anderson would understand that he was to surrender the forts in Charleston harbor rather than defend them and thus start a war. Yes, Anderson would avoid a fight, and the South would have peace yet.

Another thought occurred to Floyd. "Just for good measure," he said, "I'll send a second letter to Captain Foster, who's in command of the engineers workin' on the three forts. I'll tell him to mount Fort Sumter's cannons immediately, and as soon as he has them in place, the South Carolinians will no doubt possess the place along with Castle Pinckney. Seein' that Moultrie would be subject to a murderous fire from Sumter and that he can't retreat to either of the other two forts, Anderson will have no choice but to surrender Moultrie to the South Carolinians."

"And once the Federal presence is removed," said

Clay, "Buchanan will be forced to recognize South Carolina's independence."

"And then our states will join South Carolina in a glorious new confederacy of the South," said Wigfall.

"Caution, gentlemen," said Davis, wagging a long thin digit before them. "Let us remove the Yankee from our soil first. Then, and only then, will we have cause for celebration."

The trio of listeners realized that he was right.

5 ～

Christmas Eve, 1860

The revelries of secession continued throughout the South for days as word of South Carolina's bold step spread to every hamlet and hollow from Virginia to Florida, to Texas and Missouri and back. The celebrations and the Sabbath prevented Sarah Hammond and Rowena Randolph from leaving the region as soon as they would have liked. No matter. They had both learned long ago that very little in life could be carved in granite.

Sarah and Rowena departed Charleston on the same train as the three commissioners from South Carolina whose mission would be to negotiate the peaceful transfer of Federal property, namely the forts guarding Charleston harbor and the arsenal on the city's outskirts, to the government of their newly proclaimed republic. Sarah did this purposely, hoping to engage the gentlemen, either separately or collectively, in a serious discussion of the present situation in Charleston harbor. Specifically, she wished to learn the intentions of the recently seceded state toward the Federal garrison at Fort Moultrie. In her interviews with Governor Pickens, she had failed to extract any definite information from him; he would say only that the forts had to be surrend-

ered to South Carolina and the Federal troops removed
from the state. How this should be accomplished, he
refused to elaborate. And if the Federals should refuse
to hand over the military posts and depart the state?
Still no firm reply. Thus, she turned to dogging the
commissioners.

Also prompting Sarah to leave Charleston that Saturday morning was the advertisement in the Charleston
Mercury placed by the South Carolina Rail Road, de-
claring it would suspend service from Charleston to
Columbia and points beyond after that day. No reason
was given, but the general consensus of those interested
in such matters held the decision to be due to the holidays when few people traveled and fewer businesses
did any shipping of freight. For people like Sarah and
the commissioners, who wished to be elsewhere, the
line's declaration presented an inconvenience to their
schedules but nothing so serious that timely adjustments
couldn't be made.

The South Carolina Rail Road train pulled out of
Charleston early that morning and was due to arrive in
Columbia before noon. There Sarah and Rowena would
transfer to the Wilmington & Atlantic train that would
take them to Wilmington, North Carolina, where they
would spend the next two nights before proceeding to
Washington on Monday, the layover necessitated by the
practice of trains not running on Sundays.

Some would have called Sarah aggressive, an un-
comely trait in a woman, but she preferred to think of
herself as assertive, a virtue that she came by naturally,
being descended from Katherine Chatham, the militant
Quakeress who defied the tyrannical Puritan establish-
ment of seventeenth-century Boston; those unbending
Roundheads tried to conform the equally stubborn
Katherine to their religious practices by placing her in
the stocks and then in jail, but they failed to sway her
from the doctrines of the Society of Friends and finally

admitted defeat by banishing her to the more tolerant colony of Rhode Island. Sarah, like her courageous ancestor, refused to accept the premise that Eve was made by God from a man's rib simply to be the helpmeet of Adam and therefore all women hence should be as Eve, meaning docile subjects of men. To the contrary, she considered herself the equal of the most outstanding men of business and politics and the superior of all others. With this attitude to bolster her, she attended to the task of pursuing South Carolina's commissioners.

Although men of celebration, Robert W. Barnwell, John H. Adams, and James L. Orr restricted their movements aboard the train and kept to their own company during the short trip from Charleston to Columbia. To ensure their privacy, they instructed their youthful traveling secretary to act as a buffer between them and any fellow passengers, especially journalists, who should approach them without invitation.

Seeing how adept the young man proved to be at deflecting intruders, Sarah decided patience should direct her actions; she would wait for the most opportune time to converse with the commissioners, then seize the moment. Much to her chagrin, no such opportunity presented itself until the train arrived at the depot in Columbia, where Governor Pickens waited to greet the trio of representatives and give them his final instructions on how they should deal with President Buchanan. Peering through her compartment window as the train slowly came to a halt, she saw Pickens on the platform surrounded by an entourage of aides, other political figures, onlookers, and hangers-on. An idea struck.

"Rowena, would you take our bags and wait for me on the platform outside?" said Sarah. "I'll be along in a moment."

Rowena glanced through the window and saw Pick-

ens. "Are you thinkin' about gettin' to the commissioners through the governor?" she asked.

Sarah smiled and said, "You read my mind. That's
exactly what I plan to do."

"That could work," said Rowena. She took their
valises down from the overhead rack and exited the
compartment.

As Rowena was leaving, Sarah lowered the upper
glass of the compartment window and leaned through
the opening just enough to make herself noticeable to
the governor. The ploy worked just as Rowena said
it might.

Pickens spied Sarah, and a lascivious grin spread
across his lips. "Miss Hammond, how are you?" he
asked, more than delighted to see her again.

"I'm just fine, Governor Pickens," she replied with
forced gaiety. "Merry Christmas to you, sir."

"Thank you, Miss Hammond, and merry Christmas
to you as well. Are you returnin' North?"

"Yes, I am," she said, catching a glimpse of the
three commissioners as they stepped from the train to
the station deck. "To Washington City, actually. My
father wishes me to learn what the government intends
to do about South Carolina."

"Yes, of course," said Pickens, his good cheer sour-
ing to suspicious concern. As an afterthought, he added,
"I should also wish to learn President Buchanan's
intentions."

Adams, Barnwell, and Orr walked up to Pickens.
Their eyes shifted from the governor to the attractive
young woman still inside the train and back again. Orr
cleared his throat to gain the governor's attention away
from Sarah.

"Gentlemen, how good to see you," said Pickens,
once again effervescent as he shook hands with each
of them in succession. "I hope you had a fair trip

from Charleston. You must have, considerin' you were travelin' on the same train as Miss Hammond.''

The name Hammond shivered the senses of all three like a cold draft creeping down their spines. The specter of James Henry Hammond appeared in their minds, arousing in them a myriad of emotions, ranging from hate and disgust to admiration and gratitude, for it was James Hammond of Redcliffe who had inspired much of the South's secessionist rhetoric and who also possessed a most sordid past that included alleged affairs with the teenage daughters of his wife's brother; on the one hand, a man to be honored in Southern politics, and on the other, a wretch to be reviled by polite, aristocratic society, not so much for having done the deed but for failing to maintain decent secrecy by limiting his licentiousness to one niece or even two instead of sampling the affections of all four.

Seeing the distressed confusion on the faces of the commissioners, Pickens chortled, ''Gentlemen, you astound me. Am I to believe that you rode all this way on the same train and failed to make the acquaintance of this lovely lady?''

''We did not have the pleasure of bein' introduced to the lady,'' explained Orr, unsure of what else to say.

''Then allow me to rectify that oversight, Mr. Orr,'' said Pickens graciously. One by one, he presented the commissioners to Sarah.

John II. Adams, the man who had cast the first vote for secession at the recent convention. James L. Orr, the compromise candidate for the position he now held. Robert W. Barnwell, the fire-eater of fire-eaters from one of Carolina's most prominent, most wealthy, and above all, most powerful families.

In Sarah's eyes, they represented everything inherently malignant in the South. They were the epitome of all those slaveholding, chauvinistic, pompous, arrogant, misguided aristocrats who considered themselves the

new cavaliers, the nobility of the South, whose duty—
nay, quest—was to rule not only the Africans whom
they held in abject bondage but also the poor Anglo
and Scots farmers, husbandmen, mechanics, teamsters,
and clerks who earned their livelihoods through the
sweat of their own brows and not through the blood
and tears of the enslaved.

Sarah, although born and raised in wealth, possessed
neither ethnic nor class prejudice. People were people.
Some more intelligent, some less; some more attractive,
some not so; and thus. Economic and ancestral conditions were never given consideration when assessing a
person's worth as a human being. If she held one viru-
lent distaste, she despised bigotry in any form. With
that inner eye so focused, she saw Adams, Orr, and
Barnwell as well as Pickens and most of the South's
so-called gentry, but she knew better than to permit her
personal views to interfere with the mission at hand.

"How do you do, gentlemen?" she said as sweetly
as any Southern belle.

Pickens made further reparations by informing the
trio about exactly who Sarah Rebecca Hammond happened to be. The commissioners were duly impressed—
and relieved that she was only a distant cousin to the
Hammond they knew so well. So delighted were they
that each attempted to outdo the others in making chiv-
alrous remarks about her beauty and the prominence of
her family.

Sarah smiled and replied with all the appropriate
phrases that Southern men expected from their women-
folk but not necessarily from a Northern lady. Better,
thought Sarah, that they should consider her nothing
more than an empty-headed girl than to suspect her of
posing some sort of threat to them, their mission, or
their state. "You are too kind," she said demurely at
the conclusion of their flattery.

"Miss Hammond has let it be known that her family

will continue to do business with South Carolina," said Pickens, "in spite of our leavin' the Union."

"Very good," said Barnwell. "Now if President Buchanan and the Federal government will accept us in the same vein, then we should make the transition from state to sovereign nation with ease and peace."

"We can only pray that your wish is granted, Mr. Barnwell," said Sarah with all honest sincerity.

"Amen!" said Adams.

"Yes, of course," said Pickens. "With that in mind, we must set ourselves to work. If you will excuse us, Miss Hammond, these gentlemen and I have much to discuss before they depart for Washington City on Monday."

"Monday?" queried Sarah. "I should think you would be in a great hurry to reach Washington City and begin your negotiations with President Buchanan."

"Yes, we are eager for the negotiations to begin," said Pickens, "but the Sabbath and the holiday must be taken into consideration when makin' travel plans. Although we can conclude our deliberations this very day, the last train for the North leaves within the hour, and there will not be another until Monday mornin'."

"There is no real hurry, Miss Hammond," said Adams. "We have the personal assurance of Secretary Floyd that the Federal government will take no action concernin' the forts at Charleston prior to President Buchanan receivin' us. So you see, we have no real cause to be hasty."

"Yes, I see," said Sarah, somewhat absently because she noticed that while Adams spoke his associates frowned at the mentioning of Secretary of War Floyd. Trying to hide her own feelings, she said, "Well, I was so looking forward to making the remainder of my journey to Washington City in such distinguished company, but I suppose I shall have to endure on my own."

"The regret is all ours, dear lady," said Adams as he bowed from the waist to bid Sarah adieu.

"My sentiments exactly," said Orr.

"And mine as well," chimed Barnwell.

"Farewell then, gentlemen. Perhaps our paths shall cross again. Say in Washington City. I shall be there much of next week."

"Then we shall make a point of callin' on you, Miss Hammond," said Adams.

"Please do."

Pickens herded the commissioners away, and Sarah turned to the business of changing trains and continuing her trip to Washington.

With plenty of time on their hands the next two days, Sarah and Rowena contemplated the current situation within the country, and they speculated on the future of events.

The leaders of South Carolina had declared their state to be an independent nation, and they now demanded that the government of the United States turn over all of its property within the borders of South Carolina. This raised the question of what course of action would be taken by the United States under President Buchanan. Would he submit to the Carolinians' demands and hand over the forts in Charleston harbor? Or would he refuse to recognize South Carolina's sovereignty and risk a war with the entire South? Would the Carolinians risk a war with the United States by seizing the forts by force? Whatever the answers, the potential for evil was all too great.

Having had only limited success in Carolina, Sarah now took aim at Washington. She concluded that the commissioners' delay could work to her advantage. She would be in Washington two full days ahead of them, and this would allow her to take soundings with several government and military officials, including her own state's senators as well as certain cabinet members and other legislators.

"While I'm doing that," said Sarah, "you might visit with some of the slaves in the households of some of the Southern senators and congressmen. Find out what they've overheard recently. Who knows? One of them might have heard the one thing that might prevent this country from going to war with itself."

"I still don't understand why you're tryin' to prevent this war, Sarah," said Rowena.

"We've been over this before, Rowena. You know that my family and I are morally opposed to war, and—"

"Yes, but didn't you tell me that your granddaddy fought the British in the Revolution of '76?"

"Yes, he did, but that was my grandfather's choice. My grandmother taught her children and her grandchildren to be pacifists, to abhor war and violence, to love our fellow man, not to make war on him." As an afterthought, she added, "Or to enslave him."

Rowena shook her head with resignation and, reverting to her Virginia roots, said, "And you think you're gonna *love* these Southrons into freein' their slaves? You're dreamin', if you do. That ain't gonna never happen. There ain't gonna be no great gettin'-up-in-the-mornin' jubilee for the coloreds of the South till you do-gooders in the North stop preachin' abolition and start freein' niggers at the point of a gun."

"Rowena, you know I dislike that word."

"What? Nigger?"

"Yes, that word."

"I don't know why it should bother you so much. You're white. You ain't the one bein' called a nigger. I am. Of course, maybe you don't like bein' called a nigger-lover. Is that it, Sarah?"

"No, of course not, Rowena."

"Then what is it, Sarah?"

Sarah frowned and said, "What is it coloreds call white people when they're not around?"

"Ofays?"

"Yes, that's it. Ofays. I don't know what it means, but I know that coloreds don't use it with affection in their hearts."

"So what's your point, Sarah?" asked Rowena rather impatiently.

"It's the implication of both terms that I despise, Rowena. Both are derogatory, inflammatory, and filled with hate. I find them to be as offensive and as demeaning as the word *ugly* when applied to a person."

"Yes, Sarah, but some people are ugly."

"In whose eyes? God's? A mother's? A small child who has yet to be taught to hate, to shun, to mock, to shame anything or anybody that happens to be different? In whose eyes, Rowena? Yours?"

"No, Sarah, not mine."

"And not mine either, Rowena. That's why I choose to do everything within my power to prevent this war instead of standing idly by and watching my fellow Americans shed each other's blood needlessly. Now let us keep our sights set on that goal. Please?"

Rowena shrugged and said, "How can I say no to the woman who gave me my freedom?"

"That is not a debt to be repaid, Rowena. You are free to go your own way whenever you wish it."

"And when that time comes, I will," said Rowena with great resolve, "but now we got work to do."

Sarah patted her hand and said, "That's the spirit."

Immediately upon arriving in Washington City, Sarah hired a hansom cab to take them to the Willard Hotel at the triangular corner of Fourteenth Street and Pennsylvania Avenue. Without alighting from the hack, she tipped the doorman to take their luggage inside the hotel and help Rowena to rent a room for them. That done, she ordered the driver to take her to the residence of Senator William Henry Seward of New York.

Formerly the governor of New York and a national figure in the Whig party, Seward had gone to the Republican convention in Chicago earlier that year thinking that he would carry the party standard in the fall election. He did begin the balloting as the frontrunner, but after the second tally of votes, it became clear that he had a serious challenger in the relatively unknown backwoods lawyer and one-time congressman from Illinois, Abraham Lincoln. When all was said and done, Lincoln won the nomination, and Seward had the promise of a cabinet post should Honest Abe sweep to victory in November.

Lincoln did win, and although official announcement of Seward's nomination to the office of secretary of state had not yet been made, rumor had it that the New York senator would be the most influential man in the country, with a strong right arm around Lincoln's shoulder to aim the novice political leader in the proper direction. Seward would be the true power behind the presidential seal.

Understanding that prospect, Sarah called on Seward without requesting an interview in advance and without regard to the day and hour: Christmas Eve.

For his part, Seward would have refused to see most other visitors at this time, but Sarah Hammond was no ordinary caller. The granddaughter of the great lady who had helped to propel him to the statehouse in Albany, Sarah was also the daughter of Levi Hammond and the niece of Gideon Hammond Jr., two of the largest financial contributors to the burgeoning Republican party. Refusing to receive Sarah would be not only rude but politically unwise as well.

"To what do we owe the honor of your visit, Miss Hammond?" asked Seward, effusing a patronizing charm that annoyed Sarah as they sat in the parlor of his drably decorated home.

"Senator, I am recently come from Charleston," she said. "I left there only this past Saturday morning."

Seward gave no reaction, astute politician that he was, saying simply, "Yes, I'd heard that you were traveling in the South."

"Observing, Senator," she said, correcting him.

"Observing?" he queried, his great eyebrows rolling up his forehead.

"Yes, Senator, observing. Observing the determination of the Southerners to be separated from the Union."

"Balderdash!" pshawed Seward, instantly animated at the mention of the Union's dissolution. "This act of secession that the South Carolinians have transmitted to the rest of the nation is nothing more than the old game of the South trying to scare and bully the North into submission to Southern demands. Well, it will not work"—he pounded his right fist into his left palm for emphasis—"ever again. They threatened to bolt the Union if Lincoln won the presidency, but we were not cowed. We voted true to our consciences, and Abraham Lincoln will be President of these United States come the fourth of March in the year of our Lord eighteen hundred and sixty-one. And on that day, this nation will begin anew. Mark my words, Miss Hammond. It will begin anew."

"Yes, it will," agreed Sarah sincerely, "but Mr. Lincoln's inauguration is more than two months away. Between now and then, what is to be done to preserve the Union?"

"That question must be asked of Mr. Buchanan," said Seward flatly. "To the best of my knowledge, he plans to do nothing to incite other Southern states to secede, and he equally plans to do nothing to encourage South Carolina to renounce her declaration of secession and rejoin her sister states in the Union. He will simply sit in the White House and fidget and wring his hands like the old woman that he is.''

Ignoring Seward's castigation of the president, Sarah asked, ''What about Secretary of War Floyd? What is he doing toward preserving the peace?''

''That scoundrel!'' spat Seward. ''The man is a thief and a liar. A reprobate and a traitor to his country.''

''Southerners consider him a hero, Senator.''

''Yes, they would. That's because he's been stealing on their behalf.'' Seward snickered. ''He won't be stealing for much longer, I've heard. The word circulating through the capital is that Buchanan will ask for Floyd's resignation right after Christmas. That will put an end to his mischief on behalf of the Southern states.''

''Yes,'' said Sarah, ''but what more will he do to cripple the North and bolster the South in the interim, Senator?''

Seward frowned for the briefest of seconds, quickly changing to a benevolent, patronizing, patriarchal grin as he said, ''Now why should you worry that pretty, sweet head of yours over such matters, Miss Hammond? These are the affairs of men, and young ladies shouldn't be involved in them, don't you think?''

''No, Senator, I do not think,'' said Sarah firmly, evenly, with all the cold calculation of an executioner preparing to release the trapdoor of a gallows. ''I have brothers, cousins, and nephews who will have to fight and maybe die for their country unless you and your fellow leaders of this great nation act now to prevent a needless war between the states.''

Taken aback by her attitude, Seward disposed of his capricious smile, put on all the stolidity of his Puritan forebears, and said just as evenly and firmly as a mortician examining a corpse, ''Miss Hammond, I assure you that everything that can be done will be done to prevent a civil war between North and South. You have my word on that.''

Sarah suddenly recollected her grandmother's warning about politicians: ''When they give you their word about something, you can be assured that whatever they are promising will never come to pass.'' This was one time that Sarah wished her grandmother's wisdom would fail, but in her heart, she knew it wouldn't. Seward wanted a war with the South. Hadn't he said so in the past?

''The Union shall stand,'' said Seward in a speech, ''and slavery, under the steady, peaceful action of moral, social, and political causes, will be removed by gradual voluntary effort, and with compensation. If not, then the Union shall be dissolved and civil war ensue, bringing on violent but complete and immediate emancipation.''

In other words, the diametrically opposing forces of abolition and slavery could never find a peaceful solution to the issue because of their emotional polarity, and they would eventually collide on the battlefield in order to determine whether the United States should become either entirely a slaveholding nation or entirely a nation of free labor. Since an irrepressible conflict between the states was inevitable, Seward and his fellow abolitionists felt it should come as soon as possible.

Frustrated again, Sarah wished Seward a merry Christmas and returned to the Willard Hotel.

''How did it go with Senator Seward?'' asked Rowena.

''Not as well as I would have liked,'' said Sarah as she removed her bonnet. ''He gave me his word that everything that could be done would be done to prevent a civil war between the states. That's so much poppycock, and he knows it.''

''Poppycock?'' queried Rowena. ''What's that?''

''Fresh cow pie,'' said Sarah with a smile.

"I thought it might mean something like that. There seems to be a lot of poppycock in this town, don't you think so, Sarah?"

"Yes, I do, and it makes it so difficult to get to the truth. I suppose we'll just have to put on our knee boots and wade through it, though. That's the only way we'll get anywhere around here."

"I suppose," said Rowena. "So what are you gonna do next?"

"I'm going to church to pray to Jesus that this won't be our last Christmas to be celebrated in peace."

6

Christmas Night, 1860

Major Robert Anderson had no intention of surrendering Fort Moultrie the way his father had done before him.

Named for Colonel William Moultrie, who had defended the first fortification on Sullivan's Island from a British incursion, Fort Moultrie, a sacred spot in the hearts of all South Carolinians, traced its existence to the Revolutionary War. Later in that conflict, Major Richard Clough Anderson, a Virginia-born Kentuckian, defended Charleston when the British attacked the city a second time. He fought valiantly but unsuccessfully and was captured by the redcoats, who threw him into jail for nine months.

Over the decades since the 1783 Treaty of Paris, Fort Moultrie had fallen into disrepair. Hundreds of cracks veined its walls, and beach sand drifted so high against its landward bulwarks that stray cows often wandered atop them and into the fort. Under Colonel John L. Gardner, a veteran of the War of 1812 who spent much of his time spinning in the social whirl of Charleston, the fort had become even more decrepit. Gardner would have remained in command of the Federal garrison had he not had the colossal gall to demand weapons from the Federal arsenal in Charleston for his soldiers, thus raising the wrath of War Secretary Floyd, who ordered him to repair without delay to San Antonio, Texas, on November 15.

To replace Gardner, Floyd chose Kentucky-born Major Robert Anderson of the First Artillery, figuring that Anderson's Southern birth and sympathies would cause him to favor his homeland over the Union. Anderson, a sturdy, medium-size man, about five feet nine inches tall, with dark eyes, swarthy complexion, thinning steel-gray hair, and a military carriage, but with a warm smile and impeccable manners, was first and foremost a loyal army officer, a gentle person, yet much respected for having learned mastery in the world of men. Twice brevetted for gallantry in action, the fifty-five-year-old Anderson had fought in the Black Hawk, Seminole, and Mexican wars, being wounded by three balls at Molino del Rey, Mexico. He could have boasted of a brilliant military record without a blemish, and although promotions were difficult to come by in the peacetime army, even if one was a West Pointer, he maintained his personal decorum at all times and never reminded his superiors of his successes on and off the battlefield.

This was Major Anderson's second posting to Fort Moultrie, the first having been in 1845. He had accepted the assignment again with some misgivings. Before saying his farewells to his wife and four children in New York, he had sought the counsel of his mentor, General Winfield Scott, the army's ranking officer, at Scott's home in the city. Scott related his anger at Secretary Floyd for appointing Anderson without consulting him. Although he liked the man who had served as his aide-de-camp during the Mexican War, Scott refused to be of much assistance to Anderson, but he did advise the major that Fort Moultrie's indefensible position might make it necessary for him to move his men to Fort

Sumter out in the harbor and command Charleston from
there. Anderson said he would keep that thought in
mind.

Upon assuming command of Fort Moultrie, the major
came to the instant conclusion that the post could be
made tenable if the sand dunes were removed from the
southwest wall and if the garrison was reinforced with
several companies of infantry. Both of these requests
were refused by the secretary of war, leading Anderson
to suspect Floyd's motives. To confirm this suspicion,
the major requested permission to place a few artillerists at Castle Pinckney, the half-moon shaped fortress
situated in the harbor on marshy Shute's Folly Island,
less than three-quarters of a mile from Charleston, and
named for Charles Cotesworth Pinckney, South Carolina patriot, statesman, and framer of the Constitution,
who drafted at least thirty-two of the eighty-four provisions of that monumental document. Floyd denied the
request, instructing Anderson that his initial responsibility was the defense of Fort Moultrie.

The day before Christmas, Anderson received two
visitors: a special courier from Washington and Dr.
George Salter, a young physician from New York presently visiting in Charleston. Salter arrived first.

"What is the purpose of your visit here, Dr. Salter?"
asked Anderson as they stood outside the commander's office.

"Merely a professional call, Major Anderson," said
Salter, a stout fellow of average height, brown hair,
blue eyes, and a captivating smile. "I've come to interview your post surgeon."

"Interview, Dr. Salter?" queried Anderson.

"Yes, sir. I would like to ask your surgeon about
the military life for a physician."

"Why would you want to know about that, sir?"

"It's my opinion, Major Anderson, that our country
is headed toward a disastrous civil war. Both sides will

need all the surgeons they can find. When the time comes, I'd like to have some idea about what I'm in for.''

"I see," said Anderson. "I hope you are wrong, Dr. Salter, but I can understand your desire to be informed. You will find Captain Crawford at the post hospital. I'll have an orderly show you the way.''

"That won't be necessary, Major. Just point me in the general direction of the hospital, and I'll find it.''

"It's over there," said Anderson, pointing out the building.

Salter nodded a farewell and departed in the direction indicated by Anderson. The major failed to see the doctor stop and speak with Captain Doubleday before proceeding to the hospital.

Within a few minutes, the messenger from Washington delivered a special letter from Secretary Floyd advising Anderson not to offer any resistance to the South Carolinians should they attack Fort Moultrie in force. The major recalled General Scott's advice and decided the time had come to give it some very serious consideration.

While Anderson secluded himself in his office to mull over the difficult situation in which he'd been placed, Dr. Salter called on Captain Crawford at the post hospital. He found him sitting at the desk at the end of the cavernous wardroom.

Crawford hailed from Pennsylvania. Thin, on the short side of average height, he sported a full mustache and bushy side whiskers. Although a medical doctor by training, he aspired to military glory, having joined the army nine years earlier, serving on the frontiers of New Mexico, Texas, and Kansas as an artillery officer prior to duty at Fort Moultrie; even so, he had not yet seen any action, but he had hopes that his record would soon indicate something that he could tell his grandsons about in years to come.

Salter introduced himself. The two men shook hands, and Crawford offered Salter the straight-back chair next to the desk. Salter accepted.

"What brings you to South Carolina, Dr. Salter?" asked Crawford as soon as he was seated again.

"I have friends here," said Salter. "From college days at Columbia College in New York. I thought I would visit them one last time before the Union is torn asunder and friendships below the Mason-Dixon Line fall into disfavor in the North."

"Yes, of course," said Crawford. "I, too, have friends in the South. Like many military men, I worry about that time when we may become mortal enemies on the battlefield."

"These are difficult times for all, Captain Crawford."

"Indeed, yes." Crawford heaved a forced breath before adding, "So what is the purpose of your visit here, Dr. Salter? To Fort Moultrie, I mean."

"I've been visiting in Charleston for the past week," said Salter, "and I happened to see you coming out of the meeting hall where the secession convention was taking place. I must say that I rather admired your style and courage to wear a full dress uniform to such an event considering the mood of Carolinians toward the army and the Federal government."

"Thank you, sir. I attended the convention purely from the standpoint of a curious observer of history in the making."

"Yes, of course," said Salter. "History in the making. These Carolinians are certainly doing that, aren't they?"

"And no doubt, this is only the beginning of a long chain of historic events unfolding in our time."

"Which brings me to the purpose of my visit here, Captain. Like you, I am a physician by training, but I am hardly a man of action such as you are. I have heard about your mountain-climbing exploits in New Mexico and your visit to the Sandwich Islands to explore a live volcano. Quite an adventurous escapade, if I may say so, sir.''

Crawford held back his ego and said with proper modesty, "Thank you, Dr. Salter, but jaunts in the mountains of New Mexico and to the Sandwich Islands pale in comparison to the exploits of trailblazers such as Fremont and Marcy or that English physician Dr. Livingston.''

"Even so, they are impressive achievements, which is why I came to you. I expect the worst for our country in the near future. We Northerners can't allow the Southern states to leave the Union, and we can't allow them to stay and continue to enslave the Negro race. Either way, war is inevitable, and hundreds of thousands of good men will be forced to face death on the battlefield. Both sides will need surgeons, hundreds, maybe thousands of us. I will volunteer to serve in some regiment from New York, but I don't know whether I should serve as a soldier or as a physician. I am divided between a desire for adventure and an obligation to aid my fellow man. Clouding my decision is my meager knowledge of the army. I have no idea what to expect from the military life. Thus, I am torn between serving my country as a warrior or as a healer. Since you have made this difficult choice, I was hoping you could extend some advice on which way I should choose.''

"I can't do that, Salter," said Crawford bluntly. "That's a decision that you'll have to make on your own.''

"Yes, of course, it is, but I was hoping you might tell me why you gave up practicing medicine for the army.''

"I haven't given up practicing medicine entirely. Although I command an artillery company, I am still the post surgeon here. I hold sick call daily, and I attend to the ailing and infirm in the hospital. I also tend to my duties as a line officer.''

"And you still have time to record history in the making," interjected Salter. "I am quite impressed, Captain Crawford, but I should think that a man like you would rather be making history instead of merely writing about it.''

"That's quite true, Dr. Salter," said Crawford with forced resignation, "but until the Southrons commit some act of aggression, there is little history to be made here at Fort Moultrie.''

"*Au contraire, mon ami,*" said Salter, his eyes twinkling with mischief. He scanned the area and noted that they were out of earshot of the patients and orderlies. "We're both Northerners, aren't we, Captain, and don't we want the same things?''

"What are you getting at Salter?" asked Crawford, his suspicion growing by the second.

"I'll come straight to the point, Crawford. You're in the army, and you're easily recognized in Charleston. With or without your uniform. It's fairly hard for you to hide those whiskers and that mustache.''

"Get on with it, Salter.''

"All right. I travel in certain circles in Charleston and elsewhere. Important circles. I know or have access to several important men. Men who are making the decisions for South Carolina right this very minute as we speak.''

"Are you offering to be a spy?" asked Crawford.

Salter grinned and said, "Yes.''

"You're a fool, Salter. Don't you know that they shoot spies?''

"Only if they're caught, and I have no intention of being caught.''

"I repeat, you're a fool, Salter.''

"Just hear me out, Crawford. I can gather information in Charleston, and I can give it to you, and you can give it to Major Anderson, and he can give it to the generals in Washington, and—"

"Stop right there, Salter. Don't you know that Anderson is a Southerner?"

"Yes, but he's a loyal Union man, isn't he?"

"That has yet to be determined," said Crawford dryly.

"I see," said Salter. "Even so, you could pass the information to Washington, couldn't you?"

"Possibly, but Washington is far from Fort Moultrie. The only information that could prove valuable to me here would have to relate to any movements by the Carolinians to seize this post."

"Well, I can get you that information," said Salter boastfully.

"That information would only prove valuable if Major Anderson remains loyal to the Union, and as I have said, that has yet to be determined."

"Do you mean that you suspect Anderson of duplicity with the Carolinians?" asked Salter, suddenly serious.

"I suspect Major Anderson of nothing," said Crawford, suspicious of Salter's motives for asking such a question. "He is my superior, and as long as we wear the same uniform, I will obey his commands to the letter."

"And what if those commands are treasonous to the Union?"

"I will address that situation when it arises. Until then, I will make no speculations or hypotheses of what might occur."

"Then I take it that you are refusing my offer?"

Crawford directed his focus on Salter's right eye and said, "I didn't say that."

Salter smiled, relaxed, rose, offered his hand in parting, and said, "You will hear from me soon."

Crawford bade him farewell, watched him leave the

hospital, then returned to his duties as if nothing were
out of the ordinary.

As he passed through the parade ground, Salter noticed Captain John Foster, the engineer in charge of
repairing Fort Moultrie and fortifying Fort Sumter, entering Anderson's headquarters. He had seen Foster in
Charleston recently, but he hadn't made the gentleman's acquaintance. I must meet him soon, thought
Salter as he left the compound.

Standing before Major Anderson, Foster handed over
an envelope to the post commander and said, "I have
just received this letter from Secretary Floyd. It's dated
the twentieth instant." A West Pointer from New
Hampshire, tall, thin, and bearded, he shifted to an easy
position as Anderson accepted the communication.

The major unfolded the paper and read words that
angered and frustrated him, although neither emotion
appeared on his face, because he wished to disguise his
feelings in front of Foster. After a second perusal, he
placed the letter on the desk, looked up at Foster, and
said, "What do you make of this, Captain?"

"On the one hand," said Foster, "he tells me to
return the muskets that I requisitioned for my men from
the arsenal in Charleston, and on the other, he tells me
to complete the mounting of the guns at Fort Sumter.
No weapons for my men, but no additional men to help
me with the task of mounting Sumter's guns. I am to
hire civilians from Charleston. I tell you, sir, I am most
perplexed over these orders."

"It is not a soldier's duty to question his superiors,
Captain," said Anderson, spouting the military line as
easily as breathing air. "I suggest you follow the secretary's instructions and complete the mounting of the
guns at Sumter."

Foster focused disbelieving eyes on Anderson as he
considered questioning the major's loyalties. After all,
Anderson was a Southerner, born in Kentucky and now

the owner of a plantation in Georgia. Why wouldn't he side with the South Carolinians in their treason against the Union? Foster thought about challenging Anderson, but he held his tongue. "Yes, sir," he said without conviction.

"Very well, Captain," said Anderson. "If you have no more business with me, then you are excused."

Foster snapped to attention, clicking his heels with deliberate volume as a way of expressing his dissatisfaction with the major. "Yes, sir," he said perfunctorily, and he departed the room.

Anderson ignored Foster's mild insubordination. He had much greater thoughts to occupy his mind. He recapped the interview with Foster and reached only one obvious conclusion: Secretary Floyd wanted Sumter completed and armed so the South Carolinians could take it and train the guns on Moultrie, leaving the garrison absolutely no choice except to surrender. The major pounded his right fist into his left palm and said aloud, "By God, that will never happen."

Anderson paced his office for much of the next hour, allowing a plan of action to formulate in his mind. He recalled every incident of the past month, weighing each for implications toward the future.

Upon accepting the assignment to command Fort Moultrie, Anderson had received advice from General Scott and Captain Cullum of the Army Engineers that Fort Sumter was the most defensible fortification at Charleston. Assistant Adjutant General Major Don Carlos Buell instructed Anderson "to hold possession of the forts in this harbor and, if attacked, you are to defend yourself to the last extremity. The smallness of your force will not permit you, perhaps, to occupy more than one of the three forts, and you may put your command into either of them which you may deem most proper to increase its power of resistance." Countering Buell's communique, Floyd ordered him to surrender

Fort Moultrie rather than "make a vain and useless sacrifice of your life and the lives of the men under your command, upon a mere point of honor." And, of course, Foster's letter from Floyd also came to mind.

More important than Floyd's words were the actions of the South Carolinians. Bands of armed militia from Moultrieville patrolled the boundary of Fort Moultrie regularly, and hostile Carolinian cannon threatened the approach of any vessel that should attempt a relief mission from the sea. Captain Abner Doubleday, Anderson's second-in-command, advised the major that lines of countervallation had been quietly marked out at night, with a view of attacking the fort by regular approaches should an initial assault fail. Two thousand of South Carolina's best riflemen occupied nearby sand dunes and rooftops. The Carolinians had begun constructing batteries at Mount Pleasant on the upper end of Sullivan Island.

Anderson ceased pacing and returned to his desk. He took up a pen and wrote:

My dearest Wife,

I am sorry I have no Christmas gift to offer you. Never mind—the day may very soon come when I shall do something which will gratify you enough to make amends for all the anxiety you now feel on my account.

He lowered the pen, stared blankly at the paper, and muttered, "Or I and my command shall perish in the attempt." A shudder of foreboding stirred him to resume writing. He would give his wife no more hints to his true thoughts for now.

An hour before sundown that evening, the side-wheel freighter *Dover White,* Liverpool registered by the Levi Hammond Shipping Line, slipped her moorings from the Charleston pier and steamed off toward the bar at high tide. Her master, a direct descendant of a sixteenth-century English sea hawk who, in the company of more notable captains such as Sir Francis Drake and Sir Walter Raleigh, preyed on Spanish shipping on behalf of his queen and country, Captain Aquila Chase stood calmly beside the helmsman on the bridge, studying the horizon ahead. Stoic, dark-eyed, with black and gray whiskers that wrapped around his jaw from ear to ear, he considered Charleston harbor's geography.

To the left of the shipping channel, Fort Moultrie dominated Sullivan's Island. To the right were dilapidated Fort Johnson on James Island and Cummings Point on the tip of Morris Island. Dead ahead loomed Fort Sumter.

The *Dover White* would pass between Sumter and Moultrie, giving Chase pause for thought. No warship, no matter how heavily armed, could withstand the assault of guns from both bastions. No two frigates could survive. Possibly, no fleet either. Such a murderous fire that could be mounted from the two fortresses. On the other hand, Sumter commanded the entire harbor. Possess Sumter and the remaining posts and Charleston would be at the mercy of its gunners. Pray to God, thought Chase, that the next time we pass this way we won't have to run a gauntlet of heavy guns to reach port.

Chase took a deep breath. The heaving of his chest reminded him of the envelope he carried inside his coat. Only minutes prior to sailing, a messenger boy had brought him the letter within a letter. In the privacy of his cabin, he read the note addressed to him.

Captain Chase—

> *Please deliver the enclosed missive to Miss Sarah Hammond as soon as possible. Thank you.*

Caduceus

Sarah had informed Chase before she left Charleston that he should expect some sort of communication for her. "Accept the letter," she told him, "but do not open it. The information within might place you and the line in a compromising position. Please follow the instructions directed to you, and confide in no one that you are carrying anything for me." When Chase, a cousin of Sarah's in closer relation than James Henry Hammond, questioned her about the author of this possible letter, she replied, "The less you know at this time, Aquila, the better for you in case something should go awry." Although the master of his own ship, Chase knew his place within the extended family of Chases and Hammonds. Sarah's father employed him, and Sarah replicated the finely chiseled physical features, bold character, and keen intelligence of his great-aunt. To cross either father or daughter might prove disastrous to his career within the company. When he asked her where he should deliver the letter to her, she revealed her travel plans to him. "I will be staying in Washington City through the Christmas holiday and the immediate days afterward. I would ask you to divert the *Dover White* to Baltimore and personally bring any message to me at the Willard Hotel in the capital." Reluctantly, Chase agreed.

Heavy rains drenched Charleston and environs the next morning, Christmas Day. Fog followed.

Anderson considered cursing the weather for interfering with his plans, but he discarded the notion when he realized that the atmospheric conditions would thwart any designs of the Carolinians as well. In a brighter mood, he celebrated the holiday by attending a party given by Lieutenant and Mrs. Hall.

Every officer not on duty also attended. In particular, Captain Doubleday.

A tall, stout, slow-moving man with a thick black

mustache, a graduate of West Point, Doubleday had been at Fort Moultrie since the previous summer. His strong abolitionist views made him the most hated man in the garrison in the eyes of the Carolinians. They called him "the only Black Republican, the worst of the vile Yankee race at the fort." As a second lieutenant in the Mexican War, he had distinguished himself at Monterey and Buena Vista. His grandfather had fought at Bunker Hill, and his father had served in Congress.

The major and the captain had known each other for years before being thrown together at Fort Moultrie. They respected each other as gentlemen; courteous, honest, intelligent, and thoroughly versed in their profession. Only in politics did they truly differ. Doubleday opposed slavery; Anderson supported it strongly, although he abhorred secession. Doubleday suspected Anderson's latter position to be so much smoke, that the real fire in the major was fueled by his love of the South and its pastoral, aristocratic way of life. When the time came to be counted for the Union, the captain felt certain Anderson would be numbered among the Southrons. For this reason, he watched Anderson for any and every sign that he might betray the garrison to the Carolinians. Thus far, he had detected nothing. Perplexed, he consulted Captain Crawford the evening after Dr. Salter's visit to the fort and Captain Foster's visit to Anderson.

"What do you think our esteemed commander is planning to do about the defense of this post, Sam?"

"That is not the question, Abner. I wonder if he intends to defend the fort at all."

As much as he despised asking, Doubleday felt no other choice as he said, "Are you suggesting that he might commit treason?"

"He's a Southerner and a slaveholder. Why wouldn't he hand over the fort to the Carolinians?"

"He's said several times that he is opposed to secession. I find it difficult to believe that he would surrender the fort without firing a shot. Why, just an hour ago he indicated that he intended to defend the fort.''

Doubleday summarized his conversation with Anderson as the two ranking officers had walked the parapet at dusk only an hour earlier.

''Captain,'' Anderson had said casually, ''what do you think would be the best method for rendering the gun carriages unserviceable should the need arise?''

''Should the need arise, sir?'' Doubleday had queried.

''Yes, Captain, should the need arise. We must be prepared for all contingencies now that the Carolinians have seceded. Don't you agree, sir?''

''Yes, of course, Major, especially since the Carolinians have seceded.''

''Well, then what would be your opinion as to the best method of rendering the gun carriages unserviceable?''

''There are several methods,'' Doubleday had said, ''but my plan would be to heap pitch-pine knots around them and burn them.''

''Are you certain that would do the job, Captain?''

''The pitch-pine knots would burn hot and fast, sir,'' Doubleday had said. ''They would make short work of the gun carriages, I assure you.''

''Very good, very good.''

As Anderson had drifted into serious thought, Doubleday had considered and discarded an idea to question his superior about why he had asked about destroying the gun carriages.

Frowning, Crawford said, ''Why didn't you ask him why he asked you that?''

''I could only surmise that he intends to defend the fort or at least to abandon it and leave the Carolinians nothing serviceable. What else would you make of such a question, Sam?''

"I need more proof that he intends to defend the fort," said Crawford, "or at least deprive the Carolinians of its guns and supplies."

"There must be another way to test the major's loyalties," said Doubleday.

"Suggest a defensive plan of your own, Abner, and see how he responds to it."

Doubleday stroked his chin and said, "Good thought, Sam. I'll do it."

"Do it as soon as you can, Abner. We need to learn of his intentions before it is too late for us to act in defense of the Union."

Doubleday made no reply, realizing perfectly well that Crawford's statement bordered on mutiny. Instead, he opted to leave the question unanswered. For the moment.

The opportunity Doubleday desired to lay his plan before Anderson presented itself at the Halls' Christmas party.

"Sir, I've been considering the fort's defenses," said Doubleday, "and I've decided that a foot assault could be repulsed if the approaches were protected by an entanglement of wire."

Anderson smiled quizzically and said, "Certainly, Captain. You shall have a mile of wire should you require it."

"Thank you, sir. I'll attend to the purchase first thing tomorrow."

"Tomorrow. So soon, Doubleday?"

"Yes, sir, tomorrow."

"I should think that much wire would be cumbersome, Doubleday. Why not wait until the next day? Give the men a day to recover from today's pleasures."

"Yes, sir. Of course." Doubleday was now convinced that Anderson intended some action, but what exactly, he could only guess. Again, he consulted Crawford.

"So you think he intends to surrender the fort to the Carolinians?" queried Crawford as they spoke quietly in a corner of the Halls' parlor.

"Not only do I think he intends to surrender the fort," said Doubleday softly, "but I think he intends to do it within the next few days."

"You know we can't allow that to happen, don't you?"

As he had done before, Doubleday refused to address the question. Without another word, he walked away from Crawford to join Mrs. Hall and his wife as they reminisced about past Christmases. Although his heart was troubled with the possiblity that this might be their last Christmas for some time to come to be celebrated in peace if not in harmony, he acted as if nothing were afoot.

7 ⁓

Wednesday afternoon, December 26, 1860

Louisa Phoenix awakened alone in her bed. Not by
choice. Could she but wish it, Rafe Sims would have
been lying beside her. Or even her husband would have
sufficed. She still loved Dawse Phoenix, although she
now thought of him in the past tense; but she hated
him even more because he had preferred that seductress
of restless men, the sea, over her and all her feminine
charms. Will Rafe prove to be the same as Dawse? she
wondered. Will he choose his career over me as well?
No, not Rafe. He wants me more than some damn ship
and a voyage to God knows where. No, not Rafe.

Even so, Louisa felt a deep need for a man, any man
who could satisfy her lust. He didn't have to love her,
because she had no intention of loving him. The only
qualifications he needed for sharing her bed were a
powerful thrust, gentle hands, and a wet, adventurous
tongue. He needn't be charming and confident like
Rafe, or handsome and wonderfully muscled like
Dawse, because no matter whom he happened to be,
she would pretend that he was Rafe Sims ravishing her
and fulfilling her every sexual whim.

All these lascivious thoughts aroused Louisa to pull
her chemise up to her waist and begin caressing her

already moist pubes. The excitement of her own touch electrified her other genitalia, hardened her nipples, and tingled the fine hairs along her spine down to the crease of her buttocks. She stiffened involuntarily, her head twisting backward, then to the side as the pleasure increased with each heartbeat. She felt deeper and—

Knock, knock!

"Miss Louisa?" called Hattie from the other side of the bedroom door. "Is you awake yet, Miss Louisa?"

"Damn!" hissed Louisa through clenched teeth. "What is it, Hattie?" she shouted angrily.

"You gots company, Miss Louisa. A Lieutenant Lacy and his wife has come callin'."

Louisa searched her memory for the name and the faces to go with it. Only a vague recollection of meeting some people by that name at some boring, forgettable army-navy social function flashed through her brain. They had hardly impressed her. What are they doin' here? she wondered.

"Send them away, Hattie," she said. "Tell them I'm in mournin' for my husband."

"Yes'm, they knows that already. That's why they come here to see you. They's come to offer their sympathies and to consoles you in your hour of sorrow. Leastways, that's what they say for me to tells you."

Damn! she thought. They probably won't go away if I don't see them. "All right, Hattie," she said. "Tell them I'll be out as soon as I can get dressed. Make them comfortable. Offer them coffee and cookies or something."

"Yes'm, Miss Louisa."

Lieutenant Lacy? wondered Louisa as she removed the nightgown and slipped into her undergarments and a black dress that was meant to express the grief that she was supposed to be feeling over Dawse. She searched her memory. Army officer? Yes, that's right. Posted at Fort Jay on Governor's Island. His wife is that prissy little Yankee bitch. Skinny, too. She's got one eye that ain't quite right. Homely as they come. I think that's them. She put her hair into a matronly bun, holding it in place with several pins and a black ribbon. There, she thought as she studied herself in the mirror, a properly grieving widow. She went to the parlor to greet her guests.

Yes, Lieutenant John Lacy and his wife, Mary, were the couple that Louisa recalled, and they looked almost exactly as she remembered them. Lacy possessed a slightly pudgy build, blue eyes, sandy-brown hair and mustache, and a rather average nose and chin. He stood five feet eight inches tall, rising to his full height when Louisa entered the room. Mary remained seated on the sofa.

"Good mornin', Lieutenant Lacy," said Louisa politely. "Mrs. Lacy. Please forgive me for keepin' you waitin'. I hope Hattie has taken good care of you in the interim."

Lacy bowed from the waist and said, "Good morning, Mrs. Phoenix." He straightened up as his wife spoke the same words. He added, "Yes, your servant has taken good care of us. Thank you for asking."

"Very good," said Louisa. "It's very nice of you to call, but to what do I owe this honor?"

Lacy waited for Louisa to seat herself comfortably in a high-back wing chair, then sat down beside his wife. "First," he said, "I should apologize for our tardiness in calling on you."

"The holiday and all, you know, my dear," interjected Mary with a forced smile.

"Yes, of course," said Louisa.

"Thank you," said Lacy. "Well, anyway, Mrs. Lacy and I volunteered to express the condolences and sympathy of the officers and the ladies of the military and naval community in this vicinity, Mrs. Phoenix, and to offer you any assistance that you may require until your husband's ship arrives safely at some port.''

"I don't hold out much hope of that," said Louisa. "His ship arrivin' safely, I mean.''

"Certainly there has been nothing official yet," said Lacy with genuine concern.

"No, nothin' other than that his ship is overdue at Panama from the Sandwich Islands," said Louisa. "Commander Sims, the officer who brought me word that the *Levant* was late, he said that any number of things could have delayed the ship from makin' its destination on time. Commander Sims said that the *Levant* won't be considered lost until it's more than thirty days overdue, and that won't be until the fifth of January. As far as I'm concerned, Dawse's ship is gone forever, and so is he. I pray that I am wrong, but I must be realistic in this matter. Don't you agree?''

"You mustn't lose hope, Mrs. Phoenix," said Lacy.

"No, you shouldn't lose hope, my dear," said Mary, although not as convincingly as her husband.

"Thank you both for your concern, but I should prepare for the worst. If I continue to hope that Dawse is safe and will soon return to me but he never comes, well, I should think that would be more devastatin' than acceptin' the probability that he's never comin' home again.''

"Yes, of course," said Mary, "you are probably right to think that way. I'm sure I would, if I were in your place.''

"Let us pray, Mrs. Lacy, that you never have to be in my place," said Louisa. "Not really knowin' whether I'm a widow or a wife is most troublesome to the spirit.''

"Yes, I can see that," said Mary with a hint of iciness. She'd heard the gossip about Commander Sims and his extended visits to console Louisa, but until this very moment, she hadn't placed too much store in the veracity of such rumors. She detected the subtle difference in Louisa's tone when she spoke her husband's name and that of Rafe Sims; quite obviously, Mrs. Phoenix held the commander in greater esteem than her missing mate.

Quick to recognize a spark of friction in his wife's voice, Lacy rose and stammered, "Well, yes, Mrs. Phoenix. Of course, you are right to take this attitude. Better to expect nothing and not be disappointed should no good news come your way than to expect something and be disappointed should the news be tragic. Yes, I see your point. Well, as I said before, if you should be in need of anything to help you through this difficult period, please don't hesitate to call on Mrs. Lacy and me for assistance. We are at your disposal, madam."

"Yes, my dear," said Mary, "we are at your disposal." She stood up beside her husband. "If we can do anything, please call on us."

"Thank you, I will," said Louisa. She had Hattie fetch their coats and the lieutenant's hat, then she saw them to the door, where they said their farewells. She closed the door behind them, glad that they were gone. That Yankee bitch! she thought angrily as she returned to the chair. She could care less that Dawse's ship is missin'. She's got a man. Not much of a man, I'll admit, but he's still a man. That's more than I've got. She laughed to herself as a most obscene idea occurred to her. Why don't I just take him away from her? I'm twice the woman she is. Leastways, I've got bosoms, and I'll bet I know better what to do with them than she would even if she had half what I've got. She laughed aloud until a knock at the door interrupted her merriment.

"I'll get it, Hattie," she said, instructing the servant to remain in the kitchen. She rose, hurried to the door, and opened it, surprised to find Lacy standing there. "Did you forget something, Lieutenant?" she cooed.

"Yes, as a matter of fact, I did. I forgot to tell you, Mrs. Phoenix, that should you need to go out in public and wish to have an escort, then you need only call on me. I, or another officer from the fort or the shipyard, will be most happy to accommodate you."

"And what if all I need is someone to hold my hand and comfort me? May I call on you for that, too, Lieutenant?"

Unhorsed by her question and excited as well, Lacy cleared his throat and said, "Well, I suppose that could be arranged, if that's what you really want."

"My servant goes out to market each afternoon between two and four, leavin' me all by my little ol' lonesome self. Do you think you could come by then and keep me company until she returns?"

"Perhaps Mrs. Lacy should come by then?" he offered, although rather unconvincingly.

"No, I'd prefer the company of a man." She brushed a speck of lint from the left breast area of his uniform blouse. "A man like you, Lieutenant."

Lacy cleared his throat again, but his voice still dropped two octaves as he said, "I'll see what I can do."

"Please do, Lieutenant."

Lacy nodded, turned, and departed, a cold sweat greasing his palms.

Louisa closed the door again, placed a hand to her mouth, and giggled naughtily. Well, she told herself, he's better than no man at all. Besides bein' a man, he's also a Federal army officer. Who knows how valuable he might be to the Southern cause? I'll have to give this some thought.

Hattie left the apartment promptly at two that afternoon, and within three minutes, Lacy rapped on the door, his blood rushing like that of a dog on the scent of a bitch in heat. Louisa answered the knock and in-

vited Lacy inside. "You could have come earlier, Lieutenant," she said as she closed the door behind him.
"You didn't have to wait for Hattie to leave."

"But I thought that's what you wanted," said Lacy
defensively.

"Hattie is my servant." She took his hat and hung
it on the wall hook behind the door. "What she thinks
of you comin' here means absolutely nothin'. And as
far as sayin' something about you bein' here, she
knows better than to gossip with anyone else about
what goes on in this house."

"I see."

"Please sit down, Lieutenant." She waved toward
the sofa. "Would you like some coffee?"

"Yes, that would be nice," he stammered. He sat
down.

"Pardon me please, while I fetch the servin' tray."
She left the room but soon returned, carrying a silver
salver complete with a silver coffeepot, silver creamer,
silver sugar bowl, two china cups and saucers, and two
silverware spoons. She set the tray on the walnut coffee
table, sat down on Lacy's left, picked up the coffeepot,
and filled each cup with steaming coffee. "Would you
like cream or sugar, Lieutenant?"

"I prefer my coffee black, thank you."

She handed him a saucer with a cup of the dark
brew, then poured cream into her coffee. "Tell me,
Lieutenant," she said as she stirred the cream and coffee into complete solution, "does your wife know that
you've come here alone?"

"Why, no, of course not," said Lacy, so taken aback
by her direct question that the cup jiggled on the saucer
in his left hand. Unnerved, he returned the china to the
tray and inched a bit farther away from Louisa.

"Do you think we have something to hide,
Lieutenant?"

"Well, no, of course not."

"Well, not yet anyway," said Louisa with a smirk, "but you're hopin' we will, aren't you?"

"Whatever do you mean, Mrs. Phoenix?"

Louisa raised her cup to her lips, sipped some coffee, considered its flavor, then replaced the cup in its saucer. "You didn't only come here to hold my hand, Lieutenant," she said point-blank. "Maybe that's where you'll start, but you're hopin' to finish somewhere else on my body."

"Why, Mrs. Phoenix, I—"

She put her hand to his mouth to quiet him. "Please, Lieutenant, when we're alone, either call me Louisa or address me by some endearment that you don't use with your wife. I'm a sea widow, and you know as well as I do what that term means. And now I may be a real widow. All the more reason for me to feel the freedom to be so forward with you or any other man who should come callin'."

"Like Commander Sims?" blurted Lacy.

A black cloud shadowed Louisa's eyes. "Lieutenant, my relations with other gentlemen are not your affair," she said sternly. "You would do well to concern yourself only with what may transpire between us. Do we have that understandin', sir?"

"Yes, of course. Completely."

"Very well then," she said, smiling softly and allowing her right hand to rest on his left knee. "Now why don't we get better acquainted? Tell me about yourself, John. Where do you hail from?"

For the next hour, Lacy answered Louisa's questions about his personal and professional life. He had been born in Michigan Territory near a settlement known as Brownstown at the western end of Lake Erie, the youngest son of a federal judge. He attended the Military Academy at West Point and graduated in the bottom third of the class of '48. His first duty took him to Virginia, where he worked as an engineer on the reinforcement of the sea walls of Fort Monroe. Not finding such work to his liking, he transferred to the infantry at the earliest opportunity and spent four years at Fort Gibson in the Cherokee Nation. Showing a proclivity for organization, he was posted to Washington, where he was assigned to the lowest level of General Winfield Scott's office staff. While serving in the capital, he met Mary Hayward, a second cousin once removed to General Scott. Well aware that advancement in the army often depended on family connections, Lacy courted her for a year before proposing marriage, wanted to back out of the engagement during the traditional six months before their wedding, but went through with the nuptials for no other reason than that the union would help his career. As a wedding present, General Scott promoted him to first lieutenant and assigned him to Fort Jay on Governor's Island, where he was placed in charge of the recruit training facility. He bragged that he was very close to General Scott. "In fact," he said, "when the general is staying in New York, I am the only junior officer who gets invited to dinner at his house. At first, I got invited because of my wife's relationship to General Scott, but now I believe I've gained the general's favor. He often sends for me to listen to his ideas on various matters. I'm something of a confidant for him."

"That is impressive, John," said Louisa. "Do you and Mary have any children?"

"No, not yet," said Lacy.

"Is your wife barren?"

"No, of course not," said Lacy defensively. Then, reconsidering his reply, he added, "Well, maybe she is. I don't really know for certain. It's just . . . that . . . she's rather . . . unenthusiastic . . . about the act."

"The act?" queried Louisa with raised eyebrows. She noted Lacy's embarrassment and thought to have some fun with him. "I've heard it called a lot of things,

John, but this is the first time I've heard it called 'the act.' "

Dry-mouthed, Lacy blushed and said, "Could we please change the subject, Louisa?"

"Why should we? That's why you came here, isn't it? To do 'the act' with me?" She squeezed his thigh.

Lacy pulled away from her. "Not exactly," he said.

"Don't fool with me, John Lacy," said Louisa. "I grew up in Kentucky, where the common definition of a virgin was a girl who could outrun all her male kin. I was pretty fast on my feet, John, but only when I wanted to be." She moved closer to him. "Now, there's no need for you to be bashful when we're alone, John." She leaned against him, her right breast pressed to his left arm. "Why don't you kiss me, John dear?"

Lacy hadn't thought about kissing Louisa. In fact, he hadn't considered doing anything sexual with her. No images, no fantasies, no scenarios, nothing. Just somehow they would copulate and he would go on his way, conscience clear, as if nothing had happened between them, nothing more than what might transpire between a prostitute and a paying client, although he would never spend money on such ignominious entertainment. "Kiss you?" he stammered.

"Yes, Johnny, kiss me." She put her left hand behind his head and pulled him closer. "Put your lips to mine and kiss me like a man should kiss a woman."

They kissed. She as passionately as she could to arouse him, and he with reluctance, then with hunger as his body reacted to the scent of her. He twisted to embrace her, and she pushed herself harder against him. Their mouths separated, but he continued to kiss her cheek, then her ear, then her throat as he ran his tongue down to her shoulder. She glanced downward and noted the bulge in his trousers. A giggle escaped her lips as she realized that she had succeeded in exciting him to a sexual frenzy. She glanced at the clock on the mantel. Nearly three-thirty. *Gong!* The half hour struck.

"John, we have to stop," she said hoarsely. "There's no time today. Hattie will be home soon. We have to stop." She pushed him away.

He refused to surrender the moment and pulled her back.

She pushed as hard as she could, broke his hold, and jumped to her feet. "We have to stop now, John," she said firmly. "We don't have the time."

Lacy stood up and tried to take her into his arms.

Louisa pushed him back onto the sofa. "Calm yourself, Johnny," she said as she backed away another step. "There's no time today. Come back tomorrow." She straightened her clothing, although nothing was really out of place.

"Tomorrow?" he queried. "I don't know that I can come here tomorrow."

"Then the next day, but not today. There's no time, do you understand?"

Lacy looked grudgingly at the clock. "Yes, you're right. There's no time today. I must be getting back to the post." He stood up.

"You should leave before Hattie comes back. Although she knows better than to talk about what goes on within these walls, it's better still that she doesn't know everything."

She led him to the door, handed him his hat, and helped him into his greatcoat. They shared a farewell kiss, and she said, "Come back tomorrow, and we won't waste any time talkin'." One more kiss and he was out the door.

General Scott's confidant? thought Louisa as she leaned against the door contemplating how she could use Lacy to benefit the South. The possibility thrilled her. Rafe will be so proud of me, she told herself. A vision of Sims invaded her mind. He was naked, and so was she. A flush coursed through her, and without wasting another second, she hurried to the bedroom to quench her desire.

8 ～

Wednesday night, December 26, 1860

The inclement weather shrouding Charleston harbor with fog and dampening everything and everybody with a fine mist abated by noon the day after Christmas. The sun failed to shine, but never mind, the gloom suited the moods of all but three men.

Captain Sam Crawford awakened minutes before the post bugler tooted reveille. Invigorated with anticipation of what the day might bring, he hurried through his morning routine of tending to bodily functions, exercising to set his blood flowing rapidly, washing, and dressing. Before allowing himself to partake of a leisurely breakfast, he visited the hospital to inquire how his few patients had passed the night. With that duty completed, he joined two other officers, Captain Foster and Lieutenant Jefferson C. Davis, at mess. "Good day after Christmas, gentlemen," said Crawford with a little too much exuberance and jollity to suit Foster.

Not so Davis. "Good morning to you, too, Sam," said the junior officer. "Your spirits are certainly bright and cheery this morning."

"It's a beautiful morning, Jeff."

"What's beautiful about it?" groused Foster. "It's

damp and cold and overcast. What's beautiful about a day like that?''

"It's not the weather, Foster," said Crawford, using the engineer's last name because he wasn't as familiar with Foster as he was with Davis. "It's the time. The season, if you will. Christmas is behind us, and we have the New Year to look forward to. The prospects of the future are limitless.''

"The New Year?" queried Foster. "Prospects of the future? The only future I see is a horde of slaveholding Carolinians coming over the wall prepared to skewer all of us with bayonets.''

"Possibly," said Crawford, "but I think not. I don't think the Carolinians have that much courage. A good volley of grape would send them packing in no time. No, Captain, I don't think the Carolinians will do anything so foolhardy as to mount an infantry charge against this fort. Not as long as we have a Southerner in command here.''

Davis and Foster exchanged fearful glances. The former cleared his throat but remained unspeaking. The latter stiffened in preparation to challenge Crawford's rather insinuating and insubordinate statement. "What are you saying, Crawford?" he asked.

"I'm saying that I think the Carolinians will do nothing as long as Anderson is in command, and it behooves us, his staff and you, too, Foster, to see that he remains in command. He is a Southerner, and the Carolinians will do nothing against one of their own because they harbor the hope that he will come over to their side in due time.''

"And do you think Major Anderson will do that?" asked Davis, his voice agitated an octave higher than normal.

"It's a possibility that I have considered," said Crawford. "Haven't you done the same, Foster?''

"No, I haven't," said Foster firmly.

"I have," admitted Davis.

"So has Doubleday," said Crawford, "and I think he's prepared to seize command should Anderson show the slightest inclination toward surrendering this fort to the Carolinians."

"That's mutiny!" exclaimed Foster.

"No, Captain," said Crawford after swallowing a mouthful of black coffee. "Not mutiny. Patriotism. Loyalty to the Union." He leaned closer to Foster. "I will tell you this, sir. If Doubleday doesn't move should the need arise, then I am prepared to seize command myself. The only question I have of you"—he shifted his view to Davis—"and to you, too, Jeff, will you join me or Doubleday, for that matter, in taking a stand for the Union and freedom?"

"I will," said Davis without hesitation.

Foster leaned back, the color drained from his face as he considered the reality of Crawford's words. As a further delay, he picked up his coffee cup, drank the last of the brew, then said, "I don't think any of us will have much choice in the matter should the situation present itself."

"I'll take that as an affirmative reply," said Crawford. A great grin of satisfaction spread his lips as he anticipated what the remainder of the day might hold. If not today, he thought, then someday soon. Yes, history in the making. Just like I told that Dr. Salter. Crawford's smile grew all the wider.

Dr. George Salter awakened in a strange bed very late that morning, and his head hurt. Excruciatingly. So much so that he couldn't even open his eyes and allow the dim light of the bedroom to enter his brain. Only sensing the presence of another body curled up beside him distracted him momentarily from the throbbing between his temples. Then he recalled the night before.

Juanita was Salter's Christmas present to himself,

and she had been a good one, too. Dark eyes, dusky
complexion, jet-black hair, sensuous mouth, a Cuban
bought in Havana for the express purpose of improving
the variety of entertainers available at Madame Lisette's
menage de melange, a popular but discreet house of
flesh, located a street away from Charleston's waterfront, that catered only to gentlemen of position and
wealth.

Salter qualified in the former category, but physician
or not, he failed the test of substance. Fortunately, he
knew the right people, men of means or reputation
whose names alone could open doors. One such acquaintance he'd made at Columbia and had recently
renewed in Charleston was Tyler Harris, a scion of old
plantation money who prided himself on being a social
gadfly, even as shallow as that designation might seem
when applied to a man. Lonely, far from home, and
desiring the company of a soft woman, Salter had flattered Harris into taking him to Madame Lisette's for
an evening of comforting.

And such a comforter Juanita proved to be. Salter
could hardly move upon awakening. But maybe the
wine had caused his inertia. He considered this possibility. At the very least, the Madeira had contributed
greatly to his malaise. The lack of strength, however,
had been Juanita's doing. What an insatiable nymph
she had been! Demanding more and more from him as
the night passed in glorious debauchery. Wait a minute,
he thought. That's not right. She's the prostitute here.
She's supposed to—

Juanita stirred, rolled over, and draped a bare arm
over Salter's chest. She nuzzled against him and purred
like a Spanish kitten, "Oh, Georgie, do it to me again."

Having spent more than one night in a whorehouse
before this, Salter winced, afraid to look at the face
belonging to the limb now pulling him against a pair
of hardening breasts. He reacted by attempting to roll

away, but the strength of the woman prevented his escape.

"No, Georgie, don't go," she whispered. "Do it to me again. Like you did the second time."

The second time? wondered Salter. Panic threatened. How ugly is she? Curiosity forced his head to turn in her direction. His eyes opened involuntarily, only slightly, just enough to allow a glimpse of her features.

She smiled lasciviously, batted her almond eyes at him, and cooed, "Okay, like the third time then."

Third—? My God! She's beautiful! His eyes opened completely for a more thorough look. Yes, she's beautiful. Very beautiful. In quick succession, he relived the events of the night before. Harris had brought him there. Madame Lisette greeted them, and a Negro servant brought them wine. They drank one glass, then a second. The ladies, a few of them, joined them. He was attracted to none of them and thought about leaving. Then Juanita came into the room. More Madeira. His head spun. She took him to her room and—and—and—and what the hell happened after that? Damn! What happened after that? Obviously, we fucked. But—he punished his memory for anything resembling copulation—how? No recall. This is my penance, he thought. Probably the greatest gambol of my life, and I can't remember one sweaty moment of it. God does punish sinners. Damn!

"What time is it?" he muttered.

"It is time for you to make love to me again," she said, her voice dripping with lust. She rolled atop him, straddling his waist and gyrating her hips against his midriff.

"No," he said weakly. "I can't. Not now anyway. I'm too hung over just yet. I need the chamber pot first."

"I will empty it first," said Juanita. She threw back the covers and leaped out of bed.

Salter watched her don a red and black satin robe. Lithe and graceful, the raw form of a marble goddess of ancient Greece, a mulatto Helen of Troy. She is beautiful, he thought. He felt a deep tingling in his loins. And she thinks I'm some sort of—

Juanita banging the pot against the commode door jangled his nerves, and the accompanying rush of pain shattered his thought pattern.

She left the room.

Salter struggled to sit up on the side of the bed. No nausea, only throbbing in his head and aching in his muscles, all of them, especially those that generated the driving motion of the hips. Why can't I remember? he demanded of himself. Damn the wine! He stood, totally naked, then flopped back on the bed, the initial movement overcoming him for the moment. He heaved for more oxygen, forced himself erect again, wobbled, but remained standing. He scanned the room for his clothes, spied one piece, then another, and a third. All on the floor. That meant stooping to gather them. An unsure maneuver at best. Would he be able to rise again? Better not chance it. He stepped gingerly toward the window, thinking to open it to suck in some fresh air to clear his head. He succeeded, unlatching the glass and pulling it toward him, lifting the shutter latch, and throwing open the louvered guards. The daylight, as dim as it was on this cloudy day, burned through his eyes into his brain, bringing on more discomfort. He fought back the pain and focused on the harbor as he filled his lungs with the damp, salty air. It helped.

Staring out across the water, Salter looked in the direction of Fort Moultrie, but patchy remnants of the early morning fog bank prevented him from seeing any of the activity on the wharf near the military post. Even so, his instincts told him that something was amiss. But what? he wondered. He forgot his hangover for the moment and concentrated on the question. All sorts of things could be going on over there, he thought, and nobody here would be any the wiser. A dozen warships could be coming over the bar right now to support Anderson, and nobody in Charleston would know it. He burped a laugh at the possibility and muttered aloud, "Wouldn't that be something now?" Yes, Anderson could be up to something over there right this very moment, and nobody here would know it. But what would he be doing on a day like this?

Before he could hypothesize more answers, Juanita returned with the empty chamber pot. "I took too long," she said. "I am sorry." She replaced the pot in the commode.

A charge of energy caused by his speculation over what could be transpiring in the harbor had soothed Salter's symptoms and gave him the ability to move without the nagging ache of alcohol. He went to the toilet, lifted its lid, and relieved himself. As the stream of urine tinkled on the porcelain, he contemplated the presence of the commode in this room. It's not really a piece of furniture like a sofa or a chair, he thought. It's certainly a convenience, but it stands here all by itself offering refuge whenever it's needed. Sort of like an island in the middle of a sea. Yes, a refuge from a raging sea. An island like—

"That's it, by God!" he exclaimed without warning.

Juanita sprawled on the bed, nude again. "You will make love to me now, Georgie?"

"Not now, Juanita," said Salter as he retrieved his underwear from the floor. "There's something greater afoot than a memorable copulation with a delicious tart such as you." He stopped in the middle of pulling the garment over his shoulders and gave Juanita a good leering. "I must be mad," he scolded himself, "but like the man said, this is history in the making. I can bed you another time, but what's taking place over there will only happen once."

Juanita sat up and said, "I don't understand, Georgie. What are you talking about? What is taking place where?"

"Never mind, my dear," said Salter. He bent down to kiss her, did, then said, "I have to go now, my dear, but I'll be back. I promise."

She threw her arms around his neck and pleaded with him. "Stay with me, *por favor*. I want to feel you inside me again. Like you did last night. So many times."

Yes, my penance, he thought. Maybe the greatest fuck of my life, and I can't remember a single thrust. There is no justice.

"I have to go, Juanita," he said as he broke her hold on him. "I'll be back as soon as I can. I promise." He kissed her quickly. "Get some rest. You'll need it for when I return." Mischief curled his mouth into a smile. Don Juan, Casanova, and now George Salter, he thought. All right, maybe not George Salter. But maybe yes, if only I could remember what I did last night that was so great.

Juanita squeezed his crotch gently and said, "Yes, I know what you mean. I will rest until you return."

He took her hand, kissed the palm, and thought, Well, at least one of us remembers what I did last night. My God, am I crazy! Quite insane. To leave this for what? He released her hand, finished dressing, and left the bordello in search of a boat to carry him across the harbor to Moultrieville.

Surgeon Crawford completed his daily routine of holding sick call at Fort Moultrie, then boarded the *Raven,* one of Captain Foster's hired lighters, for the trip to Fort Sumter, where he would perform the same duty for the soldiers posted at the island fortress. As it had been the day before Christmas, the small schooner was loaded with provisions for the workers at Sumter. Crawford wondered why Major Anderson had committed so much food and materiel to a place that the Carolinians would be certain to seize at the earliest opportunity. He could only assume that Anderson planned to weaken Fort Moultrie through attrition and thus justify its peaceful surrender when the Carolinians demanded it. The man is planning treason, thought Crawford. Upon his return trip to Moultrie, he felt his assumption was confirmed when he saw the other lighter, the *Miss Penny,* being loaded with more provisions for Sumter. I must stop this traitor as soon as we land, he told himself. Even if I have to take his life to do it.

Without consulting any of his staff, Anderson had made the unilateral decision that the time had come to save his command and hopefully avert a war. For starters, he ordered the two engineer lighters to be loaded with provisions, stating that the supplies were intended for Captain Foster's laborers at Fort Sumter. He placed Lieutenant Hall in charge of this detail.

"But the one lighter has already departed for Sumter, sir," said Hall.

"No matter," said Anderson. "Load the second now, and load the other when it returns this afternoon."

"Yes, sir."

"Furthermore, I want all the wives and children of the enlisted men and the junior officers to be evacuated to Fort Johnson. I want them out of harm's way, just in case the Carolinians should misconstrue my intentions and launch an assault against Moultrie. Make no secret of this activity, Lieutenant Hall. Knowing how curious our neighbors in Moultrieville are about everything that transpires within these walls, you may inform anybody who asks that we are only concerned about the safety of the women and children. Is that understood?"

"Yes, sir. Perfectly."

"Very good. Report back to me as soon as both lighters are loaded and our dependents are on board."

Upon landing at the Fort Moultrie dock, Crawford looked for an officer and found Hall. "What's going on here?" he asked with great agitation.

"Major Anderson has ordered the evacuation of the women and children to Fort Johnson," said Hall.

"To Fort Johnson? Why?"

"He's worried that the Carolinians might attack us soon, and he wants the women and children out of the way."

"Yes, of course," said Crawford to Hall. He thought otherwise. *Their absence will also make it easier for him to surrender the fort. I must stop him before it's too late.* He stormed off to find his fellow officers from the North and to fetch his sidearm.

Hall proceeded with putting the dependents on board the *Raven* and the *Miss Penny.* As soon as the remaining provisions were loaded on the *Raven,* Hall reported to Anderson.

"Take the lighters out into the harbor," said Anderson, "and head in the direction of Fort Johnson but do not land there. I want you to anchor nearby, and await a signal of two shots from Moultrie. Once you hear the shots, you are to proceed to Fort Sumter with all haste."

"Fort Sumter, sir?" queried Hall.

"Yes, Lieutenant. I intend to occupy it by nightfall."

Hall smiled and said, "Very good, sir."

"Above all, Lieutenant, you are to keep this order to yourself until the last minute possible. Do not allow the Carolinians aboard the boats to learn of it, or I fear the plan will be doomed to failure."

Hall nodded grimly and said, "Secrecy, sir. Yes, of course."

They exchanged salutes and parted.

The lighters, with their secessionist captains and crews, pulled away from the landing, and Anderson returned to the fort's interior to inform his own officers and Captain Foster of his scheme.

Crawford returned to his quarters, where he donned his gunbelt and revolver. Now to find Foster and Davis, he thought.

Davis had the duty as officer of the day, and he was in the midst of making his rounds when Crawford met up with him on the parapet.

"What do you think of Anderson's decision to move the women and children to Fort Johnson?" asked the surgeon, coming straight to the point.

"I can appreciate his concern for their safety," said Davis. He nodded at Crawford's sidearm and said, "I take it you don't share the same evaluation as I do, Sam."

"Not quite. I'm sure he wishes no harm to come to the women and children, but I think it will make it easier for him to surrender this post when the time comes."

"Easier? How do you figure?"

"He'll have less opposition from the men and officers whose families are at Fort Johnson. They'll accept his decision in order to be reunited with their loved ones all the sooner."

"I don't think that's his motive at all."

"Let's find Foster," said Crawford, "and see how he feels about it."

Foster found them. "I say we confront Anderson," said the captain of engineers.

"Agreed," said Crawford. "Here he comes now."

Anderson approached along the parapet. "Gentlemen, I'm glad to see you together," he said. "I have something to tell you. I intend to transfer this command to Fort Sumter immediately."

Crawford gasped.

Davis swallowed hard.

"Fort Sumter, Major?" queried Foster.

"Yes, Captain," said Anderson. "It's the only truly defensible fort in the harbor, and I see no alternative except to surrender to the Carolinians. Do you have any objections to this move?"

"No, sir," said Foster. "I applaud it."

"As do I," said Crawford.

"Very good," said Anderson. "Now I must find Captain Doubleday and inform of my decision." He looked skyward. "We have very little time to achieve this without the Carolinians discovering our intentions."

"There's Captain Doubleday now," said Davis, looking beyond Anderson.

Seeing Doubleday coming near, the major broke off the conversation to greet his second in command. "I have determined to evacuate this post immediately," he informed the captain, "for the purpose of occupying Fort Sumter. I can allow you no more than twenty minutes to form your company and be in readiness to start."

Doubleday did not hesitate. He made hasty arrangements for his wife's safety, put his company into order, and reported to Anderson on the parade ground.

Salter couldn't find a willing boatman along the Charleston waterfront to take him across the harbor to Moultrieville. Inconvenienced but not dismayed, he turned to Tyler Harris to help him find transport to the wharf on Sullivan's Island. He found his old acquaintance recovering from a hangover of his own back at Madame Lisette's.

Red hair, gray eyes, freckles on his cheeks, thin, of medium height, Harris looked every bit the dandy, even in the nude. "Why would you want to go over there?" he drawled from his bed.

"I think there might be a chance for a bit of sport,"

said Salter, knowing that Harris had a penchant for the daredeviltry of the irresponsible rich.

"Such as?" queried Harris, his curiosity piqued.

"I don't know for certain," said Salter truthfully, "but I think the soldiers at Fort Moultrie might be up to something."

"Such as?"

Salter shrugged and said, "I haven't the foggiest idea what they might be up to, but—"

"But you think they're up to something?" interjected Harris. He fell back on the bed. "Count me out, George. If you want to see what the soldiers at Moultrie are up to, why don't you talk your way onto the guard boat that patrols the channel every night?"

Salter gave the suggestion some quick thought and said, "I don't think that will work, Ty. Have you forgotten that I come from New York?"

"Damn helpless Yankee! I'll bet that Cuban whore had to show you which hole to put it in last night, didn't she?" Harris allowed his head to droop a bit. "All right, I'll go with you." He stroked his chin and said, "Yes, I just might do that. Where are my clothes?"

As soon as Harris dressed, the two of them left the bordello for the waterfront.

On the very night that the secession convention passed the ordinance to dissolve the Union, Governor Pickens ordered the waters between Forts Moultrie and Sumter and Castle Pinckney to be patrolled by a guard boat throughout the hours of darkness in order to prevent the Federals from making any troop movements from Moultrie to reinforce either of the other island fortresses. For this duty, he selected the *Nina* and the *General Clinch*. The two ships took turns, alternating from that first night through Christmas Eve but with neither leaving the wharf on Christmas night because

of the foul weather. On this night, the *Nina* would draw
the watch.

"Now you let me do all the talkin' here, George,"
said Harris. "If Captain Gower hears too much of that
Yankee talk out of you, he's liable not to let us come
aboard his boat."

They met Captain Gower on the pier at the end of
the *Nina*'s gangplank just as a company of South Carolina militia boarded the craft.

"Captain, I am Tyler Harris of the Columbia *Star*,"
lied Harris, "and this is George Salter of the Baltimore
Herald. I trust you've heard of our newspapers?"

Not wishing to appear ignorant or ill-informed,
Gower stammered, "Why, yes, I have, sir. What brings
you gentlemen here this evenin'?"

"We'd like to come aboard your fine ship, sir," said
Harris, "and observe your tour of the harbor tonight
firsthand, just in case the Federals should be up to
something. And even if the Yankees are not plannin'
some mischief, I would like to inform my newspaper's
readers of the vigilance that our state's small but valiant
navy is maintainin' here in Charleston harbor."

Gower stroked his chin whiskers as he considered
the request. "Hmm. My orders don't say nothin' about
takin' any civilians with us on patrol, so I guess it'll
be okay. Come aboard, gentlemen, and I'll show you
around the *Nina*."

That was too easy, thought Salter as they walked up
the plank behind Gower and the last of the militiamen.

Within the hour as darkness settled over Charleston,
the ship had a full head of steam and was moving out
into the Cooper River with the helmsman steering toward the South Channel and the middle of the harbor.

After their tour of the craft, Harris and Salter found
a dice game among the soldiers. The former joined in
the fun, while the latter became a disinterested observer,

Salter's thoughts centering on what might be awaiting them in the night.

Major Anderson personally supervised the lowering of the flag at sundown. He tucked the folded banner under his arm and led Doubleday and twenty men of Company E out of Fort Moultrie to three long boats hidden behind an irregular pile of rocks that had once formed a seawall. Luckily, no civilians saw them marching along the shore, as most of Moultrieville was taking supper at that hour. Anderson divided the soldiers among the boats, six oarsmen to each craft; one commanded by him, the second by Lieutenant Meade, and the third by Doubleday. In one sentence, he informed the enlisted that they would be rowing to Fort Sumter, and in another curt command, he silenced their murmur of surprise and joy. They boarded the boats, placed their muskets at their feet, and awkwardly moved away from the beach into the channel.

To protect their trip across the channel to Fort Sumter, Anderson ordered Foster, Crawford, and Davis to man the guns facing Sumter with a small detail of artillerists. He directed them to fire on the state guard boat should it attempt to interfere with the progress of the long boats.

Just as Anderson had anticipated, the *Nina* made an appearance as the full moon brightened in the eastern sky, its light reflecting off the water. The Federals reached the middle of the channel. Turning back now was out of the question.

Discretion being the better part of valor, Anderson and Meade directed their boats away from the oncoming *Nina,* choosing a circuitous route to Sumter.

Not so Doubleday. Realizing that he and his men made an easy target in their brass-buttoned greatcoats and hats, he acted with resolution to reach the island fortress. Upon spying the guard boat approaching in the murky light, he said, "I want every man to remove his hat and turn his coat to hide the buttons. As soon as you can, resume rowing. Maintain a steady stroke, men. We need to give the appearance that we're in no hurry. And everybody keep quiet. No talking."

The *Nina* came within a hundred yards of Double-day's company. It came to a full stop.

"Steady, men," said Doubleday evenly. "Keep your stroke now." Sweat bubbled on his brow as he kept a wary eye on the South Carolinians, knowing how the Southerners must be scrutinizing them with great suspicion. He caught his breath and held it involuntarily. A fearful quiet, disturbed only by the gentle sloshing of water as the oars propelled the boat forward, shrouded the harbor.

The forward lookout's report of small boats in the water ahead spread quickly through the crew and militiamen aboard the *Nina*. Hearing the news, Harris and Salter hurried to the bridge to be at the forefront of the action, joining Gower, his first mate, the helmsman, and the militia commander.

"What do you make of that?" Gower asked the men gathered closely about him.

"Looks like a boatload of those workers from Sumter," said the mate.

"That would be my guess, too," said the militia captain.

"Beats me who they are," said Harris.

Salter knew who they were. Even in the darkness, he recognized the military bearing of an officer. His throat dried up on him. He swallowed hard and repeatedly, trying to get the saliva flowing again.

"I ain't so sure about that," said Gower. "They could be workers or they could be—"

"No, sir," said Salter, suddenly finding his voice and feigning a true Southern twang to his words. "It's a boat loaded with Yankees tryin' to skedaddle from Fort Moultrie before a handful of our Southern boys have to chase their sorry asses back North.''

Silence for a brief second.

Then Harris laughed.

Gower laughed, and so did the mate, the helmsman, and the militia captain.

"I guess you're right," said Gower. "Just some workers from Fort Sumter. Let's get movin' again, Mr. Tatum."

"Aye, aye, Captain," said the mate.

Harris and Salter stepped outside the *Nina*'s pilot house out of earshot of Gower and the others.

"Whatever possessed you to say something so downright foolish as that?" whispered a nervous Harris.

"I was worried that Captain Gower might fire his cannon on those poor devils," said Salter honestly.

"And he just might have fired on them if I hadn't laughed when I did. For God's sake, George, watch what you say around these men."

"Good advice, Ty," he said aloud, but to himself, he added, Fooled you, too, old friend.

The *Nina*'s paddle wheel kicked into gear, and the boat steamed off toward Mount Pleasant, its captain and crew fooled into believing that Doubleday and his soldiers were Foster's laborers returning to Sumter from Moultrie.

Doubleday exhaled his relief. "Good work, men," he said softly. "Carry on."

Doubleday's men picked up the stroke again and reached the Fort Sumter wharf ahead of Anderson and Meade because of the more direct course that Doubleday had chosen. He landed his men and immediately formed them into an offensive line with bayonets fixed to meet a crowd of secessionist workers who came to meet them.

"What the hell are these soldiers doin' here?" demanded John Lindsay, the carpenter from Moultrieville hired to finish the gun platforms. He was only one of the many men wearing the blue cockade of secession.

"Back inside the fort," ordered Doubleday.

"Go to hell, you Yankee sonofabitch!" called another.

"Go peacefully or go at the end of cold steel," said Doubleday evenly. "Fix bayonets!" He drew his side-arm for emphasis.

The Carolinians resisted with angry catcalls and threatening gestures, but their excitement soon quieted as Doubleday ordered his men to advance with force. In a few short minutes, all one hundred fifteen of the unarmed laborers had been herded inside the fort. Doubleday posted a sentinel at the landing and another on the wall, while he and the remaining four men stood guard on the workers until Anderson arrived to take command.

Anderson and Meade brought their boats to the pier. He sent Meade and four soldiers back to Fort Moultrie in one boat that towed the other two behind it. Meade would relay the message that Sumter had been secured, which meant Captain Seymour's Company H should proceed to the island immediately and Captain Foster should fire the two signal shots directing Lieutenant Hall to bring the women and children to Sumter.

Aboard the lighters *Raven* and *Miss Penny,* supposedly transporting the Fort Moultrie dependents to Fort Johnson, the Carolinian captains and their crews suspected something was amiss most of the afternoon. To allay the suspicions of the *Raven*'s captain and crew, Lieutenant Hall told them that they couldn't land the women and children until he had made certain that all the preparations to receive them had been completed at Fort Johnson. If this were so, the Carolinian patriots said among themselves, why did he continue looking back toward Moultrie? And why did he remain aboard the *Raven*? The lighter captain voiced a resounding protest.

"You are under hire, sir," responded Hall angrily, "and you will follow my instructions or forfeit your pay for this trip."

"What are you Yankees up to?" demanded the captain.

"That is not your concern, sir," replied Hall.

"You damn well better make it my concern, or this ship will go noplace else this night."

Hall turned to the two soldiers behind him and said, "I believe we'll have to take the captain in charge, men."

They nodded, seized the ship's commander, and held him prisoner.

"This is mutiny, sir!" complained the captain. "I'll press charges."

"I think not," said Hall. "You can sail this ship as its master, sir, or you can swim back to Charleston."

"The hell, you say!"

"Throw him over the side," said Hall.

The soldiers moved to obey their officer.

"No, wait!" pleaded the captain. "All right, I'll take your orders. I won't like it, but I'll do it."

"Nobody is asking you to like it, but your cooperation is appreciated." Hall saluted him. "Thank you, sir."

Two cannon shots echoed across the harbor from Fort Moultrie.

"That's the signal, Captain," said Hall. "You may take us to Fort Sumter now."

"Sumter?"

"Yes," said Hall firmly.

The captain blanched and muttered, "My God! We're goin' to war!"

"You Southrons should have thought about that be-fore you seceded from the Union," chastised Hall. "Now take us to Fort Sumter."

The captain complied.

Major Anderson saw the move differently. He was elated. He had managed to move most of his command out of Moultrie to Sumter without a single casualty and without the Carolinians knowing about it. Holding aloft a flask of brandy given to him by Lieutenant Davis, he proposed a toast: "To the success of the garrison." Then he added, "And Lieutenant Davis, should there be an inquiry and a subsequent court-martial for what we have done this night, I would be more than happy to act as your defense attorney."

Davis and his fellow officers laughed at their com-manding officer's gallows humor, all of them wonder-ing if he might be right about a court-martial. "Well," said Davis, expressing the collective feeling of all pres-ent, "what was it Benjamin Franklin said on the eve of the Revolution? 'We must all hang together, or as-suredly we shall all hang separately'?"

"Here, here!" they concurred.

That night, the God-fearing Anderson said a prayer, then sat down to write Secretary Floyd's adjutant gen-eral, Colonel Samuel Cooper, in Washington.

Colonel,

I have the honor to report that I have just com-pleted, by the blessing of God, the removal to this fort of all my garrison except the surgeon, four non-commissioned officers and seven men. We have one year's supply of hospital stores and about four months' supply of provisions for my command. I left orders to have all the guns at Fort Moultrie spiked, and the carriages of the

*thirty-two-pounders, which are old, destroyed. I
have sent orders to Captain Foster, who remains
at Fort Moultrie, to destroy all the ammunition
which he cannot send over. This step which I have
taken was, in my opinion, necessary to prevent
the effusion of blood.*

Respectfully, your obedient servant,
Robert Anderson
Major, First Artillery Co. Commanding

Major Robert Anderson slept well that night.

9 ～

Only a few people in America saw Major Anderson's maneuver as an attempt to prevent a war. Below the Mason-Dixon Line, his action was interpreted as treachery, as the gauntlet being hurled into the face of peace-loving South Carolina. Above the famed boundary between Maryland and Pennsylvania, the daring move was perceived as a delaying tactic, as a postponement of the inevitable clash between North and South. Challenge or delay. Either view served only to intensify the distrust and belligerency of each side for the other. Even fewer people thought Anderson would do anything other than sit tight at Fort Moultrie and await the outcome of negotiations between the South Carolina commissioners and President Buchanan.

Sarah Hammond placed herself among the former but not the latter. Unlike the rest of those who cared about the future of the nation and who could do something about the direction it was taking, she had a tidbit of foreknowledge that Anderson might be considering some action that would incite one side or the other to belligerence.

Captain Chase docked the *Dover White* at Baltimore on Christmas night, and first thing the next morning he boarded the predawn Baltimore & Ohio train for Washington City, arriving in the capital before eight o'clock. He hired a taxi that took him to the Willard Hotel, where he found Sarah sitting alone in the dining room enjoying breakfast.

"Good morning, Aquila," she said, delighted by his sudden appearance. "I thought I might see you sometime today. Did you bring me anything from the South?"

Chase reached inside his coat, removed the letter from the mysterious "Caduceus," and placed it on the table near Sarah's plate of half-eaten scrambled eggs, fried potatoes, ham, toast, and marmalade. "This was delivered to me just before we sailed from Charleston evening before last," he said. "I haven't opened it." He remainèd standing.

"I didn't think you would," said Sarah as she picked up the envelope. On quick examination, she noted that it had no addressee. Good, she thought as she broke the wax seal and opened the letter. "Please excuse me, Aquila, while I read this. Why don't you sit down?"

"No, thank you, Sarah. I'm not staying. I have to return to my ship as soon as possible. I have a cargo that must be in New York by tomorrow. If you will excuse me, Cousin, I'll take my leave."

"No, wait, Aquila," she said, putting the letter on the table temporarily. "How long will you be in New York before you return to Charleston?"

"The *Dover White*'s next destination is Liverpool. I'll be leaving New York a few days after the New Year and won't be returning to Charleston until February. Providing there is a Charleston to return to, that is."

"What do you mean by that?"

"Nothing. Just rumors."

"What sort of rumors?" queried Sarah, her curiosity more than piqued.

Chase cleared his throat, scanned the room for anybody who might be paying attention to them, and saw that none of the few other diners seemed to care about them. He lowered his voice to a conspiratorial level and said, "Three days ago I overheard a conversation between two deckhands from the *General Clinch,* one of the Carolinians' guard boats that patrol the harbor every night. They spoke of plans to seize Fort Sumter in the next few days." He burped a laugh. "For all I know, they might have done it already. Who knows what those hotheads are capable of doing?"

"Fort Sumter? The island fort in the harbor?"

"That's the one. It dominates the entire harbor. Its guns could level Charleston in a few hours, if somebody had a mind to do such a dastardly thing to that beautiful city."

"We've heard nothing about any such movement by the Carolinians," said Sarah. "The South Carolina commissioners are due to arrive in the city this evening with the intention of bargaining for the goverment's property in their state. I shouldn't think the Carolinians would do anything to excite President Buchanan into calling off negotiations with them."

"There's probably nothing to it, Sarah. Just the usual waterfront scuttlebutt. That's all." He shook his head with dismay. "You are certainly the image of Aunt Sarah, God rest her soul. And you act just like her, too. She must be looking down on you from heaven with a heart full of pride in you."

"I'll take that as a compliment, Aquila."

"It was meant to be a compliment. There was nobody like your grandmother. Leastwise, not until you came along."

"She taught me well."

"Maybe too well," said Chase. "She would have been wiser to teach you to stay out of politics."

"It's my country, too, Cousin."

"So it is." He shrugged. "I must be going. God be

with you, Sarah Hammond." He bent over and kissed her cheek.

"God be with you as well, Captain Chase," said Sarah with all due respect and formality that the occasion demanded. She watched him leave the dining room before picking up the letter from Caduceus and reading it.

> A behaving suspiciously. Planning something covert. May betray garrison to SCs. D no help. Valuable new ally found here. Possible help to stop A from treason. May need ship for rescue in case plan goes awry. Await your reply.
>
>   Caduceus

Without giving it much thought, Sarah left her unfinished meal and returned to her room.

Rowena greeted her at the door. "What's troubling you, Sarah?" she asked.

"This," said Sarah, waving the letter from Caduceus. "Just as I suspected, Major Anderson will probably surrender Fort Moultrie without a fight. That much is good. It's a peaceful if treacherous thing to do. At least, it will mean no blood will be shed over this. It's Caduceus that worries me. I think he's planning to stop Major Anderson from doing any such thing. That could lead to real trouble. He even asked me for a ship to rescue him just in case his plans fall through. I can't believe this, Rowena. I have to get him word right away that he's not to interfere with Anderson, no matter what Anderson plans to do." She handed the letter to Rowena and began to pace the room.

Rowena read the message and said, "What makes you think he hasn't already done something?"

"Who? Caduceus or Anderson?"

"Either one. Both. How old is this letter?"

"Captain Chase brought it to me this morning, and it was given to him two days ago." She paused as understanding set in. "Yes, I see what you mean. For all we know, Anderson may have surrendered Fort Moultrie already. Or Caduceus may have stopped him, and a battle could be raging in Charleston harbor right this very moment." She plopped down on a chair. "I feel so helpless, Rowena. I'm certain Anderson intends to do something, but I'm quite frustrated because I don't know what it might be or when he might do it."

"Why don't you let Caduceus do what he has to do and you get about your own business here in Washington?"

Sarah nodded grimly. "Yes, you're right, Rowena. That's precisely what I should do. Get your coat. We're going calling."

Sarah and Rowena spent the day visiting the offices of Washington's most powerful men, beginning with Senator Seward and finishing with Senator Clay of Alabama. In between, Sarah tried to see several other senators, including two very prominent figures from the South, Senator Davis and Senator Wigfall; but neither would make time for her. Also on her schedule were attempts to speak with Secretary of War Floyd and President Buchanan, and with them, she also failed to gain an audience. Her single greatest success was, of course, the interview with Seward.

"Senator, I suspect Major Anderson will betray the garrison at Fort Moultrie," said Sarah at the top of their conversation, "and surrender his post to the Carolinians at the earliest opportunity."

Slightly bemused by her statement, Seward asked, "On what authority do you reach such an astonishing conclusion, Miss Hammond?"

"Captain Aquila Chase, sir. He's the master of the *Dover White,* a ship of our line. I met with Captain

Chase only this morning, and he brings word that the Carolinians are planning to seize Fort Sumter.''

Now very attentive and not so patronizing, Seward leaned forward and asked, ''How does he come to know this?''

''He overheard a conversation between two Carolinians, sailors aboard a guard boat in Charleston harbor. They spoke of a plan to seize Fort Sumter and train its guns on Fort Moultrie and thus force Anderson to give up his post.''

Seward frowned and said, ''But I thought you said Major Anderson planned to surrender Fort Moultrie at the earliest opportunity. If the Carolinians seize Fort Sumter and train its guns on Fort Moultrie as you suggest, then I don't see what other option Anderson will have except to surrender his post.''

Sarah saw his point, but she refused to accept it. She tried another tack. ''Maybe so, but I have other information that Major Anderson plans to do something to betray the garrison.''

''And from where does this information come?''

Sarah hesitated for a second, then said, ''I received a letter from a friend who is very close to the situation in Charleston harbor.''

''And who is this friend, Miss Hammond?''

''To reveal his identity might compromise his position there, Senator Seward.''

''I see, but you say he's very close to the situation in Charleston harbor?''

''That's correct. He writes that he suspects Major Anderson of treason.''

''He suspects him of treason?'' queried Seward, his tone again tainted with syrupy condescension. ''How does he knows this, Miss Hammond? Is he somebody close to Major Anderson? Someone who would have Anderson's confidence? Or is he merely a casual observer of events transpiring there?''

Sarah lowered her eyes for a blink, then met Seward's gaze with forthright confidence and said, "I can't give you any more information about my friend, Senator. As I said before, to reveal his identity might compromise his position there, and considering the times and recent events, it might even endanger his life."

Seward shrugged and said, "All right, have it your way then. So what do you expect me to do with this information that you're imparting to me?"

"I should think you would take it to President Buchanan so he can act on it."

Seward chuckled at the thought and said, "Excuse me, Miss Hammond. It is not my intention to make sport of you. It's the president. For James Buchanan to act on anything would be a miracle. The man has given new meaning to the words *indecision* and *procrastination*. He fears making the wrong political move more than burning in hell in the great hereafter. He has already opined that he believes no state has the right to secede from the Union, but at the same time, he as president has no power to coerce the erring state to return to the fold. How is that for sitting on the fence, Miss Hammond? He's the master at it. I have heard that he has asked John Floyd to resign in order to avoid scandal. A president doesn't *ask* a cabinet member to resign. He dismisses him summarily. Jackson did it. As dictatorial as 'King Andrew' might have been, I'll grant him his ability to act decisively. If only Buchanan could make half as many decisions as Jackson did, or even Polk, for that matter, then maybe South Carolina might not have seceded and the country wouldn't be faced with such a terrible dilemma." He sank back in his chair, his gaze falling to the blotter on his desk. "Franklin Pierce and James Buchanan. If either of them had been blessed with half as much backbone as Jackson, the South wouldn't be so arrogant, and this nation would still be united under one flag.'' He looked up at Sarah, his expression brighter, patriarchal. ''I'm sorry, Miss Hammond. I didn't mean to deliver a speech.''

Sarah recalled something else her grandmother had once said to her: ''The politicians will always muddle through any crisis, and the people will always pay the bill of lading.'' She couldn't help thinking that Seward was no better than any other government official; he saw plainly and perfectly the past and what should have been done, but he had nary an inkling of how to deal with the present in order to preserve the future. God save us, she thought, if it's not too late for a miracle.

''That's quite all right, Senator,'' she said. ''I am very cognizant of your frustration with the president.''

''Thank you, Miss Hammond. Then you understand that there is very little I can do about the situation in Charleston harbor?''

''Yes, of course, Senator. But I still wish to do something to preserve the peace and protect the innocent who are caught up in this crisis.''

''The innocent?'' queried Seward.

''I refer to the wives and children of the soldiers at Fort Moultrie. I think it would be wise to remove them from harm's way.''

''I concur wholeheartedly. What are you proposing to do to accomplish this?''

''I would think the Carolinians would take a dim view of a warship entering Charleston harbor. Therefore, the Levi Hammond Shipping Line would be honored to send a ship to Charleston for the purpose of evacuating the wives and children of the soldiers at Fort Moultrie.''

Seward smiled and said, ''Now that's something that I can take to the president, Miss Hammond. I'll extend your offer to him as soon as I can arrange an appointment with him.''

"And will you also relate the information I've given you about Major Anderson?"

Seward chuckled and said, "You are as persistent as your late grandmother. She was quite a lady. You do her proud, Miss Hammond."

"You still haven't answered my question, Senator."

Seward sighed and said, "Yes, I will tell the president everything you've told me this morning. Now if you'll excuse me, Miss Hammond. I have other constituents waiting to press me for much more trivial favors than your request, such as jobs in the new administration."

Sarah and Rowena passed from one Northern senator's office to the next, but few were in. Those who were put her off, although all did so with great courtesy. Having exhausted the Northerners, Sarah moved on to the Southerners, all but the last of whom rebuffed her through their secretaries.

After meeting so much frustration with every other Southern political figure, Sarah found Senator Clay of Alabama refreshing. Unlike the others, Clay paid her the courtesy of apologizing in person for not having the time to receive her. "If you had only come a few minutes earlier," he said as they stood in the outer office, "I could have squeezed you in. Unfortunately, Miss Hammond, I have another appointment scheduled for this hour." He checked his pocket watch for the precise minute. "And he should be here any moment."

As if cued, the hallway door opened, and Commander Rafael Sims entered the room.

"Here he is now," said Clay. He moved to shake hands with Sims. "How good to see you again, Commander!"

Sims allowed Clay to gladhand him, but his focus fell on Sarah. He found her attractive, while also sensing an aura of danger about her. Absently, he said, "It's also good to see you again, sir."

Clay noted the look in the commander's eyes and chuckled inwardly, thinking, Good man, he knows beauty when he sees it.

Frustrated, Sarah barely noticed Sims until Clay forced her to acknowledge him.

"Miss Hammond, I would like to introduce you to Commander Rafael Sims of the United States Navy," said Clay eagerly. "Commander, allow me to introduce Miss Sarah Hammond."

Sims remained stolid as he accepted Sarah's extended hand and bowed from the waist. "It's an honor to meet you, Miss Hammond," he said with perfect Southern manners.

"Commander," said Sarah flatly.

Sims straightened up, made his eyes to go blank, and met Sarah's gaze head-on.

"Miss Hammond is the daughter of Mr. Levi Hammond of the Levi Hammond Shipping Line," said Clay.

Sims acknowledged Clay's statement with a nod and said, "I am well-acquainted with your father's company, Miss Hammond. His ships are among the safest on the high seas. Leastways, they are seldom mentioned negatively in the reports that come across my desk at the Navy Department."

Clay made another mental note, that of how Sarah made a succinct but serious appraisal of Sims as the officer spoke to her. Quite curious, he decided as he stored away this morsel of information.

Sarah thought about asking, And what reports would those be, Commander? But she discarded the notion of continuing their conversation by saying, "I don't know what reports you refer to, Commander, but I do know that our ships, their captains, and their crews carry out their duties first-rate and thus should be among the safest on the high seas. Father expects nothing less of all his employees." She turned to Clay. "Perhaps you could see me at another time, Senator. Good day, sir."

After a quick glance at Sims and a curt "Good day to you, too, Commander," she moved toward the door.

Clay hastened to the door ahead of her. He opened it, bowed from the waist, and said, "Yes, Miss Hammond, perhaps another time." A true politician, he knew better than to offend Sarah in any manner, unlike some of his colleagues. Although his state would most likely leave the Union in the near future and being polite to some Yankees would no longer be necessary, he was quite cognizant of the fact that her cousin was James Henry Hammond and that her family controlled a great deal of wealth, much of it still in the South, and that the South was somewhat financially dependent on the Hammonds—for the moment.

Sarah bustled through the doorway and into the hall. Without a word, she walked past Rowena, who had been waiting patiently for her in the corridor. From the look on Sarah's face, the determination in her step, and the direction she was headed, Rowena guessed that they were leaving the building, stood up, and followed Sarah toward the rotunda. A few steps along, they were nearly side by side, although Rowena took the caution of remaining a half-pace behind Sarah; after all, the District of Columbia lay in slave territory, and Washington was considered something of a Southern city.

"That one wouldn't see you neither, would he?" asked Rowena, her tone a touch mocking.

"This one at least saw me," said Sarah as she marched along toward the exit. "He just didn't have time to talk with me is all. Come on, Rowena. Let's get back to the hotel. I'm too tired for any more of this."

They returned to the Willard, where Sarah gave some thought to paying another call on Senator Seward at his home, but she discarded that idea upon reading in the Washington *Post* that the commissioners from South Carolina were due to arrive in the city that evening.

"Maybe I should go down to the train depot and meet them," she said, as if throwing out the suggestion for debate.

"Why would you want to do that?" challenged Rowena. "Do you think they'll talk to you any more here in Washington than they talked to you on the train back in South Carolina?"

Sarah sighed and said, "No, I suppose not, but what else can I do, Rowena?"

"You can go to bed and forget about this nonsense for one night. Sleep well and see what tomorrow brings."

"Of course, you're right."

The morning did bring something new. As Sarah and Rowena resumed their rounds of government leaders, the news that Anderson had evacuated Fort Moultrie and moved his command to Fort Sumter rocked the city. Speculation rampaged that war with South Carolina, and ultimately the entire slaveholding South, was imminent. Many expected that the next dispatches from Charleston would announce the commencement of hostilities between Anderson's forces and the South Carolina militia. Some stories did state that Anderson had used subterfuge to make the transfer of the garrison, one detailing how Anderson seduced several Carolinian authorities into oblivion with alcoholic beverages in order to achieve the maneuver.

Upon hearing the first report, Sarah hastened to Senator Seward's office, hoping to learn something of the government's reaction to the events transpiring in the South. She expected confusion and consternation from the senator but received quite the opposite.

"I am exhilarated, Miss Hammond," said Seward. "Major Anderson has stood up for the Union and has taken charge of the situation in Charleston harbor for the government. He has put the Carolinians and the other Southern states on notice that the government will not tolerate their threats. Now only that spineless Buchanan can undo what Anderson has done with this bold move.''

"And how can the president do that?'' asked Sarah.

"All he has to do is order Anderson to return to Fort Moultrie, and Anderson will have but three choices. Obey and fall prey to the Carolinians. Refuse and find himself facing charges at a military court-martial. Or resign his commission. From what I've heard about the man, he will not disobey his superior's orders. Thus, he is left with choosing between obedience to a damn fool or leaving the life that he loves.''

"Everything depends on President Buchanan now, doesn't it, Senator?''

"You're quite right, my dear. Everything is in the president's hands now.''

"And what do you think he will do?''

"Buchanan is something of an unpredictable commodity. If my guess is right, he'll give in and order Anderson to return to Fort Moultrie. That will only bolster the South's resolve to leave the Union.''

"And if the president doesn't order Major Anderson to return to Fort Moultrie?''

"Then the South will scream all the louder about the North being the aggressor.''

"The president will lose either way then.''

"Quite right, my dear. He will lose either way. He will be damned by the North if he orders Anderson back to Fort Moultrie, and he will be damned by the South if he doesn't. Whichever, we will soon discover, because the president has called an emergency cabinet meeting for this afternoon.''

At the same time that Sarah was conferring with Senator Seward, the three commissioners from South Carolina received a surprise visitor.

Senator Louis Trezevant Wigfall of Texas appeared at the home of former Assistant Secretary of State William Trescot. He had come in search of the South Carolina commissioners who were staying with Trescot while in Washington. Without bothering to knock on the front door, he burst inside and marched straight into the parlor, where Adams, Orr, and Barnwell, having slept late due to the hour of their arrival the previous evening, were enjoying their morning coffee with their host. Before any of them could speak, Wigfall said, "Have you heard the news yet?"

"The news?" queried Barnwell.

"Yes. Anderson has taken Fort Sumter."

"Taken Fort Sumter?" responded Adams.

"What are you talkin' about?" asked Orr simultaneously as he sprang erect.

"Anderson has transferred the Fort Moultrie garrison to Fort Sumter," said Wigfall, "and now he threatens to bombard Charleston if the secession convention doesn't rescind its ordinance to leave the Union."

"When did this happen?" asked Barnwell, the calmest of the three commissioners.

"Yes, Wigfall," said Trescot, "when did this happen?" Also from South Carolina, Trescot knew the senator quite well; better, in fact, than his guests, having had close contact with Wigfall during his tenure in the State Department. For a fact, unlike Barnwell, Orr, and Adams, he knew about Wigfall's hare-brained scheme to kidnap President Buchanan and hold him incommunicado until Vice-President John C. Breckinridge, a Southerner, succeeded to the presidency and did everything that the South wanted done before Lincoln took office in March. Fortunately, Floyd, Trescot, and other Southern leaders stood firm against the foolish and treacherous plan, warning Wigfall that should he attempt something so dastardly and stupid, they would disavow him and throw his carcass to the Northern wolves. Thus, the knowledge of Wigfall's penchant for the nonsensical and his understanding that the Texas senator was an easily excited hothead prone to physical displays of temper explained Trescot's hesitancy to believe this latest news.

"Last night, evidently," said Wigfall. "I don't have all the details yet, but I understand that Governor Pickens has called all the state's militia to duty to counter Anderson's movement."

"This means war," said Adams.

"Not necessarily," said Barnwell, gently rebuking his associate with a glare. Turning back to Wigfall, he stated evenly, "Governor Pickens has an agreement with President Buchanan that there will be no changes in the military situation at Charleston harbor except through negotiations with us."

"That's not quite correct," said Trescot. "The agreement was between Buchanan and Governor Gist, and Buchanan only agreed not to reinforce the garrison at Fort Moultrie. Nothin' was said about Fort Sumter or Fort Pinckney or Fort Johnson."

"That makes no difference," said Wigfall. "The Yankees have fired the first shot, and this means war!"

"Let us not be presumptuous," said Trescot. "Senator, why don't we gather some of your colleagues and call on the president at the White House?"

"A good idea," said Barnwell. "Let's all go over to the White House and see Buchanan."

Trescot held up his hands and said, "Wait a minute, Robert. That's not such a good idea. The three of you came here as South Carolina's representatives, and although our sister states of the South are sympathetic to our cause, they have not yet declared themselves free and independent nations separate from the old Union as we have. I believe we would be wiser to act separately on this matter. Although I am no longer in the government, I believe I still have the president's ear on important affairs such as this business over Fort Sumter. I can express our state's sentiments unofficially in conjunction with a delegation of Southern senators, but you can speak officially for South Carolina. Approachin' Buchanan from two different directions will surely sway him to order Anderson to return to Fort Moultrie, and as soon as he has, our militia will seize Sumter and force Anderson to surrender Moultrie. Are you agreeable to this plan, my old friend?''

Barnwell nodded and said, ''It makes perfect sense, William.'' He looked to his colleagues for their confirmation of his decision. As soon as he saw their heads bob with approval, he said, ''We'll remain here until after you've seen the president, then we'll have our turn at him tomorrow as scheduled.''

''I'll find Davis and Clay,'' said Wigfall, referring to Senators Jefferson Davis of Mississippi and Clement Clay of Alabama. ''You get a few others, Trescot, and we'll meet you at the White House. Agreed?''

''At the White House then,'' said Trescot.

In the executive mansion, tall, white-haired President James Buchanan showed the same indecisiveness that had led many journalists to brand him a ''moral coward'' and cry for his impeachment. A compromise candidate and a minority president who had failed to win a majority of the popular vote in the 1856 election, Buchanan had been a melancholy man long before this new crisis in South Carolina. When he was a young man, his fiancee had been found dead in a Philadelphia hotel room, apparently a suicide because she had heard his name linked scandalously to that of another young lady. The girl's father refused to allow the devastated, brokenhearted Buchanan to attend the girl's funeral. This tragedy, Buchanan had told friends, was a grief never to be spoken of again in his lifetime. Having lost at love, he turned to the service of his country with the

Democratic party, serving in various administrative posts under Presidents Andrew Jackson, Martin Van Buren, James Polk, and Franklin Pierce. Even so, he was never a man much admired by strong, decisive types. Former President Jackson questioned his protégé, President Polk, about naming Buchanan his secretary of state, and Polk replied, "Why, you yourself appointed him minister to Russia." To which Jackson snapped back, "It was as far as I could send him out of my sight and where he could do the least harm. I would have sent him to the North Pole if we had kept a minister there."

Buchanan defined himself as an OPF, Old Public Functionary, but the public, knowing nothing of his broken heart, thought of him as icy and distant. He was a learned constitutional lawyer, perhaps America's best, and while he considered slavery morally wrong, he believed that the Constitution protected it where it was established. At the same time, he reasoned that no state had the right to secede, but that he, as president, had no power to coerce an erring state. Thus, he placed himself and the nation between the deadly horns of a dilemma.

When the news about Anderson moving his garrison to Fort Sumter reached him, Buchanan, whose neck was so twisted that his left cheek nearly rested on his shoulder, wailed, "My God! Are calamities never to come singly!" To make matters worse, his secretary further informed him that Trescot and a group of Southern senators were waiting to see him. "I suppose I must see them," he said, "or they will turn against me as well. Go ahead and show them in."

Trescot led the legislators into the president's office. Wigfall and Clay followed close behind the former assistant secretary of state, and after them came Senators Robert Toombs of Georgia and Judah Benjamin of Lou-

isiana. Conspicuously absent from their number was
Senator Jefferson Davis of Mississippi.

"Mr. President," said Trescot as spokesman for the
group, "we have heard that Major Anderson has removed the garrison at Fort Moultrie to Fort Sumter."

"I have received the same report," said Buchanan,
seated at his desk, trying very hard to appear firm and
resolute. A cigar smoldered in an ashtray to his right.

"Then it's true," said Wigfall angrily, stepping forward as if to menace the president.

Leaning to his right to place himself between Wigfall
and Buchanan, Trescot thought to discourage the Texas
senator from further speech, saying, "Mr. President, it
is the opinion of these gentlemen and several more
senators and representatives of both Southern and
Northern states that you should not have allowed Major
Anderson to make this move."

"I did not allow it, Mr. Trescot," said Buchanan.
He slid his chair away from the desk and stood up to
his full height. "Major Anderson acted on his own accord." He picked up the cigar and puffed new life
into it.

"Then he acted against your orders, sir?" queried
Clay.

"He acted against this administration's policy," said
the president. He turned away from Trescot and the
senators and moved carefully and deliberately toward
the fireplace.

"The administration's policy, sir?" probed Clay.
"Would you please state that policy so that I might
relay it to my fellow legislators who are quite disturbed
by this turn of events at Charleston."

Buchanan threw up his hands and said, almost whin-
ing, "Gentlemen, gentlemen, please, you must give me
time to consult with the cabinet on this affair. I am
wholly unprepared to make any decision at this time."

"Are you gonna order Major Anderson to return to Fort Moultrie or not?" demanded Wigfall bitterly.

Again, Trescot moved to place himself between Wigfall and Buchanan. "Mr. President, will you be givin' the order to Major Anderson to return the garrison to Fort Moultrie posthaste?" he asked.

"I have already told you, gentlemen," said Buchanan, mustering up the courage to withstand their insistence for a decision, "I must consult with the cabinet first, then I must say my prayers over this matter. You must give me time to say my prayers, gentlemen. That is the least you can do." The president ground out his cigar in the callused palm of his left hand as was his nervous habit when confronted.

Realizing that they were accomplishing nothing, Trescot said, "Thank you, Mr. President." He turned to the senators and added, "I believe we've done all we can here, gentlemen. Shall we go?"

With great reluctance and total dissatisfaction with the interview, they departed.

Buchanan returned to the desk, dropped the cigar butt in the ashtray, slumped back into his chair, and prepared himself for the cabinet meeting.

Upon entering the president's office, the cabinet members sat down at the conference table in two groups of three: Isaac Toucey, Jeremiah Black, and Edwin Stanton, the Northerners, to Buchanan's right; and Jacob Thompson, Philip Thomas, and John Floyd, the Southerners, to his left. Stanton and Floyd chose seats opposite each other and farthest away from the president; thus, their colleagues would have no difficulty hearing them when they sparred over the question at hand.

"Thank you for coming, gentlemen," said Buchanan. "Now if you will join me in prayer?"

Collectively, they bowed their heads as the president invoked the Almighty to guide them in their deliberations. "Help us, dear Lord, to make the right and just decisions that will maintain the peace within our nation," he said. "Bless us with Your Divine Spirit and cloak us with the virtue of patience to discern Your will in these matters that we consider this day. Show us the true course for this ship of state in the days ahead that we might prevent the shedding of blood and find a peaceful and righteous solution to the difficulty we now address. Thank You, O Lord, for giving us Your only Son, in whose name we pray, amen."

Almost as a unit, the cabinet officers said, "Amen."

"Now, gentlemen," said Buchanan, "the matter at hand is the movement of the garrison from Fort Moultrie to Fort Sumter by Major Anderson. What say you on this matter?"

Floyd jumped to the attack. "Anderson must be ordered to return his command to Fort Moultrie at once," he said with firm finality. "A failure to make this order will result in disastrous consequences, Mr. President. Besides, you assured Governor Gist that no aggressive measures would be taken at Charleston harbor as long as you were president. Would you go back on your word, Mr. President?"

Buchanan hesitated.

Stanton took up the president's cause, aiming his invective directly at Floyd. "Sir, I remind you that the agreement made was between *then* Governor Gist and President Buchanan. That concord has been upheld, sir. This administration took no aggressive action toward South Carolina while Governor Gist was in office."

Floyd countered. "The agreement was made between the representatives of the Federal government and the sovereign state of South Carolina, not between two men, sir. Their words bound their respective governments, not each other."

Stanton knew Floyd was right, but he refused to

withdraw from the fray. "Oral assurances are not binding, sir. Nothing was written on paper."

"Sir, gentlemen do not need paper to hold them to their word," said Floyd.

Stanton changed his tack. "Mr. Floyd, you yourself gave Major Anderson authority to act as he has done."

"I gave him authority?" queried Floyd. "I did no such thing, Mr. Stanton."

"Were you not the secretary of war who authorized Major Anderson to move his command to another fort in the harbor should there be . . . ?" He reached inside his coat, removed a piece of paper, and read from it. "Should there be, and here I quote, 'tangible evidence of a design to proceed to a hostile act' on the part of the South Carolinians. Were you not the man who made this order to Major Anderson?"

Floyd glared at Stanton, refusing to reply to the attorney general. Instead, he turned to Buchanan. "Mr. President, you must order Anderson to return to Fort Moultrie posthaste in order to avoid the most dire consequences for this government."

Buchanan hesitated again.

Adjusting his steel-rimmed spectacles, Stanton sneered at Floyd before addressing Buchanan. "Sir, a president of the United States who would make such an order would be guilty of treason!"

The president rolled his eyes and threw up his hands. "Oh, no!" he cried. "Not so bad as that, my friend! Not so bad as that!"

"Yes, sir," said Stanton evenly. "As bad as that."

"Preposterous!" snorted Floyd. "Such an order would be hailed as the olive branch of peace."

"It would be hailed as the act of a coward and a traitor to the United States of America," rebutted Stanton.

"Gentlemen, please," said Buchanan. "We must wait until we have some official word from Charleston. For all we know, this story may only be a hoax. I have nothing yet from Anderson to confirm his movement of the garrison to Fort Sumter. Until then, we shall wait. Good day, sirs.''

Being thus dismissed, the cabinet members rose and left the president to contemplate the situation and to pray for divine guidance. Above all to pray.

10 ～

Friday morning, December 28, 1860

President Buchanan awakened stiffer than usual that morning, having slept poorly. Had he been informed of events transpiring the day before at Charleston, he might not have slept at all.

The initial inkling that something was amiss at Fort Moultrie had come with first light on the twenty-seventh. A dense black smoke from the burning gun carriages languished over Sullivan's Island, and early risers passed the word that Moultrieville or the fort was afire. Charleston Mayor Charles MacBeth ordered out the city fire department and chartered a boat to send the company to the aid of the fire's victims, but before the craft could depart, a citizen from the island rowed across the harbor with startling news. "Them Yankees has gone off and left Fort Moultrie. They done spiked the guns and burned the carriages."

"Are you certain of this?" queried a startled MacBeth.

"Certain as the sun done come up in the east. I seen it with my own eyes. Hell, they even coated the cannonballs with tar to burn them, too."

"And the soldiers have left the fort?" asked MacBeth.

"Long gone in the night."

"Where did they go?" demanded MacBeth.

"Don't know for sure," said the sweating man, "but they sure as hell is gone."

The whistle of the guard boat *Nina* silenced all further conversation. As the ship came close to the dock, a boatswain on the fore deck shouted a confirmation of the report. "The Yankees have set Fort Moultrie to burnin', and they've gone out to Fort Sumter."

Within seconds, rumors were rife among the firemen, some of whom departed immediately to spread the word. "The Yankees have burned Fort Moultrie and gone to Fort Sumter! Anderson is aimin' his guns at Charleston! The Yankees have reinforced Fort Sumter! A thousand Yankees and a fleet of warships have entered the harbor and are preparin' to attack Charleston!" The entire community was soon on the verge of panic as the people crowded onto their rooftops for a look at the distant bastion of Yankeedom in their midst.

Cooler heads regained the moment when the captain of the *Nina* made the truth known. "No warships, no guns on the walls of Fort Sumter aimed at the city. Only Yankee sentries marchin' back and forth with muskets on their shoulders."

"The governor must be told immediately," declared MacBeth, and he was the very man to relate the news to the state's top elected official.

Upon hearing that Anderson had moved the garrison from Fort Moultrie to Fort Sumter, Governor Pickens dispatched Colonel J. Johnson Pettigrew and Major Elison Capers of the South Carolina militia to Sumter to demand that Anderson remove his command back to the fort on Sullivan's Island.

The morning watch on the parapet of Fort Sumter spotted the guard boat *Nina* approaching Fort Sumter under a flag of truce and reported it to Captain Doubleday, who went down to the landing to meet the ship.

He greeted Pettigrew and Capers cordially, asking them to state their business.

"We've come to speak with Major Anderson on an urgent matter on behalf of Governor Pickens and the sovereign nation of South Carolina," said Pettigrew.

Thinking these men to be full of themselves, Doubleday nodded grimly and said, "Very good, gentlemen. Right this way." He led them to Anderson's office, where he stood by as the two emissaries spoke their piece.

"Major Anderson, Governor Pickens requests that you return your garrison to Fort Moultrie posthaste," said Pettigrew with all due courtesy and respect for a man in Anderson's position.

"Colonel Pettigrew, I cannot and will not comply with the governor's request," said Anderson in the same tone, speaking with full confidence in the presence of a majority of his staff.

Pettigrew cleared his throat to summon up the courage to speak boldy, then said, "Sir, I remind you that in movin' your command to this place that you are in violation of the agreement made between President Buchanan and Governor Gist just one month past."

"And what agreement was this, Colonel Pettigrew?" asked Anderson. "I am unaware of any agreement between our president and your former governor."

"The president gave his word to Governor Gist that no reinforcements would be sent to the Federal fortifications located at Charleston harbor," said Pettigrew.

"And none have been sent, Colonel," countered Anderson. "This post had no garrison to reinforce. I have merely transferred my command from one place to another, which is entirely my prerogative, sir, as the commander of all Federal military forces of this locality."

"Sir, the president assured Governor Gist that no soldiers would be garrisoned at this post."

"Colonel Pettigrew, as I have already stated, I am

unaware of any agreement between President Buchanan and *former* Governor Gist," said Anderson. "Therefore, until I am ordered otherwise by my superiors, I will continue to garrison this fort."

"Major Anderson, your refusal to honor the agreement between President Buchanan and Governor Gist may be construed as a hostile act by the Federal government against the state of South Carolina," argued Pettigrew.

"Colonel Pettigrew," responded Anderson firmly and with a touch of anger, "I moved my command to this post in order to avoid hostilities and unnecessary bloodshed by either side in this affair. In this controversy between North and South, my sympathies are entirely with the South." He waved a hand at his officers gathered to hear their conversation. "These gentlemen know it perfectly well. They also know that, as long as I wear this uniform, I will honor the oath that I took upon accepting my commission in the United States Army."

"Then is that your final word on the matter, sir?"

"You may tell Governor Pickens that I will not abandon my post or my country," said Anderson. "I cannot and will not go back." Turning to Doubleday, he added, "Captain, you may escort these gentlemen to the landing."

Doubleday saluted and led Pettigrew and Capers to the dock, pointing out along the way that "a mere company of men with bombs in hand could repulse any attack," and that "the walls of the fort could withstand a month-long bombardment from any quarter."

Distraught over their lack of success, the militia officers reported these "facts" to Governor Pickens, who sent word to the secession convention, then meeting in secret session, informing that body of Anderson's reply. Without wasting another minute, the delegates over-

reached their authority and voted to order Pickens to
seize the remaining Federal installations in the harbor.

Through Juanita's bedroom window, Dr. George
Salter witnessed the first act of open rebellion against
the United States government in Charleston harbor the
day after Major Anderson transferred his flag to Fort
Sumter.

Shortly after midday, Lieutenant Napoleon L. Coste,
captain aboard the United States revenue cutter *William
Aiken,* hauled down the Stars and Stripes from the mast
and raised the palmetto standard of revolt in its place.
Only two weeks earlier, Coste had informed his second
in command, Lieutenant John Underwood, that he
would never serve the Union under Lincoln and, if and
when South Carolina seceded, he would resign his commission and put the cutter under the lieutenant's authority. Without warning, Coste reneged on his word and
placed his ship and his own services at the disposal of
the insurgent Carolinians. To their honor and credit,
neither the remaining officers nor any of *William Aiken's* crew followed the captain's treacherous example.

Now suspecting that this solitary incident would
force South Carolina and the Federal government to
begin open hostilities, Salter turned away from the window, the fire of ebullience in his eyes, and announced
to Juanita, "As our English cousins so aptly put it, my
dear, the game is afoot." Disregarding her petulant
pleas to stay the day with her, he dressed and hurried
down to the waterfront, where he joined a growing as-
semblage gathering there to observe the next act of
aggression by the angry, agitated Southrons, whose
numbers increased hourly as news of the events transpiring in and around Charleston harbor circulated
throughout the nation.　　　　　•

Thinking that a show of force might convince Anderson to reconsider his position, Pickens, without the le-

gally necessary concurrence of the state legislature, dispatched three companies of elite troops from the Washington Light Infantry under Colonel Pettigrew to seize Castle Pinckney. Pettigrew assembled his troops on the Citadel green, then, amid the cheers of Charleston's citizenry, he marched them down to the docks, where they boarded the guard ship *Nina* for the short trip across the Cooper River to the dilapidated fortress. Before sundown, they gained their prize without firing a shot.

After seeing Pettigrew's force depart, Salter stayed on the wharf as the milling crowd awaited the arrival of a second contingent of South Carolina militia. Detachments of the Washington, Lafayette, Marion, and German artilleries under the command of Colonel Charles Allston and Lieutenant Colonel Wilmot G. DeSaussure assembled at the waterfront. After the return of the *Nina* from Castle Pinckney, these troops began boarding her and the *General Clinch,* alarming Salter to the possibility that the Carolinians intended to attack Fort Sumter and begin the war between the states in earnest.

"Where are they going?" he asked a stranger next to him.

"They're gonna run them Yankees out of the harbor," said the excited Southron. "Huzzah, boys! Give 'em hell now! Make 'em wish their mommas had never met their pappies!"

Damn! thought Salter. This is history in the making, and it's happening right in front of me, but I need a better seat to see everything. He searched the myriad of faces about him as he forced his brain to devise some sort of plan to get him aboard one of the two guard boats. When Tyler Harris came into view, the pieces fell into place in his mind. He broke through the crowd and forced his way through the cadre of soldiers to get to Harris.

"George, old friend," said Harris with a silly grin, "what are you doin' here? You damn fool Yankee, are you tryin' to get yourself lynched or something?"

Fortunately for Salter, few about them could hear Harris over the cheers of the multitude. Now acutely aware of his situation in the context of the moment, Salter pressed himself close to Harris and said in his ear, "I'm not trying to get myself hung, Ty, but you're gonna get me killed on the spot if you don't stop shoutin' out that I'm a Yankee."

"Oh, dear!" gasped Harris. "That hadn't occurred to me, George. I'm so sorry."

"Never mind that now, Ty. I've got more important matters on my mind. I want to get on that boat with those soldiers."

Harris burped a laugh and said, "What's the matter, George? Wasn't Juanita excitement enough for you? She didn't fuck you to death, so now you want to commit suicide by gettin' on that boat with a couple hundred angry men who intend to shoot every Yankee they see? Is that it, George? Or are you just plain crazy?"

"I'm just plain crazy, Ty."

Harris sighed and said, "You must be, to leave the bed of a sweet little raisin like Juanita to go boatin' with this bunch of killers. Man, don't you know they're not gonna let you on that boat? And even if they do let you on, what makes you think they won't throw you over the side once they're out in the middle of the harbor? This is insane, George. You're gonna get killed out there."

Salter shrugged and said, "Maybe so, Ty, but I still have to get on that boat."

"Okay, old friend. It's your funeral." He shook his head with resignation. "I can see the newspaper tomorrow. 'Yankee doctor drowns in harbor tryin' to swim home to New York.' That's how they'll see it, George. I'm tellin' you true, man."

"I'm a good swimmer, Ty."

"Okay, come on, but I'm goin' with you, if only to pay my last respects when they feed you to the fish."

"Better watch yourself, Ty. Since you're my friend, they just might toss you in with me."

"I hadn't thought about that." He chuckled and said, "You'd better be a good enough swimmer for the both of us, George, because I can't swim a lick."

"Don't worry about drowning, Ty. I'm sure they'll shoot us before they throw us in the harbor."

"No doubt." Harris laughed, slapping Salter on the back. "No doubt." He put his arm around Salter's shoulders and added, "Come on. Colonel Allston is an old friend of Daddy's."

They approached the commanding officer, and Harris made the introductions before asking the question. "Would it be possible, sir, for my friend and me to accompany you on your little sortie against the Federals?"

Allston eyed Salter with suspicion and asked, "Why do you wish to come with us, Dr. Salter?"

"In the first place, Colonel Allston," said Salter, looking Allston directly in the eyes, "I wish to witness these historic events firsthand, and in the second, I am a physician, and should there be bloodshed, I wish to offer you my services."

"But you're a Yankee," said Allston. "Why would you want to attend our wounded?"

"The Hippocratic oath said nothing about politics, sir."

Allston nodded his understanding and said, "In that case, you may join us, sir. As for you, Tyler, I'm not so sure your daddy would want you along with us. Why do you want to come with us?"

"George might need a nurse to help him," said Harris with a grin.

Allston shook his head with dismay and said, "Very

well, Tyler. You may come along as well, but both of
you stay out of the way of my men. If you don't, I'll
have them throw you both overboard. Have I made
myself clear on that point, gentlemen?''

"Yes, sir," said Salter. "Very clear."

"Go aboard then," said Allston.

The captains of the two craft set a course for Sullivan's Island, where Colonel Allston intended to make
an assault on Fort Moultrie in the dark.

Quite aware of the possibility of retaliation by the
Carolinians for transferring his command to Fort Sumter, Major Anderson established a constant watch of the
harbor with first light that morning of the twenty-seventh. He divided his officers and men into duty sections,
then assigned them times to maintain such vigilance.
The commander's first order of the day was to be notified the very instant that any unusual activity should
stir along Charleston's waterfront. When he received
word that something appeared to be out of the ordinary
aboard the *William Aiken,* he rushed to the parapet and
through a spyglass saw Captain Coste lower Old Glory
from the cutter's mast and raise the palmetto standard
of secession.

"I suppose nothing less could have been expected,"
said Anderson to the officers gathered around him, his
voice filled with resignation and frustration. "Coste did
say he would go out with South Carolina when the time
came. I suppose that time has come." He looked
askance at the faces around him.

"Coste has committed an act of treason, sir," said
Doubleday evenly, as if attempting to spur Anderson
to take some sort of action in the matter.

"I have no authority over Coste and his ship, Captain," said Anderson. "There is nothing we can do
except report his treachery to Washington."

As soon as the first company of the Washington

Light Infantry arrived on the wharf at Charleston, word was passed to Anderson that something greater than the surrender of a revenue cutter bubbled in the Carolina cauldron. He hurried to the top of the wall, where he joined the other officers. Doubelday handed him a spyglass, and standing side by side, they watched as Colonel Pettigrew led one hundred fifty men along the wharf toward Castle Pinckney.

"Damn that Pickens!" swore Anderson. "How dare he move against Federal property!"

"Look how slowly they move, sir," said Doubleday. "They must think the place is well-defended." He thought to laugh but didn't as he saw Pettigrew's men suddenly break into a run toward the castle's entrance.

"What is that damn fool doing?" growled Anderson.

"They're too late," said Doubleday. "Lieutenant Meade closed the gates as soon as the *Nina* made her destination obvious." He snorted and added, "Can you believe that, gentlemen? Now they're bringing up scaling ladders. Imagine their surprise once they get inside and find only Meade and Sergeant Skillen and his family."

"You don't suspect any harm will come to them, do you, sir?" asked Captain Crawford anxiously.

"Colonel Pettigrew is a Southerner, Surgeon Crawford," said Anderson firmly. "I am certain that neither he nor his men will do anything to dishonor themselves."

"Yes, sir," said Crawford cautiously, "but they are attacking a Federal installation. Isn't that treason, sir?"

"Treason, Captain?" said Anderson angrily. "South Carolina has seceded from the Union, and her leaders have declared her to be a sovereign republic independent of the United States of America and all other nations of this world. In no manner can this act today be considered as treason. No, sir. This is an act of war against the United States of America."

"Then what do you intend to do about it, sir?" pressed Crawford.

"There is nothing that I can do about it, Captain," said Anderson. "Not without proper orders from higher authority in Washington."

"But *you* have the authority to close the port, sir," suggested Doubleday. "It would take but the mounting of a few pieces aimed in the right directions to prevent the Carolinians from encroaching on Moultrie and Fort Johnson."

"It would do us better to blast the lighthouse out of existence, Captain," said Anderson, "and thus close the entire port instead of merely stopping water traffic between Charleston and the other forts." He turned away from Doubleday and gazed through the spyglass at Pettigrew's men storming Castle Pinckney. He lowered the telescope and bowed his head for a moment as he calmed himself inwardly. Now with less anger but with certain determination, he said, "As I have already stated, gentlemen, I can do nothing about these acts of aggression without proper orders from Washington. I will not fire our guns unless first fired upon." He searched the faces of the men around him for signs of disagreement, saw none, and added, "That is my standing order, gentlemen. No gun is to be fired from this post unless this post is fired upon first. Have I made myself clear?"

He had.

Colonel Allston's contingent of South Carolina militia landed on Sullivan's Island at half past seven that evening. Having heard rumors from the locals that Captain Foster had mined the approaches to Fort Moultrie, Allston ordered the troops to advance with great caution. Turning to Salter and Harris, he said, "You two will remain here on the wharf. If we have need of your services, Dr. Salter, I will send a man to fetch you. Is that understood, sir?''

"I'd rather go with you, Colonel," said Salter. "If there should be a fight and men are shot, the sooner I can tend to them, the more likely they are to live to fight another day."

Allston considered Salter's words for a few seconds, then said, "Very well. You may come with me. Tyler, what would—?"

"I'll be just fine right here, Colonel," said Harris.

"Very well. Come along, Dr. Salter."

Salter walked two paces behind Allston as the colonel led a small detachment of soldiers along the sole street of Moultrieville. They moved through the darkness with stealth, as Allston wished not to alarm the villagers. Within a few minutes, they halted before the gates of Fort Moultrie.

"Hello in the fort!" shouted Allston.

"Who goes there?" came a reply from within.

"I am Colonel Charles Allston of the South Carolina State Militia. I have come to demand the surrender of this fort."

The gates swung open. A Federal sergeant and a few workmen stood there.

"I have no authority to surrender anything to you, Colonel Allston," said the sergeant, "except myself, and speaking frankly, sir, I ain't worth much." He bellowed a laugh before adding, "And neither are any of this worthless bunch." He laughed all the louder. "Come on in, Colonel, and make yourselves at home. That's what you were planning to do anyway, ain't it?"

"Stand aside," said Allston angrily. He moved ahead, and the sergeant and the workmen cleared a path for him. "Follow me, men."

"I assure you, Colonel," said the sergeant as Allston stepped past him, "there ain't another soldier here. The

place is all yours, and if you don't mind, I'll be leaving
first thing in the morning.''

Allston, Salter, and the militiamen entered the fort.
The colonel scanned the walls for any sign of armed
men but saw none. Over his shoulder, he said, ''It appears the sergeant was tellin' the truth, Dr. Salter. The
place seems deserted, but even so, I don't trust those
damn Federals. Who knows what mischief they left behind to endanger us? We'll raise our own flag, then
wait for daylight.''

''That seems like the wisest choice, Colonel,'' said
Salter. ''No sense in risking any lives in the dark.''

''Yes, of course,'' said Allston. He called for the
palmetto flag to be raised above the fort, then settled
in for the night.

Salter excused himself from Allston and hurried back
to the wharf, where he found Harris sharing a bottle
of rum with a few sailors from the *Nina*. ''Back so
soon, George?''

''We wasted our time, Ty,'' said Salter. ''Major Anderson has deserted the fort completely. There will be
no fighting this night.''

''Thank God! I can't stand the sight of blood,
George.''

''That's too bad, Ty, because I've got the feeling
that it won't be long before you're gonna see plenty
of it.''

News of South Carolina's seizure of Federal property
by force had yet to reach President Buchanan when he
received the three commissioners from the seceded state
the morning of the twenty-eighth. Adams, Barnwell,
and Orr presented the president with two documents: a
copy of South Carolina's *Ordinance of Secession* and
a written demand for all Federal property to be turned
over to South Carolina and for all Federal troops to be
removed from Charleston harbor. ''Governor Pickens

wishes an immediate reply, Mr. President," said Barnwell firmly.

"You don't give me time to consider, gentlemen," cried Buchanan with dismay. "You don't give me time to say my prayers. I always say my prayers when required to act upon any great state affair. I need time, gentlemen."

"How much time, Mr. President?" pressed the impatient Barnwell. "We must tell Governor Pickens something, sir."

"I must pray on that, too, Mr. Barnwell," said Buchanan. "Now excuse me, gentlemen, so that I might tend to that very duty."

The commissioners left the White House disgruntled and dissatisfied with Buchanan's failure to make a decision.

When the news of the events at Charleston reached him, Buchanan thanked God that he had not given in to the Carolinians just yet, and he remarked wryly to his personal secretary, "If I withdraw Anderson from Sumter now, I can travel home to Wheatland by the light of my own burning effigies." For the moment, the president wavered toward the North. Then Senator Toombs of Georgia visited the White House.

"Have you made your decision yet on whether to withdraw Anderson from Sumter or not?" asked Toombs.

"Tell me, Senator," said Buchanan, thinking to sidestep the issue, "why should Georgia have such an interest in South Carolina?"

Much like the arrogant teacher who is wont to embarrass the innocent pupil with the obvious, Toombs said, "Sir, the cause of Charleston is the cause of the South."

"Good God, Mr. Toombs," sputtered Buchanan, "do you mean that I am in the midst of a revolution?"

"Yes, sir. More than that, you have been there for a year and have not yet found it out."

Buchanan was incredulous. And confused. And hurt. He dismissed Toombs without giving the senator a firm answer one way or the other, and he retired to his prayers.

While the president sought divine guidance in this national crisis facing him, Senator Wigfall, Senator Clay, and Secretary of War Floyd met with the South Carolina commissioners at William Trescot's residence.

"Damn that crooked-necked Yankee!" swore Wigfall. "I told you, Trescot, we shoulda kidnapped the sonofabitch and held on to him until Breckinridge could do the right thing for the South. Now it's too late. Those nigger-lovin' Republicans won't let Buchanan order Anderson back to Moultrie, and that damn fool Pickens will start the war before we're ready to fight. This is a fine pile of horse shit we're all fixin' to fall into."

"Calm down, Louis," said Floyd. "Nothin' is lost here just yet. I'm still the secretary of war. I still have my authority over the army. I'll order Anderson to return to Moultrie, and that will be that."

"That won't work, John," said Trescot. "The whole city knows that Buchanan has asked for your resignation."

"Yes, but Anderson is not here in Washington," countered Floyd smugly.

"If you issue such an order," said Barnwell, "whether Anderson obeys it or not, you will only succeed in turnin' the entire North against us. No, sir. The order must come from Buchanan. Then the North will turn its wrath on him instead of us."

"But how do we get Buchanan to make the order?" queried Orr. "The man never makes a decision unless prodded with a hot poker."

"I have a thought about that," said Adams. "We need another Yankee to convince him to order Anderson back to Moultrie for the sake of peace."

"For the sake of peace?" barked Wigfall. "What the hell does that mean? We're gonna hafta fight the sonsabitches sooner or later, ain't we?"

"Yes, Louis," said Adams calmly, "but we can't fight them now. We are totally unprepared for a war at this time."

"There ain't no time like the present," said Wigfall.

"James is right," said Barnwell. "We must keep the peace as long as we can so we can better prepare ourselves for war, and the first step toward that end is to have Buchanan order Anderson back to Moultrie. Now what were you sayin' about that, James?"

"He said we need another Yankee to convince Buchanan to order Anderson back to Moultrie," said Wigfall. "I ain't so sure what you mean by that, Adams, but I'm willin' to listen. Just what have you got in mind?"

"That young woman we met back in Columbia," said Adams. "That distant cousin of James Hammond. What was her name?"

"Sarah Hammond, I believe," said Barnwell.

"Yes, that's it," said Orr. "What about her?"

"Who's this Sarah Hammond?" asked Wigfall, not recalling that he had refused her request for an interview only two days earlier.

"I know her," said Clay. "She came to my office just the day before yesterday. I had another appointment at the time and couldn't see her, but we did speak briefly. She's the daughter of Levi Hammond, the shippin' magnate."

"And you say she's the distant cousin of James Hammond?" queried Wigfall, a bit bewildered by the direction the conversation was taking.

"Yes, that's correct," said Adams.

"What have you got in mind, James?" asked Barnwell, his curiosity greatly piqued now.

"I was thinkin' about what Pickens said about how she was much in favor of maintainin' the peace between North and South," said Adams.

"Yes, I recollect that," said Orr.

"Go on, James," said Barnwell, a tad perturbed at Orr for interrupting.

"I was thinkin' that we might ask the lady to speak with Buchanan for the sake of peace," said Adams.

"A brilliant suggestion, James," said Barnwell. "She's a Yankee, and she's from a prominent family. A few well-chosen words from her might be all that's needed to get Buchanan to order Anderson back to Moultrie."

"That's all well and good, gentlemen," said Wigfall, "but how do we get this Yankee woman to put a bug in Buchanan's ear?"

"I know how," said Clay, a sly grin curling his lips.

11 ~

Friday evening, December 28, 1860

Senator Clay's message read simply:

> Commander Sims,
>
>   Please come to my office at 4:00 this afternoon.
> I have a matter of state to discuss with you.
> Thank you.
>
>   C. Clay
>   U.S. Senate

Sims suspected that Clay wanted the meeting in order to learn exactly where he stood on secession. Not that Sims hadn't already made it clear that his loyalties lay with Alabama and the South, and in that order. Even so, Clay might wish to know how he could best serve their state if and when Alabama should secede. That had to be it. Yes, Clay probably wanted to discuss how a naval officer would fit into the new confederation that the Southern states were bound to form after secession. With that thought in mind, Sims reported to the senator's office.

"Come in and sit down, Commander," said Clay, offering Sims either of two upholstered armchairs that usually faced the senator's desk but that now stood opposite each other. When the commander took the seat with its back to the wall, the senator closed the curtains and sat down with the window behind him. "Are you comfortable, sir?" he asked, noting the stiffness of the commander's demeanor.

"Yes, sir, I am," said Sims mechanically.

Hoping to build some enthusiasm in Sims, Clay forced a smile and said, "Good. Good. I felt this arrangement would be less formal, considerin' the importance of the request that I wish to make of you, sir." He paused intentionally.

Sims remained stoic, although attentive.

Clay cleared his throat and continued. "I do realize that my message to you was rather terse and uninformative, but it was intended to be so ... because of the times in which we live."

"Yes, of course, sir," said Sims. "I understand."

"Do you, Commander?"

"Yes, sir. I am an officer in the United States Navy, and I am duly sworn to uphold the Constitution of the United States of America and to defend the Union against all enemies. Any action or failure to act on my part less than the fulfillment of those obligations could be construed to be an act of treason, punishable by court-martial with a possible sentence of death. Bein' fully cognizant that any fellow officer, any member of Congress, or any official of the executive branch of this government could misinterpret anything I do as treason against the flag that I am sworn to defend and how that very same person could bring charges against me, I am acutely aware of the circumstances under which we live, sir."

"Yes, of course, Commander," said Clay, feeling a tad chastised. "For that very reason, sir ... that is, your awareness of the times and the possible risk involved with any action on your part, especially with you bein' a naval officer from a Southern state . . . for those reasons, I have decided to ask you to perform a task that could serve the cause of the South as well as preserve the Union that all men of peace, both North and South, hold so dear.''

"And what task is that, sir?" asked Sims bluntly.

"Commander, I'm certain that you are well-informed on the situation at Charleston, and acceptin' that premise, I am equally certain that you are cognizant of the potential danger of war eruptin' at any hour between South Carolina and the Federal government, a war, sir, that once begun, will force every state of the Union to take up arms for one side or the other, a war that can only end in one of two ways. Either with the independence of the South from the North or with the complete destruction and domination of the South by the North. No matter which outcome should prevail, a war between the states would result in the tragedy of massive bloodlettin' on both sides. I shudder at the thought of so much death and destruction . . . a disaster, sir, that can be avoided—no, that must be avoided—that we must eschew with every ounce of our bein's.

"In that vein, Commander Sims, I am askin' you to accept a task that, on the surface, could be construed as treasonous but is actually a bold stroke for the cause of peace. Would you be willin' to accept such a task, sir?"

"Before answerin', Senator Clay, I would need to know exactly what the task is."

"Yes, of course. I understand your reluctance to accept without more detailed information, but please understand that I am not at liberty to reveal everything to you. There are certain persons involved here who must remain unnamed. You do understand that, don't you?"

"Yes, sir."

"Good. Then let me say that I represent the interests of the South in this matter. The South, as a whole,

wishes for nothin' except to resolve its differences with
the North peacefully, and that includes maintainin' the
peace between South Carolina and the Federal
government.

"Toward that end, the commissioners from South
Carolina met with President Buchanan this mornin' and
presented him with a request for the peaceful transfer
of all Federal property within the borders of their state
to their government and the complete withdrawal of all
Federal forces and agents from South Carolina. When
President Buchanan made no decision on their request,
they asked that he order the garrison now at Fort Sumter to return to Fort Moultrie as an act of good faith
on his part. On this, he also refused to make any decision at this time." Clay leaned forward and lowered
his voice as if they were in a room filled with eavesdroppers. "Let me say this, Commander. There are
those of us within the Congress and within the administration who fear that the president's procrastination will
only frustrate the Carolinians into doin' something foolish that will force the president into a counteraction
that will only lead to bloodshed. My associates and I
feel that the president has to be persuaded to order
Major Anderson and the garrison back to Fort Moultrie
before this should happen, God forbid."

Sims shrugged and said, "I hardly have the president's ear, Senator Clay. How do—?"

Clay interrupted him. "No, of course you don't,
Commander. We weren't thinkin' of that, of havin' you
speak to the president. Quite frankly, we don't believe
the president will listen to any Southerner at this time,
but we do believe that he will listen to a Northerner."

The commander twisted in his seat, smiled vaguely,
and said, "If I'm not mistaken, Senator, accordin' to
the newspapers, all Northerners are in perfect harmony
over Major Anderson remainin' right where he is at
Fort Sumter."

"Not every Northerner, Commander," said Clay, wagging a mischievous finger at Sims. "There is one who could be persuaded to speak to the president and possibly convince him that the cause of peace would best be served by Anderson returnin' to Fort Moultrie."

Feeling cornered and defensive, Sims countered, "Senator, I have no influence over politicians or political matters within this government."

"Yes, we are aware of that, too."

"Then why are you askin' me to speak with this Yankee politician? You are askin' me to speak to him, are you not, Senator?"

Clay smiled and said, "In the first place, Commander Sims, the Yankee is not a politician, and in the second, the Yankee is not a man."

"Not a man?" gasped Sims. "A woman?"

Clay grinned and said, "Yes, a woman. I believe you met her just yesterday in my outer office. You do recall bein' introduced to Miss Hammond, don't you?"

Sims remembered the moment in every detail. "It was the day before, Senator," he said, attempting to buy time in order to formulate a reasonable refusal. "Yes, I recall the lady. Miss Sarah Hammond, the daughter of Mr. Levi Hammond of the Levi Hammond Shipping Line." He now leaned forward and asked with a touch of incredulity, "Are you tellin' me, sir, that she can influence the president?"

Clay fell back in his chair and said, "Yes, I am."

"But why would she plead with President Buchanan to withdraw Major Anderson and his garrison from Fort Sumter and return to Fort Moultrie? I mean—"

Clay held up a hand to interrupt Sims and said, "Miss Hammond has taken it upon herself to maintain the peace between North and South. She has recently returned from Charleston, where she met with Governor Pickens and other dignitaries of South Carolina, includin' her distant cousin, the recently resigned Senator

James Hammond of that state. I am told that she pleaded with Governor Pickens not to commit any overt act of war that would force the Federal government to retaliate against South Carolina and thus begin a war between the states. I am also told that she has been makin' this same sort of plea here in Washington City, callin' on senators and congressmen both North and South. She's even tried to see the president, but no appointment has yet been arranged.''

The commander's brow furrowed as he queried, ''Then what would be the use in askin' her to plead with President Buchanan, if she can't get an appointment to see him?''

''A good point, sir. One well-taken. Also, one that I've already considered. Tell Miss Hammond this. If she will plead our cause with the president, I will arrange an appointment for her to see him in his private office.''

''That's all well and good, sir,'' said Sims, continuing to resist the senator's overtures, ''but what makes you think she will even meet with me to discuss this matter? More than that, Senator, why are you askin' me to do this?''

''Miss Hammond springs from a seafarin' family. I felt that since you are a man of the sea, she would be more responsive to you than to a politician.''

''I see,'' said Sims, resigning himself to accepting Clay's proposal.

''Now then, Commander. Are you willin' to perform this task for the preservation of peace between the states?''

Sims bore his gaze directly into Clay's eyes and said, ''As we discussed the day before yesterday, Senator, my sentiments lie with Alabama and the South, and I am wholly prepared to resign from the Navy should Alabama secede from the Union. But until that day comes, I will continue to serve the flag and country I have sworn to defend to the death. With both of those premises to motivate me, how could I possibly deny your request?''

Sarah Hammond came within a heartbeat of declining to see Sims when she read the card delivered to her by the bell captain of the Willard. She didn't recognize the name immediately and couldn't imagine why a naval officer would want to call on her, except possibly to ask her to speak to her father on his behalf about a position with the shipping line, a chore she refused to accept. Then Rowena reminded her that Sims was that handsome officer that she had encountered at Senator Clay's office the day before last, and the memory piqued her interest.

"Did the gentleman indicate what he wishes to speak to me about, Mr. Taylor?" Sarah asked the bell captain.

"Only that it's a matter that greatly concerns you, Miss Hammond," said Taylor, a small, thick man with a deep voice that commanded respect, although it belonged to a slave.

"And you're certain that's all he said?" she pressed.

"Yes'm."

"Very well, Mr. Taylor. Tell Commander Sims that I will meet him in the lobby in fifteen minutes."

"Yes'm." He moved toward the door, then stopped, turned around, and said, "I almost forgot. This also came for you, Miss Hammond." He held out a telegraph envelope.

Rowena took it and passed it to Sarah.

"Thank you, Mr. Taylor. Rowena, please take care of Mr. Taylor for me?"

"Certainly," said Rowena. She went to Sarah's purse, dug out a dime, and gave it to the bell captain.

"Thank you, Miss Rowena," said Taylor. He bowed to her, then left the room.

Sarah opened the envelope and read:

> *A retreated in face of SC's threat. Garrison safe at Sumter. D still no help. Trying to make contact with new ally. Still fear A will betray garrison. Will ship come for rescue if needed. Await your reply.*
>
> *Caduceus*

Sarah handed the message to Rowena to read.

"Will there be a ship to rescue those people, Sarah?" asked Rowena as soon as she finished reading the telegram.

"Senator Seward hasn't given me the president's reply yet," said Sarah. "That's out of my control for the moment anyway, so I won't give it much thought right now. I'm much more curious about this Commander Sims calling on me. I haven't the slightest idea what he wants, but I certainly intend to find out."

She primped her hair before the dresser mirror, then donned an unadorned maroon felt hat, a matching cape, and a pair of black gloves. Feeling prim, proper, and prepared to meet Sims, she went downstairs to the lobby.

Attired in a freshly brushed uniform and holding his hat in his left hand at his side, Sims watched Sarah as she casually descended the stairway from the second floor. Their initial contact had come unexpectedly, and he had hardly given her a thought at the time except to acknowledge that she possessed a particular allure complemented by a corneal glint that defined her as a thoroughly dangerous woman. Now as their eyes met again, he found himself making mental comparisons between Sarah and his wife, Annetha, back in Cincinnati, and his most recent conquest, Louisa Phoenix. This young woman intrigued him, demanded his complete interest merely on inspection of her form. Certainly, her figure was lither than that of Annetha or

Louisa, probably because Sarah had never been married
and thus had never borne a babe in her womb, unlike
his wife, who had given him nine children over their
twenty years of marriage, and Louisa, who had been
pregnant only once in her young life but who had a
tendency toward buxomness, a physical trait that contributed to her bewitching boudoir beauty but that de-
tracted from her appearance otherwise. But it wasn't
Sarah's shape that made her attractive to him. The attraction lay in her soul, an invisible quality intangible
to the eye, but an essence evident to the subconscious
spirit. Although a mysterious, unseen aura, it held him,
locked his gaze on her face.

As she descended the stairway with natural grace and
elegance, her hand lightly touching the rail, her skirt
trailing luxuriantly behind her, Sarah surveyed the
lobby until she found Sims standing in front of the
two imported chesterfields situated perpendicular to the
street windows. Strange, she hadn't noticed on their
first meeting how distinguished he looked. Handsome;
a military bearing; an air of leadership, confidence, and
inner strength about him. Most admirable and desirable
traits all, but she had known such physical specimens
before, only to have them turn out to be arrogant, con-
ceited, narcissistic, egotistic bores. Of course, every one
of them had been young and immature. This man was
a man. Or so he seemed from her point of view.

By the time Sarah reached the bottom step, Sims
wondered why his mind had made such a departure
from the mission at hand. He straightened his spine as
a reminder to maintain a military posture intended to
convey a sense of sincerity and serious purpose to
their meeting.

Sarah approached Sims without fear or reservation.
Coming within three feet of him, she smiled and said
with all due courtesy what a Southern gentleman would

expect from a lady, "Commander Sims, how nice to see you again."

Sims bowed stiffly, straightened up, and replied, "The honor is all mine, Miss Hammond." He waved his free hand toward the sofa behind him. "Shall we sit?"

"Yes, of course," said Sarah. She swept by him and sat down on the farthest end of the armed couch.

Sims waited for her to be seated before taking up the same spot on the opposite chesterfield.

"Tell me, Commander, what is this matter that greatly concerns me that you wish to speak to me about?"

Clay had warned Sims that Sarah could be forthright and blunt. Thus prepared, he decided to respond in kind. "Miss Hammond, it is my understandin' that you are quite desirous that our nation remain at peace, that a war between the states be avoided at all costs. Is this not correct?"

"You have been correctly informed, Commander. But what of it? I'm certain that I'm not the only person in America who wants to avoid a war."

"No, Miss Hammond, you're not the only person in America who wishes to avoid a war. I, for one, also wish to avoid it, and the gentlemen that I represent feel the same way."

Sarah's eyebrows twitched. "The gentlemen that you represent, Commander? And who might they be?"

"I am not at liberty to reveal their names, Miss Hammond, but suffice it to say that they are some of the leadin' statesmen of many Southern states."

"And why would a naval officer be representing some of the leading statesmen of many Southern states, Commander?"

"I am also a Southerner."

"So I gathered the other day at Senator Clay's office," said Sarah. "May I assume that these are some of the same Southern statesmen who refused to see me in their offices these past few days?''

Sims felt a slight chastisement and said defensively, ''I know nothin' about that, Miss Hammond. All I know is that they wish to avoid a war between the states, and they have asked me to speak to you on their behalf.''

''And what is it that they wish from me, Commander? I am a mere woman. A single, young woman, I might add, without the benefit of a husband with wealth or position.''

''That may be so, but you are a Hammond, the daughter of Levi Hammond, the niece of Gideon Hammond, and the cousin of Senator James Hammond of South Carolina.''

''A distant cousin, Commander, and, yes, I am a Hammond, and I do know to whom I am related, thank you. Even so, I am still a mere woman.''

''No, Miss Hammond, you are not a mere woman. You are a woman of influence. Were you less, the gentlemen that sent me here would not be so willin' to open doors for you. Specifically, one door. The door to the president's office at the White House.''

''The door to the president's office at the White House?'' she repeated. ''I see. And what would these gentlemen want me to say to the president on their behalf?''

Sims decided he had nothing to lose by coming straight to the point. ''Nothin' for them, Miss Hammond, but for the sake of peace. They would ask that you plead with President Buchanan to order Major Anderson to return his garrison to Fort Moultrie posthaste.''

''Haven't you heard, Commander? The South Carolina militia occupied Fort Moultrie last night. How can Major Anderson be expected to return his garrison to a post that is now in the hands of a foreign government?

That is how the South Carolinians are thinking of themselves these days, you know. I know because I was there in Charleston when they seceded from the Union. But that is another story, sir. The question remains: How can Major Anderson be expected to return his garrison to a post that is no longer Federal property?''

"Your point is well-taken, Miss Hammond. Perhaps the president could be persuaded to withdraw Major Anderson and his garrison from Fort Sumter and South Carolina entirely.''

"And what would that accomplish, Commander? I've been in the South recently, as I've said already. I've seen how you Southerners strut about and boast that any one of you can lick any ten Yankees in a fair fight. More so, Commander, I'm certain that most of your Southern brethren are anxious to prove their boast in the field and . . . possibly on the high seas as well?''

"I assure you, Miss Hammond, that I have no desire to take up arms against my fellow naval officers.''

"But you will if you have to. Is that not so, sir?''

Sims feared nothing in telling the truth. ''I will go where Alabama goes, Miss Hammond, and if that should be the way of South Carolina, then I will follow. And if I am called on to defend my state, then I will do so to the best of my ability, whether that duty is on land or at sea.''

Sarah recognized honesty when she heard it and when she saw it in a man's eyes, which wasn't as often as she would have liked it to be. ''Yes, I believe you, Commander,'' she said evenly. ''Let us pray that it won't come to that.''

"Yes, let us pray that it doesn't.''

"All right, Commander. Tell Senator Clay—it is Senator Clay who sent you, isn't it? I mean, who else could have sent you? He's the only one who knows both of us.''

"Yes, Senator Clay is the one.''

"And the others?"

"I don't know for certain."

Sarah studied him for a brief three seconds before saying, "Yes, I believe you don't. No matter, though. Who they are is not the issue here. You need an answer for them, and I have one for you. You can tell Senator Clay that I will gladly ask President Buchanan to withdraw Major Anderson and his garrison from Fort Sumter. I doubt that it will do any good, but I will ask him, providing Senator Clay can arrange an appointment for me."

"Consider the appointment arranged, Miss Hammond. I'll send word as to the exact time." He stood up. "Until then, I bid you adieu."

"Yes, Commander, adieu," said Sarah, "for I know we shall meet again."

Her pronouncement disturbed him, but he refused to show it. Instead, he bowed and departed without further words.

Sarah watched Sims exit, satisfied—no, excited as evidenced by the flush of her cheeks—that her estimate of him had been correct thus far. He was a man in both years and context. The pounding of her heart said so.

12 ~

Saturday morning, December 29, 1860

Jimmy Eagan saw Lieutenant John Lacy climb the steps to the brownstone on the corner of Bedford and Rodney. "The navy sets sail, and the army rides in," he muttered to no one in particular. He felt an adolescent urge in his groin at the thought of what the lovely Mrs. Phoenix did behind those closed doors with her gentlemen callers. He smiled at the thought, felt his pulse quicken, and wished to be in Lacy's shoes, if only for the next hour. Before his imagination could whip his senses into a frenzy, a sudden gust of cold wind sent a shiver through him that shriveled his rising ardor to its natural state and reminded him that such lascivious thoughts were considered a sin. "Damn!" he swore aloud. "Something else to confess to Father Gogin this afternoon." He turned away and set his mind to selling his last few copies of the *Eagle*.

Breathing heavily from climbing more stairs than he was accustomed to ascending with such rapidity, Lacy rapped his knuckles anxiously on the door to Louisa Phoenix's apartment.

"Now who could that be so early on a Saturday?"

asked Louisa, glancing at the clock on the hearth and noting the time to be ten minutes after nine.

Hattie rose from her chair to answer the call, but before she could reach the knob, another knock from without. "Whoever 'tis," drawled the servant, "he sure is in a hurry to have that door opened for him."

Him? thought Louisa. Her heart stepped up its pace. Maybe it's Rafe.

Hattie opened the door to reveal Lacy standing in the hall, slightly disheveled and in need of a shave. "May I see Mrs. Phoenix?" he asked politely, removing his hat nervously and revealing a sweaty brow.

Oh, it's only Johnny, thought Louisa, more than a bit disappointed. Then it occurred to her that he was early. He wasn't supposed to be there until that afternoon. Couldn't wait for more of what he got yesterday, I guess. Well, he'll just have to wait until I'm in the mood.

"It's Lieutenant Lacy, Miz Louisa," said Hattie.

Wary of showing any displeasure at his visit, she said, "Invite him in, Hattie," although she made no move from her chair.

The servant opened the door wider and stood aside to permit Lacy to enter the apartment.

The officer stepped past Hattie into the parlor.

"Why, Lieutenant Lacy, what brings you here this mornin'?" asked Louisa as innocently as she could, intentionally bypassing a more conventional greeting. She expected to see lasciviousness in his eyes, but instead she saw an anxiety that caused her instant concern.

Before speaking, Lacy glanced over his shoulder at Hattie as she closed the door behind him. Then to Louisa, he said, "Good morning, Mrs. Phoenix. I just wanted to see if there was anything that you needed before I depart for Washington City this afternoon."

"Washington City?" gasped Louisa.

"Yes, Washington City. General Scott received word early this morning that Secretary of War Floyd will present his resignation to the president today, and he has determined that his place is in Washington City with the president. He's only taking a skeleton staff with him, and, of course, me."

The day before, Lacy had told her that he had to attend an important meeting with General Scott that evening. When pressed for the purpose of the meeting, he'd related that it probably involved the situation at Fort Sumter. They'd discussed the possibility of something being done to aid Major Anderson and the garrison now isolated on the man-made island in the middle of Charleston harbor and how the Carolinians were already taking steps toward war with the Federal government. She had lied and said that she was against the Southern states withdrawing from the Union and that she thought the two sections of the country ought to resolve their differences in the halls of Congress. That was yesterday. Today he was going to Washington City with General Scott.

Louisa recognized a cue when she heard one. "Hattie, take Lieutenant Lacy's hat, then make us some coffee," she said as a way of dismissing an unnecessary pair of ears to their conversation. "Please sit down, Lieutenant Lacy." She motioned toward the sofa.

Lacy sat down as Hattie disappeared into the kitchen. He leaned toward Louisa and said softly, "I couldn't go without seeing you first."

Sensing something momentous in the air, Louisa sat up straight and said, "I'm so glad that you came by to tell me this, Johnny, but why are you goin' with him?"

"General Scott is going to see the president," said Lacy, "and he's taking me along because my command is an integral part of his plan."

"Integral?" queried Louisa. "What does that mean?"

"It means that I'm a major part of his plan," said Lacy, leaning back against the sofa and crossing his legs as he tried to look important. "It's a military secret, and I'm not supposed to talk about it."

"A military secret?" gasped Louisa. "Oh, Johnny, it must be real important. And you say you're goin' with General Scott to see the president?"

"Yes, that's right."

Louisa moved to the sofa and put her hand on Lacy's thigh as she said, "Oh, Johnny, that sounds so excitin'." She pressed herself against him. "How soon before you have to leave?"

"We're taking the noon train," said Lacy, the closeness of Louisa forcing him to drop his voice to a huskier tone. "The general telegraphed the president that he wanted to meet with him as soon as we arrive in Washington City tonight."

The unexpected excitement surrounding Lacy sparked a genuine arousal within Louisa. She felt the warmth, liked it, and wanted to do something about it as quickly as possible. "That doesn't give us much time, Johnny," she said. Hattie has to go, she thought, glaring at the kitchen door. An idea struck. She squeezed Lacy's leg and said, "I'll send Hattie on an errand." She kissed him quickly. "Be patient, darlin'." She sprang to her feet and went to the bedroom. Returning within seconds carrying her handbag, she called out, "Hattie, come here!" She dug into the purse and pulled out a quarter just as Hattie reappeared in the parlor. "Lieutenant Lacy hasn't had any breakfast, Hattie. So I want you to take this twenty-five cents and go to the bakery over on Lafayette Avenue and buy two sweet cakes for him. Then go by Mr. Gibbon's dairy and buy a quart of fresh milk and a half-dozen eggs. Lieutenant Lacy shouldn't have to travel all the way to Washington City on an empty stomach." She handed the coin to Hattie. "Now you be quick about it, too."

The last was intentional. Louisa knew that the surest way of slowing Hattie's pace at performing any task was to tell her to hurry.

"Yes'm," said Hattie, accepting the money and putting it in an apron pocket. She took her wrap from its peg on the wall beside the door, donned it and a bonnet that would protect her ears from the cold, and departed.

"That should take her at least an hour," said Louisa. She extended her hand to Lacy and added, "Come along now, Johnny darlin'. I don't want to waste another minute."

Lacy took her hand and allowed her to lead him to the bedroom. He closed the door behind them, turned her around, and pulled her hard against him.

"Oh, Johnny, you're so forceful," she cooed. She threw her arms around his neck and kissed him as passionately as she could. She pressed her pelvis against him and felt the proof of the fire growing within him. Breaking the kiss, she whispered, "I want you to take me, Johnny darlin'. Take me now."

Lacy kissed her throat as his fingers fumbled with the top hook-and-eye on the back of her dress.

"No, we don't have time to disrobe completely," said Louisa as she unbuttoned his uniform coat. "Just take this off." As Lacy removed the garment and dropped it on the floor beside him, she hiked up her skirt, untied the drawstring to her pantaloons, pulled them down over her knee stockings and high-top shoes to her ankles, and stepped out of them. "Come over here," she said, taking Lacy by the hand and leading him to the dressing table. She turned the chair around. "We can do it right here." She threw her arms around his neck, kissed him deeply again, and pressed her hardening body against him. As his hands drifted to her buttocks and his mouth moved to her left ear, she whispered hoarsely, "Oh, Johnny, I'm so excited to think you're goin' to Washington City with General Scott and you're gonna be an integral part of his plan to . . . to . . . to . . ."

"To reinforce Fort Sumter," he said without thinking.

Reinforce Fort Sumter? thought Louisa as she allowed Lacy to have his way for the moment. Her mind raced. War between the states? Yes, most likely. The Carolinians won't stand for Fort Sumter being reinforced. Yes, war. The possibility of a conflict increased her desire. Before she could give the idea much more consideration, she kissed Lacy harder than ever, denying him the opportunity to think about the words that he had just uttered. Feeling his lust for her intensify, she pulled his suspenders down and began unbuttoning his trousers without taking her tongue away from his. She pushed his pants down to his ankles, parted the tails of his shirt, then unbuttoned just enough of his longjohns to expose his erection. She backed a few inches away from him and said, "Sit on the chair, Johnny darlin'. Sit down and hold it up so I can fit myself on it."

Lacy complied.

Louisa pulled up her skirt, showed him what he wanted to see for a few brief seconds, then put her hands on his shoulders, straddled his legs, and eased herself down on him. "Oh, Johnny," she gasped as a shudder coursed through her, "that's so wonderful. It's so good."

He reached both hands under her skirt and squeezed her buttocks as she put her hips into motion. "Oh, God, Lou!" he hissed through clenched teeth. "You're just so much woman! Just so much woman!"

She pressed her left breast to his face and whispered, "Bite it, Johnny! Bite it!"

Lacy put his mouth around the end of the hard cone and bit down gently, thinking not to hurt her.

"No, more," she said without missing a single grind

of her hips. "Put more of it in your mouth and bite harder."

The thought of her commanding him to perform excited Lacy all the greater. He obeyed her desire, forced more of the clothed teat into his mouth, and bit down viciously as he squeezed her ample, flaccid cheeks harder, too.

"Oo-oo, oo-oo!" she gasped. "Yes—yes, that's it! Oh, yes, that's it!" She pulled his head harder against her bosom while craning her neck to get her mouth on his left ear. "Oh, Johnny, yes. You, yes. Fort Sumter. The danger. You're so much man. Oh, yes, Johnny. So much man." She bit his earlobe.

Lacy's ego erupted.

Feeling her lover stiffen with his orgasm induced Louisa to reach an uncontrollable climax of her own. She slammed herself down on him as forcefully as she could, threw back her head, and sucked for air before emitting a primitive snarl that bore the erotic resonance of a feline in heat. She continued to moan with pleasure as she squeezed his head against her breast with all her strength. Then with the last tingle of fulfillment, she snapped his head back and kissed him violently, her tongue searching his mouth for a final morsel of ecstasy and finding it as the glow of satisfaction enveloped them.

Sated, both went limp for the next minute; Louisa drooping over him and Lacy holding on to her just enough to keep her from falling off his lap.

A plan to reinforce Fort Sumter, thought Louisa as she rested on him ever so quietly and let her mind drift. Now isn't that interesting? But how?

Lacy jerked out of the dreamy haze warming him, took a deep breath, and uttered hoarsely, "Were you pleased, my dear?"

Oh, isn't that elegant? thought Louisa, bitterly sardonic. Was I pleased? Rafe would never ask that question, but hell, this isn't Rafe I got between my legs. Oh, why couldn't he be a little like Rafe? She sighed, thought, Well, he's not, and said, "Yes, Johnny darlin', I was pleased."

"That's good," said Lacy as he kneaded her buttocks.

Thinking to keep him cooperative, Louisa sat up straight, giggled, and said, "Oh, Johnny, you're so naughty. You best stop that before I get to goin' again and we start something we can't finish before Hattie comes back." She kissed him quick, and just as he began to respond, she popped erect out of his grasp and backed away from him. "Come on now," she said, "we'd best be gettin' dressed before Hattie comes home."

Disappointed and mildly embarrassed over the full exposure of his penis in front of a clothed woman, albeit a woman with whom he had copulated only minutes earlier, Lacy squirmed in the chair and turned aside to replace it within his longjohns. He glanced over his shoulder to see Louisa stepping into her pantaloons again and reluctantly reached for his trousers as he concluded that the morning's tryst was definitely culminated. He pulled the pants up to his knees as he stood up, drew them up to his waist, tucked the shirt inside, buttoned the fly, and slipped the suspenders over his shoulders.

As Lacy donned his uniform coat, Louisa finished tying up her pantaloons and lowered her shirt. She smiled at Lacy as she moved past him to the dresser mirror to primp her hair and put a touch of powder on her face to replace any that had rubbed off on her lover. Satisfied that her appearance was the same as it had been before she made love with Lacy, she turned to him and said, "Come along, Johnny. We should be in the parlor when Hattie returns." She took his hand and led him back to the living room. Turning to him, she noticed some lint and dust on his coat, flicked at it with her fingers, and said, "Please forgive me, Johnny. I'm not usually so impetuous, but I couldn't resist once you told me about goin' to Washington City to see the president with General Scott. That's so excitin', and to think that you're gonna reinforce Fort Sumter, well, I could hardly control myself." She spun away and forced a sigh. "Oh, Johnny, I mustn't think about it or I'll get all afire all over again, and you'll have to do me again right here in the parlor."

The possibility of a second union rekindled Lacy's lust. He moved up behind her, took hold of her arms, pressed his groin against her buttocks, kissed the nape of her neck, then whispered, "There's still plenty of time before Hattie returns. We could—"

Louisa leaned against him as she interrupted him. "Oh, Johnny, I'd love nothin' better than to have you do me again, but I don't think I could enjoy it as much if I had to worry about Hattie walkin' in on us." She turned around and let him embrace her. "Besides," she said as she smiled wickedly at him, "I want you to have something to look forward to when you return from Washington City."

"I don't know that we'll have enough time for us then," said Lacy.

"Why not?" she asked, her face falsely painted with the cloudy colors of disappointment and concern. "You won't be leavin' for Fort Sumter as soon as you come back from Washington City, will you? I mean, what about the New Year's Eve ball? Won't you be home for that, sugar?"

"Yes, of course, I'll be home for New Year's Eve, but I don't know if there will be time to attend any balls. If the president approves of General Scott's plan tonight, I'll only have two days to prepare my companies for debarkation."

"Debarkation?" queried Louisa. "What's that?"

"Surely, you know what that means, being the wife of a naval officer and all."

"The widow of a naval officer," she reminded him dryly. "Yes, I know what it means in naval terms, but you're in the army. I don't know what it means in military terms."

"The same as in the navy, Louisa. My companies must be prepared to debark on a warship as early as New Year's Day if the president approves of the general's plan tonight or tomorrow. Knowing General Scott, he'll press the president for a definite answer as soon as possible in order to maintain the element of surprise that his plan is contingent on, and he'll make the president give his approval so we can move ahead with all due haste."

"But why would you have to be prepared to debark your companies by New Year's Day?"

The tone of her question struck a raw chord within Lacy. His desire for her cooled instantly as he stared into her eyes with the realization that he had revealed far too much information to her. After all, hadn't General Scott told him not to reveal anything about the plan to anybody? And now he had told her nearly everything. He relaxed his hold on Louisa and said, "I shouldn't have told you any of this, Lou. It's supposed to be secret."

"I know, Johnny, but who would I tell?" She forced a giggle at his expense. "Really. Who would I tell? Suppose I said something to someone and they asked me how I came to know about General Scott's plan. What would I tell them? That my lover told me? I think not. No, Johnny, I don't dare tell anyone around here about the general's plan."

"No, I suppose not," said Lacy, although he wasn't exactly convincing, not even to himself.

13 ~

Saturday afternoon, December 29, 1860

The commissioners from South Carolina called on President Buchanan again on the last Saturday morning of 1860, and again their overtures to pass all Federal property in South Carolina to their government peacefully were rebuffed. They returned to William Trescot's home frustrated and angry that they had made no progress.

"We can only hope that this Hammond woman can achieve what we have failed to accomplish," said Barnwell. He sat in a winged chair at the head of the coffee table, his legs crossed, anxiously tapping his fingers on the heel of a boot.

"And if she should get no further than we have," said Orr, "then what?" He occupied one side of the sofa.

"We shouldn't wait," said Adams, seated at the opposite end of the couch. "We should expect the worst and prepare for it."

"And what would the worst be?" asked Trescot, standing by the hearth, holding a coffee cup in one hand and its saucer in the other.

"War," said Barnwell flatly.

"Not as long as Buchanan is in the White House," said Trescot. "He doesn't have the backbone for it."

"Yes, but what if he's goaded into it?" asked Orr. "Then what?"

"Who would do that?" rebutted Trescot. "Stanton or one of those other Yankees in the cabinet? I think not."

"General Scott," said Barnwell. "There's no one between him and the president now that Floyd has tendered his resignation. I've never met the man, but I understand his mere presence is intimidatin', and if there was ever a man who could be intimidated by another man's stature, it's Jim Buchanan."

"You might have something there, Robert," said Trescot. "I have met General Scott on several occasions, and I must admit that his size and appearance would make a weak man shake in his shoes. I must agree with you, Robert. General Scott could influence the president against us."

"Why would he do that?" asked Orr. "Isn't General Scott a Virginian?"

"Only by birth," said Trescot. "He considers himself to be an American first and foremost, and he believes in the preservation of the Union at all costs. I feel certain that he won't stand idly by and watch his country be torn asunder by secession."

"What do you think he will do?" asked Orr.

"I can't say for certain," said Trescott, "but I think we should inform Governor Pickens to prepare for trouble."

Barnwell and Orr nodded their agreement. Grimly.

Adams shook his head and said, "I think we should wait until we hear the results of the Hammond woman's interview with the president. There may be no need to concern the governor just yet. I say wait."

"Only until we hear how she does with the president," said Trescot. "Agreed?"

Now all were in agreement.

*   *   *

Senator Clay arranged Sarah's appointment with the president for one o'clock in the afternoon. She arrived fifteen minutes early. Alone. The president's secretary made her wait until the sounding of a single chime designating the hour, then he showed her into the chief executive's office.

"How do you do, Miss Hammond?" said Buchanan, his attitude condescending as he shook her hand gently. "I've heard so much about you. It's a pleasure to finally meet you in person. Won't you sit down, please?" He waved toward one of two cushioned chairs before his desk.

"If you were so anxious to meet me before," said Sarah before sitting, "why did you refuse to grant me a previous audience, sir?" Thinking she had pierced the armor of his male ego, she sat, primly folding her hands in her lap.

The president was unshaken. His smile broadened as he said, "I met your grandmother on two occasions when she was alive. I heard her say nearly the same thing to President Polk when they first met." He hacked a laugh. "I'm glad to report that my predecessor was just as much at a loss for a proper response as I am at this very moment, Miss Hammond."

"I recall my grandmother telling me about that meeting, Mr. President. She said that President Polk avoided her as long as he could because he didn't want to meet a woman who could outwit him."

Buchanan laughed fervently and said, "I don't doubt that one bit, Miss Hammond. President Polk was a man of short patience with the fairer sex." He spread the tails of his coat and sat in the chair opposite Sarah.

"That's all well and good, Mr. President, but you still haven't answered my question. Why have you put me off until now?"

The president made a futile attempt to straighten his

neck and hold his head erect as his smile vanished and a dark pall fell over his eyes. "Politics, Miss Hammond," he said. "Your people are not Democrats. I wouldn't have seen you now, if not for the very fact that several members of the Senate from my own party advised me to receive you."

Sarah nodded slowly and said, "That's honest enough, sir. Thank you. Now it's my turn to be candid." She straightened her spine all the more and proceeded.

"On my way here, Mr. President, I kept asking myself why a Southern senator would be so willing to get me an appointment with you and why a Northern senator, one with whom my family has had much truck, wouldn't even offer to make the attempt. Of course, Senator Seward is not a Democrat, but even so, I could reach but one singular conclusion, Mr. President. There are men in the North, just as there are in the South, who wish to settle the slavery issue only one way. On the battlefield. I am diametrically opposed to men on both sides who want war, Mr. President. I am descended from a long line of Quakers, sir, and although I do not actively participate in the Society of Friends, I do adhere to many of their teachings, especially those concerning war."

"And those concerning slavery as well, Miss Hammond?"

"Yes, and those teachings as well. I consider it a mortal sin for one human being to hold another in bondage against his or her will."

"But do you consider the Negro race inferior to the white?"

"No, sir, I do not," said Sarah with a touch of ire in her tone. She thought to evidence that declaration with more affirmations of her stand on the issue, but another idea intervened as she concluded that Buchanan, the one-time brilliant legal mind, was attempting to deflect her from the point of their meeting. "But that is neither here nor there, Mr. President. I haven't come here to discuss my own morality, but to make a request of you concerning the crisis in South Carolina."

Buchanan's patronizing smile returned as he said, "A request, Miss Hammond? And what would that be?"

"The Southern senators have asked me to ask you to order Major Anderson to return to Fort Moultrie. Barring that, they would ask that you withdraw Major Anderson from Charleston harbor and hand over all Federal property to the authorities of South Carolina."

"Is that what you want, Miss Hammond? Do you want Major Anderson withdrawn from Charleston harbor as well?"

"My only desire, Mr. President, is that this country should avoid a catastrophic civil war, and if withdrawing Major Anderson from Charleston harbor is necessary to achieve that end, then I am in favor of withdrawing him with all due haste."

"And if I were to tell you that withdrawing Major Anderson will do nothing to avoid such a war, what would you say then?"

"Withdrawing Major Anderson would be a peaceful gesture toward the Carolinians, Mr. President. Surely, you can see it that way."

"Yes, I can see it that way," said Buchanan, "but I fear that the Carolinians will only judge me to be a greater weakling than they already consider me to be, and my fellow Northerners will consider me to be a greater coward than they think me now, as well as a traitor to the Union. No, Miss Hammond, as long as Major Anderson remains at Fort Sumter, the Carolinians will have reason to fear the Federal government, and I will have some semblance of respect and support from the North."

"In other words," said Sarah, "you favor the status quo. Am I right, Mr. President?"

"Yes, Miss Hammond, you are. Major Anderson will not be ordered to return to Fort Moultrie, and this government has no plans to withdraw him from Fort Sumter."

"I see," said Sarah, "but will you send him additional men and supplies?"

"At this moment," said Buchanan, looking directly into Sarah's eyes, "this government has no firm plans to reinforce or resupply Fort Sumter."

"Have you told this to the commissioners from South Carolina, sir?"

"Not in those precise words, but I have made it clear to them that the government cannot do anything to force their state to return to the Union." Anticipating Sarah's next question, he raised his hand and said, "Miss Hammond, this administration intends to do nothing to provoke a war between the Federal government of the United States and the sovereign state of South Carolina. You must believe me on that point."

"And what if other Southern states should secede and join South Carolina in a new confederation of states as I've heard rumored? What then, Mr. President?"

"A confederation of Southern states will do nothing to change the posture of this administration. In my last address to the Congress, I voiced my opinion that no state has the right to secede from the Union, but I also stated that the Federal government has no legal right to force any state to remain in the Union against the will of its people. I continue to stand by those statements."

"Very well, Mr. President. You don't plan to do anything about the situation at Charleston harbor. I can understand that, but what about the Carolinians? What if they are unwilling to accept the status quo? What if

they do something more to provoke you into doing
something to retaliate against them?''

"Such as?''

"Such as attacking Fort Sumter.''

"The information available to me at this time states
clearly that the Carolinians are incapable of launching
an attack against Fort Sumter.''

"Maybe not today, Mr. President, but let me assure
you, that situation will not remain constant for very
long. I know, sir. I was in South Carolina only one
week ago, and I can tell you that those people are hell-
bent on erasing every vestige of the Union from their
state. They are convinced that God is on their side in
this dispute, and they are doing everything possible to
convince the other slave states to join them in opposing
the Federal government. Surely you can see that, sir.
Just look how they've turned Major Anderson's retreat
to Fort Sumter into an act of aggression.''

"Retreat, Miss Hammond?'' queried Buchanan
with surprise. "I hadn't thought of it that way. I
considered it to be an act of defiance in the face of
grave danger.''

"No, sir, he retreated. I have it on good authority
that he removed the garrison to Fort Sumter in order
to avoid a confrontation with the Carolinians.''

Buchanan's curiosity was suddenly piqued. "Good
authority, Miss Hammond? And who would this good
authority be?''

"His name is unimportant, Mr. President,'' said
Sarah, brushing aside his inquiry. "Suffice it to say that
he is in a position to know the truth of all that is
happening at Charleston harbor, and please let it go at
that.'' She leaned forward with determination. "The
point is, Mr. President, the Carolinians have twisted
Major Anderson's retreat into an act of aggression because they are angry that he possesses the one fort that
dominates the entire harbor, the one fort that, had they

taken possession of it first, would have forced Major Anderson into immediate and unconditional surrender. He outwitted them, Mr. President, and they are outraged by it. To cover up their own failure to move first, they have charged him with committing an act of aggression. It's all very simple, Mr. President. In order to hide their own shortcomings, the Carolinians are quick to point their accusing fingers at Major Anderson."

"I concur, Miss Hammond, but this is leading us nowhere. Major Anderson is at Fort Sumter, and he will stay there for the duration of this administration."

"I see, but what if matters at Charleston change and the Carolinians summon up the courage and the capability to attack Fort Sumter? What then, Mr. President?"

"As the old adage goes, we will cross that bridge when we come to it." He held up an index finger to accentuate his meaning. "And I might add, *if* we come to it."

Frustrated that Buchanan had blunted her, Sarah chose another tack. "Mr. President, I discussed this same situation with Senator Seward two days ago, and I told him then that I have a great concern over the safety of the wives and children of the soldiers and officers of the garrison. I volunteered to send a ship of my father's line to remove them from harm's way, and he promised to relay my offer to you. He has not yet given me your response to that proposition, Mr. President."

"I have not yet spoken to Senator Seward on this matter, Miss Hammond. In fact, I haven't spoken to him at all in recent weeks."

Sarah's brow furrowed with consternation. "You haven't spoken to him about this at all?"

"No, Miss Hammond, I have not."

"Then I will make the offer directly to you, sir."

"I will take it under consideration, Miss Hammond."

And with that, the interview came to an end.

*   *   *

Back at the Willard again, Sarah paid Mr. Taylor, the bell captain, to deliver a message to Commander Sims at the Navy Department. She instructed him to give the note only to Sims. "Nobody else, Mr. Taylor," she said firmly.

"Yes'm, Miss Hammond," said Taylor. "Nobody else 'ceptin' Commander Sims. I understand, Miss Hammond." He left but returned within an hour to report that "Commander Sims ain't at the Navy Department, Miss Hammond. They say he received a telegram from somebody and left right off without sayin' where he was goin'."

Miffed that Sims hadn't kept his promise to wait for her message on the outcome of her interview with the president, Sarah wrote a new and slightly angry note for Senator Clay and instructed Taylor to deliver it to the Alabama solon at his home. This time the bell captain was successful.

Clay read Sarah's message with great anticipation, only to be disappointed in its content. Without hesitation, he took the short letter to the home of William Trescot and presented it to the three commissioners. "The news is not good, gentlemen," he said.

Barnwell read the letter to his colleagues and their host.

Senator Clay,

   Your intermediary was unavailable to receive my letter concerning my meeting with President Buchanan, thus I write to you directly about this matter.

   I am sorry to inform you that my efforts to convince the president to withdraw Major Anderson from Fort Sumter have gone for naught. He is adamant about the status quo. He says he will do nothing either way to provoke a war or to avoid one.

Again, I offer my sincerest apologies for my failure. I remain—

> *Your friend in peace,*
> *Sarah Hammond*

"We have to telegraph Governor Pickens with this news immediately," said Trescot. He looked at Adams for an argument.

"I am in total agreement, Will," said Adams, throwing up his hands in mock surrender. "The governor must learn of this immediately."

Governor Pickens received the commissioners' telegram shortly before dusk at his temporary office at the Mills House. He read the message silently to himself, then reported the gist of it to the military commanders who had carried out his orders to seize Fort Moultrie and Castle Pinckney. "Buchanan refuses to order Anderson to return to Moultrie or to abandon Sumter," he said. "So what do we do now, gentlemen?"

"We could attack Sumter," said Allston.

"We couldn't get a boat within two hundred yards of Sumter," said DeSaussure.

"We could attack at night," said Capers. "Surprise the Yankees in the dark."

"The surprise might be ours," said Pettigrew. "I don't trust the bastards to fight fair. Who knows what sort of deviltry they're up to out on that island?"

The governor halted and said, "Attackin' Sumter is out of the question. For now, anyway. No, gentlemen, we need to show Buchanan that we're serious here, that we will not be intimidated, that we intend to defend our independence at all costs. We need another show of force, but where and how?"

"Morris Island," said Allston. "We should place a company or two at Cummings Point and begin fortifyin' it immediately."

"I agree," said Pettigrew. "If Buchanan or Anderson doesn't surrender Sumter willin'ly, then sooner or later we'll have to drive the Yankees from the harbor. To do that, we'll need batteries at Cummings Point to put Sumter in a crossfire with Moultrie."

"More than that, Governor," said DeSaussure, "we need to isolate Sumter as much as possible right now. I suggest buildin' another battery on Morris Island to control the main shippin' channel because, if the Yankees mean to stay at Sumter indefinitely, they will need resupplyin' and possibly reinforcements. A battery on Morris Island facin' the sea will prevent any help from reachin' Sumter without a serious fight."

"Then so be it, Colonel," said Pickens. "We'll get some men out there on Morris Island as soon as possible and start buildin' that battery." He turned to Pettigrew. "And the same goes for Cummings Point. Maybe if we show Anderson that he can't win a fight, he just might do the right thing and surrender Sumter without waitin' for Buchanan to tell him to give it up to us." He stroked his chin and absently resumed pacing the room. "Even with all that, I still feel we need to show Buchanan that we mean business here. What else is there, gentlemen? We've seized Moultrie, Pinckney, and the *William Aiken*. Tomorrow we'll occupy Cummings Point. That only leaves the post office, the customshouse, and the arsenal. Do we take those as well?"

"Why wait until tomorrow, sir?" said Capers. "Why not take them tonight?"

"I'd rather not approach the arsenal in the dark," said Pettigrew. "That old fart Humphreys is a cagey old badger. I wouldn't put anything past him. There's no tellin' what traps he might have set for us."

"We've had the militia guardin' the arsenal for more

than a month now," said Allston. "I see no reason to fear Captain Humphreys."

"I'd rather not risk the lives of any of our gallant boys at this point, gentlemen," said Pickens. "We can wait until tomorrow to take the arsenal, and as soon as it's done, I want word of it sent to our commissioners in Washington." A wry grin curled his lips as he added, "Excuse the pun, gentlemen, but they'll need all the ammunition they can get to deal with Buchanan."

14 ~

Saturday night, December 29, 1860

Upon arriving in Philadelphia late that afternoon, Commander Rafael Sims hired a hansom cab to take him from the Philadelphia, Wilmington & Baltimore Railroad depot to the New Jersey Railroad terminal in another part of the city, where he met the train from New York. Anxiously, he watched the passengers emerge from the coaches.

General Winfield Scott and six other army officers, including Lieutenant John Lacy, stepped onto the station platform. Lacy scurried off to see that the general's baggage, as well as that of the other members of the entourage, was brought to the taxicabs waiting to take the military men to the Philadelphia, Wilmington & Baltimore station, where they would board yet another train to continue their trip to Washington.

Standing six feet five inches tall and weighing over three hundred pounds, General Scott was dressed to the nines, as usual when in public, adorned by his self-designed gold-braided uniform and plumed hat. No one doubted his presence or his importance as he personified a wonderful mixture of gasconade, ostentation, fuss, feathers, bluster, and genuine soldierly talent and courage; a great smoking mass of flesh and blood. Little wonder he was known as "Great Scott." Although a Virginian by birth, the red-faced, heavy-jowled warhorse emphatically opposed secession, and his loyalty to the Union and the national government was beyond reproach. Widely regarded as a bold fighter known for his daring, but never foolhardy, strategy, this forthright mountain of a man was respected, if not loved, by both enlisted men and officers for his fair-minded and just discipline. At seventy-five, he was a living legend.

Sims had seen Scott before, in Washington and in New York, but had never been introduced to him. Considering the national crisis over the situation at Charleston, he was not surprised that the general was returning to the capital at this time. If anything, Sims questioned Scott's delay in removing himself and his staff from New York to Washington City. In the commander's mind, Scott should have placed himself closer to the president much sooner than this late date.

Preoccupied by the presence of General Scott, Sims nearly forgot why he had come to Philadelphia; thus, he failed to notice a veiled woman approaching him. Only the sound of her voice drew his attention to her.

"Rafe, is that you?" asked Louisa Phoenix as she came close to him. "What are you doin' here?"

"Louisa?" he queried, unable to distinguish her facial features through the black netting that hung from her hat.

"Yes, Rafe, it is I," she whispered happily, buoyed by the sound of her name coming from his lips. Disguised in the attire of mourning, she pressed herself against him in hopes that he would embrace her passionately, only to be disappointed by his lack of enthusiasm.

Awkwardly cognizant of where they were, Sims took Louisa's upper arms in his hands and held her at a discreet distance. "You shouldn't have come here," he said. "You should have stayed in New York."

"I had to see you, Rafe," said Louisa. She looked to one side, then the other, before adding, "But I hardly expected to meet you here in Philadelphia. I thought we'd be meetin' in Washington."

"No, this is better. Too many people know me in Washington. It would never do for us to be seen together there."

"I see," she said softly, stung by the implication. "Someone might tell your wife, and where would that leave you? Yes, I understand."

Sims sighed and said, "No, Louisa, that isn't what I meant. My concern goes much deeper than that." He made a quick scan of the area for a place where they could talk in some semblance of privacy. Anywhere would do as long as it was far from prying ears and eyes. "We mustn't speak of that here."

"No, of course not," said Louisa. "We must be alone when I tell you what I've learned." She glanced over her shoulder at General Scott and his staff as they moved toward the street and the cabs waiting to take them on the next leg of their journey.

Sims spotted a vacant corner to the rear of the freight office. "Come along, my dear," he said. "We'll go over there away from eavesdroppers."

Louisa turned to look at the indicated place, only to see Lacy coming toward them. "Oh, no, I think he's seen me," she gasped.

"What?" asked Sims as Louisa pressed herself harder against him, burrowing her face into his chest and feigning tears. Although uncertain of what to make of her sudden action, he played along.

Lacy hurried past them, not recognizing Louisa and not knowing Sims. The lieutenant ignored the commander and refused even to acknowledge his presence because Sims was a naval officer and a superior at that; an intentional insult of one service to the other.

As soon as Lacy was well beyond them, Louisa

ceased acting and cast a side glance at the lieutenant.
"Good," she said, "he didn't recognize me."

"Do you know that officer?" asked Sims.

"Yes," said Louisa as she looked up at him. "He's
Lieutenant John Lacy, commandin' officer of the recruit
trainin' post on Governors Island. He's part of the reason I'm here, Rafe."

The words of Louisa's telegram raced through his
mind.

> *Important news about Cousin Charles and the*
> *army. Arriving Washington nine o'clock train*
> *from New York. Meet me.*
>
> *Louisa Phoenix*

His first thought upon receiving the message was that
it was so much gibberish from a lovesick woman. Then
he recalled their parting conversation in her apartment
in Brooklyn and how Louisa had expressed a desire to
serve the Southern Cause of Freedom, and he surmised
that this was some vainglorious attempt on her part to
do just that. Thinking along those lines, he feared that
her coming to Washington might compromise him in
more ways than one; thus, he decided to intercept her
in the Quaker city instead.

Now her indication that one of General Scott's staff
was part of the explanation behind her telegram stirred
Sims to consider the possibility that Louisa might be
more than a lonely woman desirous of a man's touch.
He led her toward the vacant area behind the freight
office. As soon as they were alone, he said, "Now tell
me what this is all about, Louisa. Your telegram made
no sense at all."

Louisa lifted her veil, smiled, and said, "Of course
it did, Rafe darlin'. Cousin Charles is Charleston, and
the army just left here on its way to Washington City,

where General Scott is gonna tell the president about his plan to reinforce Fort Sumter.''

Sims was incredulous as he blurted, "What?''

"I said—''

"I heard what you said, but how do you know this? Who told you General Scott is goin' to Washington to tell the president about a plan to reinforce Fort Sumter?''

"Lieutenant John Lacy.''

"Lieutenant John Lacy?'' queried Sims. He looked off in the direction of the departing cabs, then turned back to Louisa. "That officer who just got off the train with General Scott?''

"He's married to General Scott's second cousin or somethin' like that, and he's on General Scott's staff. He told me all about the plan.''

"But why would he tell you about it?''

Louisa frowned and said, "You shouldn't ask me about that part, Rafe. Just trust me that he told me about it.''

Sims thought about pressing her for a more detailed explanation but dismissed the notion as he realized that to do so might embarrass Louisa. She was no perfect lady, but even so, she deserved to have some part of her dignity preserved. "All right,'' he said, "I'll accept that. But tell me about this plan.''

"I don't have all the details, but I do know this much. Johnny, uh, I mean, Lieutenant Lacy has to have his companies prepared to leave Governor's Island by New Year's Day. I asked him if he'd be returnin' to attend the army and navy New Year's Eve ball, and he said that he would be home for New Year's Eve, but that he doubted that he would have time to attend any balls because he has to have his companies prepared to debark from Governor's Island by New Year's Day. I would assume he meant they'd be takin' a ship to get off that island to go somewhere, but he didn't say what ship they'd be takin'. Just the same, I've been givin' that some serious thought. I'm guessin' it's some big warship. Most likely the *Brooklyn*. General Scott would only want to go with the best, and the *Brooklyn* is the best in the navy, isn't it?''

"Yes, it is," said Sims, "but I don't understand why General Scott would want to send raw recruits to reinforce Fort Sumter."

"That's puzzlin' to me, too. I should think he'd want to send more experienced men."

"Unless he intends to have them replace more seasoned companies that he's plannin' to send to Fort Sumter from some closer place. Yes, that just might be the answer. The *Brooklyn* is presently anchored at Hampton Roads near Fort Monroe, Virginia, which is only a day and a half, two days at the most from Charleston. She could hold four full companies of infantry and enough provisions to supply Fort Sumter for three months." He nodded involuntarily. "Yes, that must be Scott's strategy. With Anderson occupyin' Sumter, the Carolinians will be unable to stop the *Brooklyn* from enterin' the harbor with reinforcements."

"But they will try to stop her, won't they?"

"Yes, they will," said Sims, "and the whole South will soon follow South Carolina from the Union and come to her defense. The North will unite against us, and before too long, we will all be at war."

"You sound none too happy about that prospect, Rafe."

"I'm not. The South is hardly prepared for war. We have no army, no navy, no single government to bond us into a cohesive nation. All of these must come to fruition before we can even hope to gain our independence from the North."

"Then what are we to do, Rafe?"

"I must return to Washington with all due haste and inform Senator Clay about General Scott's plan to reinforce Fort Sumter. Possibly, he can do something to head off this disastrous turn of events.''

"What about us, Rafe? I've still got my ticket to Washington. Couldn't I come with you?''

"No, you shouldn't do that. You should be at home when Lieutenant Lacy returns to prepare his companies to leave Governor's Island. I should think that he will be callin' on you one more time before he leaves for wherever he's takin' his companies.''

"Yes, of course, you're right, Rafe darlin', and when he does leave, I'll send you another telegram.''

"No, you shouldn't send me any more telegrams, Louisa. I'm still in the United States Navy, and I could be accused of treason if any of this should become known to my superiors.''

"Can't you just resign your commission and go home to Alabama?''

"Yes, I could do that, but as long as Alabama is still a part of the Union, I must remain where I am and—'' He stopped himself from continuing the explanation. Instead, he sighed with frustration and said, ''We've been over this ground before, Louisa. Just don't send me any more telegrams, please.''

"But I have my duty to the South, Rafe. What if I should obtain more information that would help the South? Who would I tell it to?''

"I don't know, Louisa, but I do know that you shouldn't be tellin' it to me. Leastways, not with a telegram with my name on it and your name on it as well.''

"But if I can't send you the information, who should I send it to?''

"I don't know. How about Senator Wigfall from Texas? I've heard that he's a real fire-eater. He'd be glad to get a telegram from anybody workin' for the Cause of Freedom.''

"Okay, but whose name should I sign it with?''

"I don't know. You could use Smith or Jones or some other common name. Anything except Louisa Phoenix."

"Yes, of course, you're right again, Rafe darlin'. Hattie's last name is Jones. I could use that." She pressed herself against him. "Oh, how I wish I could go with you to Washington. I miss you so much, and I need your touch. The nights are so long without you."

An impulse stirred in his loins. She's such a devilishly wicked woman, he thought. If only we had the time and the place, but alas! we have neither. He pushed her away ever so gently. "No, Louisa, we can't. Not here and not now."

Her eyes and tone begged, "Then, when and where, Rafe? When and where?"

"I don't know. But for now, you must get on the next train back to New York, and I must return to Washington. If I hurry, I can catch the same train as General Scott and your Lieutenant Lacy."

"My Lieutenant Lacy? Why, Rafe, I do believe you're jealous."

"Yes, I am," said Sims. He was lying, but what was the harm? he told himself. She wants to serve the South in whatever capacity she can. So let her. He kissed her hard, his tongue darting into her mouth. She won't be the first woman to give up her body for her country. He broke the embrace and said, "I must go now. Farewell, my love." And before she could respond, he dashed away to catch a hansom back to the Philadelphia, Wilmington & Baltimore depot.

Sims rode in the same coach as General Scott and his staff, but he could sit no closer than four seats away from them and was thus denied the opportunity to overhear any conversation among the military men. He cursed his bad luck at boarding the train too late to get a better seat, but promised himself that he would not be so ill-fated when they changed trains at Baltimore.

Much the same scene as the one that Sims had witnessed in Philadelphia unfolded in the Maryland city, although this time under the illumination of the gas street lights. General Scott stepped onto the depot platform followed by his staff, and Lieutenant Lacy rushed off to see about the baggage. Scott surveyed the area, then marched off toward the line of taxis waiting to take through-passengers to the Baltimore & Ohio station, where they would make their connections for points west and south. Lacy caught up to them just as the general and the other officers began climbing into three of the four-wheeled, open hackneys.

Sims headed for a hansom. He was stopped short of his goal by an invitation.

"Won't you join us, Commander?"

Sims recognized the voice as that of General Scott. Although uneasy over being addressed by the top military man of the country, he shifted his gaze to meet the general's.

"We have room for one more, sir," said Scott, smiling, "if you don't mind riding courtesy of the army." When Sims hesitated, he added, "You are going to Washington, aren't you, Commander?"

"Yes, sir, I am."

"Then do us the honor of joining us for the ride to the B & O depot."

"The honor is all mine, General Scott," said Sims with all due military protocol, not quite believing this turn of fortune. "Thank you, sir." He started for the third hack.

"No, Commander," said Scott. "Ride with me." He turned his attention to Lacy. "You wouldn't mind riding in one of the other cabs, would you, John?"

"Of course not, General," said Lacy obediently. He

climbed down and held the door for Sims, who out-
ranked him.

"Thank you, Lieutenant," said Sims as he climbed
into the taxi. He took a place in the seat facing the
rear, sitting beside a major who sat opposite Scott.

Lacy closed the door behind Sims, then found a place
in the third carriage.

"Don Carlos Buell," said the major.

"Rafael Sims."

"Good to meet you, Commander Sims," said Scott.
"To the B & O station, driver."

The hack jerked into motion.

"You look familiar to me, Commander Sims," said
Buell. "Have we met before?"

Scott bellowed a laugh and said, "I was thinking the
same thing, Major. You do look familiar, Commander
Sims. Surely, we've crossed paths before. Are you
posted in Washington?"

"I'm a member of the Lighthouse Board, sir."

"That must be it," said Buell. "We've probably
passed each other somewhere in Washington."

"I don't get to Washington that often," said Scott.
"So why do you look so familiar to me?"

"I've attended some of the same functions as you,
General," said Sims, "but we were never introduced.
Perhaps you saw me at some of these."

"That's probably it," said Scott. He nodded absently
and allowed his view to drift toward the buildings they
were passing. Without looking back at Sims, he said,
"So you're on the Lighthouse Board in Washington,
Commander Sims. I was unaware that Philadelphia had
any lighthouses."

Sims knew a backhanded question when he heard
one. "There aren't any lighthouses in Philadelphia,
General," said Sims casually. "I was there tendin' to
a personal matter involvin' the widow of a fellow naval

officer whose ship, the corvette *Levant,* is missin' at
sea.''

"Yes, I read about that in the newspaper," said
Scott. "I don't envy you that chore, Commander Sims.
It's never easy telling a woman that her husband isn't
ever coming home again."

They rode in silence the remainder of the way to the
Baltimore & Ohio station.

Scott invited Sims to sit with his military contingent
for the hour-and-a-half trip to Washington. They talked
about the past. The general regaled the others with stories about his experiences in the War of 1812 and the
early days of the United States Army. "Before we
fought the British a second time and before the military
academy was established at West Point, the army
wasn't much better than a militia unit fighting Indians
on our borders. The Mexican War proved our need for
a larger standing army in this country."

Sims recognized bait when it was dangled in front
of him. He also saw the deadly double-barbed hook
waiting to snag him, and he refused to bite. Like most
unionists, the general advocated the extension of the
Federal government's authority over the States, and to
enforce this power, a larger standing army was absolutely essential. Sims had heard this argument before,
and being a minority of one in this situation, he resisted
the urge to defend his own belief that the states, and
thus free individuals, had the right to do as they please
as long as their actions did not harm any other state or
person. Instead, he merely nodded amicably and allowed the general to tell another story about his military career.

As soon as the train arrived in Washington, Sims
bade General Scott and his staff farewell, hired the first
hansom he saw, and rushed away to Senator Clay's
home to tell him about General Scott's plan to reinforce
Fort Sumter. A short male servant met Sims at the door.

"I's sorry, suh, but Massuh say he don't wanna be disturbed for nothin'."

"You will wake your master immediately," said Sims, "or I will buy you from him and sell you south to a rice planter in Louisiana."

The servant flinched noticeably, backed away from the door, and said, "Please come in, suh, and I'll wake Massuh right away." He closed the door behind Sims, then hurried off to awaken Clay.

A few minutes passed before Clay appeared in the foyer, the servant behind him carrying a lamp. Squinting in the dim light at his late caller, he said, "Commander Sims, is that you?"

"Yes, sir, Senator, it is."

"It's quite late, Commander. What's so urgent that you have to get me out of my bed on a cold winter's night?"

"General Scott is meetin' with President Buchanan to tell him about his plan to reinforce Fort Sumter."

Clay's eyelids rolled up into his head with disbelief. "What's this? Reinforce Fort Sumter?"

"Yes, sir."

"General Scott, you say?"

"Yes, sir."

"How did you learn this, Commander?"

"A friend who is close to one of General Scott's aides related this to me, Senator."

"One of Scott's aides?"

"Yes, sir."

"And a friend of yours told you this?"

"Yes, sir."

"When did you learn this?"

"This afternoon in Philadelphia."

"In Philadelphia?"

"Yes, sir. I went there to meet my friend."

"So that's why you were unavailable to meet with Miss Hammond after she met with the president. Are you sure about this, Commander? About General Scott plannin' to reinforce Fort Sumter, I mean.''

"Yes, sir. I rode on the same trains with General Scott and his staff from Philadelphia to Washington. I believe they are meetin' with President Buchanan at this very moment."

"At this very moment?"

"Yes, sir."

"Then we haven't a minute to lose, Commander. We must alert our fellow Southrons of this turn of events." He glanced over his shoulder at his servant. "Get me some clothes to wear, Samson. I'm goin' out." He looked back at his visitor. His face twisted with horror as he spat the words, "My God, Sims! This means war."

15 ~

Sunday, December 30, 1860

Colonel Allston bared his head as he entered the church
to look for Governor Pickens. With his hat in his right
hand, he held an envelope in the left. He surveyed the
crowd of worshippers as the minister spoke about sin,
forgiveness, and redemption in the same breath. Spot-
ting the governor and his wife sitting on the aisle near
the front of the congregation, he moved ahead slowly,
walking softly, wishing not to draw attention to himself,
but failing because his mere presence in full uniform
caused all eyes to shift in his direction.

Realizing that he was being upstaged by Allston, the
pastor ceased his oration and waited patiently for the
colonel to go about his business.

Hearing whispers behind him and noting that the par-
son had stopped speaking and was presently looking
directly at someone approaching the pulpit, Pickens
twisted around to see who was disrupting the service.

Allston was only a few feet away when the governor
turned around. He took the last two steps, halted briefly,
then bent over to speak to Pickens. "A telegram for
you, Governor," he said confidentially as he handed
off the envelope, trying to be discreet but failing at this
as well.

"Couldn't it wait, Colonel?" said Pickens irritably.

"No, sir, I do not believe it can."

Pickens huffed once before he opened the envelope, removed the single page inside, and read:

The Honorable Francis W. Pickens
Governor of South Carolina

   President Buchanan met with General Scott late last night. We suspect they plan to reinforce Sumter soon after the first with troops and warship Brooklyn. What would you have us do now?

                    Barnwell, Adams, Orr

Pickens grimaced, then folded the telegram and reinserted it in the envelope. He popped erect, sidestepped into the aisle, faced the pulpit, and said, "My sincerest apology for this interruption of your service, Pastor, but the affairs of state call." He lowered his eyes, bowed his head, and waited to be excused.

"Go with God's blessin', Governor," said the minister. "We all know what a heavy burden you bear in these most tryin' of times."

"Thank you, sir," said Pickens, looking up again. He turned to his wife, bent down close to her, and said, "Please stay for the rest of the service, my dear. I'll be along soon enough."

"Yes, dear," she said meekly.

Pickens straightened up again, searched the faces around him, found the one he wanted, and said, "Colonel Cunningham, if you would join me, sir?"

Colonel John Cunningham rose from the pew where he was sitting, asked to be excused by those people between him and the aisle as he eased past them, and fell in behind Pickens and Allston as they exited the church amid a din of whispers and hushed chattering speculating on the contents of the telegram and its possible impact on South Carolina.

Outside the church, Pickens turned to Cunningham and said, "Colonel, you will assemble your regiment and seize the Federal arsenal immediately. We need those guns now. General Scott is plannin' to reinforce Fort Sumter within the week. We must prepare ourselves for the worst. Colonel Allston, send word to General Schnierle to join me here in Charleston as soon as possible. We must prepare with all due haste to defend our homes against an invasion by the Federal army." He looked heavenward and added, "May God preserve us all."

After a short night's sleep, Barnwell, Adams, and Orr attended religious services with the Trescots, and all three prayed for a peaceful resolution to the crisis facing their independent state.

"If we can't resolve this situation peacefully," said Adams as they walked back to the Trescot home after worship, "then the least we can do is delay Buchanan from actin' as long as possible. Every day we can keep him from sendin' reinforcements to Anderson is one more day that Pickens can prepare to repel a Yankee invasion."

"Are you certain that it's all that serious, James?" asked Barnwell, his credulity stretching out. "I mean, after all, an invasion?"

"If General Scott is able to put just one more company of soldiers into Sumter," said Adams, "and get just one warship into Charleston harbor before Pickens is ready for a fight, all will be lost, Robert. Charleston will be at the mercy of Sumter's guns, as will the entire harbor. First one company of soldiers and one warship, then a regiment of soldiers and an armada of warships. No, we must delay Buchanan and give Pickens time to prepare for war."

"Not only Pickens," said Orr, "but our sister states of the South as well. Senator Wigfall says every slave state is sure to follow us out of the Union within the month, especially if Buchanan sends troops and warships to help Anderson launch an attack against Charleston."

"Buchanan will never make such a move," said Barnwell. "The man has no backbone."

"Agreed," said Adams, "but General Scott has enough courage for both of them. This midnight meetin' of theirs last night does not bode well for us, gentlemen. I fear with Floyd now gone from the cabinet that we have lost our last hope of peacefully fendin' off any more moves by the Federal government to deny us our freedom."

"We mustn't give up, gentlemen," said Orr. "We must stay the course."

"How do we do that now?" asked Barnwell.

"We must continue to press Buchanan," said Adams. "We must press him from every possible angle. We need every senator from every Southern state to call on him and impress him with one simple fact."

"And that is?" asked Barnwell.

"That every slave state will join us in drivin' the Federal army from our shores if Anderson is reinforced," said Adams.

"We need more than that to impress Buchanan that he faces dire consequences if Anderson is reinforced," said Orr. "We still need help from the North. We need the Hammond woman to call on Buchanan again and press him to remove Anderson and his garrison from Sumter and Charleston harbor."

"What makes you think she will have any more luck with Buchanan this time?" asked Barnwell bitterly.

"Her persistence just might cause Buchanan to hesitate long enough to give Governor Pickens the time he needs to build the defenses necessary to protect

Charleston," said Orr. "Remember, she does come
from a family whose name is prominent on both sides
of the Mason-Dixon Line."

"I agree with you, James," said Adams. "I say we
call on her ourselves and—"

Barnwell held up a hand to interrupt. "No, we
shouldn't do that," he said. "Senator Clay has been
dealin' with her through an intermediary. I say we
should let him continue to deal with her on this basis."

"Agreed," said Adams.

That settled any further argument. As soon as they
reached the Trescot home, the commissioners asked
their host to be their go-between with Senator Clay,
and Trescot agreed to call on the Alabama solon
immediately.

Trescot arrived at the Clay home to discover that he
was preceded there by three very prominent Southrons:
Senator Wigfall, Senator Davis, and former Secretary
of War Floyd. Clay invited him into the parlor, where
he was greeted by the other guests. "Gentlemen, I'm
glad to see all of you here," he said. "I've come to
see you, Senator Clay, on behalf of Commissioners Barnwell, Adams, and Orr, but it's just as well that you
gentlemen are also here. Perhaps you, too, can help in
this matter."

"Have the commissioners heard from Governor Pickens?" asked Clay.

"No, not yet," said Trescot, "but they feel that they
shouldn't wait for his reply, that they should be doin'
something to stall President Buchanan and General
Scott from doin' anything to reinforce Fort Sumter."

"Aw, just let them go ahead and reinforce Fort Sumter," said Wigfall. "It won't do them no good. We'll
just whup their asses, and that'll be the end of it."

"It won't be that easy," said Davis, "if General
Scott gets just one good warship into Charleston harbor.

If just one gets past the harbor's defenses, a second and third will soon follow, and Charleston will be at their mercy.''

"Precisely, Senator," said Trescot. "That's why the commissioners wish to stall President Buchanan and General Scott from doin' anything to aid Major Anderson. They feel Governor Pickens must be given time to build Charleston's defenses. Certainly, our forces possess Fort Moultrie, Fort Johnson, and Castle Pinckney, but they have no way of stoppin' any ship from enterin' the harbor. Governor Pickens needs time to build defenses against Federal warships enterin' the harbor.''

"So how can we help, Will?" asked Clay.

"The commissioners were hopin' you would ask the Hammond woman to speak to the President again," said Trescot, almost embarrassed by the request.

"But she failed the last time," said Clay. "What makes them think she might succeed this time?"

"They don't know that she will succeed, Senator," said Trescot, "but they feel certain that she can put enough doubt in the president's mind to delay him for at least one more day from approvin' General Scott's plan. And who knows how important one day can be at a time like this?''

"I don't know that I can get her another appointment," said Clay. "Especially on such short notice." He searched the faces of the other men.

"I no longer have the president's ear," said Floyd. "I can do nothin' to help you, Will."

"I think it's just a waste of time," said Wigfall. He turned his back on the others.

"I'll get her an appointment," said Davis. He wagged a bony finger at Clay and added, "You just get her to agree to see Buchanan again, Clement."

"Consider it done," said Clay.

*   *   *

"But, Senator, didn't you say Miss Hammond failed to convince President Buchanan to withdraw Major Anderson and the garrison from Fort Sumter?" asked Sims. He sat beside Senator Clay in a hansom cab wandering the streets of Washington late that winter afternoon.

"Yes, I did, Commander," said Clay, "but we feel Miss Hammond might be more successful if she's given a second chance to speak to the president."

"I don't think she will care to try again, Senator. She didn't hold out much hope of changin' the president's mind when I spoke to her last. I don't think she is a woman who would like to fail twice."

"If she knew that General Scott and the president were plannin' to reinforce Fort Sumter and that such a move would precipitate war, do you think she would try to change his mind about that, Commander?"

"Do you think we should be tellin' her that we know that General Scott is plannin' to reinforce Fort Sumter?"

Clay shook his head, shrugged, and said, "No, but it might be the only way to convince her to speak to the president again."

Sims sighed, thought for a moment, then said, "All right, Senator, I'll speak to her again, but I confess that I think it's a lost cause."

"I have confidence in you, Commander," said Clay, smiling and patting Sims on the arm. He rapped the trapdoor in the roof vigorously, and on cue, it opened. "Take us to the Willard Hotel," he ordered the cabbie.

"I agreed to meet with you again, Commander Sims, for one reason only," said Sarah, "and that was to tell you that you are rude and inconsiderate."

Sarah and Sims stood face to face in a corner of the Willard's lobby. He had arrived at the supper hour and interrupted her meal.

"I do apologize, Miss Hammond," said Sims, "for not waitin' for your message yesterday, but urgent naval business called me away from the city for the remainder of the day."

"That is unacceptable, Commander," said Sarah. "At the very least, you could have left word that you were called away and couldn't meet with me."

"I apologize for that as well, Miss Hammond."

"You needn't bother apologizing any further, Commander. It won't change anything."

Sims sighed with resignation and said, "Then can we get down to the purpose of my visit this evenin', Miss Hammond?"

"I'm not interested in anything that you have to say, sir. Farewell, Commander Sims." She turned to walk away.

Angry over being summarily dismissed by a woman, Sims reached out, grabbed her arm, and pulled her back to him. "Now who's bein' rude and inconsiderate, Miss Hammond?" he said in a low growl.

Sarah glared at his hand, then at his face as she said, "Unhand me, sir, or I shall call for a policeman."

"Go ahead and call for one," said Sims confidently, "but while we're waitin' for one to rescue you, I'll tell you why I've come to see you again."

"Very well then," said Sarah resolutely. "Unhand me, and I'll listen."

Sims released his hold on her and said, "Senator Clay sent me to ask you to speak to President Buchanan once more."

"That is a waste of time, Commander. As I wrote in my note to Senator Clay, President Buchanan will not budge from his stance. Major Anderson and the garrison are to remain at Fort Sumter indefinitely."

"That isn't what Senator Clay wants you to speak to the president about this time," said Sims.

"Then what does he want me to say to the president this time?"

"He wants you to ask him to stop General Scott from sendin' reinforcements to Anderson."

Sarah's brow furrowed as she said, "General Scott is sending reinforcements to Fort Sumter? How do you know this, Commander Sims?"

"I can't tell you that," said Sims. "Just let me say that we have it on good authority that a plan is afoot to reinforce and resupply Fort Sumter within the comin' week with two companies of infantry aboard the warship *Brooklyn,* and if such an attempt is made, the result will be war between the states within the month."

"You said 'we,' Commander Sims. Aren't you still an officer in the United States Navy? Or have you decided to betray your country now?"

Sims flushed with ire. "Dammit, woman! Don't you see what's at stake here?"

"I see it more clearly than you think, Commander."

"Then are you to do nothin' to stop this war from startin', Miss Hammond? Or was all that talk about wantin' peace just that? Talk."

Angry determination squeezed her eyelids closer together in a mean glare as she said, "I will do whatever it takes to prevent this war, sir, but now I fear nothing short of divine intervention can divert our country from a bloody civil war."

Being a very devout man, President James Buchanan usually refused to conduct the business of state on the Sabbath, but when he received word that the Carolinians had seized the arsenal at Charleston, he had no choice except to confer with General Scott on the growing crisis. "Have you heard the news, General Scott?" he asked as soon as the greetings were completed.

"Do you mean about the arsenal at Charleston?"

Noting Buchanan's slight nod, he added, "Yes, sir, I have heard."

"Then you know we must act now."

"Yes, sir."

Buchanan let his view fall on the inkblotter in front of him. He remained silent for a moment, then looked up at Scott again. "Tell me again, General," he said, "about your plan to reinforce Fort Sumter."

"It's quite simple, Mr. President," said Scott, his massive body filling over half the sofa in the president's office. "On New Year's Day, Lieutenant Lacy will muster two companies of recruits at Fort Jay on Governor's Island, put them aboard the *Macedonian,* and set sail for Fort Monroe, Virginia. At the same time, the *Brooklyn,* which now rests at anchor at Hampton Roads, will take on board three companies of infantry from Fort Monroe and set sail for Charleston to reinforce Major Anderson at Fort Sumter. The *Macedonian* should arrive at Fort Monroe the night before the *Brooklyn* enters Charleston harbor. The *Brooklyn* will cross over the bar outside the harbor at first light and enter the harbor with the rising sun at her back, making her a difficult target for the Carolina gunners to see. At the same time, Major Anderson will cover the *Brooklyn*'s arrival in the harbor by firing a steady barrage at any shore batteries in the vicinity that should fire on the *Brooklyn* first. The *Brooklyn* will discharge the infantry at Fort Sumter, then drop anchor and await further orders, which will depend on what the Carolinians do from that point."

"And what do you think they will do, General?"

"I think they will fight, Mr. President. Initially, that is."

"And what will we do about that?"

"We will have to call for more troops, sir."

"Of course we will, General, but how will we fight

them? Will we attack Charleston or will we simply maintain our defensive position on Fort Sumter?''

"The first thing we will do, Mr. President, is take back all Federal property that the Carolinians have taken illegally. What happens after that will be determined by many factors.''

"Such as?''

"Such as how many of the other slave states follow South Carolina from the Union.''

"So far, none have.''

"But they will, Mr. President, unless we act now to stop them.''

"We can't do that, General. I have said before and I say it again. I believe it is illegal for a state to secede from the Union, but I do not believe the Federal government has the right to force a state to return to the Union.''

"No, sir, we can't force a state to return to the Union, but we can defend Federal property and use force to regain possession of Federal property. That, Mr. President, is what we will be doing when we reinforce Fort Sumter. The Carolinians will have to make one of two choices. Either return the forts, the arsenal, the customshouse, and the post office peacefully, or try to keep them by force.''

"And you think the Carolinians will try to keep them by force?''

"I assess the Carolinians as nothing more than a bunch of schoolyard bullies, Mr. President. They will continue to push and press the Federal government until we either give in to their demands or we stand up to them and make them back down.''

"But you said just a moment ago that you expect them to fight if we try to reinforce Fort Sumter.''

"Yes, sir, I did, but if we should move quickly and decisively, they will withdraw.''

"And the other slave states? What will they do?''

"Some will secede, but if all do not secede and form a united front against the free states, those that do secede will be left with no alternative except to return to the Union with their tails between their legs."

Buchanan closed his eyes for a moment, a prayer running through his head. No doubts interceded. With confidence and exhilaration, he opened his eyes and said, "General, you may proceed with your plan to reinforce Fort Sumter. I will sign the order as soon as you have it ready for me."

Excited by the prospect of action, Scott felt an energy spurt putting new spring in his tired old body. He rose without the usual effort, came to attention briefly, gave the president a half-bow, straightened up again, and said, "You've made the right choice, Mr. President. I'll prepare the orders immediately."

16 ~

Sarah had slept fitfully. She looked it, too, as she was shown into President Buchanan's office for their eight o'clock appointment.

"Good morning, Miss Hammond," said Buchanan, standing behind his desk. "Won't you sit down?" He waved a beckoning hand at the two chairs in front of his desk.

"Thank you, Mr. President." Sarah chose not to sit in the same chair she had chosen during their first meeting, an ancient instinct directing her not to step where she had once fallen. She forced a petite curl to her lips and added, "It was very kind of you to see me on such short notice, sir."

"You can thank Senator Davis for that, Miss Hammond," said Buchanan, his smile patronizing, benevolent, and patriarchal all at the same time. "He was quite insistent that I see you, although he was rather vague about why you wish to see me." He sat down, rested his forearms on the ink blotter, and folded his hands. "Perhaps you could enlighten me on that subject."

"Mr. President, I've heard that the Carolinians have seized the Federal arsenal at Charleston."

"That was to be expected, Miss Hammond. They've

237

kept an armed guard on the place since the first days
after the election of Mr. Lincoln. I'm surprised they
waited this long to take it. But that's neither here nor
there, is it?''

Sarah's aspect churned to deep concern. ''Yes, it is,
Mr. President. As I said in our last interview, the Carolinians are hell-bent on removing every vestige of the
Union from their state, and they're willing to do it at
the point of a bayonet if necessary. I saw them marshal-
ing their forces while I was there earlier this month,
and they aren't the only state raising armies. Militia
companies all across the South are drilling daily in
preparation for the war that they all anticipate will come
sooner or later.''

Still grinning like a patient parent, Buchanan shook
his head ever so slightly and said, ''There will be no
war between the states as long as I am president, Miss
Hammond. You can rest assured on that fact.''

This is getting me nowhere, thought Sarah. Better
give him the broadside and hope for the best. She
heaved a sigh, thought, Here goes, and said, ''Mr. President, is that why General Scott is at this very moment
planning to reinforce Fort Sumter with two companies
of infantry aboard the warship *Brooklyn?*''

Buchanan gasped, then stiffened and stared mouth
agape at Sarah. Just as quickly, he changed his expression from surprise to outrage. ''Miss Hammond, I assure you that such a plan, if one existed, would hardly
be a subject that I would openly discuss with anyone
other than members of the cabinet and the leaders of
Congress.''

Got him, thought Sarah triumphantly. She said,
''Come now, Mr. President. The whole city knows that
General Scott arrived here Saturday night and immediately met with you. If he wasn't revealing a plan to
reinforce Fort Sumter, then what was he doing here
until the wee hours of Sunday morning?''

Anger colored Buchanan's face. "How dare you challenge this administration, Miss Hammond!"

Sarah remained calm and deliberate. "Mr. President, my family is at great financial risk in this crisis. We stand to lose everything in a war between the states. Therefore, we must protect our interests at all points, and if that means challenging the veracity of the president of the United States, then so be it."

Buchanan shifted nervously in his chair, fidgeted with his fingers, and said, "With the resignation of Secretary of War Floyd, General Scott is temporarily the top official in the War Department. Considering the situation in South Carolina, it is only natural that he and I confer. We concluded those conferences last night, and today he is returning to New York with his staff."

"Then he isn't planning to reinforce Fort Sumter within the week?"

"If he were, don't you think I would know about it?"

Sarah smiled wryly and said, "You didn't answer my question, Mr. President, which means General Scott is planning to reinforce Fort Sumter within the week."

"I did not say that," retorted the president.

"You didn't have to say it, sir." She wagged her head and added, "You mustn't let him do this, Mr. President. It will only force the other slave states to secede and join South Carolina in a war against the free states."

"Miss Hammond, most of the other slave states have already aligned themselves with South Carolina, and many of them will secede within the month. There is nothing that this administration can do to prevent it."

"But you can prevent a war, Mr. President."

"No, Miss Hammond," sighed Buchanan, "I fear I can't do that either. I can only delay it, and hopefully, I can delay it until I have vacated this thankless office."

"Then why do you intend to reinforce Fort Sumter, Mr. President, when you know to do so will only force the Carolinians to fight?"

Buchanan raised an objectioning index digit and said, "Ah, but I don't know that they will fight, Miss Hammond. General Scott and I share the opinion that the Carolinians are nothing but schoolyard bullies who will back down with the first show of force, which is exactly what we intend to do before they can prepare their defenses."

Sarah gasped with exasperation, then said, "Mr. President, I think you and General Scott are wrong in your estimation that the Carolinians will back down with the first show of force. I repeat, sir, I have seen them drilling their militia companies. They will fight."

"I do not believe so," said Buchanan, "and I am willing to take the chance that they won't."

Looking grim and feeling defeated, Sarah said, "Is that your final word on the subject, Mr. President?"

Buchanan shrugged and said, "The final word is up to General Scott. He's in command of the situation now."

Upon returning to the Willard, Sarah set Rowena to packing their belongings. "We're going to New York on the first available train," she declared. Then she sent word to Sims to meet her in the hotel lobby as soon as possible.

Sims arrived at the hotel shortly before ten, but instead of giving his card to the bell captain to deliver to Sarah, he asked the desk clerk for her room number and went upstairs to her suite unannounced.

Sarah answered the knock at her door. Upon seeing Sims, she swallowed hard, surprised, delighted, and angry that he had come up without permission. She regained her composure and said, "Commander Sims, my message said for you to meet me in the lobby."

"We've already met there twice, Miss Hammond," said Sims. "Sooner or later tongues will begin wagging if we should meet there a third time. After all, this is Washington City."

It was a flimsy excuse, but Sarah accepted it without argument, relieved that he made it instead of placing her in a position of compromise. "Yes, of course. Please come in, sir."

Sims stepped inside, and Sarah closed the door behind him without looking into the hall to see if anyone might be watching, reasoning with herself that had she looked and someone saw her, then that person might assume she had something to hide, which would certainly start tongues wagging. After all, this was Washington City.

"What did the president say?" asked Sims, coming straight to the point of their meeting.

"He tried to make believe that there is no plan afoot to reinforce Fort Sumter with two companies of infantry aboard the warship *Brooklyn*," said Sarah, "but he failed to convince me otherwise. He did say that matters are now out of his control, that General Scott has the final say on the plan."

Sims frowned and said, "We feared as much. General Scott is no man to be trifled with. He has very strong convictions about the Union, and he will do everything necessary to preserve it. He will reinforce Fort Sumter, and the Carolinians will fight. That will only put the other states in motion, and before a month is concluded, this nation will be ripped asunder with a bloody war between the states."

"I tried to convince President Buchanan of that very prospect, Commander, but he said that he and General Scott are of the opinion that the Carolinians are nothing more than schoolyard bullies who will back down with the first show of force by the Federal government."

"The fools! Don't they know that the entire South is ready to resist any such challenge?"

"They don't believe it," said Sarah, "and they aren't the only ones. Senator Seward feels the same way. In my last meeting with him, he postured that very same attitude."

"They're all fools, Miss Hammond. We Southrons will not be shackled by Northern tyranny. We will fight."

"Yes, I know," she said softly.

Their eyes met. Not for the first time, but as if for the very first time, as both looked beyond the outer edges of the other, searching for an escape from the madness that was then sweeping them and the entire nation before it. Both felt the urge to follow their instincts, the desire to surrender to a fiery passion of the moment that would offer them sanctuary from the festering tides of war. He allowed the gravity of her sensuality to draw him toward her, and she reciprocated, although involuntarily, shifting her weight onto the balls of her feet and leaning forward, hoping to meet his lips with her own. For that very instant, nothing else existed except the two of them encapsulated in an aura of primeval craving to be embraced by warm, waiting, wanting arms.

Rowena intervened. She had been watching them through the hinge space of the bedroom door and had seen what was happening between her friend and her avowed enemy, a Southern slave owner. It repelled her. She opened the door and bustled into the sitting room with their baggage, making certain to be as noisy as she could be without saying a word.

Sims and Sarah heard Rowena enter the room, and the waves of their emotions ebbed for the time being. A cloud of disappointment covered their faces for an instant, only to be replaced by the shadow of embarrassment as they shifted their gazes to Rowena; Sarah focusing directly on her friend's eyes that looked back with cold accusation in them, and Sims seeing the brown skin of Rowena's face and then the valises that she carried.

"Are you leaving Washington City?" asked Sims, returning his attention to Sarah, his tone tinged with disappointment.

"Yes," said Sarah. "General Scott and his staff are returning to New York this morning, and I thought I would go there and approach him about his decision to reinforce Fort Sumter."

"Do you think it will do any good?"

"It can't hurt."

"No, I suppose not," he said. "How soon before you leave?"

"We will depart on the next available train."

"Then you haven't a moment to lose," said Sims. "I'll be on my way then." He started to retreat toward the door, then halted. "Perhaps I could call for a carriage and drop you and your servant at the depot."

"No, I don't think that would be a wise idea, Commander Sims. As you said earlier, this is Washington City, and tongues will wag."

Sims nodded and said, "Yes, of course. Then I bid you adieu, Miss Hammond. Until we meet again."

"Until we meet again, Commander Sims."

Sims bowed gallantly to her, then left.

Rowena dropped the valises to get Sarah's attention. When she had it, she said, "Why are you getting into that with that man?"

"Getting into what?" asked Sarah with all the innocence of an anonymous feline that rubs against a table leg, shaking it until an expensive vase crashes to the floor, then walks away as if nothing had ever happened.

"I'm no fool, Sarah Hammond. I saw how you two were looking at each other."

With icy deliberation, Sarah replied, "How were we looking at each other, Rowena?"

Rowena stared at Sarah for a long second, then said, "Okay, have it your way. Go ahead and make a fool of yourself over that man, but don't you come crying to me when he breaks your heart."

Sarah sighed heavily and said, "Oh, please, Rowena! I have no intention of allowing Commander Sims, or any other man for that matter, the opportunity to break my heart. So you needn't worry about it, Rowena."

"Don't you lose any sleep worrying about me worrying about you, Sarah Hammond. I won't." She was lying, and she knew it. Fool! she thought. He's gonna break your heart as sure as the sun's gonna come up in the east, and there ain't nothin' I can do to stop it. But I'm sure as hell gonna try. You can count on that, sister.

Sims hired a hansom and went straight from the Willard to Senator Clay's office, but upon finding that the senator wasn't there, he continued on to the solon's home, where a servant informed him that Clay had gone to Mr. Trescot's house. Returning to the carriage, Sims paused to consider the situation confronting him.

If I go to Mr. Trescot's house, he thought, and I'm recognized by someone unfriendly to the Cause, I could be accused of treason. And should that happen, where would that leave me? He shook his head and waved a mental finger at himself. I think maybe that I worry too much about myself and not enough about the Cause.

Sims ordered the driver to take him to Trescot's.

A Trescot house slave asked Sims to wait just inside the front door while he informed his master that Senator Clay had a visitor. The servant parted the sliding doors to the parlor, stepped through the entrance, then closed the doors behind him. Sims paced the foyer until the servant reappeared, followed by Clay.

"Commander Sims," said Clay, "what's the news?"

"It's not good, sir," said Sims. "Miss Hammond failed to convince the president that South Carolina will fight if General Scott is allowed to reinforce Fort Sumter."

"Damn!" swore Clay, accentuating the curse by pounding his right fist into his left palm.

"Not all is lost, Senator," said Sims, trying to soften the blow. "Miss Hammond is presently on her way to New York with hopes of convincing General Scott that South Carolina will fight if he tries to reinforce Fort Sumter."

Clay snickered and said, "And do you think she will be any more successful with Ol' Fuss 'n' Feathers than she was with the president? I think not, Commander. General Scott is a much more decisive man than President Buchanan. If he has made up his mind to reinforce Fort Sumter, you can believe that no mere woman is gonna convince him to do otherwise. Not at this stage of the game. No, sir. I am afraid Miss Hammond is chasing windmills by going to New York to see General Scott."

Sims wanted to argue the point for a reason that he had yet to concede to himself, but he withheld his opinion and defense of Sarah. Instead, he said, "Well, sir, that's all I have to report."

"Thank you, Commander," said Clay. "You've served the Cause admirably, sir. It will not be forgotten."

"Thank you, sir," said Sims. He gave Clay a half-bow and excused himself.

On his hansom ride back to the Navy Department, Sims tried to focus his thoughts on the future, but he found it difficult to do so because the image of Sarah Hammond's lovely face kept getting in the way. He forced a giddy laugh and chastised himself aloud. "This is silly, Rafe Sims. You're behaving like some lovesick adolescent." He paused, then added, "But she is so alluring and so beyond my reach." He snickered and said, "Maybe that's why I want her so much."

"Did you say something, sir?" asked the driver.

Embarrassed at being caught talking to himself, Sims stammered, "Uh, no, cabbie. Just thinking out loud."

"Yes, sir."

Then to himself, Sims thought, Get a hold on yourself, man. She's a Yankee. A smile creased his lips as he added, But she's such a beautiful Yankee.

Governor Pickens pointed at a map of Charleston harbor and environs. "Here, General," he said, his finger touching a stretch of Morris Island that faced the main shipping channel to the harbor. "This is where I want you to build a battery. Out of range of Fort Sumter's guns. Set up as many guns as you can along that beach and aim them out to sea. I want this done as fast as possible. There isn't a minute to waste."

Besides General John Schnierle of the state militia, the governor's audience included Colonel Cunningham, Colonel Allston, Colonel Pettigrew, Lieutenant Colonel DeSaussure, Major Capers, Major Peter F. Stevens of the Citadel Academy, and Lieutenant William H. Ryan of the Irish Volunteers. All nodded in agreement with Pickens; a battery at this point could challenge any ship attempting to enter the harbor and at the same time would be safe from Sumter's heavy guns.

"We will name this battery Fort Morris," said Pickens. "Major Stevens, I am placin' you in command of this post. I am certain that the first shots of this war will be fired from your battery, and I wish that honor to go to our valiant cadets from the Citadel. Pick your bravest and brightest young men for this duty, sir."

"It will be an honor, sir," said Stevens.

Pickens continued giving out commands. "Lieutenant Ryan, I want you to assemble a detail of twenty men and put them aboard the *General Clinch*. You will patrol the bar between seven o'clock in the evenin' and dawn. You are to intercept and sink, if necessary, any small craft that should try to enter the harbor to reinforce Fort Sumter. You will maintain a constant contact with Major Stevens at Fort Morris or Colonel DeSaussure at Fort Moultrie, dependin', of course, on where you are at any given hour, in order to prevent their guns from firin' on you by mistake.''

"Yes, sir," said Ryan. "We'll keep a sharp eye on the sea, Governor. No invader will pass while the Irish are on duty, sir."

"Very good, Lieutenant," said Pickens. "Gentlemen, I do not have to tell you how important time is now. We do not have a minute to lose in buildin' our defenses. Just as I am attemptin' to impress that fact on you now, I wish that you would all do the same with the officers and men under your command. This is not the time for shirkers, gentlemen. Any shirkers will be dealt with severely. Make no mistake about that. How is your physics teacher from the college comin' with the battery at Cummings Point, Major Stevens?"

"Professor McCrady's makin' good progress, sir. He's aimin' his guns at Fort Sumter as well as at the shippin' channel in case there should be need to fend off a seagoin' vessel."

"Very good," said Pickens.

The door opened abruptly, and a youthful officer from Allston's brigade stomped into the room, interrupting Pickens from his speech. He carried an envelope in his hand.

"What is it, Lieutenant?" asked the governor.

"A telegram, sir." He handed the message to Pickens.

Pickens accepted the envelope, opened it, and read its vital words aloud. " 'The Honorable Francis W. Pickens, Governor of South Carolina. General Scott has

returned to New York to execute his plan to reinforce
Fort Sumter with two companies of infantry aboard the
warship *Brooklyn*. You may expect trouble any time
two days hence. God be with you. Adams, Barnwell,
Orr.' '' With slow deliberation, he refolded the telegram, replaced it in the envelope, looked up at the
officers, and said, ''There you have it, gentlemen. The
Federal government has declared war on South Carolina.'' He paused as he studied each and every grave
face before him. Nodding with confidence and satisfaction in them, he concluded, ''You have your orders,
gentlemen. To your posts, and may God be with us
all.''

17 ~

New Year's Eve, 1860

Sarah and Rowena arrived at six-thirty P.M. in Newark on the New Jersey Rail Road mail train from Philadelphia. They took the ferry across the Hudson to Manhattan and proceeded immediately to General Scott's house, where they were turned away by his orderly, who informed them that the general was dressing for the army and navy New Year's Eve ball to be held at the training facility at Fort Jay on Governor's Island.

"We have to hurry, Rowena," said Sarah as they walked back to the hackney waiting for them at the curb. "I'm going dancing tonight."

"You can't go to that ball," said Rowena as soon as they were under way. "You haven't been invited."

"That's all right. I'll be going with my cousin."

"Your cousin?"

"Yes. Cousin Susan on my grandmother's side of the family. She lives only a few blocks from here." She gave the driver the address and admonished him to make all due haste getting them there. They climbed inside the carriage, and in a few minutes they were standing in Susan Slemmer's parlor.

Susan was a Rhode Island Chase, plain, prim, proper, and petite, with an agile, meticulous mind that was quick to recognize error and the out-of-place. Her husband was First Lieutenant Andrew J. Slemmer of the First Artillery and commander of Fort Barrancas at the mouth of Pensacola harbor in Florida.

"Actually, Sarah," said Susan, "I hadn't planned on going to the ball."

"Susan, I need to be at that ball tonight," said Sarah. "I was hoping that I could go with you."

"Why do you need to be there?"

"I have to dance with General Scott."

Susan raised her eyebrows, turned her head to one side, and said, "You have to dance with General Scott? Why on earth do you have to dance with him?"

"I can't tell you that, Susan," said Sarah. Then seeing that Susan wouldn't accept that answer, she raised her hand and added, "Let's just say that my dancing with General Scott might help Andy down in Florida."

"Help Andy?" queried Susan. She shook her head, sighed, and said, "I don't know what you're up to, Sarah, but if you need me to go so badly that you have to use Andy's safety as a pretext, then I suppose I can take you to the ball."

"Thank you, Susan," said Sarah with a sigh of relief. She hugged her cousin.

"I'll have to dress first," said Susan, and after quickly inspecting Sarah's attire, she added, "and so will you. Meet me at the ferry landing as soon as you can, and I'll get you into the ball."

The navy launch from New York deposited Sarah and Susan on Governor's Island at half past nine. They were met by an officer who assigned two recruits to escort them from the landing to the mess hall that had been gaily decorated for the occasion. They were the last arrivals for the evening's festivities.

Inside the building, the soldiers took Sarah's and Susan's fur wraps and hung the garments in the cloak-room. On rejoining their assignments, they took the ladies through the greeting line, which consisted of Lieutenant Lacy, the other officers of Fort Jay, their wives and sweethearts, and Commodore Foote, his staff, and their wives and sweethearts. The soldiers presented Sarah, who wore her favorite low-cut ball gown of deep purple satin because it accented the violet of her eyes, and Susan, whose dress was the color of summer foliage. From there, the recruits led them to the refreshment table, where they served the two women cups of punch.

"There's Margaret Erben," said Susan, nodding toward a homely woman standing alone at the far end of the long table. "Her husband is first officer aboard the storeship *Supply,* which is presently anchored in Pensacola harbor. Henry, that's her husband, is a lieutenant. He's the ambitious sort. He married her because her father is a socially prominent importer. Henry is no prize either. Margaret knows why he married her, but at twenty-six and not getting any younger or prettier, she could hardly say no. As she put it, he's better than no man at all. Come on, and I'll introduce you to her."

"I'd rather meet General Scott," said Sarah, her eyes searching the great hall until she saw him sitting at a table in the far corner away from the mixed orchestra of musicians from the military and naval bands from the area.

Susan shrugged and said, "All right, if you insist." She turned to her escort, slid her hand through the crook of his elbow, and said, "Private, to General Scott's table, and hurry."

Sarah did likewise with her recruit, and the two soldiers led them tentatively to Scott's table, where they snapped to attention in the presence of the general and his adjutant, Colonel Lorenzo Thomas, and Mrs. Thomas.

"Sir," said Susan's soldier, raising his voice over the din of the ball, "may I present Mrs. Susan Slemmer, wife of Lieutenant Andrew Slemmer of the First Artillery?"

Thomas rose from the table.

"Thank you, son," said Scott. "I already know Mrs. Slemmer. Excuse me if I don't rise, Susan, but I've had a long day. A touch of the gout, you now."

"That's quite all right, General," said Susan.

"And who is this lovely young woman with you, Susan?" asked Scott, his face beaming with lechery.

"General Scott, may I introduce my cousin, Miss Sarah Hammond, the daughter of Levi Hammond of the Levi Hammond Shipping Line?"

"Miss Hammond, how nice to meet you!" said Scott.

"The honor is all mine, General Scott," said Sarah.

"So your father is Levi Hammond. I've never met him, but I did meet your grandmother once." He thought for a moment, then added, "No, twice. Maybe three times." He burped a chuckle. "Well, whatever. An incredible woman. The kind you never forget." He shook his large head softly, frowned with a memory, and concluded, "I understand she passed away a few years back."

"Yes, that's right, she did," said Sarah. "We all miss her still."

"An incredible woman. Had she been a man, no doubt she would have been a senator or a governor."

"Had she been a man, General Scott, she would have been president, and had she been president, our country wouldn't be facing this terrible crisis confronting it now."

Scott tilted his head and smiled cautiously as he said, "You sound much like her, Miss Hammond."

"Thank you, General Scott. I will take that as a compliment."

"As it was intended."

Thomas cleared his throat.

"How remiss of me, ladies," said Scott. "Allow me to introduce Colonel Lorenzo Thomas, my adjutant, and Mrs. Thomas."

Thomas bowed from the waist and said, "Ladies."

"Colonel Thomas," said Susan, curtsying. "Mrs. Thomas."

"Colonel," said Sarah curtly as Thomas straightened up again. She didn't bother to curtsy. "Mrs. Thomas." Then looking back at Scott, she said, "I'm sorry that you're bothered by the gout, General. I was hoping to have at least one dance with you, sir."

"Why, Miss Hammond, I'm quite flattered," said Scott, eyebrows rolling up his massive forehead.

"It was not my intention to flatter you, General. From the looks of your uniform, you hardly need any greater blandishment."

"Why, Sarah!" gasped Susan.

Thomas stepped forward a pace and said, "Miss Hammond, do you know to whom you are speaking?"

The general guffawed and said, "My God, you are just like your grandmother. Only she would've had the effrontery to speak to a man in my position in that manner." He let out a louder laugh that rose above the music and the chatter of the revelers. He added, "It's true, you know. The apple doesn't fall far from the tree."

"No, General, it doesn't," said Sarah.

"So, Miss Hammond, to paraphrase Shakespeare, 'You came not to praise Scott, but to dance with him.' Why?"

"I wish to speak to you without being interrupted, and the likelihood of that happening on the dance floor is high, General."

"Quite right, Miss Hammond. Quite right. Who would have the temerity to cut in on the General of the

Army? So what is it, Miss Hammond, that you wish to speak to me about without being interrupted?''

"What I have to say to you, General Scott, is for your ears only."

"This sounds serious," said Scott, his tone mocking.

"It is, General," said Sarah sternly. "So serious that I will offer you two words to define the gravity of my request."

"Two words, Miss Hammond?"

Sarah bore her gaze into Scott's right eye and said, "*Brooklyn* and Sumter."

Scott never flinched, remaining unmoved for a good three seconds before the orchestra struck up a lively melody, bringing a smile to his face. "Ah, yes," he said. "*The Virginia Reel.* Colonel Thomas, I think Mrs. Thomas would enjoy dancing to this tune. Don't you agree?"

"Yes, sir," said Thomas, taking his cue to leave the table. He took his wife's hand and led her onto the dance floor.

"Susan, would you please excuse us?" asked Scott.

"Certainly, General," said Susan. She turned to her escort and said, "I think I need another cup of punch." She took his arm, and they departed.

Sarah turned to her soldier and said, "I can find my own way back to the refreshment table. Thank you, Private."

The enlisted man bowed and left.

"Please sit down, Miss Hammond," said Scott, indicating the chair to his right, the closest one to him.

Sarah sat down and said, "Thank you, sir."

"All right, Miss Hammond. You've got my undivided attention. What is it that you wish to say to me?"

"General Scott, I have just come from Washington City, the same as you have. And like you, I have just come from visiting with President Buchanan. I saw him last this morning when I went to plead with him not to reinforce Fort Sumter.''

''And what did the president say, Miss Hammond?''

''He said that any decision on Fort Sumter now lies with you, General, that only you can change the plan now, and that is why I am here. To ask you not to do this thing.''

Scott considered her words for a few seconds, then said, ''First of all, Miss Hammond, how do you know that there is a plan to reinforce Fort Sumter?''

Quite evenly and with forthright direction, she replied, ''I heard gossip in Washington City that you had come to the capital to see the president about the situation at Fort Sumter, and I confronted the president with that rumor. He conceded that your visit did concern the national crisis because you are the General of the Army, but he tried to convince me that he had no knowledge of any strategy to reinforce Fort Sumter. However, being a religious man, he refused to commit to an outright canard, instead resorting to the ways of politicians who weave their words in such tangled webs that they make denials without actually denying or admitting anything. I saw right through this tactic, challenged him on it, and that is when he said that you are now in charge of the situation with South Carolina.''

''All right, Miss Hammond, let us suppose there is a plan to reinforce Fort Sumter. What business is it of yours if this government should wish to do so?''

''My family and I are trying to prevent a war between the states, General Scott.''

''And don't you think that President Buchanan and I are trying to do the very same thing, Miss Hammond?''

''If you are, then you're going about it the wrong way,'' said Sarah. ''Sending more soldiers to Fort Sumter will only add fuel to the fire started by Major Anderson when he retreated from Fort Moultrie.''

''Retreated from Fort Moultrie, Miss Hammond?''

queried Scott. "Why would you use that term in reference to Major Anderson's maneuver?"

"How else would you describe his movement from Fort Moultrie to Fort Sumter, General? He moved his command out of harm's way to Fort Sumter. Isn't that retreating?"

"Yes, I suppose it is," said Scott.

"And now you are planning to attack the Carolinians with the *Brooklyn* and two companies of infantry."

"Attack the Carolinians?"

"That's how the Carolinians will look at it, General. The Carolinians, the Georgians, and every other Southerner. All will consider the reinforcement of Fort Sumter by the *Brooklyn* to be an act of aggression by the Federal government against South Carolina, and every Southern state will come to the aid of the Carolinians. In short, General, you will provoke a war between the states."

"Major Anderson needs more men and supplies in order to defend Fort Sumter properly. How else am I to get him more men and supplies except by the sea?"

"I see your point, General, but don't you realize that sending more men and supplies to Anderson will only provoke the South to rise against the Federal government en masse?"

"They won't do it," said Scott. "They'll back down with the first show of force."

"How do you know that for certain, General?"

Scott wiped his open hand across his mouth, then said, "I don't."

"Then why run the risk of starting a war?"

"What would you have me do, Miss Hammond? Abandon Major Anderson completely? He needs those reinforcements and supplies to defend Fort Sumter."

"All right, I'll grant you that much, but do you have to send them there aboard the most powerful warship in the fleet?"

"How else do I get them there? Should I put them on an unarmed civilian ship and have them run into Charleston harbor without protection?"

"Yes, you should," said Sarah. "The Carolinians are less likely to fire on a civilian ship than they are on a man-of-war. My father has a ship in port right now that would be most suitable for the task. The *Dover White*, captained by my cousin Aquila Chase. He knows the harbor. He could land your soldiers and the supplies at Fort Sumter during the night, and the Carolinians will be none the wiser until the next morning."

Scott pursed his lips and stroked his chin in thought as he considered Sarah's suggestion. "You just might have something there, Miss Hammond," he said. "Hmm. A civilian ship landing troops under cover of darkness. That just might work. I'll take your suggestion under advisement, Miss Hammond. I'll discuss it with my staff at the earliest possible opportunity."

"General, I would prefer that you consider not sending any more soldiers into Charleston harbor first."

"That is completely out of the question. Anderson needs those reinforcements and supplies, and the government must show the Southern states that it will not tolerate rebellion against its authority over them."

Sarah shook her head with resignation, sighed heavily, then made one last attempt to sway Scott to see matters her way. "At the very worst, General," she said, "employing a civilian ship should be perceived as a peaceful gesture by the other Southern states."

The orchestra ceased playing, and the dancers applauded them.

Clapping his hands politely, Scott leaned closer to Sarah and said, "I fear the time for peaceful gestures is past, Miss Hammond, but I'm willing to make one if it will help prevent bloodshed."

The applause subsided.

"General, I must impress—"

Scott raised his hand to stop her. "Miss Hammond, you said you wanted to dance with me in order to speak to me in private. Well, you've had your 'dance.' Now if you don't mind, I'd like to relax and enjoy the remainder of the year in peace, for I fear it will be our last for some time to come."

Louisa Phoenix accompanied the Lacys to the ball. To many, her presence seemed out of place, considering the fact that her husband remained missing in the Pacific, but she disregarded their opinions without a second thought. Other than her secret moments with Rafe Sims and her use of John Lacy, she hadn't had much fun lately. In her estimation, she deserved a night out, even if she had to spend it with a bunch of Yankees.

Attending the ball was one thing, but actually dancing was another. Was she a widow or not? If she was, then she should have been mourning her loss instead of waltzing the night away. If she wasn't, she should have been behaving like a respectable married woman whose husband was missing at sea instead of waltzing the night away. She cared for neither mantle, not when there were music and dancing and brightly colored decorations and a reason to celebrate and be gay. She was young, alive, and unfettered—for the moment—widow or not. She would dance if she wished, and that was that.

To that point in the evening, Louisa hadn't chosen to make a spectacle of herself just yet. Like the other unaccompanied ladies in attendance, those with husbands posted elsewhere or doing their duty aboard ship, Louisa had a young private from the training center to wait on her. She sat on one of the chairs lining the wall opposite the main door, telling her soldier to stay within earshot in case she needed him, which she didn't until she saw Sarah and Susan talking to General Scott. Before that moment, she hadn't given much thought to the general, except to admire the cut of his colorful uniform. Now seeing Sarah and Susan speaking to General Scott aroused her curiosity. She beckoned her recruit with a summoning finger.

"Yes, mum?" he queried, his accent suggesting that his origins lay across the Atlantic in Ireland. He stood ramrod straight, his Celtic gray-green eyes focused on the wall behind her.

"What was your name again, Private?" she asked, raising her voice to be heard over the music.

"Killoy, mum."

"Your first name, Private Killoy."

"Michael, mum."

Louisa motioned for Killoy to come closer, to bend down so that she wouldn't have to yell at him. As soon as he complied, she said, "Michael, do you know who those two ladies are over there with General Scott and Colonel Thomas?"

Killoy looked over his shoulder, spotted Sarah and Susan standing in front of Scott's table, studied them for a few seconds, then turned back to Louisa. "No, mum," he said, "I don't recognize either one of them."

"I've seen the one," said Louisa. "I believe her husband is an army officer. But the other woman I've never seen before. Would you be a dear, Michael, and inquire as to her identity please?"

"Yes, mum." He straightened up.

"Be discreet when you ask, Michael. I wouldn't wish anyone to think me to be nosy."

"Yes, mum," said Killoy. He clicked his heels, then departed.

Nothing seemed out of the ordinary until Colonel Thomas led his wife onto the dance floor and Susan took her escort's arm and left Sarah alone with Scott. Isn't that odd? thought Louisa. Seeing the general motion to Sarah to seat herself set Louisa's mouth agape. Who is that woman that she should sit down with General Winfield Scott all by herself? I must find out who she is. She looked after Killoy. Where is that boy? She returned her attention to Sarah and General Scott. Who is that woman? she wondered. How tempting to cross the room and ask Sarah herself, but Louisa restrained herself from acting impetuously.

Killoy returned. He leaned close to Louisa and said, "The one lady is Mrs. Slemmer, mum. She's the wife of Lieutenant Slemmer, the commanding officer of Fort Barrancas down in Florida, wherever that is. The other lady seems to be a bit of a mystery. Her escort tells me her name is Miss Sarah Hammond. Beyond that, mum, he knows nothing."

"Are you certain of that, Michael? Her name, I mean."

"That's what he said, mum."

"Very well then, thank you, Michael." She felt frustrated for the moment, then an idea occurred to her. "I need some punch." She stood up, took his arm, and added, "Let's go, Michael."

Killoy led Louisa around the perimeter of the dancers to the refreshment table. He poured a cup of punch and handed it to her, Louisa keeping an eye on Sarah and General Scott the whole time.

The music ended. The dancers applauded the orchestra. Gentlemen bowed and ladies curtsied to their partners. The orchestra leader tapped his baton on the music stand in front of him, and the musicians struck up another number.

Louisa drank the punch absently until she saw Sarah rise and leave General Scott without making any courteous gestures of farewell. Noting the stern set to Scott's jaw, she surmised that Sarah had said something to displease the general, and seeing Sarah storm off in a huff roused her suspicion that Ol' Fuss 'n' Feathers had been equally disagreeable. My, my, thought Louisa.

Isn't she having a tizzy? I must learn what those two said to each other. An idea came clear in her mind.

"Michael," said Louisa, turning to Killoy, "would you find Lieutenant Lacy and ask him to come to me?"

Killoy clicked his heels, bowed, and said, "Yes, mum!" He went in search of his commanding officer and found him in the company of Mrs. Lacy and Lieutenant and Mrs. Charles R. Woods. The private snapped to attention and addressed Lacy. "Sir, Mrs. Phoenix wishes to speak with you, sir," he said.

Lacy shifted his eyes nervously in the direction of his wife, then looked back at Killoy and said, "Did she say what she wanted to speak to me about, Private?"

"No, sir. Only that I was to find you, sir, and pass that message to you, sir."

Feigning displeasure, Lacy frowned and said, "Very well then. I suppose I'll go speak with her." He forced a sigh to accentuate his charade of annoyance. "If you will excuse me, ladies? Charles?" He gave Mrs. Woods a curt nod that substituted for a bow. Then back to Killoy, he said, "Lead the way, Private." He followed the recruit to the refreshment table, where he excused the soldier before speaking to Louisa. "Did you need something, Mrs. Phoenix?" he asked, trying to mask his desire to take her elsewhere so he could ravish her repeatedly—or so he imagined his sexual prowess to be often enough.

"Lieutenant Lacy, I wish to dance," she said evenly, making it sound like a command.

"I don't think that would be such a good idea, Mrs. Phoenix," said Lacy, maintaining the deception that they were nothing more than acquaintances. "People might talk."

"I don't give a damn what people might say. I want to dance."

Realizing that arguing with her would prove a waste

of time, Lacy groaned and said, "All right, I'll get Private Killoy to dance with you."

"John Lacy, I want to dance with you."

A cold sweat bubbled up on Lacy's forehead as he rubbed his equally moist palms on his trousers. "Louisa, be reasonable," he pleaded. "How would that look?"

"I don't care how it would look," she said, then lowering her voice, she added, "and if you meant all those things you've been saying to me, then you wouldn't care either."

Lacy heaved a real sigh and said, "I just can't."

"Very well. If you won't dance with me, then I'll just go find somebody else. Perhaps General Scott would like to dance with me." She looked in Scott's direction. "He's just sittin' there doin' nothin'. I think I'll go ask him." She started toward the general's table.

"No, wait!" said Lacy, reaching out and grabbing her arm.

Louisa stopped, glared at his hand, and said, "Either dance with me or let me go."

He did neither. Instead, he grimaced and said, "You just can't walk up to the General of the Army and ask him to dance with you. You have to be introduced first."

"Very well," said Louisa. "Then introduce me to him."

Lacy went rigid with fear. What have I done? he asked himself. Introduce this strumpet to General Scott? My God, what foolhardiness is this?

"Either take me to him or let me go, Johnny."

Her words echoed in his head, forcing him to focus on the moment. "All right, I will," he said unwillingly. He released her and crooked his arm to her. "This way, Mrs. Phoenix," he added stiffly.

Louisa put her hand on Lacy's arm and allowed him to lead her to Scott's table, where he introduced her to the general as well as to Colonel and Mrs. Thomas. In two breaths, he explained how Louisa's husband was missing at sea and how she wanted to meet the general.

"Well, well!" said Scott. "This is turning out to be quite an evening. First the pretty Miss Sarah Hammond wants to meet me, and now the lovely Mrs. Phoenix. Either I'm younger and handsomer than I thought, or I'm so old and senile that my mind and eyes deceive me into believing that young women still find me irresistible."

"The former, I assure you, General Scott," said Louisa.

Scott chuckled and said, "Flattery will get you everywhere, Mrs. Phoenix."

"Will it get me a dance with you, General?"

"Miss Hammond wanted me to dance with her as well, Mrs. Phoenix, but, alas, I had to decline her request, as I must decline yours. The gout, you know."

"Oh, you poor man! Does it hurt much?"

"Not as much as it hurts me to think that I may be missing the night of my life dancing with the likes of Miss Hammond and you, Mrs. Phoenix. A pity, isn't it?"

"Yes, sir, it is. But maybe not so much for you as for me. Possibly, I am missin' the most in this bargain. Or perhaps not. I would have to share you with this Miss Hammond of whom you spoke, and I should think that I would be jealous of that possibility, General."

Scott guffawed and said, "I don't think you would have to worry yourself too much on that account, Mrs. Phoenix. Miss Sarah Hammond is not the kind to dote on an old man such as I, General of the Army or not. She is a Northerner and the daughter of a seafaring family, no insult intended toward your husband and our valiant navy. I mean to say that she lacks the gentility of a Southern lady, such as yourself. You are a Southerner, are you not, Mrs. Phoenix?"

"I hail from Kentucky, sir. I am a Lee by birth, and a kinswoman of Colonel Robert Lee of Virginia."

"A good man, Colonel Lee," said Scott. "Wouldn't you say so, Colonel Thomas?"

"Absolutely, General," said Thomas.

"Yes, he is," reiterated Scott. "Anyway, as I was saying, Miss Hammond is not interested in me so much as a man as she is interested in me as the General of the Army, the man who now controls the fate of this nation, or so she would have me believe."

"The fate of the nation, General?" queried Louisa, dipping her line into deeper waters for a bigger fish.

"Politics, my dear," said Scott. "Politics. Nothing for a Southern lady to worry her pretty head over."

Politics? wondered Louisa. Aloud she said, "No, I shouldn't think politics would be somethin' for a Southern lady to concern herself with."

"Not when there's music and dancing," said Scott.

"I quite agree, General, but you can't dance with me, so what am I to do?"

"No, I can't dance with you, but John here can. Go ahead and dance with her, John. Mary won't mind, and besides, it's an order from me. She can't argue with you on that one." He laughed raucously.

"Yes, sir," said Lacy meekly.

The music stopped, and the dancers applauded again, Louisa, Lacy, Scott, and the Thomases joining in politely.

Why would this Northern woman be interested in politics? Louisa asked herself. And why would she be so interested in General Scott? Does she know about the plan to reinforce Fort Sumter? How would she know? It's supposed to be a secret, isn't it? Or is it? I must find out.

18 ❧

Tuesday, New Year's Day, 1861

Lacy was late.

Louisa was unhappy about it. She busied herself with knitting to pass the time as she waited for his arrival, trying not to let Hattie see her displeasure over Lacy's tardiness.

Near the end of the previous evening's festivities at Fort Jay, Louisa had coaxed Lacy into promising to come by her apartment the next day. "I need you, Johnny," she whispered into his ear as they danced. She knew he understood her meaning by the sudden stutter in his step. "Come by in the mornin'. Not too early. I'll send Hattie on an errand that will take her hours to complete, and we can be at our leisure." She almost giggled when he stumbled again. He's so easily excited, she thought.

"I'll make some excuse to Mary and be there around ten," he said.

"Promise?" urged Louisa.

"Promise," said Lacy.

That was the night before. This was today. The mantel clock had already struck eleven. Still no Lacy.

Damn that Yankee! thought Louisa. I ought not to give him any when he gets here. That would teach him to be on time in the future. Rafe would never leave me waitin' like this. The thought of Sims aroused her to squirm in her seat involuntarily.

"Somethin' givin' you an itch, Miz Louisa?" asked Hattie.

"Just tired of sittin' so long in one place," said Louisa. She forgot about Lacy and Sims for the moment and considered an alternate method of learning more about Sarah Hammond. All she really knew was the little bit that General Scott had given her: Sarah Hammond was a Yankee and the daughter of a seafaring family who was interested in politics. Yankee, politics, seafarin' family? wondered Louisa. Nothin' particular about bein' a Yankee. That only makes her peculiar like all Yankees. Bein' interested in politics is certainly odd for a lady, but bein' a Yankee means she's most likely not much of a lady. Then again, there was that senator whose name was Hammond, but he was from South Carolina. She couldn't be related to him. So that leaves a seafarin' family. Let's see here. Ships, the ocean, the harbor, the docks. Yes, that's it! She put her knitting aside, stood up, and stretched. Looking through the street window, she thought, Damn! it would have to be winter and so cold. She pouted aloud, "I wish it was warmer outside. I'd sure like to go for a stroll down to the waterfront."

"We could bundle up against what little cold there is, Miz Louisa. The sun shinin' enough to help keep you warm, if you was to wear that black coat with the fur collar."

"Yes, why not?" said Louisa, resigning herself to the fact that Lacy wasn't coming and she'd have to do some investigating on her own if she wanted to learn more about Sarah Hammond. "That's what I'll do. I'll go for a walk down to the waterfront. You can go with me, Hattie. Get our wraps."

Hattie obeyed the command, and in a few minutes

they were walking briskly along the avenue toward the ferry landing. The sun shone brightly on them, giving false promise of a glorious year to come. They reached the waterfront just as the ferry arrived from Manhattan.

"I have an idea, Hattie. It's such a beautiful day. Why don't we take the boat over to New York and go window-shoppin'? We can make a day of it."

"Yes'm, if you say so, Miz Louisa."

They boarded the ferry and took the casual trip across the East River to the New York side. After docking, they took the roundabout route to the shopping district by walking along the waterfront. Louisa looked for signs that might bear the name of Hammond but saw none until they came to the wharf at the foot of Warren Street. Opposite the corner building of the M. O. Roberts Shipping Line, declared by two-foot block letters, was the headquarters of the Levi Hammond Shipping Line.

A seafarin' family, thought Louisa. She smiled to herself, smug that she had made this discovery.

Louisa failed to notice the two side-wheel steamers tied up in their slips beside the wharf at the end of the street until she heard a familiar male voice that drew her attention to one craft, the *Dover White*.

"Ain't that Lieutenant Lacy on that ship, Miz Louisa?" queried Hattie.

Louisa stopped to take a better look at a knot of five men in civilian clothing facing two merchant marine officers on the deck of the ship. "Yes, I believe it is," she said. Quickly, she recognized another man as Lieutenant Woods and a third as Colonel Thomas. Two others she had seen at the ball the night before, but she couldn't recall their names. The ship's captain, Aquila Chase, and his first officer were strangers to her.

So this is where Johnny's been, she thought. What's he doin' aboard that ship with those other officers? I wonder if it's got anything to do with General Scott's plan to reinforce Fort Sumter. Must be. They're all dressed in regular clothes. Probably tryin' to be secret about this. Maybe Johnny was lyin' to me when he said the general was sendin' the *Brooklyn* to Fort Sumter. She caught sight of the gangplank to the *Dover White* and read the name of the shipping company on its white canvas sides. Levi Hammond Shipping Line? she thought. Sarah Hammond. Maybe Johnny was tellin' me true and the general has since changed his plan. Maybe he's still sendin' the *Brooklyn* to protect this ship. Or maybe . . . Aw, hell! this is all so confusin'. But I must find out what's goin' on here and get word of it to Rafe.

Seeing that Lacy and the other officers would soon leave the *Dover White* and would be coming their way, Louisa turned to Hattie and said, "Come along, Hattie. I want to be home before dark, so we don't have too much time to look at store windows."

They scurried away.

Lacy failed to see Louisa and Hattie; likewise, his fellow officers. Their attention focused on inspecting the *Dover White* and listening to her captain.

"Gentlemen, although my employer has entered into negotiations with you for the use of my ship," said Chase, "I must tell you that I will not be a part of your plan. I am a Quaker and thus I am relieved of taking part in any act of war. You can lease the *Dover White* from Levi Hammond, but you cannot rent me."

"Captain," said Thomas, "we have been informed that you know Charleston harbor so well that you don't need a pilot to enter or leave it. We would need your services as well as your ship. One without the other would be superfluous."

"I repeat, gentlemen, I am a Quaker. I will not take part in an act of war."

"You won't be taking part in an act of war," said

Thomas. "You will merely be delivering men and supplies to Fort Sumter."

"Soldiers and war materiel, Colonel. Pawns and tools for waging war. I will have no part in it."

"But don't you see, Captain Chase?" argued Thomas. "Using a civilian ship to deliver reinforcements and supplies to Fort Sumter is intended as a peaceful gesture to the Carolinians. You would be serving the cause of peace in this matter."

"I doubt that the Carolinians will construe your gesture as peaceful any more than they took Major Anderson's investment of Fort Sumter as a peaceful gesture. No, sir, the Carolinians will fire on any ship attempting to bring aid to Fort Sumter, even under the cover of darkness. My employer has the right to risk his property in such a venture, but he does not have the right to risk my life or the lives of my crew without their consent."

"We are prepared to pay you handsomely, Captain Chase," said Lacy.

"Keep your money, sir. I have made my position on this matter perfectly clear. Find yourselves another man, and while you're at it, why don't you find yourselves another ship? I'm rather attached to this one, and I'd hate to see any harm come to her." He turned and looked at the craft tied up in the next slip. "Why not take the *Star?* She's seen this sort of action before."

"The *Star?*" queried Thomas.

"Yes," said Chase. "The *Star of the West*. Surely you remember how the *Star* was used to transport William Walker and his filibusters to Nicaragua back in '55?"

"I recall Walker," said Thomas, "but I've never heard of the ship until now."

"If you recall Walker, sir," said Chase, "then don't you think it appropriate that the same ship that carried so many Southern filibusters to Nicaragua to enslave that tiny nation should be the ship to carry stores and soldiers to Fort Sumter to pound a stake in the heart of Southern slavocracy? Think of the irony of it, Colonel.''

Thomas smiled and said, ''Yes, it would be most ironic that Walker's ship should be the one to reinforce Anderson. You know, Captain Chase, I believe General Scott would appreciate the irony of it as well. Thank you, sir, for suggesting it. Is this ship owned by your company?''

''No, sir. The *Star* is owned by the M. O. Roberts Shipping Line. Mr. Roberts lives in an apartment above his offices.'' He pointed out the building.

''Very good, Captain. I thank you again.''

''Although I am a man of peace,'' said Chase, ''I wish you well in this venture, Colonel Thomas.''

''Thank you, Captain Chase,'' said Thomas. Over his shoulder, he said, ''Come along, gentlemen. We must find Mr. Roberts and see if he will rent his ship to us.''

Colonel Thomas and his entourage found Marshall O. Roberts at home that forenoon. The shipping magnate was just sitting down to lunch when they knocked at his door.

''Mr. Roberts?'' queried Thomas.

''Who wants to know?'' groused Roberts. He was a man well past his prime with tufts of gray hair at his temples and practically no hair at all elsewhere. His face was severely lined with age, and his shoulders bowed inward, putting a hunch in his spine.

''Are you Marshall Roberts?'' insisted Thomas.

''And I said, who wants to know?''

''I am an agent for the United States government, sir,'' said Thomas, ''and I have come here on a most important matter of business.''

''Government agent?'' queried Roberts. He squinted a palsied eye at Thomas, then at the other officers.

"You look like military men to me. What would the army want from me?"

"Mr. Roberts, may we come in?" asked Thomas. "Our business with you needs to be conducted in privacy."

"There's nobody here except me, but if you need to talk in private, then come in and we'll talk."

Thomas led the group into the sparsely furnished parlor of the shipping magnate's living quarters. The room resembled the captain's cabin on a clipper ship with the single exception of a sofa in the place of a bunk.

"Mr. Roberts," said the general, "you must swear to me that the business we are about to transact will be kept in the utmost secrecy. No one other than yourself is to be made party to these discussions, no matter what their outcome. Is that understood, sir?"

"Got something to do with Fort Sumter, I'll bet."

Thomas blanched, regained his composure, and said, "A very astute supposition, sir. I take my hat off to you."

Roberts glared at the plug hat on the general's head and said, "Then why don't you?"

Thomas removed his hat, and the other officers did likewise.

Roberts sat in the only chair at the captain's table, looked up at Thomas, and said, "Let's see here. We've established that you are military men who want to do business with me, probably rent one of my ships to take supplies to Fort Sumter. Am I right so far?" Before Thomas could reply, he added, "Oh, yes, and all this is supposed to be kept secret."

"That's correct, sir," said Thomas.

"Out with it, man!" snapped Roberts. "Who are you and exactly what is it that you want?"

"Do you swear to keep our business here secret, Mr. Roberts?"

"I don't tell anybody my business, sir. Ask anybody on the waterfront. They'll tell you."

Thomas nodded and said, "Very well then. I am Colonel Lorenzo Thomas, adjutant to General Scott." He performed a half-turn and waved a casual arm toward the other officers. "These gentlemen are posted here in New York. We have come to rent your ship the *Star of the West*. We understand that it is most suited for the task we have in mind for it."

"*Star of the West*, you say? You must want her to carry a lot more than just supplies to Fort Sumter. I understand Walker put a couple hundred men on her when he went down to Nicaragua. Is that how many you're planning to send to Anderson?"

"Possibly," said Thomas.

Roberts nodded grimly and said, "Two hundred men and supplies. How many warships are going with her?"

"None," said Thomas.

"No warships? Are you planning to get my ship sunk in Charleston harbor?"

"No, sir. The *Star of the West* will enter the harbor during the night and unload her cargo and return to the open sea before daylight."

"My captain doesn't know Charleston harbor very well," said Roberts. "You'll need to hire a pilot to go along."

"Do you know one?" asked Thomas.

"I can get one for you, but first there's the matter of the *Star*. She'll cost you fifteen hundred dollars a day and fuel costs."

"Your government is only willing to pay you one thousand dollars a day," said Thomas, "and no fuel costs."

"I'll need at least twelve hundred fifty dollars a day and fuel costs," said Roberts, "and insurance by the government against the *Star* being damaged or lost."

"Twelve hundred fifty dollars and our word that

should anything happen to your ship, the government will compensate you accordingly. That is my final offer, sir."

"How many days?" asked Roberts.

"Eight," said Thomas.

"Ten," said Roberts, "and I'll pay the pilot, captain, and crew."

Thomas thrust out his hand and said, "We have a bargain, sir."

Sarah Hammond was furious with Aquila Chase. "Father had the contracts all prepared, Cousin," she said as she paced his cabin aboard the *Dover White*. "All you had to do was cooperate."

"I will not be a party to an act of war," said Chase calmly, "and I'm surprised and just a little disappointed that you, Sarah Hammond, would want to be a part of this business with the army."

"Part of it? I'm at the center of it. I'm the one who suggested to General Scott that he employ a civilian ship to convey supplies and soldiers to Fort Sumter under cover of darkness. He would have used a warship and gone into Charleston harbor in broad daylight with all guns firing. That, dear cousin, would have been an act of war. The *Dover White* entering the harbor during the night would pass the guard boats without a problem because it's a Hammond ship."

"A Hammond ship?" queried Chase. "What does that have to do with anything?"

"During my recent journey in the South, I made it quite clear to the governors of several states that, politics to the contrary, we still intend to do business with the planters and factors of their states. The Carolinians would never fire on a Hammond ship, especially after I send word to Governor Pickens that you are coming."

"But we would be going to Fort Sumter," said

Chase. "Don't you think Governor Pickens would feel betrayed once he learns of the deception?"

"Only if he learns of it, Cousin," said Sarah. "Part of my message to him would be that you would be removing the dependents of the garrison from Fort Sumter, which you would do. Remember Caduceus? My ally whose message you delivered to me in Washington?"

"Yes, I recall that."

"Part of my plan is to send him word that you would be coming to Fort Sumter, and he is to ready the dependents for departure on the *Dover White*. You would convey soldiers and supplies to Fort Sumter, then remove the innocent children and wives of the garrison to safety in the North. That, dear cousin, would have been a humanitarian deed."

"Why wasn't I told this before?"

"I didn't think it would be necessary," said Sarah. "I thought surely that you would cooperate with Colonel Thomas, and that would be that. On the day that you would have departed, I would have given the details of the plan in a letter that you would not read until you were at sea and it was too late to turn back."

"You should have told me this before, Sarah."

"I realize that now, but the time is already past for regrets. We must move ahead. Somehow, we must use the *Star of the West* to carry out my plan to rescue those women and children from harm's way."

19~

Wednesday, January 2, 1861

"As of last night," said Governor Pickens to the gathering of military men in his office, "the U.S.S. *Brooklyn* still lay at anchor at Hampton Roads, Virginia. Three companies of infantry from Fort Monroe and enough provisions for three months remain on board. I expect to hear from our informant at any moment about whether the *Brooklyn* weighed anchor durin' the night and set a course for our harbor. If she has, then the earliest we can expect her is tomorrow afternoon. More likely, if she left Hampton Roads last night, she will attempt to enter the harbor at first light on Friday. My question to you all is this: Will we be ready to repulse the invader?"

"The *General Clinch* will spread the alarm, sir," said Lieutenant Ryan of the Irish Volunteers, "as soon as the *Brooklyn* comes into sight. We'll run into the harbor firin' rockets to alert the batteries and the city, then we'll come about and face the enemy head on."

"Very commendable, Lieutenant Ryan," said Pickens, "but the *General Clinch* would better serve us by continuin' to the docks of Charleston and stayin' out of the *Brooklyn*'s way. From what I understand, she has more than enough armament to defeat ten steamers

the likes of the *Nina* and the *General Clinch*. If the
Brooklyn comes in sight, you just spread the alarm,
then take cover up the Cooper.'' He focused on another
officer. ''What about your batteries on Morris Island,
Major Stevens? Are your cadets ready for a fight?''

''We drill them constantly, sir,'' said Stevens. ''The
Brooklyn will be hard-pressed to get past our brave
boys from the Citadel.''

''Confidence is good, Major,'' said Pickens, ''but I
hardly think your four howitzers along the channel or
your thirty-two-pounders at Cummings Point will do
little more than slow the *Brooklyn*'s progress through
the channel. I suggest you get in as many shots at the
invader as you can before he can find the range to your
guns, and as soon as he does mark the distance, you
take those boys of yours and get them the hell out of
there. We'll need them more than ever, if the *Brooklyn*
should make it safely into our harbor.''

Stevens nodded, his face grim with cold reality.

''How are you comin' at remountin' the guns of Fort
Moultrie, Colonel DeSaussure?'' asked Pickens.

''A few are ready for a fight right now, Governor,''
said DeSaussure, ''and a few more will be ready on
the morrow. Not enough, I'm afraid to say, to hold off
the *Brooklyn* or even put up a good fight against Fort
Sumter. In fact, sir, I doubt if all the guns were ready
that we could defeat the *Brooklyn* by herself or Fort
Sumter alone. Facin' both of them simultaneously could
prove disastrous for us.''

''You will have your men work on those guns day
and night until all are ready for battle, Colonel,'' said
Pickens. ''What you say in this room may be true.
Maybe they won't be enough to defeat the *Brooklyn* or
Fort Sumter, but then again, if your boys get in a few
good licks, just maybe the *Brooklyn* will turn tail and
run on out of here again. No matter though. For now,
you keep your assessment of the situation under your

hat. The same goes for all of you. We mustn't let the people or our valiant soldiers know that we face a grave danger in the *Brooklyn* as well as Fort Sumter. We must continue to reassure them that we have the situation well in hand. Is that clear, gentlemen?''

All nodded their understanding.

''Governor,'' said Ryan, ''if I might make a suggestion on how to deal with the *Brooklyn* if she should try to enter the harbor?''

''By all means, Lieutenant, make your suggestion,'' said Pickens. ''I'm more than willin' to listen to any fresh ideas on how we can defend this fair city from the Yankee invader. It's why I called you all here.''

''Thank you, sir,'' said Ryan. ''Well, sir, it came to me that we could block the channel by scuttlin' the *General Clinch* as soon as the *Brooklyn* shows her colors on the horizon. No ship would be able to pass through the channel, and that would afford us the time to deal with Fort Sumter.''

''Not a bad idea, Lieutenant,'' said Pickens, ''but better than that, we could scuttle the *General Clinch* in front of the *Brooklyn* and the *Nina* behind her. Then we'd have the *Brooklyn* trapped, a sittin' duck, if you will, for Major Stevens and his cadets.''

''What about the infantry aboard the *Brooklyn,* Governor?'' asked Colonel Cunningham. ''Surely, they would be landed on Morris Island, if the *Brooklyn* were trapped in the channel. Three hundred seasoned soldiers would make short work of the cadets. We must address that possibility as well, sir.''

Before Pickens could formulate a reply, Colonel Allston entered the room bearing a message for the governor. His face beamed with good news.

''What is the word, Colonel Allston?'' asked Pickens.

''At daylight this mornin','' said Allston, ''the

Brooklyn was still ridin' her anchor at Hampton Roads, Governor.''

A collective sigh of relief filled the room, followed immediately by a chorus of cheers.

"Gentlemen, if you please?" asked Pickens, restoring decorum to the meeting. "We are not out of the woods yet. Just because the fox is still in his lair doesn't mean we can quit guardin' the chicken coop. It only means we've got us another full day to prepare for the *Brooklyn*'s arrival. Now let's get to it." His eye caught a questioning look on Cunningham's face. "Oh, yes, Colonel Cunningham, your concern about Yankee infantry landin' on Morris Island. I'll give it some thought, and I'd like each of you gentlemen to do likewise. Think about how we should deal with that possibility, and we'll discuss it at tomorrow mornin's meetin'."

"Thank you, Governor," said Cunningham, "but there's also the matter of Fort Johnson. It just sits there, waitin' to be occupied."

"And it faces Fort Sumter," said Pickens. "Very good, Colonel. Send a detachment to occupy Fort Johnson and begin mountin' guns there as well."

"Yes, sir."

"Now let's get to work on our defenses while we still have time to build them."

"We have done all that we could," said Orr as he sipped coffee in the Trescot parlor with his host, his fellow commissioners, and Senators Clay and Wigfall. "Buchanan will not budge from his stance on Fort Sumter. We have no choice except to return to home and admit our defeat to Governor Pickens."

"I can't believe he doesn't think Fort Sumter is a threat to Charleston," said Barnwell. "How did he put it in his letter, James?"

"He said Fort Sumter would be defended," said Orr,

"and that he did not, and I quote, 'perceive how such a defense can be construed into a menace of the city of Charleston.' "

"Isn't that incredible?" said Barnwell. "Fort Sumter's guns could level Charleston at any time Major Anderson should wish to do so, and he doesn't perceive that as a menace to Charleston. What was his justification for takin' this stance, James?"

"Our so-called armed action against Federal property," said Orr.

"Yes, that's it," said Barnwell. "Anderson makes the first hostile move by occupyin' Fort Sumter, and he has the audacity to tell us that we started it."

"He accuses us of bullyin' him," said Adams, "by statin' that we have urged him to withdraw the troops from the harbor of Charleston, and until he does, we have said that negotiation is impossible. I don't recall any of us puttin' it exactly like that."

"It makes no difference now," said Orr. "The die is cast. He will not remove Anderson from our midst, and he intends to reinforce and resupply Fort Sumter within the week. As we wrote to him already, my friends, he has most likely rendered civil war between the states inevitable."

"My state will secede within the week," said Clay. "I expect the announcement at any time."

"You can bet that Georgia, Florida, Louisiana, and Mississippi will also secede in the next week or so," said Wigfall. "Texas and the rest of the South will soon follow, and before spring, we will forge a new and greater nation on this continent. A confederacy where the rights of the states will be observed by the national government. When you gentlemen return to South Carolina, tell your people that they stand alone today, but very soon they will be standin' shoulder to shoulder with the rest of the South against the tyranny of the Yankees."

"We will certainly do that, Senator," said Orr.

"In the meantime," said Wigfall, "we will keep a close watch on our enemies here in Washington City."

"And elsewhere," said Clay.

"Yes, of course," said Wigfall. "Floyd has men watchin' the *Brooklyn* around the clock. The moment she pulls up her anchor, the word will be spread across the South like a prairie fire bein' whipped up by a cyclone. You will not have to face the Yankees alone, gentlemen. As God is my witness, you can bank on that much."

Lacy never did come around to Louisa's apartment on New Year's Day, leaving Louisa with only her imagination.

After returning home from Manhattan, Louisa put pen to paper and wrote a letter to Rafe Sims, telling him about what she and Hattie had witnessed that afternoon and offering speculation on its meaning. She assumed that the *Dover White* would convey the soldiers from Fort Jay to Fort Monroe to replace those being sent to Fort Sumter aboard the *Brooklyn,* and she surmised that the sailing of the *Dover White* would precipitate the movement of the *Brooklyn*. However, she didn't expect this movement to come any earlier than Thursday, the third of January, because the *Dover White* appeared to be unprepared for going to sea.

The next morning, Louisa awakened early, dressed in a hurry, and without telling Hattie where she was going, rushed off to the ferry landing to take the first boat across the East River to New York. She caught a hansom at the Manhattan dock and told the driver to swing by the Warren Street wharf before taking her to the Jersey City ferry. As the cab passed the *Dover White*'s slip, she noted little activity around the ship and no cargo waiting on the pier to be loaded on the steamer.

Maybe I was wrong about this ship, she thought. No, I couldn't be. I saw Johnny and Colonel Thomas and those other officers aboard her only yesterday. If they weren't plannin' to hire the *Dover White,* then what were they doin' aboard her? They must be up to something, and the *Dover White* and that Hammond woman are involved in it some way. That Hammond woman. Maybe I should find out more about her before I go off half-cocked about the *Dover White* and look foolish. Yes, better to be sure than have Rafe think me a silly girl buttin' in where I shouldn't be.

"Driver, take me back to the Brooklyn ferry landin'," she said through the screen behind her head. A second thought occurred to her. "No, forget that. Take me to the offices of the Levi Hammond Shipping Line instead."

In a few minutes, the cabbie reined in his horse in front of the Hammond building. He dismounted and helped Louisa from the carriage. She paid him the exact fare and nothing more.

The hour had yet to reach seven when the workday would begin on the waterfront, but already several stevedores were assembling near the doors of the shipping companies, hoping to find work that day. As starting time approached, they increased in number, until the cargo boss magically appeared in their midst and began signing them on for a day's labor.

Louisa waited patiently for the longshoremen to leave for the wharves, then she stepped up to the cargo boss. "Excuse me, sir," she said, "but might I inquire about this company from you?"

The burly, bearded, pot-bellied foreman tipped his hat and said, "Yes, ma'am. Frank Roderus at your service. Ask me anything you like. I know this company like the back of my hand. What is it you want to know?"

Louisa could see that he was taken in by her looks,

and she intended to take advantage of his surge of desire. "I attended a New Year's ball where a lady was pointed out to me as being the daughter of the owner of this company. Her name was Sarah, I believe. I didn't get an opportunity to meet her, so I thought I would come down here and inquire after her. Do you know of her?"

"Yes, ma'am, that would be Miss Sarah Hammond, Mr. Hammond's daughter," said the cargo boss. "She's just like her grandmother. She's named for her, too. Quite a young woman, Miss Sarah. She knows the business as well as her father. Maybe even better than he does."

"You make it sound like she works here."

"She used to. Not anymore though. She quit some time back and went into the family banking business for a while. Then she quit that last year to travel. Spent a lot of time in the South, I hear. Even bought herself a female slave down to New Orleans and freed her as soon as they got back to New York. Of course, that's not surprising. Miss Sarah is a Quaker, you know. Quakers are opposed to slavery and all such things."

"Isn't that interestin'?" said Louisa. "Her buyin' and freein' a slave, I mean. Not many people have that kind of money to throw away on a Negress."

"The Hammonds have lots of money. Wouldn't surprise me none if they bought a whole plantation full of slaves and set them free."

"From what you're sayin'," said Louisa, "I take it the Hammonds are fairly influential people."

"You'd be right there, ma'am. It was Miss Sarah's grandmother who got Bill Seward elected to the statehouse back when, and Mr. Hammond and his brothers helped Mr. Lincoln carry New York in the last election."

"I thought as much just from looking at Miss Hammond at the ball. She seemed like such a regal lady, attired as she was and the way she carried herself.''

"*Regal* is a good word for Miss Sarah. A good word for all the Hammond ladies that I've met over the years.''

"And from what I've seen, it's a good word for the Hammond ships. Like the one tied up over yonder.''

"You mean the *Dover White,* ma'am?''

"Yes, that one. It seems to be a regal ship. One that would sail the seas with pride.''

"Yes, ma'am. The *Dover White* is a proud ship. She recently returned from Charleston. Her master is Captain Aquila Chase, a cousin of Miss Sarah.''

"And will she be returning to Charleston soon?''

"No, her next destination is Liverpool.''

"I see.'' Louisa wanted to make a few inquiries about the *Dover White,* but she resisted the urge, thinking she shouldn't press her luck with this man; he might get suspicious if she asked too many questions. Instead of asking him anything else, she said, "Well, you've been most helpful, Mr. Roderus. Thank you and good day.''

"You're most welcome, ma'am, and good day to you, too.''

Louisa walked away thinking that she had struck pay-dirt. A rich Yankee bitch, she thought. Rich enough to buy a nigra wench and set her free without givin' it a second thought. A rich, nigra-lovin', Black Republican Yankee from a seafarin' family that helped get that Black Republican Lincoln elected to the White House. And her daddy owns a ship that recently came from Charleston, and never mind what that fool said about the *Dover White* goin' off to Liverpool next. That's just a story to make folks think nothin's doin' with the *Dover White* reinforcin' Fort Sumter. I was right. Miss Sarah Hammond and her family are involved with reinforcin' Fort Sumter. I think I'll have to rewrite my letter to Rafe. He'll be real interested in readin' this.

"Please sit down, Colonel Thomas," said Buchanan.

"Thank you, Mr. President," said Thomas, taking the right chair in front of the president's desk.

Occupying the other was Joseph Holt, formerly the postmaster general and now Buchanan's secretary of war.

"You look exhausted, Colonel," said Buchanan. "May I have my secretary get you a cup of coffee or some other libation?"

"Coffee would be fine, sir," said Thomas. "I took the first train from New York this morning, and with everything else yesterday, it's been a long year already."

"And I don't think it will get any shorter with the passing of the calendar," said Buchanan. "Excuse me for just a moment, Colonel." He stepped around the desk, went to the door, opened it, and told his secretary to order some coffee and cookies for Thomas. In another few seconds, he was seated behind his desk again. "If you wish, you can begin your briefing now, Colonel."

"Yes, sir," said Thomas. "General Scott sends his apologies, Mr. President. He would have come himself, but the gout has him laid up for the moment."

"We all have our frailties and infirmities, don't we, Colonel?" said Holt.

"Yes, sir, I suppose we do," said Thomas, trying not to look directly at the president's twisted neck.

"Proceed, Colonel," said Buchanan, just a little annoyed by Holt's interruption.

"Yes, sir." Thomas cleared his throat, then said, "Sir, General Scott wishes to modify the plan to reinforce Major Anderson at Fort Sumter."

Buchanan frowned and said, "How so?"

"Instead of sending the *Brooklyn* with three companies of infantry from Fort Monroe, General Scott would like to send two companies of infantry from Fort Jay aboard an unarmed civilian ship."

"An unarmed civilian ship?" queried Holt. "Has Scott gone mad?"

"No, sir, quite the contrary," said Thomas. "General Scott fears that removing the *Brooklyn* from Hampton Roads and troops from Fort Monroe will weaken the defenses of the Norfolk Navy Yard and Washington City, and he believes a civilian ship is less likely to be fired upon by the rebels than a ship of the line, sir."

"Rebels, Colonel?" asked Holt. "Is that what we are calling the secessionists now?"

"The New York newspapers are using the term, sir," said Thomas, "and naturally, the people are adopting it. Of course, the actions of the Carolinians are those of rebels against the Federal government, are they not, sir?"

"Yes, I suppose they are," said Holt, "which is exactly why we need to send the *Brooklyn* into Charleston harbor with supplies and reinforcements for Major Anderson. An unarmed civilian ship won't be able to withstand an artillery barrage from the Carolinians guns at Fort Moultrie."

"General Scott has thought of that contingency, sir," said Thomas. "It's his intention to have the *Star of the West* enter the harbor—"

"The *Star of the West?*" interjected Holt. "Isn't that the ship that took Walker and his filibusters to Nicaragua?"

"Yes, sir, it is," said Thomas. "General Scott charged me with hiring a civilian ship for this task, recommending the *Dover White* of the Levi Hammond Shipping Line, but her captain balked at accepting the mission. However, he did recommend the *Star of the West,* and we thought it would be ironic that the same ship that Walker used to spread slavery to Nicaragua should be the one to convey our soldiers into the heart of the slave states.''

Buchanan smiled and said, ''Yes, I see the irony of it as well. Proceed, Colonel.''

''Well, sir, General Scott intends to have the *Star of the West* enter the harbor just before daylight and discharge the troops and supplies under the covering fire of Fort Sumter. It's the general's summation that even if the Carolinians are able to remount all of Fort Moultrie's guns, they will still be no match for Anderson's artillery. He's confident that the Carolinians will have no choice except to cease fire and allow the landing of the reinforcements and the unloading of the supplies.''

''Tell me, Colonel,'' said Buchanan, ''why did General Scott change his mind about the *Brooklyn?* When we spoke Sunday last right here in this office, he seemed so positive that a warship was absolutely essential to his strategy to reinforce and resupply Major Anderson. What changed his mind? You mentioned the Levi Hammond Shipping Line. Did Miss Sarah Hammond have something to do with it?''

''Yes, sir, she did,'' said Thomas.

A wry smile curled Buchanan's lips as he said, ''I should have known that she would badger him into changing his plan. When did she do this, Colonel?''

''She attended the army-navy ball at Fort Jay on New Year's Eve, sir,'' said Thomas.

''And how much had General Scott had to drink when he conversed with her?'' asked Buchanan.

''Not so much as one drink, sir. His gout worried him too much to imbibe that night.''

''I see,'' said Buchanan.

The president's secretary brought a silver coffee service into the room and served Buchanan and his guests. As soon as he departed, the briefing continued.

''It seems to me,'' said Holt, ''that this plan is

fraught with danger. An unarmed civilian ship is not made to withstand cannonballs. We would be putting two hundred soldiers at hazard, not to mention the captain and crew of the ship.''

''The ship will be commanded by Captain John McGowan of the Revenue Service,'' said Thomas. ''He is much experienced in this sort of thing.''

''If I understand you correctly, Colonel,'' said the president, ''the success of this plan is contingent upon Major Anderson protecting the *Star of the West* once it enters Charleston harbor. Is that not correct?''

''Yes, sir, it is,'' said Thomas. ''A message detailing the plan should be sent to Major Anderson so he can make preparations for defending the *Star of the West*.''

''Yes, of course,'' said Buchanan, ''Major Anderson must be notified of the change in plan.'' He smirked and added, ''Good God, we haven't even told him about the original plan yet, and now we shall notify him of the change in it. He will certainly think us daft, won't he?''

''You needn't worry about that, Mr. President,'' said Holt. ''If you approve of this change, I will send a detailed message of it to Major Anderson.''

''Thank you, Joseph,'' said Buchanan. ''I confess my reluctance to approve this plan, but I have to put my trust in General Scott in these matters. All right, Colonel Thomas, do you have orders for us to sign?''

20 ～

Thursday, January 3, 1861

Scuttlebutt travels faster than a tidal wave from bow to stern on even the largest ships of the line. On land it takes a little longer.

Commander Sims heard about the order for the *Brooklyn* to stand down from its preparations to go to sea as soon as he walked into the Navy Department Thursday morning. Trying not to raise suspicion about his motives for asking, he verified the truth to the rumor within the hour, then made an excuse for leaving the building. He had to tell Senator Clay about the *Brooklyn*'s new orders as soon as possible.

"Are you certain of this news, Commander?" asked Clay. He and Sims stood in the library of the senator's home.

"Yes, sir," said Sims. "The order was issued last night, and it was signed by the president himself. The three companies of infantry were ordered back to Fort Monroe, and the supplies aboard *Brooklyn* are to be returned to the supply depot at Norfolk."

"I wonder," said Clay. "Does this mean that Buchanan is backin' down? That he won't try to reinforce Fort Sumter at all? Maybe the Hammond woman was able to convince him after all?"

"Perhaps she was successful in convincin' General Scott to revise his plan to reinforce Anderson," said Sims.

"Yes, that's probably it. You did say she was goin' to New York to speak with him, didn't you?"

"Yes, sir, and yesterday, General Scott's adjutant, Colonel Thomas, visited the White House. Perhaps he brought word from General Scott that there would be a change of their plan."

"Most likely," said Clay. He smiled and added, "This is good news, Commander. I've been plannin' to return to Alabama within the week, and now I can go home secure in the knowledge that war between the states has been averted. If not forever, then at least for the time bein'." He slapped Sims on the shoulder and said, "Yes, Commander, this is wonderful news."

Sims frowned as he said, "You're returnin' home, sir? Does that mean Alabama will secede soon?"

Clay's smile vanished as he said, "Senator Davis has already left for Mississippi, and Senator Toombs is plannin' to leave for Georgia soon. Senator Benjamin left for Louisiana this mornin', but before departin', he met with Buchanan and told him that within the week Mississippi, Florida, and Alabama would leave the Union. He also told the president that he felt civil war between the states was inevitable, and he vowed that the South would never surrender to Yankee tyranny. He gave me a copy of the letter he left with Buchanan. Allow me to read the last of it to you."

Clay picked up a folded sheet of paper from his desk, spread it between his hands, and read: "You may carry desolation into our peaceful land, and with torch and firebrand may set our cities in flames; you may even emulate the atrocities of those who in the days of our Revolution hounded on the bloodthirsty savage; you may give the protection of your advancing armies to the furious fanatics who desire nothing more than to add the horrors of servile insurrection to civil war; you may do this and more, but you can never subjugate us: you can never degrade us into a servile and inferior race—never, never, never!''

A brief silence.

''Strong words, sir,'' said Sims softly.

''Senator Benjamin only expressed what so many of us in the South feel so deeply in our hearts. The separation of North and South is inevitable, Commander. Several states have already called for conventions to decide not *whether* they shall secede from the Union but *when*. I expect the votes for secession will be near unanimous in every state of the South, Alabama included.''

''But how soon, sir, before Alabama takes a vote?''

Clay shrugged and said, ''I can only reiterate what Senator Benjamin told the president. Within the week, maybe two weeks, but not much longer than that. Don't you worry about it, Commander. We need you here in Washington for the time bein', listenin' and watchin' those men who would wish us ill. When you're needed elsewhere, word will be sent to you and hundreds of other officers of the navy and army throughout the country. First, secession, then the forgin' of a confederation of slaveholding states. After that, we'll need officers for an army and a navy to defend our new nation against Yankee tyranny. Be patient, Commander. You will be called . . . in due time.''

Governor Pickens received Senator Wigfall's telegram with great relief. The Southron informant at Hampton Roads had sent a message earlier in the day that the *Brooklyn* had been ordered to stand down and that the three infantry companies had been ordered back to Fort Monroe, but until more official word was received, the Carolinians refused to rejoice over what they perceived as a victory, especially since Pickens had heard that Adams, Barnwell, and Orr were returning to South Carolina, having conceded that their negotiations with President Buchanan had proven fruitless.

"We have accomplished nothin' yet," the governor cautioned his staff and the militia officers gathered about him in his office at the Mills House. "Major Anderson continues to occupy Fort Sumter, and the threat of his guns being brought to bear on Charleston still exists. We must remain vigilant against the possibility that the Federals will still send a warship to his aid. For all we know, Buchanan and Scott may be plannin' to send the entire fleet against us. We have no way of knowin' what all their ships are up to."

Colonel Alston burst into the room. "Governor, there's news from Georgia," he said, his voice quavering with excitement. "The Georgia militia has seized Fort Pulaski, Fort Jackson, and the Federal arsenal at Savannah."

"Are you certain of this, Colonel?" asked Pickens, not fully believing Allston.

"Yes, sir. Here is the telegram from Governor Brown." He handed the message to Pickens.

The governor smiled as he read the words, then said, "We are no longer alone, gentlemen. Georgia is with us now."

"Huzzah!" they cheered. "Huzzah!"

Within the hour, the news had spread throughout the city, causing widespread celebration among the citizenry, the din of which awakened George Salter from an alcohol-induced slumber. He rolled over in Juanita's bed, felt her naked warmth radiating against his bare chest, opened his eyes to confirm his consciousness, then tentatively reached for his aching head as someone most unwelcome and most unforgiving pounded on the door.

"George, are you in there, ol' friend?"

Damn! thought Salter. It's Ty. "Go away!" he

shouted without thinking of the consequences: his brain slamming against the interior wall of his cranium.

"Quit fuckin' that girl, George," said Harris through the door, "and get on out here. There's history happenin' again. The Georgia militia just took Fort Pulaski from the Federals."

Fort Pulaski? wondered Salter, the fog in his head beginning to burn away. "Where's that?" he asked aloud. He struggled to sit up.

"What is it, Georgie?" asked Juanita, stirring in the bed beside him. Backside to him, she lifted her head enough to look over her shoulder at him.

Salter patted her buttocks affectionately and said, "It's only Ty, *cara mia*. You go back to sleep while I talk to him."

"Come on, George," said Harris. "Open up."

"No, you stay with me today," she said, sitting up and gripping his arm firmly. "We make love today without the wine."

"We will, Juanita, we will. I promise. But first I must talk to Ty."

"George, you're missin' it," said Harris.

"I'm coming, Ty."

"Fine," said Harris. "Shoot your wad, then get your Yankee ass out of that bed and come on out here."

"I meant I'm up, Ty."

"Well, you'd better be if you're comin'," said Harris before bursting into laughter.

"Stay with me, Georgie," said Juanita, pouting.

"I came back the last time I said I would, didn't I?" Seeing her nod, he continued, "Well, I promise I'll come back again. I promise, *cara mia*." He slid out of bed, found his clothes, and dressed hurriedly. His head hurt, but a desire to be a witness to history, if not a part of it, overwhelmed the debilitating effects of the previous night's wine. As he reached for the door handle, he took one last look at Juanita and said, "I'll be back, and this time no wine." As he opened the door, he thought, Who are you fooling, Georgie boy? Without Madeira, you're just another short-horned buck in the rut.

"It's about time, George," said Harris when Salter finally emerged from Juanita's boudoir.

"Now what's this all about, Ty?" asked Salter as he closed the door behind him. "Where's this Fort Pulaski you're talking about?"

"It's in Georgia. Why would the Georgia militia bother capturin' it if it was somewhere else?"

"Where at in Georgia?"

"Savannah. It's in the harbor there, the same as Fort Sumter is here. Leastways, I think it is."

"How did you find this out?" asked Salter.

"I just came from the newspaper, the *Mercury*. Mr. Robert Barnwell Rhett, the owner and editor, just got it off the telegraph wires, and he's spreadin' the word. The South is risin', son."

"I hear music outside," said Salter, his eyes shifting toward the window at the end of the hall. "Has someone struck up a band because the Georgians took Fort Pulaski?"

"That's only part of it, George. The Georgians also captured Fort Jackson and the Federal arsenal at Savannah. And there's more. You know those stories we've been hearin' about Buchanan sendin' a warship down here to reinforce Anderson?"

"What about them?"

"Well, they were true, but now they're not. I mean, there was a warship comin' here, but now there isn't. It's stayin' up in Virginia instead of comin' here."

"It is?" queried Salter. It is? he asked himself as well. Now what?

"Sure, it is," said Harris. "Those Yankees know better than to come down here lookin' for a fight. Present company excepted, of course, because you're not lookin' for a fight, just a little piece of history and a good piece of ass.'' He glanced back at Juanita's door. ''And I'd say you've pretty much found the latter.''

To hide his real thoughts, Salter said, ''That's right, Ty, and now that I've found the one, let's go find some more of the other. What do you say we hire a boat to take us out to Fort Sumter so we can see what Anderson thinks about being cut adrift by President Buchanan?''

''Oh, we can't do that, George. Governor Pickens has cut off all communications with Fort Sumter except through his own couriers. He's stopped the mail from bein' delivered, and he's passed the word that nobody's to sell any food to the Yankees. Only the workers the Federals hired are allowed to go out to Fort Sumter.''

''I guess the governor wants the fort finished before he takes it away from Anderson.''

''More than that, the militia is mountin' more guns at Fort Johnson and Cummings Point. It looks to me like the governor's plannin' to lay siege to Fort Sumter.''

''Yes, I guess it does,'' said Salter. To himself, he added, And those poor bastards out there on that rock don't even know it.

Frustration seemed to be dogging Sarah Hammond's every step. First, Buchanan wouldn't order Anderson back to Fort Moultrie, then he and General Scott came up with a plan to reinforce Fort Sumter. After she made some headway by convincing Scott to employ a civilian ship instead of using a frigate, Scott's adjutant passed over the *Dover White* for the *Star of the West*. Now Sarah wanted to speak to Scott about hiring Aquila Chase as the pilot for the *Star of the West*, and she was making no progress whatsoever.

Sarah went to General Scott's home in New York the day after New Year's, but she was turned away by an orderly who said the general wasn't receiving any visitors due to his condition. "The gout, you know. Try again tomorrow, Miss." Out of disappointment, she called on her father at his office on Warren Street.

"Father, I need your help again," she said as she stood in front of his desk instead of sitting in the hardest, most uncomfortable chair in the building, the one Levi Hammond was given by his mother as a lesson in business: "Never let anybody get the upper hand in a negotiation, Levi. You start by putting them ill-at-ease when they sit across the table from you." The elder Sarah Hammond gave each of her other sons an identical chair.

"Certainly, Sally, but what more can we do? We offered the *Dover White* to General Scott, but Colonel Thomas went elsewhere. What more can we do than that?"

"I want Aquila to be the pilot on the *Star of the West.*"

"Aquila the pilot on the *Star of the West?* Whatever on earth for, Sally?"

"Father, I have a spy in Charleston, and he informed me long ago that the dependents of the garrison at Fort Moultrie, now at Fort Sumter, are in grave danger should there be a battle. I am hoping that Aquila, with the aid of my spy, can convince Major Anderson to evacuate those women and children from Fort Sumter aboard the *Star of the West*. Then no innocents will be left in harm's way."

"I see," said Levi. "That explains why you were so vehement about General Scott hiring the *Dover White* from us."

"Yes, it does. It's too late for that now, but it's not too late to get Aquila aboard the *Star of the West.*"

"But why talk to me about this now, Sally? You should have said something sooner about this. I could have told Aquila to mind his manners with Colonel Thomas and accept the charter."

"Yes, Father, I know. I've already had this discussion with Aquila. That time is past. Now we must move in another direction, and that is to put Aquila on the *Star of the West* as the pilot."

"And how do you intend to do that?" asked Levi.

"I went to General Scott's home this morning to make that request, but I was turned away by his orderly. I left my card with a note on it about using Aquila as the pilot, but I don't think it did much good. During our conversation the other night at the ball, I got the impression that General Scott wasn't too enamored with me. He's a Southerner with Southern attitudes about women being seen and not heard, especially when it comes to politics and business. I don't think he will respond to my call this morning, and that is where you come in, Father. I would like you to call on him and request that Aquila be hired as the pilot of the *Star of the West*. Would you be willing to do that, Father?"

"Certainly, Sally. I'll go by his house first thing this afternoon."

Good to his word, Levi Hammond called on Scott that afternoon, but he was no more successful at seeing the general than his daughter had been that morning. The next morning he reported his failure to Sarah at his office.

"I gave the orderly my card," said Levi, "and he gave me the same excuse that he gave you. 'The general is seeing no one, sir,' he said. 'The gout, you know. Try again tomorrow, sir.' And with that he closed the door in my face. I suspect General Scott is deliberately avoiding us, Sally. Perhaps he's embarrassed that Colonel Thomas went to Roberts instead of using the *Dover White*."

"That could be, Father, but I don't care about that now. All I want is for Aquila to be the pilot for the *Star of the West*. I should think General Scott would wonder why I've made this request and give me an audience to hear me out. At the very least, I should think he would wonder why you called on him and give you an audience to find out. After all, you are a wealthy shipping magnate, and the government will be much in need of this line in the future, if future events unfold in the same vein as they have transpired in recent months.''

"Yes, I concur, Sally, but he wouldn't see either of us, and that is that.''

"This is most disheartening, Father. I'm not sure what to do now. I suppose I could go by his house again and ask to see him like the orderly advised me to do.''

"Why don't you do that? And if you don't have any more success than you had yesterday, send me word of it, and I'll go by again. If we show him persistence, he just might give in to one of us.''

"Thank you, Father.''

Sarah left his office, and on her way out of the building, she met Frank Roderus, the cargo boss.

"Good morning, Miss Sarah,'' said Roderus as he tipped his hat politely.

"Mr. Roderus,'' said Sarah stiffly.

"Coming back to work here, Miss Sarah?''

"No, Mr. Roderus, I was only visiting my father.''

"Too bad. We certainly do miss you around here, Miss Sarah. If you was still working here, that lady who came by asking after you yesterday would have been able to talk to you herself.''

"Someone was here asking about me, Mr. Roderus?''

"Yes, miss. She didn't give her name, but she did say that she saw you at a ball on New Year's Eve. She said you were a regal lady.''

"That was kind of her. Did she say why she was looking for me?''

"No, miss, she didn't, but I gathered that she was

disappointed that she hadn't been introduced to you at the ball.''

"Probably some social climber. Most military wives are like that, my cousin Susan being an exception."

"She also seemed interested in the fact that you'd bought a female slave and had set her free. She remarked that . . . how did she put that . . ." He rubbed his jaw in thought. ". . . that not many folks have the money to throw away on a Negress. That's not exact, Miss Sarah, but it's pretty close."

"It makes no difference, Mr. Roderus. As I said, she was probably some social-climbing military wife, but thank you for telling me about her. I'll mention her to my cousin Susan the next time I see her. Maybe she'll know who this woman might be. Good day, Mr. Roderus."

Roderus tipped his hat again and said, "Good day, Miss Sarah."

Sarah hailed a hackney and ordered the driver to take her to General Scott's house, where she was greeted by the same orderly, who told her the exact same thing, almost word for word, as he had the day before. As she rode away in the hired carriage, a thought occurred to her. *It's almost like the man was repeating lines in a play. I wonder what General Scott is up to. I must find out.*

Louisa's letter was special-delivered to Sims that afternoon. He accepted it tentatively and read it very privately.

> *January 2, 1861*
> *Williamsburgh, New York*

My dearest Rafe,

> *The army is showing some unusual interest in a civilian ship named the* Dover White *and be-*

*longing to the Levi Hammond Shipping Line. I
think the* Dover White *will be conveying the soldiers from Fort Jay to Fort Monroe to relieve the
soldiers being sent to Fort Sumter aboard the*
Brooklyn. *I think this because I saw the daughter
of Levi Hammond conversing privately with General Scott at the New Year's Eve ball at Fort Jay,
and the next day I saw Lieutenant Lacy and Colonel Thomas with three other officers aboard the*
Dover White *talking with the captain. Today I
visited the waterfront and asked about the daughter of Levi Hammond and learned that she is a
Quaker, a Black Republican, and an abolitionist.
She is also involved in her father's business. I
believe she was the agent for her father with General Scott. Tomorrow I will go back to the waterfront and try to learn more about the* Dover
White *and when she will be sailing for Virginia.
Wish me luck.*

> *With all my love,*
> *Louisa*

Sims wadded the letter in his hand angrily. Damn
that woman! he thought, furious with Louisa for writing
to him at the Navy Department. And damn Sarah Hammond! If Louisa's words were true, then Sarah Hammond must be a Yankee spy. But is she? he heard a
little voice ask. Hadn't she said she was going to New
York to see General Scott about changing his plan to
reinforce Fort Sumter? The *Brooklyn* had ceased preparing for sea, and the infantry companies had been returned to Fort Monroe. She must have succeeded in
convincing Scott to change his plan, but change it to
what? Now Louisa had written of this civilian ship belonging to the Levi Hammond line, Sarah's father's
company. Had Scott decided to send supplies and rein-

forcements by a civilian ship? That would be madness. He would never do such a thing, thought Sims. It was too preposterous even to think about. Or was it? God, if I only knew for certain, maybe a disaster could be averted. If I only knew for certain.

21 ~

Friday, January 4, 1861

Louisa hadn't seen Lacy since the New Year's Eve ball at Fort Jay. His absence worried her.

When she visited the waterfront on Thursday morning, Louisa overheard a rumor that the *Star of the West* would be making a side trip to Charleston during the steamer's regular run to New Orleans and Havana. She asked several stevedores and even some of the ship's crew about the gossip, but every last man refused to tell her anything concerning the *Star*. Rebuffed by so many tight-mouthed longshoremen and sailors, she made her own observations and tried to reach her own conclusion. She noticed that crates and boxes being loaded aboard other ships were marked with various ports of call: Amsterdam, Southampton, Baltimore, Galveston, Le Havre, and dozens of lesser points around the globe. But the cargo being stowed in the holds of the *Star* bore no markings whatsoever. Furthermore, the *Dover White*'s freight did display the customary destination stenciling, designating it to be delivered to Liverpool. The final piece of the riddle confronting Louisa was the presence of a Revenue Service officer aboard the *Star*. When she asked about his identity, she was told that his name was Captain John McGowan, a man who had spent years on cutters patrolling the American coast chasing smugglers.

Is the *Star of the West* a ruse, Louisa asked herself, to cover the true relief ship, the *Dover White?* Or are these Yankees so stupid as to be this obvious?

Both questions vexed Louisa, and she wished that Lacy would come calling to confirm one suspicion or the other. When he hadn't made any contact with her by Friday morning, she decided to proceed with caution. She wrote him a note asking him to come by and escort her to New York City to do some shopping; the ploy for the benefit of Mary Lacy, in case she should intercept the message. She followed that with a letter to Rafe Sims, informing him about the possibility that the *Star,* and not the *Dover White,* was preparing to sail to Charleston with soldiers and supplies for Fort Sumter.

As she addressed two envelopes and folded the sheets of paper to be inserted in them, Louisa heard Jimmy Eagan hawking his newspapers on the street corner below her window.

"Rebels seize Fort Pulaski!" shouted Eagan.

Fort Pulaski? wondered Louisa. Now where would that place be? Virginia? No, Mississippi. Or is it? She stuffed the envelopes quickly, rose from the desk, went to the window, opened it, and called down to the newsie. "Oh, boy! Boy!"

Eagan looked up at Louisa and said, "Yes, Mrs. Phoenix. Would you like a paper, mum?"

"Possibly, but first tell me what you were sayin' just now."

"You mean about the Rebels seizing Fort Pulaski?"

"Yes, that's it. Where is Fort Pulaski?"

"Says here it's in Georgia, mum." He held up a copy of the *Times.* "A place called Savannah."

Savannah, hmm, thought Louisa. I guess this means

Georgia will be leavin' the Union quite soon. This is wonderful news.

"Do you want a paper, Mrs. Phoenix?" yelled Eagan.

"Oh, yes, of course. Just a minute and I'll send my servant down to get one." She closed the window and went back to the desk. She sealed the two envelopes, then called for Hattie to come to her. In the seconds before Hattie appeared in the room, Louisa removed a nickel from her purse.

"Yes'm, Miz Louisa?"

"Hattie, I want you to take this nickel down to the street and buy a newspaper from that boy on the corner. Then I want you to take this note over to the Lacys over on Atlantic Street. They live at Number 205." She held up the envelope. "See? I've written the address on the envelope. If you can't find it, then just show this address to someone and they'll help you find it. Understand?"

"Yes'm, Miz Louisa." She took the nickel. "I'll get the paper first, then go deliver that note for you."

"Very good, Hattie. In the meantime, I have to take a letter to the post office." She put the note to Lacy on the desk beside the letter to Sims.

While Hattie purchased the newspaper, Louisa went to the bedroom to don her hat, coat, and gloves for the walk to the post office. As soon as she was dressed, she returned to the parlor desk to pick up the letter to Sims, only to discover that the newspaper was there but not the missive to Sims or the note for Lacy. Hearing Hattie emerge from her room, she turned and said, "Did you pick up the note for the Lacys, Hattie?"

"Yes'm, I did, and I put the other letter in your purse, Miz Louisa, so as you wouldn't go off and forget it."

"That was very thoughtful of you, Hattie. Now you hurry along and deliver that note to the Lacys. I've asked Lieutenant Lacy to escort me over to New York to do some shoppin', and I'm hopin' he can do it this afternoon. So don't you dilly-dally along the way. You go straight to their house, then come straight home. You hear?''

"Yes'm, Miz Louisa." Hattie wrapped a muffler around her neck, pulled on her coat, and tied a scarf around her head. "Are you sure you is warm enough, Miz Louisa? Ain't no good for you to go and catch a nasty cold now."

"I'll be fine."

The two women left the apartment without another word. At the street, they parted, Hattie going west to find the Lacy residence and Louisa walking toward the waterfront to deliver the letter to the post office.

Louisa arrived at her destination in less than a quarter hour. She went to the service window, removed an envelope from her purse, and presented it to the balding, mustachioed clerk. "I would like this letter to be sent special delivery," she said. "How much would that be, sir?''

The clerk examined the address on the envelope and said, "That depends, ma'am, on where you want it delivered."

"Where I want it delivered?" puzzled Louisa. "Why, it says right there that it's to go to Washington City."

The clerk held up the letter for Louisa to read the address and said, "You must have forgotten to write that on here, ma'am."

For a few seconds, Louisa felt as if she were trapped in a vacuum, weightless and unable to move. Confusion squinted her eyes together as she studied the envelope, then they widened as she realized that this letter was addressed to Lieutenant John Lacy. "O lordy!" she gasped. "Hattie!" She snatched the envelope from the clerk, turned, and ran out of the post office.

On the street, she saw an available hansom cab, hailed it, climbed inside, and ordered the driver to take her to 205 Atlantic Street as fast as possible. The cabbie complied as best as he could, directing the horse's gait and maneuvering the carriage according to the traffic, slowing and yielding the right-of-way at intersections when necessary and almost racing when the opportunity presented itself. Only a few minutes passed before the hansom turned onto Atlantic Street, but to Louisa, the time seemed endless.

My God! thought Louisa over and over. Hattie has the wrong letter. I must stop her before she can deliver it. But what if she does? It's addressed to Rafe. Johnny wouldn't open it, and certainly Mary wouldn't either. But she might. He might. Whichever, I can't take that risk. I've got to stop Hattie.

The words to command the driver to greater speed formed in her head, but before she could utter them, she saw Hattie on the sidewalk of the 500 block, obviously coming from the Lacy home. She made eye contact with the servant.

"Stop here!" shouted Louisa.

The hack halted the carriage at the curb.

"Wait here," said Louisa as she climbed down. She stepped onto the sidewalk and stormed up to Hattie. "Where's the letter you took?"

Hattie smiled proudly and said, "I done delivered it like you said, Miz Louisa. I give it to Mrs. Lacy herself only a few minutes ago."

Louisa lashed out with an open hand and slapped Hattie across her cheek. "You stupid nigra bitch!" she screeched. "You took the wrong letter." She held up the note to Lacy. "This is the letter you were supposed to deliver."

Hattie cringed.

Other pedestrians stopped to watch and listen to them.

"I's sorry, Miz Louisa, I's sorry."

Louisa raised her hand to strike Hattie again, but the murmurings of a growing audience stayed the blow. Instead, she grabbed Hattie's jaw between the thumb and fingers of her left hand, squeezed it as hard as she could, and snarled, "I'll deal with you at home. Now you git!" She pushed Hattie away from her.

Crying, Hattie ran off toward the apartment on Bedford.

More conscious of the crowd around her, Louisa thought to stare them down, but when that failed, she squinted at one older man and said, "What's the matter with you? Ain't you never seen a nigra put in her proper place before?" Before the man could answer, she climbed back into the cab and simply sat there.

Somewhat perplexed, the driver asked cautiously, "Where to, ma'am?"

Catatonia seized Louisa for the moment. Her body as rigid as a marble statue, she sat there. But her mind was in full motion, filled with a kaleidoscope of images and thoughts: Rafe Sims and desire, John Lacy and deception, General Scott and anger, Colonel Thomas and confusion, the *Dover White* and Sarah Hammond and hate, Captain McGowan and the *Star of the West* and more confusion, Hattie and guilt, Mary Lacy and fear. Above all fear. Fear of discovery. Fear of failure. Fear of losing all hope of ever making Rafe Sims her man forever.

"Where to now, ma'am?"

The driver's voice echoed in Louisa's brain, scrambling the myriad of emotions running amok within her. She forced herself to concentrate on the issue at hand.

I must get that letter back, thought Louisa. I'll go to Johnny's house and get it. I'm sure he wouldn't read somebody else's mail. Neither would Mary. But she took it from Hattie. Surely, she read the address and realized it was a mistake for Hattie to bring it to her.

If she had, she should have given it back to Hattie and
told her it was a mistake and that she should bring it
back to me. But she didn't give it back to Hattie. She
kept it. Why? To read it, of course! That scrawny bitch!
I'll scratch her eyes out if she did. I'll—

"Where to now, ma'am?" repeated the driver.

"What?" she muttered without thinking.

"Where do you want to go now, ma'am?"

Thinking clearly now, Louisa said firmly, "I already
gave you the address, you stupid man. Number 205
Atlantic Street, and hurry."

The driver snapped the reins over his horse, and the
carriage lurched forward. In two minutes, he stopped
in front of the Lacy residence. "Here you are, ma'am,"
said the cabbie. "That'll be twenty-five cents."

"Twenty-five cents?" protested Louisa.

"Yes, ma'am," said the driver firmly.

"That's highway robbery."

"Pay it willingly, or I'll get that policeman on the
corner to make you pay it."

Louisa spotted the lawman, frowned, then paid the
fare. "I'm the one who should be callin' for a policeman," she said. "You lowdown, good-for-nothin'
thief!"

The driver took the coin from Louisa and said, "The
ride was only a dime, lady. The rest was for the abuse
you gave me and that poor black woman." He tipped
his hat and added, "Good day, ma'am." He drove
away before she could spew any more epithets at him.

To hell with him! thought Louisa as she turned away
from watching the hansom move down the street. Looking at the brownstone building before her, she told herself, I've got a much more important chore to do here.
She marched up the eight steps of the stoop to the front
door of the Lacys' house and knocked on it soundly.
In less than a minute, it opened, and Mary Lacy glared
at her from the shadowy interior without saying a word.

"Good mornin', Mrs. Lacy," said Louisa.

"Mrs. Phoenix," said Mary evenly, without emotion.

"I'm sorry to bother you, Mrs. Lacy, but my servant, Hattie, delivered the wrong letter to you." She dug into her purse and produced the note for John Lacy. "She was supposed to deliver this one." She held it out to Mary.

"No doubt she was," said Mary deliberately, not making any move to take the note.

"Well, I'd like to have the other one returned to me, please."

"I'm sure you would."

Louisa scowled and said, "What does that mean?"

Mary's lips barely moved as she said, "You know perfectly well what that means, you brazen hussy!"

She's read it! thought Louisa. She stepped forward and said, "Give me my letter."

Mary tried to close the door in Louisa's face. "Stay out of my house," she said, her voice an octave higher with a touch of agitation.

Still holding the letter to Lacy, Louisa pushed the door open, forcing Mary to move back, although awkwardly. "I want my letter," hissed Louisa. "Give it to me."

"No," said Mary, retreating into the hall. "I'm saving it to show John as soon as this business with Fort Sumter is concluded. I want him to see that you're not only a traitor but also an adultress."

"He already knows that much about me," said Louisa as she followed Mary into the corridor and closed the door behind her.

"What?" gasped Mary.

"That's right. He already knows. He knows because he's been with me more than once, and I mean that in the biblical sense, Mary."

"You're a liar," screeched Mary as she continued

to back away from Louisa. "John would never have anything to do with a woman like you."

Louisa burped a laugh that bordered on the maniacal and said, "Every man wants something to do with a woman like me. They want me because I do the thing that women like you don't do. I fuck them, and I enjoy it as much as they do."

Her Christian morality and sensibility gored by Louisa's words, Mary nearly choked before swallowing hard and screaming, "Liar! Not my John! My John loves me! He'd never have any truck with a woman like you."

Louisa laughed loudly now, then, gloating, said, "Oh, but he has, Mary. I let him have his way with me, and he told me all about General Scott's plan to reinforce Fort Sumter. It was a fair bargain, Mary. He got what he wanted, and I got what I wanted."

"John would never betray his country."

"But he did, Mary. You have proof of it in my letter to Rafe, and now I want that proof returned to me. So give me my letter, Mary."

"I won't do it. I'm sending it to John as soon as you leave, which I must insist you do right this minute."

Louisa put the note to Lacy in her purse and said, "I'm not goin' anywhere, Mary. Not until you give me my letter to Rafe."

"Never!" said Mary just before turning and darting into the parlor.

Louisa followed. "Where's my letter?" she demanded.

Mary retrieved the letter to Sims from the butler's table, where she had left it beside a decanter of brandy and a snifter that had a half-inch of the liquor in it. "Get out of my house," she said, "or I'll call the policeman on the corner."

"You're not callin' anybody, you skinny bitch!" hissed Louisa half a second before attacking Mary. She pushed Mary onto the sofa, then grabbed for the letter, lurching forward and falling on the couch awkwardly, losing her purse in the process.

Mary rolled away, bumping the lamp on the end table, knocking the chimney free, and tumbling it to the lower level of the table, where a thick doily preserved it from shattering. She jumped to her feet and backed away toward the cold hearth, keeping an eye on the doorway to the hall, hoping to escape and go for the policeman.

Louisa regained her feet and placed herself between Mary and the doorway. "You're not gettin' out of here with my letter," she said. She stepped slowly toward Mary.

Mary continued to back away toward the fireplace, bumping into the rack of fire tools. Thinking quickly, she reached down and picked up the poker. Brandishing the brass rod, she said, "Get away from me, you dirty whore, or I'll bash your head in." To better control the poker, she stuffed the letter to Sims inside her dress between two midriff buttons.

Louisa retreated a step.

Mary threatened to strike.

Louisa stepped backward, her dress brushing against the end table. She glanced sideways and saw the base of the unlit lamp, recognizing it as a weapon. She reached for it without taking her eyes from Mary and grabbed it by the wick holder, which she pulled free.

Mary swung the poker at Louisa, aiming for her left arm.

Louisa fell backward onto the sofa, avoiding the blow from the brass shaft. She threw the wick holder at Mary, missing her head by several inches.

Mary swung the poker backhanded and missed again when Louisa anticipated the attempt and leaned to her right to avoid it successfully. The momentum of the swing carried Mary over the butler's table. She lost her balance and fell over it onto the floor, landing on her side at Louisa's feet.

Louisa pounced on Mary, straddling her thighs, grabbing her by the hair and yanking it as hard she could, bringing a terrible scream of pain from Mary. "Call me a dirty whore, will you?" she said. "I'll show you, you scrawny bitch." She pulled on Mary's hair all the harder.

Mary couldn't use the poker, but she could throw a strong elbow, which she landed soundly against Louisa's rib cage, driving the wind from her assailant's lungs, forcing Louisa backward, and breaking Louisa's hold on her hair. She rolled onto her back and tried to bring the poker into play, but she was too close to use it effectively.

The letter to Sims worked its way out of Mary's dress and slid to the floor beside Mary, unnoticed by the combatants.

Louisa stayed the blow of the poker by grabbing Mary's wrist, then struggled with her for control of the weapon. As they fought, she caught sight of the lamp base again. She reached for it with her left hand, got it, and tried to crash it on Mary's head.

Mary saw the lamp base coming. She released her right hand from the poker and used it to hold off the potentially fatal strike.

Kerosene sloshed out of the lamp base and splashed on Mary, some of it landing in her hair and eyes, most of the combustible soaking into the bodice of her dress.

Mary screamed as the kerosene burned her eyes, blurring her vision but not her spirit. The agony sent a rush of energy into her limbs. She broke Louisa's grip on the lamp base, and it fell harmlessly on the sofa, landing and staying upright on the cushion. With another surge of strength, she rolled sideways and banged Louisa into the butler's table, freeing herself from the heavier woman's weight. She scrambled onto her hands and knees, and still holding the poker in her left hand, she crawled away toward the door, tears washing the kerosene from her eyes.

"No, you don't," said Louisa hoarsely between gasps for air. She stumbled to her feet.

Mary pushed herself erect, turned, and faced Louisa, menacing her with the poker. "Stay away from me, whore!" she growled, her eyes blinking rapidly to fight the burning of the kerosene. "I'll kill you if you come near me again. Do you hear me, whore? I'll kill you." Her vision still blurred, she swung the poker wildly, not coming within three feet of Louisa, but the lethal weapon came close enough to make Louisa keep a respectful distance between them.

With Mary backing toward the doorway and swinging the poker in defense, Louisa knew she had to do something drastic and soon. She saw the box of lucifers on the mantle. Yes, that's it, she thought. She darted to the fireplace and grabbed the matches.

"What are you doing there?" said Mary, not seeing clearly at all.

Louisa took a lucifer from the box and took a stealthy step toward Mary. "You should have been more reasonable, Mary," she said. "Now you leave me no choice." She struck the match on the box.

Mary saw the hazy light, smelled the burning sulphur, and knew what that meant. "No, you wouldn't," she gasped.

"You shouldn't have read my letter, Mary. You should have given it back to Hattie, and nothing would have happened to you."

"My God, no!" screamed Mary. She turned to run but stumbled into the side of the doorway.

Louisa threw the burning match.

The lucifer landed in Mary's hair, setting it afire with a whoosh and spreading instantly to her dress.

Mary screamed with horror and pain, dropped the

poker, burst into a run through the doorway, opened the front door, and raced outside, still screaming as the flames consumed her.

The policeman on the corner saw Mary almost as soon as he heard her screams. He ran to aid her, as did several passersby, but she fought them until one of them tackled her in the street.

O lordy! thought Louisa. What have I done? I must get away from here. I must flee. She dropped the matches on the sofa beside the lamp base. She started for the door, stepped on the wick holder, backed away, saw it on the floor, and without thinking about why she was doing it, replaced it in the lamp base on the sofa. She saw her letter to Sims on the floor beside her purse. She retrieved them. After quickly examining the envelope to determine positively that it was hers, she stuffed it in the handbag, then moved to the doorway again and went down the hall to the front door. She stopped short of the open exit and saw the anxious crowd gathered in the street around Mary Lacy, she assumed. She caught her reflection in the hall mirror. I'm a mess, she thought. She straightened her hat and coat, brushed back her hair in case even a single strand was out of place, then steeled herself with courage before emerging from the house. Certain that nobody was paying any attention to her in all the confusion, she stepped quietly down the stoop to the sidewalk, and joined the frenzied scene.

"Stand back!" ordered the policeman. "The poor woman's dead. Stand back, I tell you."

Louisa obeyed. Without speaking to anybody, she walked away toward her own apartment—and sanctuary—as if absolutely nothing out of the ordinary had happened.

22 ～

Saturday, January 5, 1861

The news about Mary Lacy's death appeared in the
next day's newspapers.

BROOKLYN ITEM

> Mary Lacy, residing at 205 Atlantic Street,
> while in a state of intoxication last evening,
> attempted to light a fire. Her clothing caught
> fire, and before assistance could be rendered,
> she was burned to death.

They got it wrong, thought Louisa. She died yesterday morning, not last night. Or did she? Maybe the
policeman was wrong. Maybe she wasn't dead when I
left there. Maybe she lived long enough to tell the policeman that I'm the one who set her afire. O lordy!
What am I to do? What am I to do?

Now wait a minute here, Louisa. Let's read that item
again. It said she was lightin' a fire, and her clothes
caught on fire, and it said she was intoxicated. Now,
where'd they get an idea like that. I was the only one
around when it happened. Let's see here. What would
make the police think it was an accident? The lamp on

the sofa, the brandy on the table, the box of lucifers, the spilled kerosene. Nothin' else was burned. Why *wouldn't* they think she was lightin' a fire and set herself to burnin' instead? I think I might if I hadn't seen what really happened.

For the past twenty-four hours, Louisa had held herself a prisoner inside her apartment, fearful that venturing out might lead to her arrest for Mary Lacy's murder. According to the newspaper, it wasn't a murder but an accident. Her fears were groundless. She was free after all. She could go outside again; she could leave her apartment and mail the letter to Rafe Sims. But what good would that do now? A whole day had passed. The news contained in the letter was now stale. She needed fresh information for Sims. She must go to the waterfront and see if the *Star of the West* or the *Dover White* had sailed yet. That's exactly what she would do now that she was free again.

Louisa finished dressing by noon and walked down to the ferry landing in time to catch the twelve-thirty boat to New York. After debarking at the Manhattan dock, she hired a hansom cab and ordered the driver to swing by the Warren Street docks before delivering her to the Hammond building. As the hack drove by the wharf, she noted that the *Dover White* had little activity around it, but the *Star of the West* was busier than ever. The cabbie halted his rig in front of Louisa's destination, where she saw Frank Roderus leaving the shipping company's offices. She hailed him from the carriage, then alighted.

Roderus turned at the sound of his name, saw Louisa, and smiled naturally, delighted to see her again. After all, he was a man, and she was an attractive woman. Besides that, he thought to ingratiate himself to Sarah Hammond by learning the lady's name for her. "Afternoon, ma'am," he said, tipping his hat in greeting. He waited for Louisa to pay the driver before adding,

"How nice to see you, ma'am! Come looking for Miss Sarah again?"

"Not exactly, Mr. Roderus," said Louisa. "But why do you ask? Is she here?"

"Not yet today, but she was here the other day. Thursday, the day after you came by inquiring about her."

"I'm sorry I missed her."

"She was, too," said Roderus, "when I told her you was here looking for her."

Louisa stiffened as she said, "You told her I was here looking for her?"

"Yes, ma'am, but I couldn't tell her who you are because you didn't leave your name with me. I could only tell her about our speaking with each other."

Still tense, Louisa forced herself to breathe as she said, "Yes, of course. How silly of me not to tell you my name!" She heard the voice of her lover, Rafe Sims, telling her, *You could use Smith or Jones and some other common name. Anything except Louisa Phoenix.* She cleared her throat, took a deep breath, and said, "It's Jones. Mrs. Harriet Jones."

"It's an honor to make your acquaintance, Mrs. Jones. When I see Miss Sarah again, I'll be sure to tell her that you came by looking for her again."

"Well, actually, Mr. Roderus, as I intimated before, I didn't exactly come down here lookin' for Miss Hammond."

"That's right. You did say that. So what does bring you down to the docks on a day like this?"

"The other day you mentioned that the *Dover White* would be leavin' for Liverpool soon, but I see she's still here, and I haven't read anything in the newspapers about her leavin'. Has her next port of call changed?"

"No, ma'am, it hasn't. The boys will finish loading the *Dover White* first thing Monday morning, and she'll be sailing for England just before sundown Tuesday."

"But I saw a lot of crates and boxes on the pier as I went by in the hansom cab."

"Yes, ma'am, but those are going aboard the *Star of the West* bound for New Orleans and Havana."

"Oh? I haven't read anything in the newspapers about her leavin' either. Do you know when this ship will be departing New York?"

"Not until Monday, ma'am. With tomorrow being the Sabbath, ships departing on Monday have to be loaded up by dark on Saturday." He chuckled and added, "Stevedores work no harder than the Lord, you know. They have to rest one day in seven, too."

Louisa smiled and said, "Yes, of course they do. Well, thank you, Mr. Roderus. Once again, you've been quite helpful and so charmin'. Good day, sir."

"Thank you, Mrs. Jones, and good day to you, too." He tipped his hat, then added, "I'll be sure to tell Miss Sarah you came by again."

"You do that now," said Louisa with a flirtatious wink.

Roderus puffed himself up and said, "Yes, ma'am."

Louisa walked away, thinking, The *Star of the West* doesn't sail until Monday, and the *Dover White* doesn't sail until Tuesday. That's very good to know. I'm sure Rafe would like to know this, too. I'll write him immediately and tell him about these two ships. She stopped as a stiff thought occurred to her. This time I won't sign my own name to the letter just in case it should fall into the wrong hands. She resumed walking toward the waiting hansom. Yes, I must learn to take better care in these matters at all times. I must be careful not to expose myself again. Yes, I must be very cautious every minute. I must, for my own sake as well as Rafe's and the South's.

Susan Slemmer also read the newspaper that morning. The news of Mary Lacy's death startled her and brought tears to her eyes. Her first reaction was to disbelieve the article, but reason quickly convinced her that the item had to be true; the address was correct, and Mary did have a tendency to imbibe. She and Mary hadn't been close, but they did share the commonality of being military wives, making them sisters of a sort. Thus, cause for Susan to dress and take the ferry to Brooklyn, to the Lacy residence to offer comfort and consolation to the bereaved husband.

No one answered the Lacys' door when Susan knocked on it just past noon. She rapped on it thrice more, but still no reply from within. Either Lacy wasn't home, or his grief was so great that he wasn't cognizant of the ongoing world around him. Frustrated, she turned to leave, only to be confronted by a plump woman in a brown cloth coat and black scarf covering her head, waiting patiently on the sidewalk at the bottom of the steps.

"There's no one to home at that house, mum," said the plump matron, her accent heavy with the brogue of Ireland.

"I'm Mrs. Susan Slemmer. Mary was a friend of mine."

"Then you know about the terrible tragedy that struck this house yesterday." She crossed herself and added, "Saints preserve us all."

"Yes, I read about it in the newspaper this morning," said Susan.

"I saw the whole thing. Mrs. Michael Colgan is me name, mum. We live two doors down. I was just comin' home from the grocer's when the poor thing come a-runnin' from that very door with her hair and clothes all afire, and her a-screamin' and wailin' so, it was terrifyin' and a horror to see. She ran right out into the street and collapsed right there." She pointed out the exact spot. "Mulligan, the copper on the corner, tried to help her, he did. Put out the fire with his very own hands. Of course, he was wearin' gloves, but no matter, he still did it. But it was too late. The poor thing was already gone. And without the last rites.'' She crossed herself again. ''But she wasn't Catholic, now was she?''

''No, she wasn't,'' said Susan.

''No, I didn't think so. Never saw her at Mass.''

''Where was Lieutenant Lacy when this happened?''

''His worship hasn't been around here since New Year's Day, Mrs. Slemmer. He's posted out on Governor's Island, you know.''

''Yes, I know,'' said Susan.

''Mulligan and O'Leary, the copper from two streets over, carried Mrs. Lacy's body inside her house, and me and some other ladies from the neighborhood put her on her bed and covered her with a sheet. O'Leary stood guard over the place until Mulligan made his report and other coppers came to relieve them. We told the coppers who she was and her husband's name and where he could be found, and they said they'd take care of notifyin' Lieutenant Lacy. When they come to take the body to the city morgue, the coppers said they couldn't get word to Lieutenant Lacy because he was restricted to his post the same as the rest of the soldiers out on Governor's Island.''

''Restricted to his post?'' queried Susan. Then she recalled the rumors about men at Fort Jay being sent to relieve the soldiers at Fort Monroe who would be reinforcing Fort Sumter. ''Even so,'' she added, ''they should have been able to get word to Lieutenant Lacy. I mean, his wife has died. Surely, that has some meaning to the army.''

''I don't know, Mrs. Slemmer. All I know is what the coppers said. They couldn't get no word to Fort Jay, and that was that.''

''Well, we'll just see about that. Thank you, Mrs. Colgan. It was nice to make your acquaintance.''

"Likewise, Mrs. Slemmer."

Susan hurried away toward the ferry landing. She would take the ferry to Fort Jay and tell John Lacy herself that his wife had met with a fatal accident.

"Is this the ferry to Governor's Island?" she asked a boatman at the landing.

"Yes, it is," said the bearded fellow.

"When does it next leave for Fort Jay?"

"We go over there on the even hours and come back on the odd hours. Our next run will be at two o'clock."

"Very good," said Susan. "I'm just in time."

"I'm sorry, ma'am, but the army says nobody goes over to Fort Jay without orders from General Scott himself."

"Without orders from General Scott?" she repeated. "But he's in Washington City."

"Yes, ma'am, I know."

"But I must go to Fort Jay," she protested. "I have some sad news for one of the officers posted there. His wife has had a fatal accident. You must take me over there so I can tell him."

"I'm sorry, ma'am, but we can't do that. Not without orders from General Scott."

Susan could see that he meant what he said and that she would have no luck changing his mind. But she was not to be denied. Another idea came to mind. "Very well, then," she said. "You can deliver a message to him for me."

"No, ma'am, we can't do that either. The army says all communications with the men on the island has to go through channels, meaning army channels."

Much to her chagrin, Susan knew exactly what he meant. She wanted to protest, but thought better of it, saying, "I see. Very well then, if I have to go through channels to get Lieutenant Lacy a message, then I suppose I will. Thank you, sir."

"Ma'am."

Susan left the ferry and hired a hansom cab to take her to the New York Navy Yard in Brooklyn, where she called on Commodore Foote at his residence.

"Sir, I wish to send a message to an officer at Fort Jay," she said as they stood in the foyer of the large frame house.

"Why do you come to me with this?" asked Foote.

"As you must know, Commodore, Governor's Island is now restricted because of this business concerning Fort Sumter, and this prevents me from communicating a message of sorrow to Lieutenant John Lacy, who is the commanding officer of the recruit training facility at Fort Jay."

"A message of sorrow, Mrs. Slemmer?" queried Foote.

"Yes, sir. Lieutenant Lacy's wife has met with a fatal accident, and I believe he is unaware of it."

"A fatal accident? What happened to her?"

"I'm not fully acquainted with all the details, except that her clothes caught fire while she was trying to light a fire in her home."

"That's terrible. How utterly tragic. And you say you can't get word of this to Lieutenant Lacy?"

"Yes, sir, that's correct. I tried to send him a note by way of the ferry to Governor's Island, but the ferryman refused to deliver it because the army has forbidden any communications with the island except through proper channels. To do that, I would have to return to New York and search out whoever is in command there and make the request. I thought I would have an easier time of it by coming to you, sir."

"And you shall," said Foote. "Just write out your message for Lieutenant Lacy, Mrs. Slemmer, and I'll have it delivered to him as quickly as possible. I believe the *Lockwood* is getting up steam for Governor's Island right now." He glanced at the tall cabinet clock. "Yes, I'm certain of it." Then he realized that he was speaking out of turn. "No, wait. I could be mistaken about that. The *Lockwood* won't be going to Governor's Island until the morning. But never mind, Mrs. Slemmer. You just write out your message, and I'll see to it that Lieutenant Lacy receives it as soon as possible. You have my word on it. If you need paper and ink, I have plenty in the library."

"Tomorrow morning?" queried Susan. "But his wife died yesterday. The man should be informed immediately."

"I am sympathetic, Mrs. Slemmer, but there is nothing else I can do. I have no other boat available at this time. Your message must wait until the morning, or you will have to find another way of getting it to him. Considering the hour, I doubt that you will have the time today. The decision is yours, Mrs. Slemmer."

"Very well then. I suppose I have no other choice." Susan wrote the note to Lacy and gave it to Foote. She thanked the commodore for his assistance and returned to New York with the satisfaction that she had done all she could in the matter.

Secretary of War Holt handed the official document to President Buchanan and said, "Mr. President, I believe we are making a grievous error sending the *Star of the West* to Charleston." Holt had requested this meeting with the president and General Scott, expressing dire urgency in his message to both leaders that they had not a minute to waste.

"A grievous error, Joseph?" queried Buchanan, holding the report but not looking at it.

"Yes, sir," said Holt. He pointed at the sheaf of papers in Buchanan's hand. "That is Major Anderson's latest communication with the Department of War. It's dated 31 December. I received it only a few hours ago. If you would read it, sir, you will discover the *Star* will be sailing into a trap."

"A trap?" inquired Scott.

"Yes, General," said Holt. "At the very time he was writing this, Major Anderson has advised me, the Carolinians were constructing one or two batteries on Morris Island commanding the main shipping channel into Charleston harbor. I can only assume that these guns will be ready for duty by the time the *Star* should arrive at the harbor entrance, making the reinforcement of Fort Sumter extremely dangerous to Captain McGowan, his crew, and the soldiers aboard the *Star*. Therefore, before leaving my office, I sent word to New York for the *Star* to remain in port until further notice."

"I agree with Mr. Holt's assumption, Mr. President," said Scott. "We must assume the Carolinians have these batteries operational by now, which means the *Star of the West* would be in great peril if allowed to proceed." He turned to Holt and added, "I congratulate you, sir, on taking swift and decisive action in this matter."

Levi Hammond read in the *Evening Post* that General Scott and his staff had gone to Washington to confer with the president. He circled the item, then sent the newspaper and a note to Sarah, stating simply:

> *It would appear that we have been duped. General Scott has been in Washington these past two days. I am afraid that our efforts were for naught.*
>
> *Father*

Not ready to admit defeat, Sarah made immediate plans to go to Washington to see Scott and, if necessary, the president, too. "We'll go by my father's office first," she informed Rowena. "There will still be time to catch the six o'clock train. We won't get to Washington until tomorrow, but I don't care. I must get Aquila on that ship."

Sarah and Rowena arrived at the Warren Street dock at a quarter before five. Sarah told the driver to wait for them; they wouldn't be long.

Neither woman noticed anything unusual about the *Dover White* or the *Star of the West* as they climbed down from the carriage and entered the Hammond building, where they encountered the company cargo boss.

"Good evening, Miss Sarah," said Roderus. "I'm rather surprised to see you here."

"I've come to see my father," she said. "Is he here?"

"No, I'm sorry, Miss Sarah," said Roderus. "He's not here. He's gone home until Monday morning."

Sarah frowned and said, "Foiled again. I wanted to tell him that I'm going to Washington to see General Scott. I guess I'll have to write him a note. Would you mind delivering it to him for me, Mr. Roderus?"

"I'd be pleased to do so, Miss Sarah."

"Thank you, Mr. Roderus. I'll go up to my father's office and write it. Would you please wait here for us?"

Roderus tipped his hat and said, "Certainly, Miss Sarah."

Sarah climbed the stairs to her father's second-floor office with Rowena trailing behind her. Sarah sat in her father's high-backed upholstered chair, while Rowena went to the window to look out at the harbor, specifically at the *Star of the West* and the *Dover White*. Sarah wrote, and Rowena observed, her eye caught by the activity aboard the *Star* and along the dock, men preparing to cast off lines and set the ship free from its moorings. Sarah continued to write, and Rowena noted that black smoke billowed copiously from the funnel of the *Star,* but the *Dover White*'s stacks emitted nothing.

"Sarah?" said Rowena.

"Yes."

"You don't have to write that note to your father."

Sarah stopped writing, shifted in the chair to look at Rowena, and saw that her friend's attention was focused out the window. She stood up, pen still in her hand, and moved closer to the window. In the next instant, she understood exactly what Rowena meant. "This can't be," she said ever so softly. "This can't be."

"But it is," said Rowena. "The *Star* is getting under way right this very minute."

"We have to stop them. They can't leave without Aquila. They just can't."

"They can, and they are, Sarah. And there's nothing you can do now to stop them."

"But I have to try," said Sarah. She turned for the door, but Rowena caught her by the arm.

"No, Sarah, you don't have to try. Let them go."

"But they're starting a war, Rowena."

"What of it?"

"What of it?" repeated Sarah, her tone expressing a disbelief that Rowena had said those words.

"Yes, what of it? So what if they start a war? It'll be a war between the North and the South, a war between the slave states and the free states, a war that just might bring an end to slavery, a war that might free my people from bondage."

"It will still be a war, and men will still die. We have to do everything we can to stop it."

"No, Sarah, *we* don't." She released Sarah's arm.

Sarah was speechless.

Rowena wasn't. "Sarah, there's nothing more you can do. It's all out of your hands now. The *Star of the West* is getting under way, and you can't stop it."

"I can go to Washington and—"

"By the time you get to Washington, that ship will be half the way to Charleston, and nobody will be able to stop it except those rebels in South Carolina. Face it, Sarah. You've done everything that you could do, and now there's nothing more to do except to wait and see how it all comes out.''

Sarah shifted her eyes from Rowena to the window. She watched the *Star of the West* get up steam and ease away from her slip out into the channel. A new thought crossed her mind. ''There are still women and children at Fort Sumter,'' she said calmly. ''I can still do something about removing them from harm's way. Come on. We're going to see my father.''

They went downstairs, where Roderus and the hansom cab waited patiently for them.

''Thank you, Mr. Roderus,'' said Sarah, ''but we won't be needing you after all. We're going to my father's house instead.''

''In that case, Miss Sarah,'' said Roderus, ''I'll be going, but before I do, I thought you'd like to know that woman came by again.''

''That woman?''

''Yes, the one I told you about the other day. The one who said she saw you at the New Year's Eve ball?''

''Oh, yes, now I remember. What about her?''

''Well, I got her name this time. It's Jones. Mrs. Harriet Jones.''

Sarah thought about it for a second, then said, ''I'm afraid I don't know anyone by that name, but thank you, Mr. Roderus, for learning it for me.''

''You're welcome, Miss Sarah.'' He helped both women into the carriage, then watched it disappear around the corner of Warren Street. As soon as it was out of sight, he wondered, Maybe I should have told Miss Sarah that Mrs. Jones was asking questions about the *Dover White*. Aw, why bother her with that? She didn't seem too interested in Mrs. Jones anyway. Better to let it be, Frank. Head bowed, he strolled away toward his favorite watering hole.

''Pardon me, mister,'' said a young male voice.

Roderus turned to see a military courier. "What is it, son?" he asked.

"Could you tell me where I might find the *Star of the West,* sir?"

The cargo boss pointed out to sea and said, "By now, she should be passing Staten Island on her starboard side and Governor's Island on her port."

"Damn!" swore the courier. "I'm too late." He glanced at the pouch hanging at his side. "There's gonna be hell to pay now."

Roderus stroked his chin, studied the soldier, and thought, I wonder what he meant by that.

Commodore Foote had lied to Susan Slemmer. The *Lockwood* was going to Governor's Island that evening, but good to his word, he gave Susan Slemmer's message to Lacy to Ensign Marcus Holt, the first officer of the harbor steamer *Lockwood,* taking care of the matter personally and enjoining the man to "hand it to Lieutenant Lacy yourself. Do not trust it to anybody else. It's not good news for him, and no one else should learn about it before he does. Is that understood, Ensign?"

"Yes, sir," said Holt. He accepted the letter, then saluted Foote, who didn't bother to return the courtesy.

The *Lockwood* chugged away from the navy yard pier at a quarter after five o'clock, her destination the landing on the west side of Governor's Island, where two hundred soldiers and officers were assembling in the fading light. Once the craft entered the main channel, the captain ordered all but the minimum running lights extinguished; no sense drawing attention to the ship unnecessarily. At a speed of five knots, the three-mile trip down the East River took an uneventful half-hour. Near darkness had descended on the harbor by the time the steamer tied up at the poorly lit pier at Governor's Island.

Ensign Holt debarked the *Lockwood* before the soldiers started filing aboard. He approached the first army
officer he encountered and said, "Sir, I'm looking for
Lieutenant John Lacy. I have a personal message for
him."

"I'll take it," said Lieutenant Charles R. Woods.

"I'm sorry, sir," said Holt, "but my orders are to
deliver it to Lieutenant Lacy and no one else."

"Very well then," said Woods. He scanned the shadowy faces on the pier, found the one he wanted, and
said, "That's him over there, talking to Surgeon Ten
Broeck."

"Thank you," said Holt. He saluted the superior
rank, then approached Lacy. "Lieutenant Lacy?"

"Yes?"

Holt saluted, then produced the envelope from Susan
Slemmer. "I was instructed to deliver this letter to you
personally, sir."

Lacy grinned and said, "More orders from the War
Department, no doubt."

"No, sir. I believe it's personal business for you.
Leastways, Commodore Foote indicated that it was."

Lacy took the envelope, moved closer to one of the
few lanterns lighting the landing, opened the letter,
and read:

Lieutenant John Lacy
Fort Jay, Governor's Island

Dear John,

*With the deepest sympathy and with the great-
est sorrow in my heart, I regretfully have to inform you that your wife, Mary, met with a fatal
accident in your home on Thursday evening, January 4. I do not know all the details, but the
newspaper account stated her clothes caught fire*

while she was trying to light a fire. A neighbor woman of yours has told me that her body was taken to the Brooklyn city morgue.

I am terribly sorry to impart this tragic news to you in this manner, but I thought you should know as soon as possible, and no other means was available. Please forgive me for not delivering this message in person. If there is anything that I can do further, please do not hesitate to contact me.

> *Yours most sincerely,*
> *Mrs. Susan Slemmer*

With slow deliberate moves, Lacy refolded the letter, placed it inside the envelope again, then stuck it neatly inside his overcoat. He turned to Ten Broeck and said, "Excuse me, Doctor, but I have to speak to Lieutenant Woods immediately."

"Bad news, sir?" queried Ten Broeck.

"Yes," said Lacy, showing no emotion whatsoever. Without another word, he went to Woods. "Charles, I am turning command of this expedition over to you," he said flatly.

"What?"

"Mary is dead," said Lacy softly, "and I must go to her. You are now in command." He held his hand out. "Good luck."

"Mary is dead?" asked Woods, absently accepting the handshake.

"Don't make a fuss about it, Charles," said Lacy. "The men mustn't learn about this or they're certain to construe it as a bad omen of things to come. From this moment forward, you are in charge. Now act like it."

"I'm so sorry, John."

"Thank you. Now take command."

"Certainly."

Lacy disappeared into the dark, and Woods obeyed the order, commanding the two companies of infantry to begin boarding the *Lockwood* for an appointment with destiny.

Sarah told the driver to take them to her father's house on Fifth Avenue beyond Thirty-second Street. They arrived there almost an hour later.

"I thought you would be on your way to Washington City by now," said Levi Hammond, looking up from the book he was reading when his daughter and her friend entered his library.

"That was my intention," said Sarah, "but when we stopped by your office to tell you my plans, we saw the *Star of the West* cast off her lines and pull away from the dock."

"What's this?" quizzed Hammond. "The *Star* has sailed?"

"That's right, Father. An hour ago."

"I didn't think they would be embarking this soon," said Hammond. "Let's see now. The *Star* departed today. The usual steaming time to Charleston is three and a half days. That would put her outside the bar sometime Tuesday night. With a good pilot who knows the harbor lights, she could slip into Fort Sumter before anybody was the wiser."

"But that's just it, Father," said Sarah. "Didn't you see the article on the back page of the newspaper that you sent to me? The one about Fort Sumter being under siege?"

"Yes, but it reported nothing special. It was only *rumored* that Fort Sumter was under siege."

"Rumor or not, it did state unequivocally that Major Anderson's communications with the outside have been cut."

"So what is your point, Sally?"

"The dispatch was dated January 2, three days ago."

"So?"

"So if the report is true, how will Major Anderson learn that the *Star of the West* is bringing him supplies and reinforcements?"

"I see your point," said Hammond, "but don't you think General Scott has taken care of that?"

"Yes, I'm certain he's sent word to Major Anderson that the *Star* is coming, but I wonder if the Carolinians will permit the message to be delivered."

"That is not our concern, Sally."

"But it is, Father. Major Anderson must know that the *Star* is coming so he can be prepared to evacuate the wives and children of the garrison when the *Star* returns to New York. I propose that we send a telegram to our agent in Charleston and have him pass the word to Major Anderson."

"If Fort Sumter is under siege as the newspaper reports," said Hammond, "how do you think Mr. Crenshaw is going to deliver a message to Major Anderson?"

"I don't know, but I'm sure he can find a way."

Hammond heaved a sigh, closed the book on his lap, and said, "Sally, we've done all that we can in this matter. It's out of our hands now. We tried to influence events in order to prevent a war, but I fear we can do no more. We must simply sit back now and see what unfolds."

Sarah looked at Rowena, remembering her friend saying nearly the same exact words. She lowered her head, heaved a deep breath, and said, "Yes, I suppose you're right. All we can do now is wait."

23 ⁓

John Lacy buried his wife. A few fellow officers—army and navy—with their wives, several friends, and neighbors of the Lacys attended the funeral. The cortege included Mrs. Colgan, Susan Slemmer, and Louisa Phoenix.

Mrs. Colgan, busybody that she was by nature, wept appropriately, while judiciously observing the other mourners, looking for signs of impiety and inspecting their attire for proper taste and elegance, particularly in the ladies. She saw Susan Slemmer, nodded at her during the graveside service, and spoke to her afterward as if they were old friends. However, she failed consciously to recognize Louisa through the double black veil that Louisa wore, but she did sense an odd familiarity about this mysterious woman, especially when Louisa stepped up to Lacy to offer her condolences. She strained to overhear their conversation, but the effort proved unsuccessful.

"I'm so terribly sorry, Johnny," said Louisa in words intentionally spoken softly, intended only for his ears. She touched his arm to convey to any suspicious onlookers that she was truly grieved for his loss.

"I'll bet you are," said Lacy, his voice low, abrasive,

on the brink of cracking; his eyes tearful and stricken with pain, refusing to look at her. "You're probably the reason Mary's dead."

A wave of fear rolled through Louisa, but she fought it off, disguising her true feelings by acting the hurt party when she pouted. "How can you blame me for her death, Johnny darlin'?"

"You sinful, wicked bitch!" he hissed, hoping no one else heard him. "You led me to sin, and Mary's death is my punishment. I never want to see you again. Now go away from me and never come near me again."

Louisa knew better, that he didn't really mean those words, that sooner or later this wound would heal and he would want her again; it was only a matter of time. But for now, she would accommodate him. "Very well, Johnny," she whispered. "I'll go, but I will never forget the moments we had together." As she turned and moved a few feet away, she smiled behind her veil and thought, He's right; I am wicked.

Wishing to conceal his anger with Louisa, Lacy sought refuge in Susan, moving to meet her as she approached him to express her sympathy for him. "Mrs. Slemmer," he said, "I haven't thanked you properly for what you did." His voice was loud enough for everybody within several feet to hear him clearly, including Louisa. "If not for your thoughtful letter, I would this minute be aboard the *Star of the West* somewhere out on the Atlantic, ignorant of Mary's death, and she would ... still ... be lying ... in the city morgue." He broke into uncontrollable tears.

Susan offered him her shoulder and a gentle, comforting embrace, while others came closer to touch him with tender hands, consoling hearts, and sincere words. Only Louisa kept a discreet distance.

Star of the West on the Atlantic? wondered Louisa. That Mr. Roderus had said that the *Star of the West* would be departing that morning, and that her first port of call would be New Orleans, then Havana. But why would Johnny be aboard a ship bound for New Orleans? Her heart fluttered as the answer came to her. He wouldn't unless New Orleans was just a ruse and the *Star of the West* was actually bound for Charleston and Fort Sumter. She gasped, but nobody noticed. O lordy, that's it! The *Star of the West* is takin' soldiers to reinforce Fort Sumter. A sense of urgency sped through her. I must inform Rafe about this right away.

Louisa hurried from the cemetery to the waiting hansom cab that had brought her there. She told the driver to take her home, then thought better of it. "No, take me to the ferry landin' instead," she said. Then to herself, she added, This news is far too important to trust the words of a grievin' man. I must be certain that the *Star of the West* has sailed before I send word of it to Rafe.

An hour later, Louisa arrived at the Warren Street pier to discover the *Star*'s slip vacant. After removing her veil, she saw Frank Roderus supervising the loading of the *Dover White,* ordered the cab driver to wait for her, then alighted to speak with the cargo boss. She worked her way along the congested wharf toward Roderus, but before she could get too far, she caught his eye and waved for him to come to her.

Roderus flattered himself with lusty thoughts that the woman must be interested in him to come down to the docks so often. Like an obedient puppy, he beckoned to her signal. "How nice to see you again, Mrs. Jones!" he said. He tried to disregard her attire but couldn't. "Are you going to a funeral or something?"

"And it's nice to see you again, Mr. Roderus," she said cheerfully. "I've already been to a funeral, but I hardly knew the departed woman. I went out of courtesy to the widower, bein' a widow myself and him bein' an army officer and all."

"I didn't realize that you're a widow, Mrs. Jones."

"Yes, my late husband was a seafarin' man. He was lost at sea."

"I'm so sorry to hear that."

"Thank you, Mr. Roderus."

Roderus heaved a sigh to clear the air and said, "So what brings you down here today, Mrs. Jones?"

"I was just passin' by when I noticed that the *Star of the West* was not here, and I was quite perplexed by her absence because I thought you said she wouldn't be departin' New York until tomorrow."

"Well, no, Mrs. Jones, I didn't quite say that. I said the *Star* would be leaving today, but I was wrong about that. She left Saturday evening."

"Saturday evenin'?" gasped Louisa.

"Surprised me, too. I thought for sure she—"

Louisa didn't wait around to hear the rest of what he had to say. Without saying farewell, she turned and hurried back to the waiting hansom.

Roderus was dumbfounded. His only thought, Well, I guess she wasn't interested in me after all. Women!

Louisa wasted no more time. She hurried to the nearest telegraph office to send a wire to Rafe Sims in Washington.

The president paced his office.

General Scott and Secretary of War Holt watched.

Buchanan paused at the hearth, removed the cigar from his mouth, and stubbed it out in his left palm without a sign of pain but certainly with anguish. He stared first at Scott, then at Holt, while in his mind he reviewed the events of the past few days.

When the military commander in New York informed Holt that the message for Captain McGowan hadn't been delivered because the *Star of the West* had sailed at the appointed hour, the war secretary met immediately with Buchanan and Scott, and together they decided their next action should be to order the *Brooklyn* to intercept the *Star of the West* at sea and assist her in any way possible in her mission to reinforce Fort Sumter. Much to their collective chagrin, the secret order wasn't delivered to Captain Farragut aboard the *Brooklyn* until Monday morning, and Farragut telegraphed back to Holt that the earliest the warship could get under way would be the next day, most likely the day after.

And so matters stood.

"So what do you suggest we do now, gentlemen?" asked Buchanan.

"I believe we have done all we can do, Mr. President," said Holt. "The *Brooklyn* will sail as soon as possible and follow the order already given. Farragut will either find the *Star* or he won't. If he succeeds, all the better. If not, then he will have done all that he could. As for the *Star,* we can only hope for the best."

"I feel we should mount another expedition immediately, Mr. President," said Scott. "If the Carolinians fire on the *Star of the West* and do her and the men on board harm, we will have no choice but to consider South Carolina to be in a state of insurrection against the United States government, and it will be our sworn duty to quell the rebellion with as much haste as possible. I feel we should prepare now for that eventuality."

"I concur with General Scott on the point that it will be our sworn duty to quell the insurrection with haste, Mr. President," said Holt, "but I disagree as to the timing. We can't assume the Carolinians will do any harm to the *Star* and the men on board."

"And we can't assume that they will allow the *Star* to pass peacefully, either," said Scott.

"No, we can't," said Holt, "which is precisely my point, General. We can only wait for the outcome of Captain McGowan's mission. We don't have the luxury of anticipation in this matter."

"I see your point, Joseph," said Buchanan. "For all we know at this juncture, Captain McGowan may very well succeed in his mission, and should he meet with success, I believe the Carolinians will recognize the resolve of this government to maintain the Union and resign themselves to rescinding their ordinance of secession."

"And if Captain McGowan fails?" asked Scott. "What then, Mr. President?"

"As the old adage goes, General," said Buchanan, "we will cross that bridge when we get to it. Until then, we will wait. We will wait and hope and pray. Above all, pray."

Commander Rafael Sims knew nothing about the *Brooklyn*'s secret orders, but he had heard the rumors concerning a civilian ship taking soldiers and supplies from New York to Fort Sumter, though he had given them little credibility until he received a special-delivery letter Monday morning.

Sir:

Today, a great deal of activity was observed on the wharf where the Dover White *is tied up, but it centered around another ship, the* Star of the West. *This ship was being loaded with unmarked crates and boxes, and she has a new captain, an officer from the Revenue Service named John McGowan. The cargo boss said the former will not be sailing until Tuesday next and the latter will sail on Monday morning next. The* Dover White *is supposed to be going to England, and the* Star of the West *is supposed to be going to New Orleans and Havana.*

It is believed that these two ships are actually in the employ of the Federal army and that one of them is headed to Charleston to reinforce Fort

*Sumter, while the other is a ruse by the Yankees
to throw us off the track. A watch on these two
ships will continue, and you will be informed of
their departures from New York.*

God bless the South,
Jones

Jones, eh? wondered Sims. This smacks of Louisa
Phoenix. He burped a chuckle as another thought came
to him. *That girl is finally wisin' up. How audacious
of her to use the name of her own slave! Possibly I've
misjudged her. She might be as clever on her feet as
she is on her back.*

These thoughts aside, the letter upset Sims through
the day as much for the news it revealed as for the fact
that he felt positively that he knew the identity of its
author. He wanted to pass this information to those who
needed to know, but he couldn't. He had no way of
verifying the truth of the report without arousing the
suspicions of his superiors about his loyalties, and to
let on that he had any knowledge of civilian ships being
in the employ of the United States Army would certainly force him to reveal his connection to "Jones,"
a course he refused to choose because a gentleman,
especially a Southern gentleman, never compromises a
lady, particularly when that lady's virtue might be in
question. Thus, he destroyed the letter and tried to forget its contents until a telegram was delivered to him
late that afternoon.

Sir:

Star of the West *sailed Saturday with soldiers
for Fort Sumter.* Dover White *still in port.
Warn Charleston.*

Jones

This was information that Sims couldn't keep to himself. He had to tell the only loyal Southerner he knew still to be in Washington.

"Who is this Jones?" asked Senator Wigfall after reading the telegram.

"A patriot, Senator," said Sims.

The two men stood in front of the hearth in the parlor of the senator's home. A small fire warmed them.

Wigfall grunted and said, "I see. Of course, his identity should remain as secret as possible. I withdraw the question, Commander."

"Thank you, sir."

"Who else has seen this telegram?"

"Nobody."

"Good. Let's keep it that way." Wigfall wadded the paper into a ball and served it to the hungry flames. "You've done well to come to me with this, Commander, but I think it would be wiser in the future that this Jones would communicate with me directly for as long as I'm here in Washington." He winked at Sims. "Senatorial privilege offers me a certain amount of protection that is unavailable to you as a member of the navy. It would never do to have you accused of treason at this stage of the game. The South will have great need of you in the years ahead."

"I will send word to Jones to contact you henceforth, Senator," said Sims.

"Good. Good. You do that, and you can rest assured that I will act on this information and any more reports from this Jones with all due haste. As for now, I think you would be wise to keep your distance from me and all other Southern legislators remainin' in Washington. As I have said already, the South will have need of your services in the future."

Sims agreed, deciding then and there to put as much distance as possible between himself and the Southern Cause until the call to duty should come his way.

*   *   *

Ty Harris left the offices of the Charleston *Mercury* and sought out George Salter to tell him the latest news from New York. He found Salter on the Cooper River waterfront, talking to crew members of the *General Clinch* as they prepared to go on evening patrol in the main shipping channel to the harbor.

"Have you heard the news yet, George?" asked Harris.

"What news would that be, Ty?"

"The New York *Times* has run a story about a ship called the *Star of the West* preparin' to leave New York this past Saturday night bound for Charleston."

"Yes, I heard about that, Ty," said Salter. "What of it?"

"There's more. The governor has received a telegram from some mysterious person who simply calls himself Jones, confirmin' the *Times* story that the *Star of the West* sailed from New York with two hundred Federal soldiers bound for Fort Sumter."

"The *Star of the West?*" queried Salter. "Isn't that the ship that transported that rogue Walker and his filibusters to Nicaragua or someplace like that?"

"I wouldn't know about that," said Harris. "I only know that the Yankees are comin', and there's gonna be hell to pay once they're sighted in the channel."

"You better believe that, friend," said one of the sailors.

"No doubt, there will be," said Salter, staring out at Fort Sumter in the distance. He imagined an artillery battle, seeing in his mind the powder flashes from the Federal guns followed by the puffs of bluish-gray smoke, then hearing the long reports echoing across the water as Major Anderson's gunners returned the fire of the Carolinian batteries at Fort Moultrie, Fort Johnson, and Cummings Point. What a spectacle it will be! he thought. And men will die doing their duty. Also, innocent women and children will perish in this calamity. My God! what a pitiful tragedy that will be! Good people dying because their political leaders have lost the art of compromise. Before he could go too deeply into the vision unfolding in his head, Salter realized that no ships dotted the scenario. Returning to reality, he turned to his friend and said, "Ty, this newspaper story, did it mention any warships coming with the *Star of the West?*"

"Yes, what about the warships?" asked the sailor.

"No, it didn't say anything about warships," said Harris, "but I can't imagine the Federals to be so foolish as to send a solitary unarmed civilian ship to reinforce Major Anderson. They must be sendin' at least one warship with the *Star of the West*. I should think it would be the *Brooklyn*. Don't you think so, too, George?"

"I think you give President Buchanan and General Scott too much credit, Ty. Of course they would send a single unarmed civilian ship with reinforcements for Fort Sumter. What better way to make them look like the peacemakers and the Carolinians look like warmongers?"

"Maybe so, but I'll tell you this much. Unarmed civilian ship or not, Governor Pickens has no intentions of allowin' it into the harbor, and if that means firin' on Fort Sumter and commencin' a war with the Federal government, then he is duty-bound to do it."

"You can say that again," said the sailor.

"Which will only lead to the destruction of this beautiful city," said Salter, gesturing broadly with a sweep of his left arm, "and that will be tragic in itself."

"I doubt that Major Anderson will order his gunners to fire on the city," said Harris. "He is a Southerner by birth and breedin', a man of honor. He would never make war on the good citizens of this city."

"No, I suppose not. He'll probably only fire at the batteries firing at the *Star of the West.*"

"I doubt that he even knows the *Star of the West* is comin' here. After all, the Federals have been penned up on that island without any communications with Washington since the day before the New Year began."

Salter took Harris by the arm and said, "Walk with me, Ty." To the crewmen of the *General Clinch,* he nodded and added, "See you, boys. Have a safe watch tonight."

"Thankee, Dr. Salter," they said severally.

"Governor Pickens has only prevented the mail from going through," said Salter as they walked along the wharf. "Surely, he hasn't interfered with military couriers, too?"

"It's my understandin' that Washington has made no effort to contact Major Anderson except through the mails since well before Christmas."

"Are you sure about this, Ty?" asked Salter anxiously.

"Well, I'm not one hundred percent certain of it, but I know for sure that I can find out if he's received any communications from Washington recently."

"Then do it, will you, Ty?"

"Whatever for, George? You aren't plannin' to send a message to Major Anderson yourself, are you now?"

Mischief curled the corners of Salter's mouth as he said, "Ty, you are such a clever fellow. You've found me out. I am a Northern agent."

Harris frowned at Salter as he said, "You know, George, for the longest time, I've had my suspicions that you were a Yankee spy."

Salter heaved a theatrical sigh and said, "I should have known that I couldn't keep up the charade forever. Not with you, Ty. But tell me. Would you consider me to be more like Major André, or am I Nathan Hale reborn?"

"Neither," said Harris, a wry grin twisting his lips. "I would have to say that you're the second comin' of Benedict Arnold."

"You cut me to the quick, my good and dear friend."

"Enough, George. It's a good thing that you're a man of medicine."

"It is?"

"Yes, it is."

"Why is that?"

"You would starve if you had to earn your living on the stage."

"I suppose you are only right, Ty. I am definitely no threat to the Booth brothers."

Harris jostled Salter, then said, "Come along now, and let's find us some wine and women and maybe a song or two, and for tonight we'll put aside all this talk of war. What do you say, George?"

"Why not?" shrugged Salter. I know why not, he told himself. Someone has to warn Anderson that the *Star of the West* is coming, so it might as well be me. But how do I do it? How?

24～

Tuesday, January 8, 1861

Daybreak found George Salter sleeping in the house of John Lindsay, the carpenter who lived in Moultrieville and worked for the U.S. Army garrisoned at Fort Sumter.

The doctor had met the woodworker the night before at a local drinking spot, bought him a few drafts of ale, and learned that he was a true believer in secession. "So why do you continue to work for the army?" asked Salter.

"They pay well," replied Lindsay, "and they pay on time in silver and gold. I can't always get that from folks around here, you know."

"No, I suppose not," said Salter. He lifted the mug to his lips and drank.

"So what brings you over to Moultrieville, Mr. Salter?" asked Lindsay, continuing to eye his drinking companion with the suspicion that residents everywhere reserve for visitors to their area, especially talkative strangers who seem to be more inquisitive than they should be.

Salter swallowed slowly as he considered whether to tell the absolute truth or something less. Replacing the mug on the bar, he opted for the former and said, "Actually, it's Doctor Salter. I'm a physician from New York, and I came down here to spend the holidays with an old college friend. Perhaps you've heard of him? Tyler Harris? The grandson of Samuel Harris, the planter?''

"I've heard of the old man. Involved in railroads at one time, wasn't he?''

"That's him," said Salter, nodding to accent his reply. "Anyway, since coming here, I have made the acquaintance of Dr. Samuel Crawford, assistant surgeon with the Federal garrison.''

"I know him," said Lindsay, head bobbing. "A good doctor, but he wishes he was a soldier." He squinted at Salter dubiously and asked, "What about him?''

Salter grinned and said, "Well, I can see that there's no sense beating around the bush with you, Mr. Lindsay.''

The carpenter lowered one eyebrow at the doctor and said, "Strangers don't buy less'n they want somethin'.''

"A fair observance, sir," said Salter. "So I'll get right to the point. Since Governor Pickens has cut off mail delivery to Fort Sumter and nobody except you workers from Moultrieville are allowed to go out to Fort Sumter, I have been unable to communicate with my newfound friend and colleague Dr. Crawford.''

Lindsay leaned away from Salter as if he had some sort of contagion and interjected, "You ain't askin' me to deliver any letters for you, are you, Dr. Salter? Because if you are, I ain't doin' it. No, sir.''

"Well, I confess that was my first thought, Mr. Lindsay, but since you've made your stand perfectly clear on delivering personal letters, I will respect your integrity and not ask you to do such a thing for me." A twinkle entered his eye. "But how do you feel about taking a newspaper to Dr. Crawford for me?''

Lindsay frowned and said, "A newspaper? Which one?"

"A copy of Mr. Rhett's Charleston *Mercury*."

"Mr. Rhett's *Mercury*, you say?"

"That's right," said Salter, feeling his way and seeing a glimmer of light at the end of the tunnel.

"A true patriot, Mr. Rhett," said Lindsay. "What's in his newspaper that's so important for Dr. Crawford to read?"

"There's an advertisement for an asthma remedy that he might wish to read," said Salter eagerly. "The last time we spoke, he made mention of the problems with respiratory problems among the garrison and the workers. This particular remedy could also be used in treating the catarrh and other such maladies."

Suspicious by nature, Lindsay said, "Show it to me."

"Certainly," said Salter without hesitation. He pulled the newspaper from his coat pocket, opened it to the third page, spread it on the bar, and indicated the advertisment for Jonas Whitcomb's Remedy for Asthma with a forefinger. He studied Lindsay's eyes as they concentrated on the page for several anxious seconds, and when the man's orbs failed to move side to side in an orderly fashion but flittered up and down and all around, the physician surmised the carpenter to be illiterate or poor-sighted but too proud to admit either case.

Lindsay shifted his gaze to Salter and said, "That ain't all that's in that newspaper."

"That's true," said Salter. "There's news in here about the other states preparing to secede. There's news from other cities such as Washington, Philadelphia, New York, and even Paris, France. I'm sure Dr. Crawford would be interested in reading those items, too, but the only thing I'm interested in having him read is the advertisment for Jonas Whitcomb's Remedy for Asthma."

The carpenter gave Salter a hard look, then said, "I suppose there's nothin' in there that could do any harm to South Carolina. I mean, Mr. Rhett wouldn't print nothin' that would help the Federals, now would he?"

"Not knowingly," said Salter with a broad smile.

"All right, Dr. Salter. I'll take your newspaper out to Dr. Crawford when I go to work at sunup. Speakin' of mornin', it'll be here before you know it." He downed the last few drops from his mug and plopped the glass on the bar. "Thank you for the ale, sir. I'll be seein' you."

"Before you go, Mr. Lindsay, could you recommend a good hotel in this town?"

Lindsay chuckled and said, "Dr. Salter, this is Moultrieville, not Charleston. The nearest sleepin'-over place to here is over to Mount Pleasant, but you can't get there from here."

"I can't?"

"No, sir, not at this time of night. Hell, you can't even get back to Charleston tonight unless you're plannin' on swimmin' back."

"No, I hadn't planned on that."

"Well, you could probably sleep in the back of this place, but the rats might not like your company." He winked at Salter and added, "You see, they're Southron rats, and they might not cotton to a Yankee sleepin' with them."

"I see," said Salter with a grin.

"But hell, I ain't so particular as the rats. You can sleep over to my house. Me and the missus don't get to entertain gentle folk too often. It'll cost you, though. My wife's got a little somethin' growin' on her back that I'd like you to take a gander at. Fair enough for a warm bed and a good breakfast?"

Salter's grin widened as he said, "Fair enough, Mr. Lindsay." He drank the last of his ale and added, "Lead on, sir."

True to his word, Lindsay took Salter's copy of the *Mercury* with him to work the next morning, and at the earliest opportunity, he gave it to Crawford with a brief explanation that it came from "a Yankee sawbones named Dr. George Salter. Says he knows you."

"Yes, I have made Dr. Salter's acquaintance," said Crawford.

"That's what he said, too. He said there's an item in there about some asthma cure that you should read."

"An asthma cure?"

"That's what he said."

"Well then, I suppose I'll have to read it, won't I? Thank you, Mr. Lindsay, and thank Dr. Salter for me when you see him next."

"I'll do that, Dr. Crawford. Now I got to get back to work."

As Lindsay returned to his job, Crawford perused the newspaper, soon discovering the article detailing the mission of the *Star of the West*. Cure for asthma, my foot! thought the assistant surgeon with great agitation. He leaped to his feet and immediately sought out Captain Doubleday, finding him on the parapet scanning the harbor for any sign of hostility from the Carolinians. "You won't believe this," he said as he presented the *Mercury* to Doubleday. "I'm not sure I do."

Doubleday lowered his spyglass, glanced at the paper, then stared at Crawford. "I won't believe what, Sam?" he inquired.

"There's an expedition on its way here to reinforce us," said Crawford. "It's all here in this newspaper."

Doubleday's face twisted with curiosity and disbelief. "You're jesting, aren't you?" he said.

Crawford shook his head slowly.

Doubleday took the newspaper and read the article. When finished with it, he said, "Come on. We have to show this to Anderson."

They took the newspaper to the commanding officer,

who read the article with great doubt to its veracity. "This is preposterous," he said. "A civilian ship bringing soldiers of the United States Army to reinforce us? How ridiculous can these journalists be?"

"My thought exactly, sir," said Doubleday. "To publish all the details of an expedition of this kind, which ought to be kept a profound secret, is virtually telling South Carolina to prepare her guns to sink this vessel. It is inconceivable that our government would send a mercantile steamer, a mere transport, utterly unfitted to contend with shore batteries, when it could dispatch a man-of-war furnished with all the means and appliances to repel force by force. Why, I believe the *Brooklyn* alone could go straight to the wharf in Charleston and put an end to this insurrection for once and all time."

"I wholly concur, Captain," said Anderson. "General Scott would never send a civilian ship with reinforcements. Surely, he would place them aboard a war vessel that could defend itself against shore batteries. This story is merely another stupid rumor in this rumormongering sheet. I refuse to believe it."

"What if we are wrong, sir?" asked Crawford.

"Wrong, Captain?" queried Anderson. "I will believe this ship"—he tapped the newspaper for emphasis—"this *Star of the West,* is coming to reinforce us when I see it tying up to our dock."

Oddly, Governor Pickens held the same concerns as Major Anderson about the accuracy of the article in Rhett's *Mercury.* He called a meeting of officers at Charleston's city hall to discuss the matter with them. "Gentlemen, you've all read the story in the newspapers," he said, "and most of you are aware of the telegram from this fellow Jones in New York. It is my gut feelin' that the Yankees have sent a ship with soldiers for Major Anderson, but I have serious doubts that they would employ a civilian ship to bring them here. What say you, gentlemen?''

"I would think General Scott would have sent the *Brooklyn*,'' said General Schnierle. "Why would he risk the lives of four or three or even two companies of good infantry aboard a civilian ship? It makes no sense, sir.''

"I agree with the general,'' said Colonel Allston. "Surely, the enemy would send a warship of some kind. Possibly even the *Harriet Lane*. Didn't that New York newspaper report she was at the navy yard there?''

"I recall that, too, Governor,'' said Colonel De Saussure. "The *Harriet Lane* would be nearly as effective as the *Brooklyn*. It would only make sense that General Scott would send her with this civilian steamer if not instead of it.''

Pickens nodded as he considered their statements. He searched their faces for answers to the questions he hoped his eyes were conveying to them, but finding none, he said, "If this story is true, gentlemen, whether it's a civilian ship or a naval vessel comin' our way, are we prepared to meet the enemy with force?''

General James Simons of the state militia, ordered by Pickens to survey the harbor's defenses, spoke up. "Sir, I have carried out your orders,'' he said, "and it is my opinion that should the enemy send a warship against us to relieve Fort Sumter, we will be helpless to prevent it.''

"Helpless, General?'' queried Pickens uneasily. "How so, sir?''

"Governor, the cadets at the Morris Island battery have never fired a twenty-four-pounder or even seen one fired. At Fort Johnson, we have raw militiamen who have never handled a heavy gun. At Fort Moultrie, the guns the Yankees so poorly spiked upon their departure for Fort Sumter have been repaired, but I can safely say that there probably isn't a man in our garrison there who has ever loaded a siege gun. Moreover, the position is indefensible against the superior arms of Fort Sumter. We have made great preparation at a great expense to defend ourselves, sir, but for what end, if it should all end in failure? The enemy can demolish our posts whenever he pleases from one of the most impregnable fortresses in the world, and so our posts live at his will and remain in our possession at his sufferance.''

Simons cleared his throat and continued. ''Should the enemy attempt to reinforce Fort Sumter and we draw his fire, we shall have no choice except to withdraw our forces to positions of safety out of the range of his guns.'' He paused again before dotting all the *I*'s and crossing all the *T*'s of his speech. ''Therefore, sir, I urge you to permit the enemy to reinforce Fort Sumter without interference from us.''

''I shall do no such thing!'' raged Pickens. ''Although our soldiers may be inexperienced in battle, I am certain that they would rise to the occasion and fight as well as those regulars inside Fort Sumter. We are Carolinians, sir, and let us not forget that.''

Several officers chorused the governor's sentiment.

''Besides, General,'' Pickens continued, ''we have made great strides toward total independence, and I have no intentions of takin' a step backward now. Is that understood, gentlemen? We shall not retreat.''

A courier entered the room carrying an envelope. He gave it to Colonel Cunningham, who quickly discerned that it contained a telegram for Pickens. Without hesitation, the colonel stepped forward and handed it to the governor.

Pickens read his name, then tore open the envelope and removed the message. He read:

Sir:

 Steamer Star of the West *departed New York*

on the 5th instant with two hundred Federal soldiers to reinforce Fort Sumter. Be prepared.

Senator L. T. Wigfall

Pickens held the telegram over his head for all to see as he said, "Gentlemen, we have confirmation. The *Star of the West* has sailed from New York as Jones reported yesterday. She is carrying two hundred soldiers to reinforce Fort Sumter." He surveyed the faces before him. "Gentlemen, we must not let this ship into our harbor. Is that clear?"

To a man, they agreed.

25 ~

Wednesday, January 9, 1861

William Conant Church, a reporter for the New York
Evening Post and a stowaway aboard the *Star of the
West,* awakened at three in the morning and went immediately to the upper deck of the steamer, where he
found Captain McGowan, the first mate, the pilot, and
two army officers on the bridge.

"Good morning, Mr. Church," said McGowan. "Sleep
well?"

"As well as could be expected," said Church.
"Where are we now?"

"We're somewhere off the Charleston bar," said
McGowan. "We've been here since midnight looking
for the harbor lights and the main channel, but thus far,
we've been unsuccessful." He waved an arm toward
the blackened coast. "No lights out there. It is evident
from these indications that the hospitable Carolinians
do not mean for us to go in without a salute."

"Captain, I believe I see something," said Mr.
Brewer, the pilot. He pointed to a hazy glow on the
starboard horizon. "I believe that to be the light of
Fort Sumter."

"Are you certain?" asked McGowan.

"Yes," said Brewer firmly.

"Can you find the channel now?" asked McGowan.

"No, I still need the location of the lighthouse," said Brewer, "but I don't think we will find it in the night. I believe the Carolinians have extinguished it."

"I believe you are correct, sir," said McGowan. "We will heave to until daybreak."

Church returned below decks, where he recounted the *Star*'s journey since leaving the slip at the foot of Warren Street. From his journal, he read:

> *On board the* Star of the West,
> *Saturday, January 5th, 1861*

> *The steamship* Star of the West *sailed from the foot of Warren Street, New York, this afternoon, at about five o'clock, under command of Captain McGowan, an experienced officer, who for many years was in the United States Revenue Service.*

> *The vessel cleared for New Orleans and Havana, but this was only a precautionary measure, as the real object of this expedition was to convey provisions and troops to Major Anderson, at Fort Sumter. The plan of the movement seems to be to convey these troops and stores as they would be conveyed in a time of profound peace, except that it is intended to go in early in the morning, if possible, without the knowledge of the South Carolinians. In accordance with this plan, the greatest precautions possible have been employed to keep the movement wholly secret.*

> *The vessel left the wharf before dark, as it was thought her sailing would attract less attention and be less liable to create suspicion by following such a course. It was as much as to say, we have nothing to conceal. We sailed out leisurely, until dark, when came almost to dead stop, and finally, off the Robin's Reef lighthouse, she was allowed to drift; and here*

*we awaited the arrival of the two hundred troops
from Governor's Island. They did not come quite as
soon as was expected. The delay, however, was only
temporary, and at five minutes before seven o'clock,
we detected the approach of the steamship* Lockwood. *At seven o'clock precisely, that boat was
alongside our vessel. The night was clear and beautiful, though moonless, and I watched the approach
of the* Lockwood *from the upper deck. She displayed
no lights, and I could see no one, as the men had
been purposely kept out of sight. But as the boat
came near, the deck suddenly became alive with
soldiers.*

The transfer of the men and baggage from the
Lockwood *to the* Star of the West *commenced immediately, and was conducted with as much expedition
and silence as possible. I placed myself at the head
of the gangway, and although our lights were dim,
I could see the soldiers distinctly as they came up,
in their gray overcoats and dark caps. Officers and
privates were as fine-looking fellows as one could
wish to see. I learned, however, that about one hundred and fifty of the men are recruits.*

*It was found that the vessel was drifting too near
the Staten Island shore; and to remedy this both
vessels steamed away. This, of course, caused a temporary suspension of the unloading and reloading;
but the entire labor, including this delay, was accomplished in fifteen minutes. The* Lockwood *then
put off, and the* Star of the West *steamed away for
Charleston.*

*Such secrecy has been observed in starting out the
expedition that officers and command were wholly
ignorant of their destination until a few hours previous to the departure. After they were informed of it,
they were not permitted to leave the island until they
set foot upon the* Lockwood. *All communications, in*

*fact, between the island and the city were cut off.
One of them showed me an order issued but a few
days since, directing him to California, and he had
been home and made preparations for his journey.
Now his baggage is in New England, and he is on
the* Star of the West *bound for Fort Sumter.*

*Privates, of course, were wholly ignorant when
they came on board this evening, and it was curious
to hear their conversation.*

"Halloo, Billy, are you here?"

"Yes, Jim, this is me."

"Well, where are we?"

"I don't know, Jimmy."

*"Well, I don't care. I'd go to the d—— quick
enough to get off that old island."*

*It may well be questioned whether "Jimmy" will
find it pleasanter to be shut up in Fort Sumter six
months or a year, more or less, than he has found
it on "that old island."*

*But shall we get to Fort Sumter? That is the ques-
tion which has been freely discussed this evening.
Here we are, with two hundred soldiers, good and
true it may be, led by experienced officers, with
plenty of muskets and ammunition. But what of that,
should they open fire on us from the batteries of
Fort Moultrie, or should send a vessel or two outside
to capture us? What would our muskets avail against
a twelve-pounder? A hole in our machinery, and we
are probably at the mercy of the palmetto chivalry.
We have, of course, absolutely no means of resistance out of musket range; but must run in under a
full head of steam if possible. There is a small brass
piece on our deck, but we have no balls for it, and
the captain says if a ball were to be fired from it, it
would kick clean over, and be more likely to kill the
man who should stand behind it than the enemy. Our
principal hope is in the ignorance of the Charles-*

tonians; and if they get no whisper of our plan, we hope to slip into Fort Sumter, without opposition or hindrance, on Wednesday morning next at daybreak. But the belief is prevalent that the Charlestonians are not ignorant of our movement. There were rumors on the dock, in fact, before we started, that our destination was Charleston, and that we were to convey troops from Governor's Island. It is not to be presumed that no good friend of the palmetto state will immediately telegraph this rumor to Charleston; nor is it to be presumed that, with such an intimation, authorities there will not be on the lookout for the Star of the West.

But if they do hear of our approach—if they do actually learn, beyond doubt, that we have reinforcements and provisions for Major Anderson, that they are actually under way, will they resist our passage to Fort Sumter, either by opening fire upon us from Fort Moultrie, or by sending one or more vessels out to capture us? If I echoed the sentiment of every man on this vessel who has expressed an opinion on the subject, I shall answer: "Yes." The belief here seems to be unanimous that if our object is known, we shall be fired upon.

Sunday, January 6

We have had a most delightful day; the water is smooth as a lake, and this evening we caught the warm breezes of the South.

You will easily see that the chief subject of conversation has been our chance of getting into Fort Sumter; and the more the subject is discussed, the more probable it seems that we shall have to take our chances against the South Carolina batteries. There are several steamers in her service which can be sent out to disable us. Then, will the lights be burn-

*ing in the lighthouses, and will the buoys be
unmolested?*

*Is it not probable, it is asked, that the government
has ordered the* Brooklyn *to Charleston, and that
we shall find her there to cover our entrance, in
case of an attack? The theory has been freely discussed, but as we have no means of knowing anything about it, you will hardly need to be informed
that we have arrived at no satisfactory conclusion.*

*If we are attacked, will Fort Sumter protect us?
It is said it can silence the guns of Moultrie in a
few hours, and if it shall do so, we can lie off until
the job is accomplished, and then perform our work.
We fully expect the protection of Fort Sumter. The
captain has an immense American flag, twenty feet
by forty feet, and has been instructed to raise this
at his masthead the moment the first shot is fired.
There is already an ordinary United States flag aft,
and raising this large one forward can hardly fail
to inform Major Anderson that we consider ourselves under his protection.*

*At a few minutes past eleven o'clock this evening,
we met the steamer* Columbia, *from Charleston,
bound for New York. Captain Berry, who is a zeal-
ous secessionist, let off nine rockets, but our captain
did not respond. We display but few lights, and the
soldiers are not permitted to remain on deck while
a vessel is in sight.*

*We took an experienced pilot from New York, as
a Charleston pilot was not to be thought of; but he
is not familiar with the Charleston harbor, and this
adds much to the embarrassment of our captain.*

Monday, January 7

*We made Cape Hatteras at ten o'clock this morning.
We had a decided "sensation" on board today.*

One of the officers was reading aloud from Saturday's evening edition of one of the New York morning papers, when he stumbled upon a paragraph, announcing that there was reason to believe that the steamship Star of the West would sail that afternoon with troops and provisions for Fort Sumter. Of course, there is no longer any doubt that the chivalric palmetto soldiery will be after us, and that we shall have to run their guns or be sunk. Our captain, who has seen much service, assures us that it is very unpleasant business to be shot at a great while, without any chance to shoot back. In confirmation of this opinion, he relates how a vessel which he was once on was fired into from a Mexican battery for about half an hour before the ship had any opportunity of returning the compliment. He says it was very unpleasant. I am not a military man, but the assertion appears quite reasonable to me.

I observe that "Dixie" is the prevailing air on board, and there seems to be something appropriate which I hear twenty times a day:

> Away down South in the land of cotton,
> Where old friends are not forgotten,
> Away, away, away, away!
> I wish I was in Dixie,
> Hurrah! hurrah!
> In Dixie's land I'll take my stand,
> And live and die in Dixie's land.
> Away! away! away down South in Dixie,
> Away! away! away down South in Dixie.

Tuesday, January 8

We made Cape Fear about eight o'clock this morning. We have moved slowly, as the captain's instruc-

tions are to cross the bar early in the morning and
run up to Fort Sumter at daybreak, and we wish to
approach the harbor by night. This afternoon we
stopped about seventy miles from the bar for three
hours or more, and had some fishing. The day has
been delightful, and our success in enticing unsus-
pecting bass was quite satisfactory.

Toward night, we put on steam, anxious for the
result of tomorrow morning's experiment. In the
"Recollections of a Zouave," I have read that on
the morning of a battle the bravest soldier, while
nothing would tempt him to be elsewhere, seriously
wishes himself eighteen hours older, and I doubt not
that is now the prevailing sentiment on board the
Star of the West. At any rate, we wish ourselves
safely within the walls of Fort Sumter, where all
hands say we are bound to be in a few hours, unless
we are in the bottom of Charleston harbor, or pris-
oners of war. Every arrangement within the power
of those in charge has been made to secure the success of the enterprise, and anxious interest increases
every hour. Every light has been extinguished; even
our staterooms are in utter darkness, and in the
cabin we have only one lantern, by the dim light of
which one of the officers has this evening been reading The Adventures of Captain Simon Suggs, for the
entertainment of his companions.

The provisions have been brought from below and
placed in the cabin and on deck. If Moultrie disables
us, the captain is determined to run the vessel
aground as near Fort Sumter as possible; then the
boats, which are all in readiness, will be instantly
lowered, and the men conveyed to Fort Sumter as
rapidly as possible. It is hoped, also, that by bringing the provisions up, much of them may be conveyed to Major Anderson. We have six boats,
capable of holding ninety men. They have all been

overhauled since we left New York, and are in perfect order. Arrangements have been made for steering the boat from the lower deck in case the wheelhouse should be shot away. Men will be stationed below with mattresses to fill up shot holes. In short, everything has been done that can be done to secure the accomplishment of our mission.

The Officers
The following are the military officers on board:
Charles R. Woods, 1st Lieutenant, 9th Infantry.
Wm. A. Webb, 1st Lieutenant, 5th Infantry.
Chas. W. Thomas, 2d Lieutenant, 1st Infantry.
Assistant Surgeon, P.G.S. Ten Broeck, Medical Department.

Lieutenant Woods, a fine, soldierly-appearing man, has the command. He has served on the frontiers, and in 1855 was dispatched to Walla-Walla, in Washington territory. He drove the Indians out of Walla-Walla Valley, in 1856, after their attack upon Governor Stevens.

Lieutenant Webb has served in Washington territory, Texas, and Florida, and went to Utah in the winter of 1857. He was detached from his regiment and had charge of a heavy battery. He also constructed the works at Fort Bridger, and was subsequently on General Johnston's staff for a year. He left Utah in April, and since has been at Governor's Island.

Lieutenant Thomas has served mostly in Texas, and has been, at different times, at nearly every post in that state.

Dr. Ten Broeck was graduated at the College of Physicians and Surgeons, and entered the service in 1847, shortly after the battle of Cerro Gordo. He served in the Castle of San Juan and Vera Cruz,

*and subsequently in the city of Mexico. After peace
was declared, he served on the Texan frontiers.*

Church dozed until first daylight, when the shudder
of the ship's engine increasing speed to cross the bar
awakened him. He returned to the open deck to observe
the dawn. A finer morning I've never seen, he thought
as he stared at the clear blue sky. In the distance, he
saw the spires of Charleston and the cold walls of Fort
Sumter, atop which the American flag floated in the
gentle breeze. To starboard, the light that the pilot had
suspected to be that of Fort Sumter turned out to belong
to another steamer.

Captain Doubleday walked the parapet of Fort Sumter with first light. The previous evening, he had seen
the harbor pilot boat flash a signal to the guard boat
General Clinch that hinted something must be amiss,
that the Carolinians expected trouble in the morning.
He had risen early to see firsthand what this disturbance
might possibly be.
Scanning the gray horizon with his spyglass, Doubleday spotted the *Star of the West* passing over the bar
into the Morris Island channel. He satisfied himself that
the ship flew the American flag but that it was a civilian
craft and not a warship. No reason to awaken his commanding officer. Not yet, anyway.

A sailor aboard the harbor pilot boat spied the *Star
of the West* as Captain McGowan guided his ship toward the bar. "Ship ahoy!" he cried, and within seconds, the captain ordered the craft to full speed for the
run into the harbor to alert the city.

The watch aboard the guard boat *General Clinch* was
next to see the approaching *Star of the West*. He rousted

Lieutenant Ryan, commander of the Irish Volunteers aboard the ship, and pointed out the oncoming steamer.

"Fire off the rockets," ordered Ryan as the captain of the ship followed the example of the pilot boat and called for full speed into the harbor.

A single red rocket streaked into the peaceful sky and burst over the channel, alerting everybody awake and outside for several miles around.

The Citadel cadets, under the command of Major Peter F. Stevens, slept fitfully between the sand dunes of Morris Island. One of the lonely sentries who patrolled the isolated beach, Cadet William S. Simkins, saw the rocket fired from the *General Clinch*. Realizing its significance immediately, and without hesitation, he awakened his companions, who rushed to their guns without confusion as their training had taught them to do. The boy soldiers waited rigidly and patiently at attention as their officers decided what to do.

"My orders are to fire upon any strange ship trying to enter the main channel," said Major Stevens. "We will do just that." He sighted the number-one gun, then turned it over to Cadet George Edward Haynesworth from Sumter County. His gaze fell on the face of Cadet Captain John M. Whilden, to whom he gave the order, "Commence firing!"

With perfect precision, Whilden barked, "Number one, fire!"

Cadet Haynesworth, barely sixteen years old, snapped one end of the firing lanyard into the ring of the friction primer protruding from the gun's vent, uncoiled it full length, and drew it taut.

"Fire!" shouted Stevens again.

Haynesworth obeyed the order.

Moments earlier, notice was taken aboard the *Star of*

the West of a village on Morris Island, presumably at Cummings Point, only a mile or so from Fort Sumter.

"Is it possible that the Carolinians have a battery near there?" asked Lieutenant Webb.

"No," said Lieutenant Thomas, "there is no battery there."

He was wrong.

Lieutenant Woods saw a puff of smoke appear suddenly over the beach of Morris Island, and from it came the shot fired by the Citadel cadets. As the cannon's report echoed over the harbor, a ball the size of a man's head skipped over the water along a line that would have put it in front of the ship if it had more propulsion.

Captain McGowan accepted the ball for what it was: a shot across his bow, a warning to heave to. He was not to be deterred. "More speed!" he demanded from the engine room. "Raise the garrison flag!" he shouted to Lieutenant Woods.

The infantry officer obeyed, and the twenty-by-forty-foot ensign was unfurled at the fore.

Captain Doubleday didn't wait for the results of the shot fired on the *Star of the West*. As soon as he heard the report from Morris Island, he dashed down the back stairs to Major Anderson's room, pounded on the door thrice, then burst into the room.

Anderson popped erect in his bed, startled from his slumber, and demanded, "What is it?"

"The Carolinians are firing on a merchantman coming over the bar," said Anderson, his words coming between puffs of breath.

"What's this?" asked Anderson, outraged and confused by the sudden announcement.

"I believe it to be the *Star of the West*," said Doubleday. "The newspaper may have been telling the truth."

Anderson sat motionless for a moment, then threw

back the covers and said, "Return to your post, Captain. I'll be along as soon as I can."

Doubleday said, "Yes, sir," then disappeared to carry out the order.

Usually a fastidious man, Anderson dressed hastily to join his officers in conference as the rumbling of the Morris Island battery's guns pierced the solitude of his quarters. My God! he wondered. Are we at war?

At Fort Moultrie, Lieutenant Colonel Roswell Ripley, a West Pointer and Northerner who had joined the secessionist movement, asked himself the same question when he was alerted that the *Star of the West* had entered the channel and the Morris Island battery had commenced firing upon the civilian ship. He gave the order for all crews to man their guns and prepare for action. Like Doubleday at Sumter, he mounted the parapet to keep watch on the *Star* through a spyglass.

Having heard the echoes of the Morris Island battery, the people of Charleston flocked to the waterfront in hopes of watching the battle in the harbor.

The cannonade didn't disturb George Salter from his sleep that morning. He was already awake, awaiting history. He stood on the roof of Madame Lisette's bordello, a borrowed spyglass to his right eye, surveying the channel for signs of death and destruction and silently praying that he would see none.

Seeing the huge American flag flapping in the wind at the head of the *Star of the West* stirred a single emotion in Major Stevens. With a deep-set hatred for a government that would place itself above his own beloved South Carolina, he shouted, "Fire!"

Without hesitation, Cadet Whilden yelled, "Number two, fire!"

Boom! The cannon was fired, and its ball sped over the water to land short of the *Star*'s bow.

"Boom!" chortled Captain McGowan. "You must give us bigger guns than that, boys, or you cannot hurt us."

A third shot rose from Morris Island. All eyes on board watched as it descended toward the ship and crashed into the fore chains about two feet above the waterline, scaring the life out of the seaman taking soundings directly above the hit. He dropped the line and sought out safety.

McGowan saw him running and yelled, "Get back! You're much safer where you were, Jack. Lightning never strikes twice in the same place."

Reluctantly, the sailor returned to his post.

Major Anderson went to the laundry room that opened up on the terreplein of the sea flank of Fort Sumter. He was joined there by Captain Foster, Lieutenant Meade, Lieutenant Talbot, and Assistant Surgeon Crawford.

"It's the *Star of the West*," said Foster. "The newspaper article was true. We are being reinforced by a civilian ship."

"We don't know that for certain," said Anderson. "This could be a Carolinian ruse to lure us into war."

"Impossible!" said Foster.

"I have no orders concerning a civilian ship conveying reinforcements to this post," said Anderson.

"But she's flying the flag, Major," said Foster. "Our flag! And the Carolinians are firing upon it. We must defend this ship whether she is bringing us reinforcements or not."

"I have no orders, Captain," said Anderson flatly.

Foster threw up his hands and stormed from the room, bounding up the steps that led to the terreplein, mashing his hat in his hands and muttering, "Those damn rebels trample on our flag, and he allows it. My God! I've half a mind to . . ." He let his words trail off, realizing nearby enlisted men were listening.

"Fire at will!" said Major Stevens.

The cadets fired, reloaded, fired, reloaded, and fired again, sending shot after shot toward the *Star of the West* as Captain McGowan negotiated the channel.

"Why doesn't Sumter answer them?" demanded McGowan. "I see the flag above the fort, but maybe the Carolinians have the place." A thought struck. "Signal the fort with our flag," he ordered. "Let Anderson know who we are."

The captain was obeyed.

Doubleday saw the *Star*'s distress signal and announced to his fellow officers that this indeed was the ship mentioned in the *Mercury*. Without waiting for Anderson's approval, he shouted, "Run out the guns!"

Every gunnery crew turned a hand, and every cannon within the fort was moved into position to be fired. Each disciplined man waited for the order.

Lieutenant Davis ran up to Anderson and said, "Sir, the battery on Morris Island is beyond our range. We can do nothing to it. I believe we must concentrate our fire on Fort Moultrie before she can bring her guns to bear against the merchantman."

"Lieutenant," said Anderson calmly, "go below and take charge of the forty-two-pounders. Aim them at Moultrie, but wait for the order from me before firing. Understood?"

"Yes, sir," said Davis. He snapped off a salute, then followed the order.

"Sir, we can't fire on Fort Moultrie," said Lieutenant Meade. "I can't believe this is the work of the South Carolina government. It must be some secessionist hotheads trying to stir up trouble. If we retaliate for it, we will begin a terrible civil war between the states. I urge you to restrain our men, sir.''

The *Star of the West* was rapidly moving out of range of the Morris Island battery, and just as fast, the steamer was coming within striking distance of Moultrie's guns.

"Now, boys, we'll give 'em a shot or two," cried Colonel Ripley atop the parapet of the fort on Sullivan's Island. He shifted his view to Sumter and saw that its guns had been run out. With less valor, he added, "And then we'll catch the devil from Sumter."

The huge Columbiad nicknamed Edith roared and spewed her ball toward the *Star,* but the shot went wild, the ship still far out of range.

"Moultrie is firing at the merchantman!" shouted Lieutenant Talbot.

"Do let us give them one, sir!" pleaded Captain Foster.

"Patience, Captain," replied Anderson. "Be patient. We have no orders, and thus far, no harm has come to the merchantman."

"The ship is still signaling us, Major," said Doubleday. "Shall we reply?"

"Yes, do," said Anderson.

Doubleday tended to this chore himself, but much to his chagrin, the halyards were fouled and inoperative. He reported the failure to Anderson.

"Why doesn't Anderson answer us?" demanded McGowan.

A second shot from Edith at Fort Moultrie fell short of the bow.

Noting the shots coming from Fort Moultrie, Lieutenant Woods said, "We will soon be within their range, Captain. Will you still run us into Sumter?"

McGowan heaved a sigh and said, "I cannot run that risk. It is too great without support from Sumter." He stared angrily at the island fortress now little more than a mile away, then made the fateful decision. "Helm, out of port!" he shouted.

Brewer spun the wheel, and the *Star of the West* made a tight turn to come about and head for the open sea.

One final ball from Edith bade the merchantman farewell.

Frustration and anger saturated Fort Sumter, overriding the relief that Major Anderson felt because the onset of civil war had been averted, if not forever, then at least for the moment.

Jubilation permeated Charleston as the word was passed that the *Star of the West* had turned around and was steaming out to sea. Relieved that a bloodly battle had failed to materialize, George Salter found Ty Harris, and both of them got gloriously drunk for three days.

The cadets on Morris Island gave the *Star* a lasting sendoff, firing continuously until the steamer was well out of range. Throwing their hats in the air, they cheered their commander, their flag, and their Cause, believing God was on their side after all.

When news of the expedition's outcome reached the outside world, Louisa Phoenix danced about her apartment with joy over a Southern victory, and Rafe Sims, dining alone, raised his glass in silent toast to the valor of his fellow Southrons who had repulsed the first wave of invasion by the very government that he had served for most of his adult life.

In the New York *Evening Post,* after the *Star of the West* returned safely to its berth at the foot of Warren Street, William Conant Church wrote:

The war has begun in earnest . . . I do not believe anymore that this tremendous question can be settled peacefully. I rather anticipate civil war, fratricidal horror—hell let loose on earth—for a season.

Yet hope lived on in the breast of Sarah Hammond. It was only a faint glimmer that this catastrophic conflict could yet be prevented, but it was better than no hope at all. She knelt in prayer to thank the Almighty for giving the peacemakers another chance to prohibit a horrific war that so many thought inevitable as long as slavery existed.

The flag of the Union—the ensign aboard the *Star of the West*—had been fired upon, but it still waved unscathed over Fort Sumter in the very eye of the maelstrom. The first tides of war had ebbed.

HISTORY'S
CHRONOLOGY~

November 6, 1860

Abraham Lincoln was elected president of the United States.

November 21, 1860

Major Robert Anderson took command of Federal troops in Charleston harbor from Colonel John L. Gardner.

December 3, 1860

President Buchanan delivered a message to Congress that argued against the right of secession, but expressed doubt as to the constitutional power of Congress to make war upon an individual state.

December 6, 1860

Select Committee of Thirty-three was appointed by the House of Representatives to take measures for the perpetuity of the Union.

December 10, 1860

Howell Cobb of Georgia, secretary of the treasury in
Buchanan's cabinet, a Southerner who didn't like President Buchanan's action or inaction, resigned from the
cabinet.

December 12, 1860

Chief of Staff General Winfield Scott arrived in Washington to confer with Buchanan.

December 14, 1860

Lewis Cass of Michigan, secretary of state, a Northerner who didn't like President Buchanan's action or
inaction, resigned from the cabinet.

December 20, 1860

South Carolina seceded from the Union.

December 26, 1860

U.S. troops commanded by Major Robert Anderson
moved from Fort Moultrie to Fort Sumter under cover
of darkness.

December 27, 1860

Robert Barnwell, James Orr, and John Adams, commissioners from South Carolina, arrived in Washington to
treat with Buchanan for the peaceful transfer of Federal
property to their state's government control.

   The U.S. revenue cutter *William Aiken* was surrendered to South Carolina by her captain.

Castle Pinckney and Fort Moultrie in Charleston harbor were seized by South Carolina authorities.

December 29, 1860

John B. Floyd of Virginia, secretary of war, resigned at the request of Buchanan because of the scandal rising around Floyd's misuse of his office to arm the South and disarm the North.

December 30, 1860

The U.S. arsenal, customshouse, and post office at Charleston were seized by state authorities.

January 2, 1861

Fort Johnson in Charleston harbor was occupied by state authorities.

January 3, 1861

Fort Pulaski, Georgia, was seized by state authorities.

The War Department reversed earlier orders by former Secretary of War Floyd to move big guns from Pittsburgh to forts in the South.

January 4, 1861

The U.S. arsenal at Mount Vernon, Alabama, was seized by state authorities.

January 5, 1861

Fort Morgan and Fort Gaines at Mobile Bay, Alabama, were seized by state authorities.

The first expedition for the relief of Fort Sumter, sailed from New York City on the side-wheeler *Star of the West*.

January 6, 1861

The U.S. arsenal at Apalachicola, Florida, was seized by state authorities.

January 7, 1861

Fort Marion, St. Augustine, Florida, was seized by state authorities.

January 8, 1861

Jacob Thompson of Mississippi, secretary of the interior, resigned from the cabinet.

A Federal guard at Fort Barrancas, Pensacola, Florida, opened fire on twenty state militiamen advancing toward him in the dark. The militiamen fled.

January 9, 1861

Fort Caswell, North Carolina, was seized by citizens of Smithville and Wilmington.

Mississippi seceded from the Union.

The *Star of the West,* carrying relief troops for Fort Sumter, was attacked at the entrance of Charleston harbor and forced to turn back.